ANOTHER PATH

BY CAITLIN LYNAGH

THE SOUL PROPHECIES BOOKS 1 & 2
HIDDEN VARIABLES / ANOMALY

(REWRITE INCLUDING PAGES FROM SOPHIA LETO'S JOURNAL)

First Edition 2019
Outlet Publishing. Bulloch House, 10 Rumford Place
Liverpool. L3 9DG. UK.
www.outletpublishinggroup.com

Requests to publish work from this book should be sent to:
info@outletpublishinggroup.com

This book is a work of fiction.
Any resemblance to actual events or persons, living or dead, is entirely coincidental.
Another Path (The Soul Prophecies) copyright ©2019 Caitlin Lynagh

Cover design by Serena Daphn

ISBN: 978-1-9995965-2-1 eBook: 978-1-9995965-3-8

*Dedicated to Mark and Evelyn Westwood
of Westwood Books, Sedbergh.*

PREFACE

When I started writing *Anomaly* in 2014 I had an idea of where I wanted **The Soul Prophecies** series to go. I wanted to write about Arhl's world and I had a vision for how the series would end. The series was always going to be a trilogy but half way through *Anomaly* I realised that I needed to explain Sophia's story too. I wrote *Hidden Variables* as a prequel to *Anomaly* for that purpose.

Four years later and I have finished writing the series; I know where the story travels and its ultimate destination. Outlet Publishing offered me the release of a deluxe edition of *Hidden Variables/ Anomaly* to include my science notes (Sophia's journal) and suggested editorial changes to tie in with the rest of the series.

This was the perfect opportunity for me to make some changes to the original books and tidy up any loose ends. Thus *Another Path* was born.

The basic stories behind the original *Anomaly* and *Hidden Variables* remain unchanged, though some sections and ideas have been modified. For those of you who have already read *Anomaly* and *Hidden Variables* I hope you will also enjoy reading *Another Path*. We plan to release the next books in the series all within a year of this one. The original *Anomaly* and *Hidden Variables* books will be discontinued after the current press run ends, so I guess that will make them collectable in the future.

Thank you all for your patience and for your continued support as well as all the kind reviews. I'm always overwhelmed, and motivated, by the positive feedback for my books and I'm looking forward to sharing my new work with you.

CAITLIN

HIDDEN VARIABLES

ONE

Ahrl watched the world burn. Wars played out across a decimated land and explosions and flashes tore up the ground. Undiscovered weapons, machines and humanoid, metallic figures ran across the blood-soaked Earth. One of these figures paused and turned towards Ahrl's vision, with the face of a near-perfect human, it stared up from the fountain's surface, and the light of self-awareness gleamed from within its eyes. Ahrl pulled his mind away and lifted his gaze from the fountain. This vision was as unsettling to Ahrl now as it had been the first time he had seen it millions of years ago, and as much as they could try to avoid certain scenarios, they could not avoid everything. He felt the cool ground beneath his bare feet and gripped the stone column as he stared out across the garden. Tiny purple and golden flowers danced between grassy blades on the gentle sloping hills like little boats on vibrant green waves, stretching out in all directions towards a horizon that existed solely within his mind.

Existence was complicated, but consciousness was far worse. Humans had been lucky so far. Their blue and green gem of the universe was a relatively pleasant and easy planet on which to evolve. Humanity had won greater odds in the cosmic, quantum lottery than Ahrl's home planet had ever done, but Ahrl wasted no time with envious thoughts. The past could not be changed. Yet, like

Ahrl's world, humanity's downfall would largely depend on nature, luck and the collective decisions made by each individual.

If it had not been for the scientist from Ahrl's world, who had jumped through time and created both the garden and fountain from their memories, Ahrl and the rest of the thirteen may never have known anything about Earth or its conscious lifeforms. The fountain revealed many things, both Positive and Negative. It held humanity's past, present and future, and, just as it was impossible to look away from a vulnerable child stumbling into the world, it was impossible for the Thirteen to turn away from Earth. They knew too much, and their consciences would make them pay for it.

Despite their godlike knowledge, the Thirteen were not gods or goddesses, or any form of deity in any description or words. The Thirteen, and all of the deceased humans, were souls; they simply existed beyond life and their biological machines. Their minds, thoughts and emotions accrued throughout life dictated their existence in the afterlife. All that stood between a person's immortality and destruction were their choices. The energy for existing beyond life came from maintaining a balance with one's conscience, and the conscience could not be tricked, misguided or unheard in death; it was always heard. If you made a choice which had negative consequences for others, then it would undoubtedly upset the fragile balance of energy within your soul, and sometimes there was no way to recover. That's why the fountain was as much a curse as it was a blessing; knowing too much was sometimes just as bad as knowing too little.

Family and friends created bonds of love between the living and the dead, and sometimes it was possible to guide a living soul. The living usually called it a feeling, a hunch, intuition, or put it down to luck. For this reason, Ahrl and all the deceased souls were cautious when it came to matters of the living. They had interfered directly once before, and the effects of that interference, both good and bad, still shaped the world. Many souls had spent centuries rationalising their thoughts and feelings in the aftermath; some had been luckier than others – and despite the plethora of geniuses and creative minds, and the knowledge that the fountain gave, they still didn't know everything.

Ahrl's being tingled with energy from the tips of his imagined fingers to the bottom of his toes. He gazed down into the small pool, held within a bronzed bowl on the top of the crenulated column of stone. Flashes of light and colour danced across and over Ahrl's features as images were painted on the pool's surface, one after the other. He let his mind drift over the images like a paper plane sailing on an unfelt breeze. There were so many emotions, so many people, so many lives finely intertwined and connected to one another in the great and messy tapestry of life. Every decision made by every individual had a knock-on effect for the rest of the world and even inaction was a decision in itself. Faces appeared across the pool; young and old, male and female, from all cultures and countries; all reacting to what happened around them. And justice and injustice were sometimes heavy weights to shift in such an unbalanced world.

Ahrl's mind paused for a moment on a future possibility that he and many others hoped would come to pass. It was their bright hope for humanity and the afterlife, the best Positive possibility in a minefield of Negatives ones, and they had had much success willing certain choices for specific individuals over the years. There were some moments in time that were more important than others; crucial moments, which had dictated the entire course of human history, and this was to be one of them. In a lab, a small group of physicists would follow in the footsteps of the scientist from Ahrl's world. They would discover the answers to one of the biggest questions in the world and ultimately they would find answers to questions they hadn't even thought of yet.

It was dangerous and it came with its own consequences, but humans would make this discovery regardless; the fountain showed no possibility where humans didn't. It was important that the right people came together in the right way to make this discovery, as their subsequent actions would ensure the best chance for a Positive future for both humanity and the afterlife. This meant tracing through lines of ancestors and guiding specific people towards certain places and choices. They could never guide a person against their needs and desires so long as these were Positive. But with so many lives all tangled together and the unpredictable whims of nature, there were many hidden pitfalls along the way.

Despite all their concerns over the centuries, Ahrl was optimistic that the path was Positive and the world would not burn. However, with all great discoveries, the idea had to come from somewhere, from someone. The images flickered to a closer point in the future, a boy and a girl, meeting by chance, over a heavy cardboard box. It was these two minds, bouncing off one another, that would cause a chain reaction in the thoughts and ideas behind the discovery. *Alice. Kyle.* Ahrl smiled at the pair. Their souls at the centre of their bodies, invisible to the majority of the living but very much visible to the dead, shone like stars with multiple colours, some overlapping as though two supernovas were colliding, but they weren't the only two involved in this discovery.

He willed the fountain to a closer point in the future and the images switched again like fish fliting beneath the pool's surface. He saw another girl, a girl who caused both a frown and a smile to appear on his face. *Sophia.* She was just as important as Alice and Kyle, and without her and her unusual family, they would not make the choices that they needed to make.

Ahrl gazed at Sophia's future as he had done a thousand times before, watching the images drift lazily over the surface of the pool. A flash of darkness, of Negative, caused him to straighten up; this time, something was wrong. He saw Sophia, as a teenager, but unlike the happy and bright teenager he had seen so many times before; this version of Sophia showed immense sadness. Negative emotions weighed her down and he could sense her sorrow and confusion as though it were his own, clutching at his insides with blade-like fingers. *Why?* Ahrl nudged his thoughts and the fountain back to the vision in the lab but it was different this time, only Sophia was there. Ahrl watched as Sophia, accompanied by the wrong individuals, made the same discovery. He followed the thread of this pathway and witnessed the subsequent decisions and actions. He saw arguments and corrupted individuals exploiting the new information and the resulting technological advances. Ethics and concerns were ignored or pushed under paperwork and institutional rules. The same terrifying scenes as before claimed the pool's surface and he pulled his mind away from the vision of the burning world.

No, this isn't the path we willed. What's going on? What has changed? Ahrl felt as though invisible hands had grasped onto his mind. He saw a man standing before a mirror, his face red as tears fell from his bright green eyes and his mouth stretched over gritted teeth as though he were struggling to contain his desperate cries. He held an electric razor and shaved brown locks from his head, letting each curl and tuft fall into the sink. The vision shifted and he saw the man again; this time he was dressed in black with a hood pulled up over his head and he was running through the woods with a small box in his arms. The man stopped by a tree, pulled out a small trowel and began digging. *Who is this man? Why am I seeing him now?*

The edges of his mind buzzed with activity; it troubled him how easily Negative's mindless purpose of destruction warped the human mind and conscience. The images shifted once more and Ahrl froze as though he had been turned to stone, snared by the Medusa's gaze. This one scene was another future possibility which would lead to the burning world, and it jumped across the surface of the pool again and again like a jammed zoetrope. He knew what this meant; the more times the fountain showed it, the more likely this future scenario would come to pass. His jaw fell loose and his eyes widened for a second before what felt like a tidal wave of steel slammed into his being. Yet he stood rigid under the avalanche of pain and emotion. The fountain released him suddenly and he sagged forwards, realising that even with all the pathways, and all the times they had managed to avoid Negative interferences, they still couldn't prepare for everything or account for everyone.

No, there must be someone, there must be something we can do. He searched the fountain, and through the many twists and turns, until he found that a Positive future for humanity was still possible.

He paused for thought. It would take a lot of luck, and a lot of chance, and there would probably be several disturbances along the way, but it was there. He let his mind branch down several pathways all at once and focussed his energy; sometimes the impossibilities were simply misunderstood possibilities, but others required extraordinarily long odds to succeed.

TWO

A memory slipped through her mind like reflections on water; one moment sharp, the next disturbed and chaotic. She caught a glimpse of herself as a child, crouched on the floor with her face buried in her muddy knees. Her small body shook and her breathing came out in choked gasps as the tears rolled down her face. Her brother, Elias, crouched down beside her and held her shoulder.

'I told you, Sophia, I told you not to tell anyone,' he said. A crease between his brows marked his smooth, rounded features.

'But why?' She scrubbed at her eyes but the tears would not stop and her lungs heaved for air.

'People don't believe us anymore.'

'But I thought... I thought Kirsty believed me.' Her lips wobbled, as she fought to contain her emotions. 'She said she believed me, she said she was my friend.' Elias pulled her towards him and cradled his younger sister in his skinny arms.

'Hey, it's alright, Sophia, it's alright,' he said, stroking her head. 'Grandma just says that people are afraid, they're afraid of what they don't know.' Her sobs hitched up and down, muffled as she buried her face into her brother's t-shirt. The memory splintered into different thoughts, sounds and emotions and faded from her dreams.

Sophia twisted, her feet and legs tying knots in her bedsheets. She felt a warm tingling sensation spread out from her chest and rise up into her head. Her mind was pulled sharply from her hazy dream memories to a place that lingered for the most part on the outer edges of her awareness; a dream formed with such crystal clear clarity that her mind believed for a moment that she must be awake and firmly rooted in reality. Two teenagers appeared, a girl with eyes as blue as the summer sky and a boy with a warm smile. They sat side-by-side on the edge of a concrete skate ramp, talking and laughing. Sophia knew this pair well, she had dreamt about them for as long as she could remember. She drew closer, just to be near the pair who seemed to pull peace and calmness to their very presence like gravity. She could see their souls shining brightly at the centre of their bodies – two golden spheres casting their light across the ground in wide overlapping circles around them. Sophia absorbed all the details; the greenery of the park around them, the large detached houses set back from the skate park on the higher ground behind them. She looked over her shoulder and her gaze fell on a large lake and then moved further beyond to hedgerows and fields. The colours began to fade and blur into hues of grey at the corners of her vision and she turned back to the pair, only to be confronted by a wall of grey nothingness. Her mind retracted from her sub-conscious and back to the intangible realms of sleep.

Sophia's eyes opened to a thankless world full of light, colour and sound. A soft heaviness settled upon her, as though the energy in her body had been drained out through the soles of her feet overnight. Her dreams had darted in and out of her awareness, leaving her groggy and disorientated. She clasped a hand to her forehead, closed her eyes and exhaled deeply. She recalled the pair, the clarity of the vision that had forced its way between her dreams and memories. A faint smile curved her lips and she rolled over on to her side. Her dark gaze drifted to the alarm clock on her nightstand, her eyelids threatening to close again. But it was ten to eight. Her eyes snapped open as she launched herself from her bed.

She grabbed the blue uniform from her desk chair and began the impossible task of putting everything on all at once. She ran her hairbrush through her dark waves and then gripped the handle between her teeth and pulled up her knee-high socks as she half-hopped, half-stumbled to the bedroom door. She threw her brush back in the general direction of her bed and then ran across the landing to the bathroom to clean her teeth. She hurried back to her room to pick up her school work and dashed down the stairs.

The Letos lived in a large family home on the outskirts of an average, bustling town. Sophia lived with her parents, her older brother, grandmother, aunt and uncle, though they were rarely all present at the same time. She skidded into the kitchen just as her mother Louise pulled a tray of cheesy toast out from under the grill. Without missing a beat, Sophia grabbed a piece of toast, singeing her fingers.

'Good morning, Sophia,' Louise said. Sophia blew on her fingers and toast and then stuffed as much as she could into her mouth.

'Gooph Mornoph,' she managed to say as she gulped down the hot, buttery and cheesy mess, wincing slightly as the heat stung the back of her throat. Louise's dark brows dipped together.

'You could at least chew before you swallow and maybe let it cool first,' she said, as her dark chocolate gaze travelled up and down her daughter in amusement. 'Have you just woken up?'

'Yoph,' Sophia said as she propelled the rest of her breakfast to her stomach. She gulped again. 'Alarm didn't go off.' She shrugged and reached for another slice of cheesy toast.

'You're not even dressed properly.' Louise clucked her tongue. 'Did you dream?'

'Yes, I saw Alice and Kyle again, but the rest were just memories.' Sophia whisked away from her mother's grasp and grabbed a piece of kitchen roll to wipe the grease from her mouth and fingers.

'Sophia, you need to tuck your shirt in, and your tie? Where is your tie?'

'Top pocket,' Sophia said. She binned the tissue and ran for the door.

'Sophia…' she heard Louise call.

'I've got to go, sorry, Mum!' She shut the door behind her.

* * *

'Good morning,' Sophia said with hurried breath to the coach driver as she stepped on board. The driver smiled and the door slid shut behind her. She found a cluster of empty seats, a little way back on the left hand side, dumped her bags and sat down by the window. She rubbed a clear circle in the fogged up window and gazed out at the world. Parents tugged small children along the pavements to school, teenagers walked in groups, or alone with their heads encased in headphones, and adults in smart business attire marched by. Everyone was busy, following worn routes to familiar destinations with similar purposes every day, and no one questioned the sanity of it all. She pulled out a hairband and attempted to tie back her long hair; giving up after several failed attempts.

The roads grew busier and the houses both shrank and multiplied as the coach travelled closer to town. Sophia's gaze swept over the world, lazily drinking in details but committing nothing to memory. It wasn't long before the coach stopped again before a row of smart red-bricked houses with well-kept gardens and shiny family cars. It was the pleasant side of the road. Opposite, bordered by a muddy football pitch, was the unpleasant side. It was a poor residential area, notoriously frequented by police cars and debt collectors. Sophia turned her attention to the red-bricked side; she knew this stop well and she made no attempt to hide her smile.

Annie White may have been small but her presence could match that of a storybook giant. She stepped on board, dwarfed by a blue sports bag, a bulging school bag, and a clarinet case. How an earth she managed to carry all her bags with her tiny frame was baffling but she was far stronger and wiser than she appeared. Her dark eyes zoned in on Sophia and a huge smile lit up her round face as she navigated the narrow aisle, dumped her bags and knelt on the seat in front of Sophia.

Annie shook her head. 'I see you're championing the bedhead look.' She whisked a tiny brush from one of the many pockets within her blazer and offered it to Sophia.

'Thanks.' Sophia smiled gratefully. 'Alarm didn't go off and the usual.' She slipped a band around her hair, securing it into a ponytail. Annie's eyes widened and a smile teased her lips as she clutched the back of the chair and leant towards Sophia.

'What did you dream?' she whispered.

'Well, I dreamt about that pair again, they were at the skate park…'

Annie groaned and rolled her eyes.

'Those two, again?'

Sophia smiled.

'They're important, Annie…'

'I know, I know, you're going to meet them someday and they're going to help humanity with some discovery, blah, blah, blah. You dream about them all the time. I was hoping you might have seen something different and a bit more exciting than the predictable Romeo and Juliet.' Annie flashed Sophia a grin.

'Exciting?' Sophia arched a brow.

'Yes, like maybe something extraordinary, unexpected, or unnatural?' Sophia shook her head.

'Only if it's Positive. The ordinary good things may seem boring and normal to us but I'd rather have that than anything bad or alarming.'

'Safe and predictable. Where's your sense of adventure?' Annie giggled. 'But I guess you're right.' A mischievous smile broke onto her face and she asked, almost innocently, 'How am I looking today?' Sophia worried the inside of her cheek with her teeth for a moment, her gaze orbiting the coach. She blinked and let her vision switch. It was as though the curtains had been flung back from her eyes, or perhaps some sort of invisible lens had fallen across her sight; whatever it was, the world burst into otherworldly colours. Little, round spheres the size of a grapefruit appeared at the centre of every person's body, ghostly and semi-transparent but filled with different colours which surrounded a central, tiny, black pill-shape like the planets orbiting the sun. These colours were often in layers, but they would mix and wrap around one another, and some layers were bigger than others. The Letos referred to these spheres as souls, and the outermost layer often shone on the surface of a person's body, producing their own personal glow.

Sophia's gaze dropped to Annie's soul; pretty average for a teenage soul, she had all the colours but it was mainly white where it still had plenty of emotional learning to do. It was rare to see a soul without white or with very little white; Sophia knew from experience that even the majority of adults and the elderly still carried vast amounts of whiteness. Sophia could see big bands of deep red for love and dark blue for compassion, a little bit of lilac and aqua hues for creativity and imagination and a small amount of pink for lust or desire and green for envy; but surrounding these colours, a warm golden yellow shone out from Annie as though she was being backlit on a darkened stage. This showed calmness and joy. There were a few splurges of grey that dimmed her brilliance like dirt being thrown into a crystal clear pond. Sophia blinked again and let her otherworldly vision fade.

'You're in a good mood today but…'

'But?'

'You have some grey, but I don't think you're too upset; you're missing someone, Joe?'

'Of course I'm in a good mood, it's not been a full week yet.' Annie glanced away sheepishly. 'Joe called yesterday; he's coming back from uni for a visit soon.' Annie leant towards the coach window as they passed a pretty blue café with a cursive lettered sign reading "Mary's Café". 'We should go and get ice cream there.

I went with Mum last weekend and they do these amazing ice creams with sherbet and sprinkles.'

'Sure. We could go after school?' Sophia said.

Annie tore her gaze away and grinned.

'It's a deal.'

THREE

Annie and Sophia stepped off the bus following clusters of students up a long tarmacked driveway framed by sloping green lawns, the sports fields, and netball and tennis courts. The school loomed above them. They trailed behind the other students through two double doors and then wound their way up a flight of stairs to their registration classroom. The coach was always early so they sat down at their single desks, Annie twisting round in her seat to talk to Sophia. Sophia kept half an eye on the door and the clock above the whiteboard; her heart stuttered each time the door swung open.

'Would you relax,' Annie said. 'You're making me nervous.'

'Sorry.'

'They can't do anything and Kirsty would be a damned fool if she tried.'

'I know, I'm just always aware of them,' Sophia said. 'We must be the unluckiest people in the world to end up in the same form class as those three again.'

'You said it,' Annie said. 'But at least we're still together.' The door swung open again and Kirsty, Bianca and Sarah appeared, laughing and chatting. Kirsty paused for a brief moment, her gaze slanting down to Sophia and Annie. The corner of her mouth stretched into a long crooked smile, and her lips parted.

'Alright girls, find your seats,' Mrs Joyce said. Kirsty's blonde curls whipped about her face as she clamped her mouth shut and turned her head. The three giggled and made their way to their desks. Mrs Joyce dumped a bag exploding with papers onto her desk and then leant over to switch on the computer. 'Alright, answer when I call your names.' She wrestled a pen and clipboard from her bag. She stopped twice to scold Kirsty and her friends for talking, but the three just smiled innocently and resumed their conversation in whispers. Just as Mrs Joyce finished the register there was a knock on the classroom door and it was pushed open by the school's headmaster. A light sheen decorated his brow and receding hairline.

'Sorry to bother you, Mrs Joyce,' he said. 'I have another student for you.'

'Oh, but there are no other names on the register,' Mrs Joyce said.

'It was a last minute addition due to exceptional circumstances.' The headmaster stepped into the classroom and a male student stepped in behind him. The student gazed at the ground and a curtain of sandy blonde hair formed a barrier between him and the rest of the class.

'Oh, I see, of course…' Mrs Joyce's words died in her throat as she gazed at the new student.

'Go on, take a seat, Avery,' the headmaster said, gesturing to a seat at the back of the class. Whispers erupted around the classroom and Sophia heard the same name muttered under every breath, Avery Richmond. The other students stared at him, turning in their seats as he walked to his new desk.

'Settle down now,' the headmaster said, drawing the students' attention back to the front of the class. 'I don't feel like I need to explain the situation, you are all aware. I hope you all respect Avery and make him feel welcome again. Mrs Joyce.' The headmaster held his hands behind his back and nodded at her. 'I'll see you all in the hall for assembly in a few minutes.' He strode out of the room. Mrs Joyce eyed Avery in the corner of the room but made no further comments.

'Alright class, you heard the headmaster, make your way to the hall please.' The students stood up and a wave of discussion flew throughout the classroom as students filed out and cast hurried glances in Avery's direction. Annie stood and turned round to face Sophia.

'Well, I didn't expect him to come back again,' she said, keeping her voice low and gesturing with her head towards Avery.

'Yeah, I'm surprised,' Sophia replied, rising from her seat.

'I wish your dreams had shown you that instead.'

'I wish I had more control over them.' Sophia glanced back at Avery who sat in his seat with his head bent over his desk. He showed no signs or inclination of joining the other students for assembly.

'I know, it would have been way more interesting though,' Annie said. Sophia bit her lower lip and followed Annie out of the classroom.

* * *

Sophia's trainers thumped against the sunset-tinged tarmac. Her teammates called out to her and she moved into position, dodging and twisting to evade her marker. She caught the ball and froze briefly before passing it onto another teammate. Her muscles ached and her stomach grumbled quietly as the hours stretched into the evening. Situated on the far side of town, and arguably the wealthiest part, the impressive school building backed onto protected woodland. The students were forbidden to enter the woods during school hours and were discouraged after school hours, but they often turned deaf ears to the warnings.

Sophia ran down the edge of the court; she had been put in her favourite position, wing-attack. There were two games taking place on the courts that evening and Sophia was grateful that she had been placed in a team with Annie and not Kirsty and her friends, who were playing on the other court. Annie ran up ahead, quick and agile in goal-defence, evading her marker with ease. Sophia, on the other hand, struggled to get past the opposition's wing-defence, Heather Langley, otherwise known as Heather long-legs. Mrs Berns, their coach, stood in a narrow section between the courts, but she could only watch one game at a time and, contrary to popular belief, she didn't have eyes in the back of her head. As their team neared the opposition's hoop, Sophia felt her bib constrict around her chest, and suddenly she was tugged backwards. Heather leapt past her and Sophia realised all too late that Heather had fouled whilst Mrs Berns' back was turned. Sophia regained her footing and Heather glanced back with a small smirk. Sophia glowered at her but then a tingling sensation brushed across her left ear, continuing up and over her scalp. She paused, her breath catching in her throat as warmth bloomed from her chest, reaching through her body like the branches and roots of a tree. She recognised this feeling, recognised the static quality of the air that no one else seemed to notice. It was faint, very faint, but it was there.

Sophia's gaze darted between her teammates, the ball, and then around her as she tried to locate the source. She moved across the court and jumped to deflect a pass from the other team; she missed and the effervescent sensation grew, buzzing pleasantly around her skull. She stopped suddenly and looked up through the tall fencing surrounding the courts and up above her to the school's sloping front lawns. A figure lay stretched out on the grass. However, this figure was nowhere near as interesting as the semi-transparent figure standing beside them. A shiver ran down Sophia's spine; there was no doubt about it, there was a deceased soul, standing on the school lawns. Sophia stared up at the deceased woman; her ghostly figure appeared to be waning, as though she couldn't quite hold onto her form.

Sophia looked down to the figure on the grass. She recognised the boy instantly, answering one of her many questions whilst simultaneously producing several more. Sophia's thoughts raced ahead. It was impossible, surely? That event had been over a year ago, she would have definitely noticed this deceased soul by now. She stared, but unless her eyes were betraying her, the boy was Avery Richmond, which meant the woman was…

'Sophia!' she heard Annie shriek. Sophia turned instinctively to the sound of her friend's voice, the sensations freeing her mind and body, snapping like an elastic band, and then something hard hit her face, smothering her airways with the scent of rubber, sweat and tarmac. Gravity seemed to grab up and pull as her legs crumpled. She hit the ground hard on her backside, just saving the back of her head from the same fate as she caught herself on her elbows. The pain jarred up and down her body and condensed into the areas which had taken the most impact. She stared up at the wispy clouds dragging themselves across a forever-changing sky and one thought went through her mind before the pain fully kicked in. *Why?*

FOUR

He could recall her smile, the warmth of her arms and the sweet smell of her perfume. He remembered their long conversations and the hours they had spent reading poetry and visiting museums and galleries when his father had been too busy. Avery's mother had worked hard but she had still managed to find the time for him. Avery sat up as soon as he heard the strange thud; it was incredible how a person could ignore familiar sounds all day but react so quickly to something that was even just a little bit *off*. He saw the girl fall to the floor and the netball flying through the air and for a moment he was concerned. He thought he recognised her from registration; she looked vaguely like the girl who may have been sat behind Joe's sister, but he wasn't sure. His concern was short lived; there were plenty of students around her and their teacher was already pushing through the crowd. His gaze snagged on three girls, failing to hide their laughter behind their hands. Again he thought he vaguely recognised them, but their laughter twisted their pretty faces and made them hideous to him now.

He lay back down on the grass again, lifted his hand up and stared at the lines on his palm, separating the sky with his fingers. Coming back to school had been a mistake; he could feel it deep within his bones and gut. The halls and rooms were hazy echoes in his clouded mind with the odd indisputable familiar place, object or person striking through like lightning. Joe's sister was one of these lightning strikes but no, she had a name, it was on the tip of his tongue, it began with A. *Annie.*

He dropped his hand and clutched his head, threading his fingers through his hair. Everything was so difficult. His mind felt oddly detached, but then this was nothing new. Sometimes he would feel light and his body would relax as it remembered a happier time, and in other moments he would feel heavy as though he had just fallen to the bottom of a deep well, the way out a pinprick of light above him, if it was there at all. He fought constantly to distract himself, numb his body and cast these painful feelings aside. Despite this, he somehow knew that he could never truly discard them; he was beyond sadness and despair, beyond anger and frustration, beyond hurt and betrayal. No one ever told you that these emotions were just layers, often mixed and mashed together, but still layers. And no one ever told you that there was a place past these layers, a terrible place that you didn't want to find, because if you did somehow find this place, you were, without a doubt, lost. Avery knew this place and he welcomed the numbness that it brought. It was as though his insides had been carved out like a pumpkin and now he just sat on the side watching the world go by. He had lived in this place for the past twenty months and twenty-two days exactly.

His psychiatrist and father had both agreed that sending him back to school would somehow do him some good, but Avery couldn't see it, even starting a year behind, with new faces. Tragedy wasn't a real concept for the majority of teenagers outside of history and classical studies. It was a race to get through exams, rack up points on a CV and burst out into the workforce, no waiting, no gaps. Perhaps immersing himself in his studies would help to distract his mind from the gaping hole inside, the empty chair at the dinner table, the one forever-closed door at home. He closed his eyes and inhaled deeply. He didn't want to go back home but the reason was calling to him, pulling him back into feelings he didn't want to feel. Tomorrow was the day when the clock had started ticking; it was the day that had ruined everything. Tomorrow was her birthday.

He exhaled. *Too soon, I should have waited until after her birthday.* He could remember her smile, the warmth of her hugs, the love behind her every word, but he also remembered why she had been singled out, and that crushed him more than any amount of earthly measurement. *They let him go, why did they let that creature go?* He felt the sudden sting of a hundred emotions like the lashes of a whip and he was prepared for it. He clenched his fists, believing for the most part that he deserved the pain and that he didn't deserve to be happy when she couldn't be. When the emotions threatened to bubble up and over his carefully constructed defences, he retreated back to the numb, empty place inside.

He sat up again and blinked. A violet and blue sky hung above him; netball practice was long over. He stood up slowly and made his way to the school's carpark, where a single black, sporty hatchback sat alone, away from the lampposts and under the branches of the treeline. Passing his test was the only thing he had managed to do since his world fell apart. It was escapism – or a potential way out. He paused for a moment with his hand on the driver's door and gazed into the woods behind the school. The woods belonged to some rich toff, likely one of his father's friends. Technically, even though it was private ground, there were public walkways through the forest for the occasional trekker and ambitious dog walker. Of course, the students never paid much attention to the rules and the more rebellious ones often escaped to smoke and drink at all hours. For a second he yearned to disappear amongst the trees and escape to the place he now called *sanctuary*, but he got into the car and drove the long way home instead.

An orange light flashed and a large timber gate slid to the side to reveal an expansive driveway and a house that was all glass, steel and timber rectangles. An architectural masterpiece, his father had proudly called it, though his mother had always said that it looked a bit cold. Avery parked beside his father's gunmetal grey Bentley.

He slammed his car door a little too forcefully and marched up to the porch. He opened the door but didn't reach for the light switch. An eerie blue glow dimly illuminated the hallway which could only mean two things: the television was on, and his father was home. He crept inside, closing the door quietly behind him, slipped off his shoes and padded softly towards the lounge. Sure enough the television was on but muted, and his father was lying sprawled on the sofa in his dressing gown, surrounded by empty whiskey bottles. He was out cold and his snores ripped through the air like a chainsaw. Avery saw the mess of fast-food and empty bottles; he shook his head and retreated down a second hallway to his bedroom. People had different ways of dealing with pain, Avery had realised; his father chose to knock himself out with alcohol and Avery chose to shut out the rest of the world entirely.

FIVE

People's lives were very much like stones in a hurricane. You could be picked up, dropped, tossed around and reach the highest and lowest of levels. You could knock against other stones, have near misses, and sometimes have encounters that would send you spinning onto a different course entirely. Ahrl had often thought this when observing people and their encounters with others. He had seen it before; the thread of people's lives becoming entangled and forever changed, even if the encounter lasted only a couple of minutes and the individuals involved never saw each other again. A minority of encounters became extremes regardless of whether they were good or bad, but the majority were simply normal and changed very little.

Ahrl tapped his fingers along the edges of the fountain and felt his concern grow. He had tried his best to protect Sophia Leto over the years, considering her extraordinary circumstances and family history. He had even willed Annie's family to move from the other side of the world, a move they had already been contemplating, but had required a little extra encouragement. The Thirteen were very careful about interfering and revealing their knowledge to the world, even to those who shared unique gifts like the Letos. Humans were afflicted with a desire for knowledge that could never be fully satisfied, and there was always the danger of knowing too much before the time was right – or too little.

Ahrl closed his eyes and let his mind slip into the pool. A faint murmuring swarmed around him, growing louder as individual voices leapt out of the void. Faces appeared, scenarios arose, circumstances clashed and Ahrl skipped from point to point, his mind jumping through the timelines in his quest to find an external variable. *No, not that one;* he moved onto another person, another time, *no;* he moved on again. He searched through hundreds of options, glanced over thousands of lives, felt millions of possibilities, and then he paused, *Wait, what is this?* He dove deeper into the possibility and the garden shifted around him, its colours darkened and blurred, transforming into earthly shapes. Ahrl opened his eyes and found himself standing beneath a bridge beside a river. The damp stench of rot and bodily odours forced him to switch off his smelling sense and concentrate firmly on his vision.

An elderly man squatted by the dirty, mossy bricks, a wiry beard drooping from his grimy face as he held his hands above a small fire. The man wouldn't notice Ahrl, for he wasn't truly there and never would be. Ahrl studied the unkempt man with his mismatched clothing riddled with tears and holes. The man's soul shone out with sickly, painful hues of browns and greys, but the golden band of Positive which encased his soul was unmistakable and strong. Ahrl smiled. *Yes, this is the one.* Ahrl stretched out a hand and concentrated on the man and the Positive scenarios he hoped would come to pass. Ahrl cleared his mind, bringing all his good intentions, memories and emotions to the forefront and felt a familiar warmth blossom in his chest. Ahrl's soul began to shine, illuminating his entire body. He felt the invisible timelines swell and flex around him and a tendril of golden light stretched down his arm and flowed from his fingers, reaching out to the man and sinking down into his soul. The old man froze and gazed up through Ahrl as his cracked lips spread into a smile and Ahrl pushed the last of his energy into the Positive purpose he had for this old man. His soul glowed almost on a par with Ahrl's. *I may not be able to change your life for you, but you may be able to change another's life.*

Ahrl felt a tug on his mind which tingled and nudged at him

as though someone was standing next to him, incessantly tapping on his shoulder. He dropped his connection with the old man and lowered his arm. The earthly possibility and the old man faded from Ahrl's vision and the brightness of the garden returned to Ahrl's existence. The pool flashed before him with a dozen possibilities before once again falling calm and silent. Ahrl straightened up, closed his eyes and responded to the call by filtering out all his other thoughts and focusing solely on the connection; he gave a mental push in his mind. When he opened his eyes his gaze was drawn to his left where his old friend, Ioel, stood.

'You were at a meeting?' Ahrl asked, noting Ioel's crisp white robes. Ioel inclined his head.

'Hello, Ahrl, and yes, it seems that these meetings are becoming a regular occurrence.'

'Haven't they always been?'

'Not as frequent as they are now.'

'Did you voice my concerns?'

'Yes, I did, though I wish you would attend for yourself instead of staring into the fountain for unknown lengths of time.'

'How can I not?' Ahrl asked. 'The fountain is becoming more unsettled by the day and Sophia just can't help but be involved with all future possibilities. I just wish we could do more to help her.'

'You know we can't, interfering could cost us dearly in our conscience-determined existence, don't forget, it's how we lost so many from our home…'

'I know,' Ahrl said. 'You don't need to remind me.'

'We do what we can with our subtle methods of suggestion,' Ioel said.

'I can think of our less subtle moments,' Ahrl replied. Ioel frowned.

'It has to be that way, we can't cast the final decision, we can only guide. It is up to the individual whether or not they choose to follow our guidance and what they do when they get there. The Thirteen are troubled by the fountain, there could be… complications.' Ahrl nodded, his lips pinching into a thin line.

'A certain possibility is becoming more frequent. Florence Leto saw it too, years ago, though the others seem to be divided about it,' Ahrl said.

'It could knock us from the path we have hoped for. They still haven't told Sophia, have they?'

'It appears not, though I cannot say for sure, the fountain reveals conflicting, often disjointed images.' Ahrl smiled at Ioel. 'It's why I spend so much time studying the fountain, searching for wisdom and guidance.' The corners of Ioel's lips twitched and he shook his head.

'I shall let you get back to your gazing then. One other thing before I go, I was told to remind you that the rest of us would like to see you sometime this century.'

'Of course,' Ahrl said. 'I shall see you all soon.'

SIX

The sharp tang of chemicals tickled Sophia's airways as she surveyed the chemistry classroom. The students stood in pairs with Bunsen burners, test tubes and conical flasks lined up on the desks beside them. Everything felt familiar to Sophia, the old dark desks, the whiteboard, the students, and yet her gaze snagged on a pair of students that just didn't quite fit. Avery sat paired with a girl called Emily, and Emily's usual partner Beth was nowhere to be found. Avery leant heavily on one elbow and gazed out the window whilst Emily lifted a conical flask with tongs and set it on top of the Bunsen burner. Sophia caught her chemistry teacher walking between the desks and she saw herself with Annie. There was a popping sound like a muted gunshot and Emily squealed and cowered whilst Avery barely moved beside her. The vision faded just as quickly as it had arrived and the classroom bleached out into a sleepy residential street. An elderly man, who Sophia knew as Mr Gilliam, was being hoisted on a stretcher into the back of an ambulance under a pre-dawn sky. She stood beside the back doors of the ambulance as the cool breeze grazed her skin. Mr Gilliam's grey eyes seemed to stare at her for a moment as his chest fell up and down in small movements.

Sophia's alarm cut through her dreams and she groaned as she blindly stuck out an arm to silence it. She sat up slowly; her brain felt as though it was listing from side to side. She shivered as a warm and cold static energy crawled over her skin. She reluctantly pulled herself from her bed and made her way into the bathroom. She caught sight of herself in the bathroom mirror and grimaced at her reflection. Despite the icepack Mrs Berns had practically glued to the bridge of Sophia's nose, bruises had emerged and now decorated the top of her nose and stretched to the tired skin around her eyes. *I look like hell.* She still remembered the smell of grit and rubber as the netball collided with her face and she still remembered who had commandeered her attention… *Avery's mother. How could she be there? Avery had returned to school briefly following his loss, before the other incident, but I didn't see her then. Why haven't I seen her before?*

Avery's mother wasn't the only problem, her dreams had been more than dreams again; she recognised the familiar buzz of energy, the tingling sensations which ran through her nerves. It was enough to tell her that the visions hadn't been completely Negative but neither were they Positive. Sophia was just a casual bystander as always in her dream visions, or like a single audience member at the cinema engrossed in the film, but utterly alone and powerless to intervene with the characters' lives. There was nothing she could do, but watch and hope that no one would be seriously hurt. Sometimes the dream visions had already come to pass by the time she woke up, and other times it could take weeks, if not years. She waited for the buzz of energy clinging to her skin to die down and then she stepped into the shower.

'Good morning, Sophia,' Flo said as she sat at the dining table holding a steaming cup of her favourite coffee.

'Morning, Grandma,' Sophia said as she pulled out a bowl, poured cereal and flicked on the kettle.

'How's your nose?'

'Sore.' Sophia made a cup of tea, poured milk on her breakfast and joined her grandma at the table.

'Did you dream last night?'

Sophia nodded. 'I dreamt about a minor explosion in my chemistry classroom, though I don't think anyone will be hurt by it.'

'Hmm, OK.'

'Oh, and I saw Mr Gilliam being put into the back of an ambulance but he didn't look like he'd been in any sort of accident, and he was definitely alive.'

'Your mother will probably know more about that one, should it come to pass.' Flo opened her eyes and placed her hands around her coffee cup again. 'Anything else?'

'No, nothing else.'

'Good. Seeing too much puts a lot of strain on the mind. Some of our ancestors went crazy you know, because they saw too much.'

'I know.' Sophia sighed. 'I wish I'd dreamt about Alice and Kyle instead; I wonder how many years it will be until I actually meet them.'

'You'll meet them when it's time, no need to rush these things. You've seen many random things lately and there are simply too many people and pathways for your mind to potentially get lost in.'

'They might not be that random,' Sophia said.

'No, you could be right. Our gifts have often been focussed on important events, but I'm not convinced that anything you've seen lately will change the course of humanity in any great way.'

'But you're always saying that everyone's actions affects everyone else no matter who they are,' Sophia said.

'Yes, they do, we all do, but we usually have our energy focussed.'

'What should I do about Mrs Richmond?' Sophia asked, thinking of Avery's mother. Flo stood up, picked up her empty mug and moved over to the kettle.

'There isn't much you can do,' she said, pulling a blue and silver coffee tin from the corner cupboard. 'We have to be very careful who we speak to, what we do and what we say.' She shook the coffee tin and a little rustling sounded from inside. 'If only ordinary humans did the same, eh?'

* * *

'Looks like your dream was right last night, the dark lord has forced Emily to pair up with Avery,' Annie said, tilting her head towards their chemistry teacher as she dumped a test-tube rack on their bench.

'I wish I could tell her to be careful,' Sophia said, her dark gaze darting nervously between Emily and her lab partner. Annie rolled her eyes.

'Why? Do you think she'll get hurt?'

Sophia's brow creased.

'Well, I didn't see her getting hurt but that doesn't mean that she won't.' Annie watched Emily set up her tripod and Bunsen burner and carefully place her conical flask on top of the flame. Sophia continued to mutter under her breath, her eyes darting between their own experiment, Emily's Bunsen burner, and Avery. She hadn't seen Avery's mother since being hit in the face with the netball. Every time she let her vision switch with Avery in her sights, his mother hadn't appeared. She knew it could only mean one thing, Mrs Richmond was a very weak soul and she was already fading in and out of the living world. One day in the near future, she would fade out completely and enter a sleep-like state until Avery crossed too. Such was the fate for most Deykashee souls, albeit a temporary one.

'Miss White, do you intend to stare across the lab all day or are you going to participate in this experiment?' Mr Armfield said as he strode between the rows of lab benches with his nose in the air. He looked down at Annie through narrow spectacles. 'Do I have to remind you that part of your final mark includes practical assessment?'

'I'm sorry, sir,' Annie said.

'Hmmm. Well, sorry will not get you an A in Chemistry.'

'I know, sir,' Annie said, nodding and adopting a fake sombre expression.

There was a loud "popping" sound almost instantly followed by a high-pitched scream. Mr Armfield whirled round to the source. All eyes in the room were fixed on a pale-faced Emily, who slowly uncurled her hands from her ears and straightened up. 'What was that?' Mr Armfield said as he marched over to Emily and Avery's lab bench. Colour returned to Emily's cheeks and her lips parted as she stared at her conical flask.

'I think… I think I left the cork in the flask by mistake,' Emily said as her bottom lip quivered.

'Did you not read the instructions?' Mr Armfield said, wagging a finger at the whiteboard. 'And Mr Richmond…' He turned to Avery but his vocal chords appeared to fail him. 'Ah… yes… well…' He licked his lips and then coughed into a fist. He turned away and marched back to the front of the room. 'OK, class, get on with your work.'

Annie pressed a hand over her mouth to stifle her giggles and looked over at Sophia. Sophia sighed and wiped her forehead with the back of her hand.

'Like anyone can even read that, it looks like an army of ants took some LSD and fell into an inkpot,' Annie whispered as she sidled up to Sophia. 'That was amazing, it's got to be like the fiftieth time now your dreams have been right.'

'I don't know,' Sophia said as she lifted their conical flask carefully from the top of the tripod. 'It's not like I keep count.'

'You know your family could really prove you had gifts if you went to someone official in the science world. Surely your dad would be able to do it.'

Sophia shook her head. 'No one would believe us; humanity hasn't discovered the missing connection yet, and there's not much we can say,' Sophia said.

'Well, you were right about Emily so far today, now it's just Mr Gilliam who's left.'

'I'm not even sure we can really find out about that one.'

They continued with their experiment and Sophia cast glances in Avery's direction. He seemed to be in his own little world again, staring out of the window like he did in the majority of the lessons they shared together. Just as Annie finished recording the last result, Mr Armfield signalled an end to the lesson.

'Alright, that's enough for today,' he said from the front of the lab. 'Remember to dispose of the contents of your experiment in the chemical waste bin, and don't forget your homework; page eighteen, section six in your textbooks.' A muted groan escaped through Annie's teeth as she helped Sophia to clear away their experiment.

They followed their classmates out into the corridor and made their way through the tides of students to the locker room. As they rounded the corner, they saw Kirsty, Sarah and Bianca hanging around Kirsty's locker. Sarah dropped her gaze to her feet but an evil smile appeared on Bianca's face and she tapped Kirsty on the shoulder. Kirsty glanced briefly at her friends and then cast her gaze towards Annie and Sophia.

'Oh, look who it is,' Kirsty said. The edges of her lips jerked upwards at harsh angles and her eyes glinted. 'Still up to your childish games?' Sophia ignored them and looked straight ahead. She had been here before enough times; it hurt more in her dreams than it could now but she could do without the confrontation. 'Go on, witch,' Kirsty said as she shut her locker. 'What colour am I today?'

'She's the witch,' Annie muttered. 'And she's another word, which rhymes too.' Sophia looked down.

'What? Can't you see anymore? Have your stupid little gifts deserted you?' Kirsty said. Annie clenched her firsts and Sophia stuck out an arm to stop her from stepping forwards. Kirsty haughtily raised one eyebrow. 'Though I guess you are a witch, since your family are all gypsies.' Kirsty's voice drawled as though it were an effort just to pronounce every word. 'Given your foreign heritage, why don't you just go back home and live in a horse-drawn caravan with your own kind?' Kirsty threw her head back and a noise which was more of a cackle than a laugh bubbled out through her lips. Anger rose up and over Sophia like a wave; she didn't bother to reply, or argue the fact that she had been born in England and held a British passport, her home was right here. Instead, she turned to Sarah and did something Flo had warned her not to do.

'How's your grandfather, Sarah?' Sarah's head snapped up and her hazel eyes widened as the colour fled from her face. 'He's at the hospital, isn't he?'

'How… how…. He only just went in today.' *Good,* Sophia thought as she supressed a victorious smile. *I was right.* Surprise flashed briefly across all of their faces and Sophia wondered for a small moment if just perhaps they might believe her this time. Not that she dared hope the name-calling would stop and that things would be at least bearable between them, but then she felt a cold numbness spread across her skin and in the next heartbeat Kirsty had composed herself.

'Her mother must have told her, she works at the hospital,' Kirsty said. She smiled a though she'd just solved a major case and had locked away a murderous psychopath.

'Oh yeah, of course,' Sarah said, relaxing her taut body and bobbing her head up and down like a puppet. Kirsty's eyes narrowed into razor-thin lines.

'Come on, let's go,' Kirsty said. 'She's not even worth the airspace.' She led the way, her heels clicking on the floor; she paused briefly when she reached Sophia. 'Nice try, witch,' she hissed before following her friends out.

'I shouldn't have done that,' Sophia said.

'I can't believe that…'

'Annie, its wasted energy,' Sophia said as she stepped forwards towards her locker and sought out her physics' text book.

'I don't know why you just put up with it,' Annie said. 'You should go to the headmaster and complain.'

'If Kirsty and her barnacles want to be nasty then it's up to them. They'll regret it later,' Sophia said. 'I can deal with it and ignore their words as long as they don't get in my way. One day we'll all enter the real world outside of school and I think some people are going to be in for a shock.'

'I wish I could be as calm as you, but they just make me so angry,' Annie said.

'I'm not always calm, but anger doesn't solve anything,' Sophia said. A loud clang rang out from the other side of the locker room and they both jumped and turned to the source. They caught the back of a boy's head with sandy-coloured hair as he disappeared around the corner of the boy's locker room on the opposite side.

'Who was that?' Sophia said.

'I'm not sure,' Annie said.

'Do you think he heard anything?'

'No, I don't think so,' Annie said. Sophia let out a sigh and shouldered her bag. 'Well one thing's for sure, I guess - you were right about Mr Gilliam.'

SEVEN

Sophia had only just dropped her schoolbags by the front door when Elias appeared at the end of the hallway.

'Turn around, we're going shopping,' he said, brandishing a small piece of paper.

'Huh?' was all Sophia could say before Elias marched her back out the door. 'Wait, where are we going?' Sophia asked. She didn't want to go shopping, all she wanted to do was lie on her bed, preferably with an icepack on top of her eyes, and forget the world for a couple of hours.

'Grandma Flo is making dinner and she asked me to get a couple of things for her, you know what she's like,' Elias said as he opened the door to the Leto's garage. They heard the crunching of footsteps and turned to see a handsome man in a suit approaching their house. Sophia immediately felt a rush of warmth seep into her body; it was like being cocooned within a fleecy blanket on a cold winter's day. She smiled and let her vision switch; beside the man in the suit appeared another man who looked almost exactly the same, only his clothes were casual and his body wasn't completely opaque.

'Thomas, Ollie,' Elias said as a smile broke across his face. Sophia could see the twins' souls, alike in many ways and full of Positive energy. Oliver was a Deykashee soul to Thomas, and his soul's colours were adorned with more of the creative and imaginary, aqua and lilac hues. Thomas's soul had much less creativity but greater bands of compassion and love, a deep blue and red.

'Good evening,' Thomas said as he smoothed down his suit. Oliver rolled his eyes.

'Hey guys,' Oliver said.

'What are you doing here?' Elias said.

'We've come to talk to Florence,' Thomas said.

'Thomas's got some visions to share with Flo,' Oliver said. 'Where are you two off to?'

'We've got some last minute shopping to do,' Elias said.

'Well, we won't delay you anymore. Come on Oliver.' Thomas approached the house and rang on the doorbell.

'See you guys later,' Ollie said. He grinned and then dashed through the door into the house. Sophia's vision switched back and she blinked a few times to adjust.

'We're taking Dad's car then?'

'Yes, since he's not here to use it himself at the moment, I thought I'd give it a run,' Elias said.

'I take it Mum's on nightshift again?' Sophia said as Elias pulled out of their driveway and headed down to the main road.

'Yeah. Grandma Flo decided that there wasn't anything decent to eat. So we lucky, lucky people get to go food shopping.' Elias smirked and pushed back the unruly locks hanging in front of his eyes.

'Great.' Sophia rolled her eyes.

Cars crawled into the busy supermarket carpark but Elias found a space near the door. He picked up a basket and cool, stale air blasted them as they walked in. It was mayhem. Young children screamed in trollies, older children zipped around in colourful school uniforms and tired parents leaned on trollies for support as they yelled at their children to behave. The noise and stench of body odour was enough to persuade Sophia that she didn't want to stay here any longer than necessary. She squeezed the tip of her tongue between her teeth for a moment.

'We need to split up; it'll take us forever otherwise. What do we need?' Sophia asked. Elias scanned the store and nodded.

'If you could get some of that cheese Grandma always raves about and a bottle of red, I'll get the vegetables.'

'OK, I'll come and find you,' Sophia said before darting off into the crowds. She squeezed her way between parked trolleys and twisted around children. She reached the foot of the dairy aisle, saw a roadblock of trolleys and so headed down to the wine aisle instead. Alcohol appeared to be just as popular as milk and cheese. After a few minutes of scanning the shelves, Sophia managed to find a familiar-looking bottle of red. She tucked the wine under her arm and returned to brave the dairy aisle.

After a few moments she found the cheese Grandma Flo liked; it was circular and wrapped in a floral, orange paper. Sophia grabbed the cheese, turned sharply and felt her knees smack into a soft, yet unforgiving lump. She heard an "oomph" sound and then a bald head, attached to shoulders and a skinny body, rose up in front of her. Guilt gripped her.

'I'm so sorry. I didn't see you there…' Sophia's croaky words trailed off as a pair of green eyes blazed back at her. The cool refrigerated air suddenly plummeted and Sophia's vision flickered. *What the hell is this?* She felt her weight shift beneath her and her body tilted dangerously towards the cold dairy shelves. The man's eyes widened, concern briefly flashed through them and he grasped her arm. Sophia bit back a gasp as an icy numbness sprouted from where he touched her and flowed up through her veins. The man's mouth moved but all Sophia could hear was a faint ringing sound. She cast her gaze around but her vision swayed, dipped and bobbed as she searched for any sign of deceased souls. Static energy tingled across her scalp and her vision switched completely. A soul, as black as coal, appeared within the man before her. The black void reached out, engulfing his body in what looked like shadowy flames, and every so often another colour would try and fail to break free like sparks from a bonfire. *Negative! It's a dark soul!* Her mouth fell open and her mind seemed to freeze and detach itself, caught up within the chilling currents of the man's presence. The darkness reached out for her, brushing against her skin, probing for any weakness in her character. She instinctively recoiled from the man, trying to break whatever invisible connection had latched onto her mind. She stepped backwards and felt an instant pain all over her scalp as though thousands of tiny icy needles had been struck into her skull all at once.

Images forced their way behind her eyes and suddenly she was no longer in the crowded dairy aisle at the supermarket. *What the...* Her gaze fixed on the scene before her; she saw a man and a woman who at first glance appeared to be embracing. However, as Sophia's eyes absorbed the details she realised the pair were struggling and that the man was pressing a gloved hand over the woman's mouth. Sophia gasped and tried to move towards them but her legs were like stone pillars, they refused to budge. Fear shone through the woman's pale blue eyes and her cries were muffled. She was beautiful, elegant and regal in appearance, despite the wild strands of dark hair that had escaped from the clasp behind her head.

From Sophia's close-up view she could see the wet, slushy ground and the dirty brickwork behind the woman and the man. Although brown curls framed this man's face, his toxic green eyes were unmistakable; he was definitely the same bald man from the supermarket. She studied his expression; his pale brow was wrinkled and his pupils were tiny dark dots in a stormy sea of greens. Sophia's gaze dropped and trailed the bent angle of his arm and then her eyes widened. He held the handle of a knife, buried deep into the folds of this woman's coat, just above her stomach. Blood dribbled down the length of the knife's handle and dripped to the damp ground. The woman fell slowly and Sophia watched in horror as the sharp blueness in the woman's eyes vanished, as though they were freezing in the clutches of death. Sophia knew this woman. A terrible thought passed through her mind and her stomach dropped as she looked back at the man. The woman was Mrs Richmond, Avery's mother.

The sounds and colours of the supermarket returned and Sophia stared up into two dark, deep green pools. The man stared down at her as the life seemed to drain out of his pale skin, turning his complexion grey.

'It was you,' Sophia said before she could think. She blinked the last remnants of the vision away. 'You killed her.' The man's mouth dropped open and he released her quickly.

'Sophia,' she heard Elias call. The man glanced up and then gave Sophia a hard stare before turning on his heel and walking as swiftly as possible down the aisle. 'Sophia?' Elias said, touching her arm as he reached her. She felt warmth rush immediately from his fingertips and the supermarket returned in all its energetic clarity. 'What happened? Who was that? We're supposed to stay away from Negative souls.' His gaze softened and his grip relaxed as he studied Sophia's face.

'Elias, I've screwed up,' Sophia said.

'What are you talking about?'

'I saw something,' Sophia said quietly through trembling lips. 'I saw something awful.'

EIGHT

Her words felt like bullets puncturing Den's chest as he recalled that fateful day, the one day he had been desperately trying to forget. *How does she know? There was no one else there.* He didn't dare look around to see who might have overheard her.

'Sophia!' he heard a male voice shout. *Sophia? So that's her name.* Den glanced up and saw a young man, with similar features to the girl before him, hurrying towards them. Den let go of her arm and spun on his heel. He walked away in the opposite direction as quickly as he could without arousing suspicion. He rounded the corner at the bottom of the aisle and cradled his face in his hands. *Who the hell is she? What does she know?*

He glanced around the corner and then snatched his head back as he saw them standing together. *She couldn't possibly know? Could she?* Den's head ached as a vein throbbed beside his right eye. He began to sweat and his arms trembled. He rubbed his eyes and took a deep breath. *You're just being paranoid, Den,* he told himself as he picked up a pizza. He had nothing to be worried about; she hadn't been there all that time ago. There was no way she could know, and besides, the so-called justice system had nothing more to go on. *It was you, you killed her.* Her voice echoed between his ears and he shook his head. *It must be a mistake, there's no way she could know,* he told himself, but there was no mistaking her words. *Had she been there?* He tried desperately to remember who had been around when he had left the alleyway, but it was futile, his head had felt like it was on fire in the moments after, nothing had made sense. His mind began to wander to the past again and his grip tightened as a spasm of pain ripped at his insides. He pushed the memories back and blinked back tears.

'It's not fair, I didn't mean to… I didn't…' he said aloud. He heard someone clear their throat and his gaze darted to a woman tapping her foot beside him. He moved away and looked down at the plastic-wrapped pizza; it was a little pricey for his meagre budget but what could he do? He dumped the pizza into his basket, on top of several cans of cheap beans and a reduced-priced loaf of bread, and then he got out of there as swiftly as possible.

It rained on the walk home and Den let his tears fall freely as he hunched his shoulders to the elements. He cursed under his breath as the cold misty rain quickly soaked his clothes. The flimsy plastic bag strained under the weight of bean cans and he eyed it nervously. After what felt like forever, his home finally appeared in the distance. He quickened his pace, passing row upon row of pretty and tidy houses before crossing over the road and onto a muddy field. A row of brown-bricked terraced houses were squashed together at the far end of this field. Den's tiny one-bed flat occupied the upper part of one of these houses, the third terrace from the end. *A wonderful gift from those soulless council pigs.* His worn trainers squelched against the grass. Den's gaze found the window to his lounge; the curtains were still drawn and white marks stained the shoddy brickwork. It wasn't much to look at but it was a roof over his head and somewhat safe. He pulled out his keys and hurried to open his door. Just as his feet hit a pile of envelopes on the floor, the bag split and the cans rolled across the threadbare doormat. He let out a frustrated cry and fought the urge to punch something.

'Great, just great,' he muttered. He shut the door and awkwardly scooped up the tins and the post. He trudged up the dirty carpeted stairway, passed through his lounge, and dumped everything onto the kitchen counter. Out of habit he checked the electricity meter on the wall, thankfully there was still some credit left. He turned on the oven and ripped open the plastic surrounding the pizza before placing his meal inside. After he'd put the beans away he finally picked up his post. The envelopes were all official looking with urgent stamped in red capitals below his address. He glowered at them and shut them in a drawer where they appeared to be breeding. One envelope remained, the only one he had been waiting for. Den's fingers trembled as he opened it.

As his gaze fell upon the company's blue curved logo adorning the top of the letter, Den recalled the interview. He had dressed nicely in the only suit he owned, rehearsed his lines for days and researched the company on the library's computer. The job was an admin position and he thought the interview had gone well; the pretty female interviewer was friendly. He gulped and tried to steady his shaking hands; this must have been the hundredth job he had applied for in the last couple of months. *This will be the one, Den, you've already had all the rejections now, this will be the one* he told himself. He took a deep breath and read the first few lines…

Dear Mr. Boothe,

Thank you for your interest in working with Tele-Air Communications. Unfortunately, after careful consideration, we are unable to offer you a position at this time…

Den's shaking intensified. He let out another frustrated cry and crumpled the rejection letter into a tight ball. *Why? Why does this always happen to me?* He gritted his teeth and kicked the kitchen door; the door swung and slammed shut. He thumped his hands down onto the counter then hissed through his teeth at his throbbing hands. He hated his current part-time job and he hated his boss, an insufferable nightmare who Den was sure enjoyed tormenting him. Den's thoughts began to sink into dark places; he felt as though the air around him had grown dense, squashing him from all sides. It was always the same, why did everything go wrong all the time? Why couldn't he catch a break? He pressed his head into his right hand and leant heavily onto the counter. He felt heavy and his thoughts raced back through his past, spiralling down and down. She appeared in his mind, the beautiful woman with the expensive necklace. He recalled her muffled cries, the blood. He let out a pitiful moan, *No, not now, please not now.* Warm tears slipped from the corners of his eyes as he sobbed. He drew in a shaky breath and clenched his right hand into a fist before a scream forced its way out between his teeth and he brought his fist down hard on the countertop. *You deserve to feel this,* a voice said from the back of his mind, it was his voice, but somehow it was different. *You're a monster.*

'No, no, it wasn't my fault,' Den said to himself.

Ultimately it was, the knife was in your hands.

NINE

Flo, Elias and Louise sat in silence and Sophia felt the weight of their gazes pressing down on her from all sides.

'Elias, you fool,' Flo said, lightly cuffing Elias' ear.

'Ow,' Elias said, scowling at Flo.

'It wasn't Elias' fault,' Sophia said. 'I should've checked. I should've been paying more attention.'

'Hmmph,'

'I caught hold of a Negative pocket of energy, didn't I?' Sophia said. Flo glanced around her study, her gaze lingering on her bookshelves before returning to Sophia.

'Yes, it seems like you caught a pocket of extreme energy, an imprinted memory so to speak. It happens sometimes, that's why people think that they see ghosts if they're in the right mind-set, in the right place at the right time. What they're actually seeing is a memory; they're usually formed if an extreme emotion was felt at the time the memory was created, and they can linger, sometimes within people or at certain places. It doesn't happen often, but it's why we rarely visit historic sites.'

'But why did I see it? I wasn't thinking about Mrs Richmond or Avery or death…'

'Probably because of our weird family,' Elias said, narrowly dodging another swipe from Flo. 'We're more in tune to certain frequencies than the rest of the living world.'

'The past, present and the future are all connected, and even though the past collapses it still affects the present and future,' Flo said.

'The man you described, Sophia, what did you say he looked like again?' Louise asked.

'He was about Elias' height and build, but Caucasian. He was completely bald and he had these vivid green eyes.' A deep crease formed between Louise's eyebrows and her eyes darkened. 'What's wrong, Mum?'

'He sounds like he could be one of the suspects,' Louise said.

'I was thinking the same thing,' Elias said.

'Suspects?' Sophia asked.

'No one was actually convicted for Mrs Richmond's murder,' Louise said. 'But they had two suspects; the first looked nothing like the man you've described but the second…'

'The second?'

'Well, they never found him,' Louise said. 'The police had video footage of the suspect, but there were no leads.'

'So the man at the supermarket did it and he's the second suspect?'

'Not necessarily,' Flo said. 'A memory isn't always one hundred percent accurate. Memories can be tweaked over time by the imagination, and you can have a memory of an imaginary memory too.'

'What do you mean?' Sophia asked.

'I mean, he might just be a complete nut job who likes the idea of killing people but imagines it rather than carries out the act. That in itself is an extreme and highly likely with a Negative soul, though I daresay it's not always just Negative souls, all humans have dark thoughts from time to time - it's how you deal with and react to them that defines you.'

'So you're saying he might not have done it after all?' Sophia asked.

'It's possible you saw something from his imagination, rather than something that's actually happened. It's still an extreme pocket of Negative energy.' Sophia's shoulders shuddered as a cold chill ran down her spine.

'Why would anyone imagine that?'

'Some people are messed up,' Elias said.

'My point is you don't know for certain, and it's probably better to keep it that way,' Flo said, cutting a sharp glance at Elias.

'But what if I'm right? What if it is him?'

Flo dropped her shoulders and let out a low breath.

'There isn't much we can do about it.'

'We could try and look at the case from the public records,' Louise said. 'But I don't think we'd find anything of interest. We may never see him again.'

'It's probably a dead end,' Flo said. 'But I don't like it because of what you said. You would have freaked him out and I don't think you should be going about on your own anywhere for a while.' Sophia opened her mouth to protest. 'No, Sophia, we don't know who that man from the supermarket is, and if he is unstable, I don't want you to run into him again and for you to be on your own. There's no telling what he might do if he feels remotely threatened, and don't forget his Negative energy will try and attack your Positive energy; it could only take the slightest wayward thought or extreme emotion for him to act dangerously. If you need to go anywhere then Elias will take you, and Elias will also walk you to and from the bus stop.'

'Grandma, the bus stop is barely a hundred yards away,' Sophia said.

'Distance has no meaning to Negative events,' Flo said. 'Plus, you will have worried him with your comments, guilty or not.'

'I agree with your grandma, Sophia,' Louise said. 'Perhaps Elias should drive you to and from school...'

'Annie gets the coach, Mum; I'm not alone on the school coach.' Louise bit her lip and no one said anything for a few moments.

'What about Mrs Richmond?' Elias said, breaking the silence.

'She's fading, but it sounds like she's fighting it,' Flo said. 'I'm amazed she's lasted this long though. Less than one percent of souls come back and attach themselves as Deykashee souls, and less than five percent of those make it past two or three years before fading, or rather, zoning out.'

'She must be really worried about her son,' Louise said.

'What's he like at school, Sophia? You see him, don't you?' Flo asked.

'He's in my year now and he's in lots of my classes, but he doesn't really speak to anyone. He keeps himself to himself and doesn't seem to have any friends. I keep trying to see Mrs Richmond, but she never appears.'

'Hmm, it's just as I suspected. This could become complicated,' Flo said. 'I think it's best if you continue to give Avery a wide berth. Losing a loved one under normal circumstances is always difficult, let alone the circumstances which took Mrs Richmond. It's even more difficult when Deykashee souls occur since most people can't see them.'

'That won't be a problem,' Sophia said. 'He glares at anybody who even tries to get close.'

'Avery can't know about your gifts or that his mother is still around. I would imagine that he's emotionally fragile right now. It's a wonder he's been allowed to return to school at all if he's still behaving like that,' Flo said. 'It's affected him badly.'

'They probably thought human contact and socialising would help,' Louise said. Flo rolled her eyes.

'What if I do see Mrs Richmond again?' Sophia asked.

'Ignore her if you can, unless she speaks to you and tells you something important.' Flo massaged her temples. 'This is giving me a headache. For now we'll just have to be extra cautious. Which means you, Sophia, need to listen and be careful too.' Flo pinned her granddaughter with her stare.

'OK, OK,' Sophia said.

'For now we should just focus on our visions,' Flo said.

'Yeah, yeah. Alice and Kyle, Alice and Kyle...' Elias said, standing up. 'We know. I'll be in my room if anyone needs me.' Flo frowned as Elias headed upstairs.

'I better get ready for work,' Louise said.

'Come on, Sophia, join me. Let's try and focus your mind,' Flo said as she sat cross-legged on the floor. Sophia sighed and joined her grandma.

TEN

Kyle and Alice grasped a heavy cardboard box between them; their eyes locked for a brief moment in a world where only they seemed to exist. Their souls shimmered in golden hues, the light illuminating their bodies from within and breaking through from their skin. This light bounced and shifted as though it was shining through droplets of rain and little rainbows cast their colours around the pair. Peace, warmth, compassion flooded every fibre and cell of Sophia's being. She sighed in her sleep as every troublesome and weary thought was lifted from her shoulders.

Their clothes gradually changed and the box disappeared but the pair still stood facing each other. She saw them in black graduation gowns with red sashes lined with dark green at a university. Alice's gown faded from black to a white dress and Kyle's gown morphed into a suit as they stood beneath a stained glassed window before all their friends and family. The scene changed again and their clothes became lab coats, as they stood amongst computers and high-tech machines.

The images kept coming, changing faster and faster as their entire lives were mapped out before Sophia's eyes. She saw their homes, their children and grandchildren and everything in between with every new line that painted itself across their faces. Every achievement, every mistake and every loss but despite it all their happiness seemed unquenchable. They left a mark of hope and nurtured seeds of compassion with every person's path they crossed and every heart they touched. It was as though the whole world would be moved by this pair, who would probably join the ranks of the millions of unsung heroes left out of the history books.

The dream began to fade back to the original scene with the box, the corners of Sophia's vision began to blacken and she cried out to the young couple. *Wait, tell me where you are.* Sophia heard her own voice echo around her. The couple's eyes bulged and their heads whipped from side to side. *Where are you?* Sophia cried again, but it was no use, the dream faded further from her mind and a new scene painted itself into her subconscious. She stood in a room with impressive furnishings and long windows. Behind a dark, polished desk a man sat in a fitted suit, shuffling papers; every so often he would pause to read, his eyebrows furrowing together and his lips pinching into a tight line. Sophia stared at the man, there was no mistaking the slight crook in his nose or his sharp icy blue eyes and sandy-coloured locks. It was Avery Richmond – an older Avery, who sported a five o'clock shadow across his jawline. *Where are we?* Sophia wondered as her gaze drifted towards the windows. *Why are my visions showing me Avery Richmond?* She moved closer to the window and saw lots of tall buildings, a large muddy river and, over to the left, the London Eye. *London? He's in London?* She turned back to the older Avery. *I guess he must have done well for himself then, but what is this place?* She pressed her face up against the cool glass and tried to peer at the building but before she could locate herself the vision collapsed around her, the colours running and pooling on the floor as the walls and objects disappeared. She turned back to Avery just as his body faded away.

Sophia awoke with her alarm. She washed and dressed then went down to the kitchen. Her cheeks ached as she smiled and sorted out her breakfast before joining Flo at the dining room table.

'You dreamt about Alice and Kyle again, didn't you?' Flo said as she sipped her morning cup of coffee.

'Yes, they're adorable,' Sophia said. 'I saw their entire futures again. They look so happy together; I'm a little envious actually.'

'Any clues on where they might be?'

'No, nothing.'

'Do you ever see anything bad happening to them?'

'No! Of course not. Why would I?'

'I'm not saying you would, it's just some freak event might prevent them or delay them from meeting, anything could happen really. We know they must meet for humanity's sake, so we have to look out for anything that might stop them.'

'Ah, I see. No, I didn't see anything like that,' Sophia said. She twirled her spoon around in her cereal but made no move to eat it. 'I saw something else though.'

'Oh?'

'It was Avery. I think I saw something from his future.'

'A possibility from his future; was it Negative?' Flo asked.

'No,' Sophia said. 'He was in this smart-looking office, somewhere in London I think because I could see the London Eye.'

'Interesting. Did you see anything of note?'

'No, I don't think so,' Sophia said. 'You don't think it's important, do you?'

'I don't think so. It could be that your sub-consciousness is fixated on Avery and his mother since your encounter at the supermarket,' Flo said. 'We just need to refocus your mind and do some more training. I hope you're still writing your dream visions down.'

'Yes, I'll do it after school.'

'Good. It's not just tradition you know, you never know when an overlooked vision might be useful to us in the future.'

'Yes, like the vision I had in the supermarket,' Sophia muttered.

'You should write that one down too and the one you had of Avery last night.'

'Grandma, why do we have visions?'

'Why? I don't know why, it's just a gift that we have, or a curse depending on how you look at it. Your grandad had a theory actually; he thought that the universe was trying to find the right balance between conscious species with souls and the right planet with the right sort of environment.'

'Is that because of the Thirteen?'

'Yes,' Flo said. 'We know they exist and we know they're not human. We believe our souls were formed from a sudden spark in emotion, like lust, fear or guilt, but the Thirteen came from a world which existed millions of years ago.'

'What happened to the Thirteen? I mean, before their souls found their way to Earth?'

'Their planet was destroyed. Through ignorance and just plain bad luck,' Flo said. 'Though we don't know an awful lot about it, only bits and pieces our ancestors have managed to gather from Deykashee souls over the years. There's not much we can do about our gifts now. We have them and that's that; we just have to do the best we can with what we're given.'

'But if the choices we make affect our souls, which then determine our final existence, doesn't that mean that the choices and decisions we make from what we see will also affect our souls?'

'Yes,' Flo said.

'But most people aren't aware, and doing nothing is also a decision, wouldn't that affect the soul too?'

Flo hesitated and took a big gulp of coffee.

'Yes, potentially.'

'It would be better if we could switch our gifts off,' Sophia said.

'Not necessarily. Don't confuse ignorance with control. Some people are ignorant because they have little control over their lives and circumstances; others are ignorant because they won't open their minds to ideas, opinions and advice from others. Ignorance as a choice is never a good thing, but sometimes it is better to remain blissfully unaware, so long as you're not hurting anyone.'

'Then we're damned if we do and damned if we don't, all because of what we see, and that's out of our control,' Sophia said.

'It's not very fair.' Flo's face creased as she smiled.

'No, it's not fair,' Flo said. 'But that doesn't mean purposefully going out of your way to look for trouble. All we can do is try our best and act within our own conscience and be kind to everyone, even if they don't deserve it. Your kindness will be a reflection of you and not them in the end. I can see that you're troubled, Sophia.' Flo's eyes darted down to Sophia's soul. 'Penny for your thoughts?'

'It's nothing,' Sophia said, taking another spoonful of cereal. *But I'm not blissfully unaware, and doesn't that mean I should find out more about the man at the supermarket? What if he did really do it? If I ignore it and he walks around free then won't that weigh on my soul forever?* Flo raised a dark grey brow at her and Sophia looked away.

ELEVEN

He sat within the cracked frame of the glassless window, one knee bent up as he gazed out across the treetops and the sunlight caressed the autumn leaves. Cupped in one hand he held some birdseed. He sat perfectly still as the woodland birds descended upon his spot, his little piece of sanctuary in this unfair world. A robin hopped up onto his knee and he held his breath as the little bird descended and perched on the side of his hand. A second later, a magpie landed upon the watchstrap on his wrist and the robin flew away. The magpie's claws scratched at his wrist as it pecked at the seeds within Avery's hand.

'Now that was a bit mean, Bob,' Avery said. The magpie turned, tilted its head and cackled at Avery. It pecked at the metal clasp shining in the sunlight and then went back to plucking seeds from Avery's hand. Avery leant his head back against the crumbling brickwork and closed his eyes. He could remember the day he had picked out the beautiful necklace for his mother at Adamantem, the jewellers. Impressive stones had shone under the bright lights within the glass boxes; rubies, emeralds, diamonds in different colours, some as large as coins. He could also recall the restaurant that the Richmonds had dined in for his mother's birthday, and the smile which had lit up her face when she had opened the box his father had procured from the inside of his suit jacket.

His mother had gasped and then smiled as she gazed at the necklace.

'Oh, this is beautiful, Graham,' she had said as she looked up at

Avery's father. 'You shouldn't have, this is too much.' She placed a gloved hand upon her chest.

'It's your birthday and cause for a special celebration. Nothing is too much for you, my dear,' Graham said. 'I'm glad you like it. Avery actually picked it out.'

'He did?' his mother said, turning her attention to Avery. 'I'm impressed. You made a magnificent choice, my darling, it's beautiful.' Avery felt his chest swell and couldn't stop the grin from spreading across his lips.

'Here, I'll help you put it on,' Avery said. He stood and gently lifted the necklace from its box and fastened it around his mother's slender neck.

'It really suits you, Tallulah,' his father said as a small smile teased the edges of his lips. Avery resumed his seat and nodded in agreement as the necklace flashed under the dimmed lights like soft twinkling stars. It was a double, interlinked, chained necklace; the smaller chain held a row of small but brilliantly blue, colour changing, sapphires cut into squares. The slightly longer, daintier chain hung in sweeping curves from the first and held slightly larger, round diamonds at regular intervals. A single, larger, teardrop diamond hung at the centre point. The necklace sat neatly across his mother's collarbone and just above the v-neckline of her black satin dress.

'You boys spoil me,' she said lightly, touching the teardrop diamond.

'That's not all,' Avery said as he pulled a brown paper bag from his jacket hanging on the back of his chair.

'There's more?'

'You didn't tell me about this, Avery,' Graham said.

'It was a last minute buy. I'm sorry, I didn't have time to wrap it.' Avery handed over the slim package to his mother.

'Oh, you didn't have to get me anything else, you two didn't need to get me anything. The meal was wonderful and spending time with you both is all I could wish for.'

'Careful,' Avery said as his mother opened the bag. 'It's a bit old.' She carefully slid out a slim, tattered, brown book. 'It's a poetry book,' Avery said. 'One I haven't seen before; I think it's pretty rare.'

'Oh my,' she said. 'Thank you, Avery. Thank you.' A violinist began to play in the corner of the restaurant and Avery turned to watch the woman. He had always been entranced by musicians, but in particular violinists. It was a musical instrument that few had the patience to conquer as it was virtually impossible to get a pleasant sound out of it as a beginner.

'How are your violin lessons going?' his father asked.

'Good, but I still sound terrible,' Avery said. 'Suzanne says I make her violin sound like a donkey.'

'You don't sound that bad. Practise makes perfect,' Tallulah said. 'You'll need your own violin soon.'

'I have to say I'm impressed, Avery,' Graham said, 'I thought you would have given up long before now.'

'No.' Avery laughed. 'I'm determined to master it now.'

'Oh, Graham, Avery,' Tallulah said. 'I can finally tell you a little more about the new exhibition that I was involved in putting together for the museum.'

'What is it?' Avery asked. Tallulah smiled, her gaze darting between Avery and Graham.

'The museum has managed to acquire a previously unknown painting by a particular famous artist, on a temporary basis. It's expected to cause quite a stir amongst the community and we've been invited to the opening night along with the museum's curators, board of directors and other donors. It would be lovely if you two could be there.'

'No need to ask,' Graham said. 'Of course we will.'

Avery opened his eyes and clenched his fist; the seeds crunched in his palm and the magpie cackled loudly before launching itself into the air and disappearing amongst the trees. Tears carved tracks down the sides of Avery's cheeks and he wiped them away with the cuff of his sleeve. He lay his hand back down on the windowsill and uncurled his fist.

'Sorry,' he mumbled, to no one in particular. He glanced down at the violin case propped up against the wall beneath him. A familiar hopeless feeling, one he had felt almost every day since she had been taken away, lay heavy over his body, as though the old brickwork sucked the life out of him. He gazed out across the trees as the sun played peekaboo behind their branches on its slow descent to the horizon. Even the light and warmth of the sun was fading from him now. He remembered the night the police had called his father to tell him the news; he remembered the man who they had taken in as a suspect but later released due to lack of evidence, despite finding traces of his mother's blood on his clothes. It was obvious to Avery; he had killed her and they had let him go. 'Asim Umar, damn him. I bet they only let him go because he's a doctor. He's not even…' Avery held his tongue and the thought as a strangled sob escaped from his lips. He pressed his other hand over his mouth to contain it. *If I hadn't picked out that necklace.*

He emptied the seeds from his hand, brought both his legs up to his chest and buried his face in his knees. His shoulders shook and he held himself tightly. Every tear that fell was a liquid form of his anger, hatred and despair. He didn't know how long he cried but when he uncurled himself, dark clouds obscured the stars. 'I hate this,' he whispered as he gazed up at the sky. He closed his eyes and gulped past the raw lump in his throat. 'I just want this to be over.' He sat numb as the cool night air sapped the warmth from his skin. Eventually he pulled himself away from his sanctuary and, using the small torch on his phone, trod the familiar route back to his car in the school's carpark. He drove home, pulled up next to his father's Bentley and then crept inside. He found his father passed out on the sofa again with an empty whiskey bottle on its side next to him. *I hate this.*

TWELVE

Den breathed through his mouth as he scrubbed the floor of the men's toilets at The King's Cockerel. The stench of sweat, cigarette smoke and other foul odours could make even those with the strongest dispositions gag. He battled through the chore, the endless layers of grime turning the water in the mop bucket black. The women's toilets were no better. He paused and wiped his forehead with the back of his arm. It had taken all of Den's willpower to not snap the mop in half and walk out when he had cleaned the toilet stalls. *Damn this job, why should I have to do this?* He flared his nostrils and inhaled accidently, choking on the putrid air laced with a barely detectable hint of cleaning agent. He scrubbed harder. The only thing that lightened Den's mood in this god-forsaken place was the graffiti-riddled walls. He read a few lines describing his employer, sniggered, accidently inhaled through his nose and choked again. *Breathe through your mouth, Den!*

He gripped the mop tighter and eyed the door. He knew Mr Hobbs, a hairy man shaped like a barrel, would be behind the bar pretending to clean glasses but in reality would be watching whatever was on the tiny television hoisted up in the top corner of the bar. Den hated the man with a passion; it was always *'Den, clean the toilets, Den, take out the trash, Den, get the gum off the seats, Den, Den, Den.'* Not once had Hobbs let him use the cash register or taught him anything useful about running a pub. *How an earth am I supposed to better myself when you only give me the crappy jobs?* Den fumed as his mop slapped against the grey-tiled floor. *You wouldn't be so happy if the pigs knew about your dodgy setup with Weedy Sam.* He had often fantasized about telling the police but then he wouldn't even have a part-time job and it would be the same crappy circle all over again; on the dole, applying for benefits, pressurised into getting any dead end job, always looked down on by those who had been born with spoons in their mouths - some of them may not have been gold or silver spoons but at least it was a spoon.

He finished cleaning as best as he could and stepped out to pour the water down the drain outside. He gazed up at the exterior of the pub as a nearby lamppost flickered, casting its sickly yellow light intermittently on the brickwork. One of the windows had been broken and boarded up and the toilet artists had done a similar job outside with the pub's golden lettered sign. It was late; the night time darkness had peaked and the last few stragglers were sat inside nursing their drinks. Den glanced up and down the street; the homes were all dark, the shops closed and a fox skittered across the road in the distance.

'Den!' he heard Hobbs yell. Den hung his head and brought the mop bucket back inside. 'There you are. Take out the trash before you go,' Mr Hobbs said, without looking up from the television. Den ground his teeth and glanced at the clock hanging behind the bar; his shift had finished fifteen minutes ago.

'Sure,' Den said, forcing the word out of his mouth. He put the mop bucket away and then picked up two black sacks and carried them to the alleyway behind the pub. The smell of rotting rubbish was enough to bring back memories of that day; he remembered the way she struggled, her rich perfume and the panic in her eyes. He shook his head and pushed the memories aside. The bin lid creaked as he opened it and he hoisted the sacks inside.

'Den, Den, Denny,' a voice said. Den let go of the bin lid and whirled round. 'Or should I say Lucian?' Den bent his elbows and knees slightly and kept his hands open. Three men stood before him; the first was huge and round and was wearing a tattered tracksuit, the second was spindly and lean with a mop of greasy hair. The third man stood in the middle; he was shorter than the other two but broad across the shoulders and much better dressed. Den knew this man well - Mr Cooper. 'Where's your father, Lucian?' Mr Cooper asked. His voice was heavy and rumbled around the edges of his slippery words.

'It's Den.' Den tried to still his trembling muscles by clutching his hands into fists. Mr Cooper's lips curled at the edges. He ran a hand through his short greying hair, a chunky gold signet ring glinting in the light from the lamppost.

'I'm sorry,' Mr Cooper said. 'Where's your father, Den?'

'I don't know,' Den said, eyeing Mr Cooper's bodyguards.

'He's lying,' the spindly man said. He spoke as though he were trying to smear his words through the gaps in his discoloured teeth.

'I'm not lying. I don't have anything to do with my father.' The conversation fell silent, Mr Cooper and his bodyguards staring at Den and Den returning their stares. Mr Cooper broke the silence first by coughing politely into a fist, then he clasped his meaty hands together.

'Well, that's unfortunate, Den. Your father still owes me and I'm led to believe that you two are still quite close.' He cracked his knuckles.

'I haven't seen him for months, and besides, you got your payment.'

Mr Cooper's mouth dropped into a grim, tight line.

'It was quite unusual really, your father turning up with a woman's necklace. You can imagine my surprise when I realised the woman had only died less than twenty-four hours before, murdered in fact. Your father doesn't seem like the type, Den, but then again, neither do you. Then he just happens to take off out of the blue and no one seems to know where he went. I know he was with you the day she died, Den. I have eyes, everywhere.'

'Whatever my father owes you is between you and him; that

necklace should have been more than enough.'

'No one wanted to touch the damn thing after that's woman's death made the national news. I finally got rid of it but it had to be dismantled. It was worth a lot less in the end.'

'That's not my fault,' Den said. 'You could have waited, you could have…'

'Could have what? Waited for somebody to find it?' Mr Cooper cracked his knuckles. 'Besides, I've added interest to your father's debts after all the hassle that damn necklace gave me.'

'You can't do that,' Den said as his gaze darted around the narrow alley; it was too small, too dark, too similar to that night. The smell of rotting rubbish reminded him of the smell of her blood and the way the knife had slid so effortlessly into her soft form.

'Perhaps I need to be a little more persuasive, Den,' Mr Cooper said, placing his hands behinds his back. He began to walk up and down as though he were deep in thought and contemplating a difficult question. 'I don't know what happened that night but I can imagine it. It's such a pity that you have such bad taste in women, Den.' Den didn't reply but his shoulders tightened. Mr Cooper smiled like a shark. 'They never did find the murder weapon, did they? It would be a shame if somebody were to find it now, wouldn't it?' Mr Cooper stroked his chin. 'You see, a little birdy told me they saw you running into the woods, Den. I never thought you were a runner.' Den remained silent and gripped his hands into fists. Mr Cooper sighed. 'It's only a matter of time, Den. You can tell me where your father is and then I can forget what I know about your woodland adventure. Understand what I'm saying?'

'I told you, I don't know where he is.'

'Den, you're not making this easy for me, and I'm not the bad guy. I don't like being the bad guy; I just want to get back what I'm owed.' Mr Cooper stopped his pacing and sighed, then smiled at Den. 'I wonder what would happen if someone set fire to that little flat of yours, Den. It would be a terrible accident now, wouldn't it?'

Mr Cooper inspected the dirt under his nails. 'Perhaps you'd be inside or perhaps you wouldn't.' Den gulped and took a half-step backwards. 'If you're not going to talk, well…' Mr Cooper's eyes flashed between his bodyguards.

'I already told you, I don't know where he is. I have nothing to do with him.'

Mr Cooper shook his head.

'Boys,' was all he said as he turned his back on Den. The two bodyguards grinned and Den recognised a chilling absence in their eager eyes. They advanced slowly towards him.

'Wait, I told you, I don't know anything.' Den's voice quaked and he felt the blood drain from his face.

'That's too bad, Den, too bad,' Mr Cooper said as he walked away.

THIRTEEN

The students' royal blue uniforms seemed exceptionally vibrant and crisp and the off-white lunch tables gleamed. She clutched her lunch tray tightly with both hands. The lunch hall was nowhere near its full capacity, but it was loud, and several boys were knocking a paper ball around. They ran around the tables, flinging their bodies here, there, and everywhere, desperate to keep their makeshift ball aloft, whilst the other diners scowled or laughed at them. Sophia scowled; it was hard enough trying to balance the flimsy tray without trying to dodge overexcited boys.

Hot steam wafted up to her face, carrying the smell of tomato and herbs. She knew what she had picked up without even looking at it; pasta, served with a spicy tomato sauce, Annie's favourite. She glanced back over her shoulder; Annie was just behind her, following Sophia's lead. Sophia let out a deep breath and let her feet carry her subconsciously to their usual lunch table at the back of the hall. She was several steps behind another male student, navigating the maze of tables, chairs and diners, when she felt a niggling of unease stir in the pit of her stomach. A cold stabbing sensation spread outwards from her chest and into her fingertips and toes. A pressure built up around her head, behind her eyes and nose, as though she were diving too deep. She paused as time seemed to slow around her; the conversations became muted echoes and bodies drifted like distant clouds across the sky. Her limbs felt awkward and heavy as she tried to push her legs forwards.

One of the boys from the paper ball group, a boy who Sophia

knew as Harry, staggered backwards as the ball sailed in an arc towards him. The student in front of Sophia didn't see Harry and in that split-second when flying objects lose their inertia and just seem to float in the air, Harry leapt backwards to catch the ball. His body curved like a dancer in slow motion and then he collided with the student. It happened within seconds, and time caught up with itself, jerking forwards violently. Red sauce and pasta splattered everywhere, all down the student's shirt, blazer and trousers. The plastic plate bounced, his cup went spinning and the tray clattered against the linoleum floor. The lunch hall fell deathly silent, and in that moment, Sophia caught the side profile of the student before her.

She recognised the sandy hair and icy blue eyes, the strong jawline and the slight crook in his nose; it was Avery Richmond. A shudder ran down her spine and she felt something deep inside her recoil from his presence. She saw the detached look in his eyes, lined with a veil of sadness that no amount of time could ever heal. The uncomfortable stiffness in his shoulders and neck barely seemed to affect him as he looked down at his tomato-soaked shirt. Then the laughter started from somewhere behind them, cruel, sharp, and deadly contagious. It quickly washed over the entire room, until nearly every student's mouth mimicked the sound. Sophia thought she heard Annie snort, but her gaze zeroed in on the little ghostly, grey sphere at the centre of Avery's torso. Darkness bloomed out from his soul in black smoke-like tendrils, casting a heavy weight of despair and anger. The temperature seemed to drop by a couple of degrees and the hairs on the back of Sophia's arms stood on end. She felt a sense of hopelessness and self-loathing as a light blush raced up the back of Avery's neck and into his cheeks; he bowed his head and stormed out of the hall, shoving past Harry as he left.

The Negative energy vanished with Avery but there was no time to breathe a sigh of relief. The scene jumped forwards and Sophia no longer stood in the lunch hall at school. She was in what appeared to be a large double garage; there were no cars parked inside, but one half of the garage was filled with cardboard boxes. There was also a treadmill, weights, and work tools hanging from the whitewashed walls. Her eyes were drawn to the centre of the room, and she saw Avery, slightly above her, as though he were standing on something. An almost feral, yet destroyed look had claimed his red-rimmed eyes, and raw tear-tracks adorned his pale cheeks like battle scars. She couldn't see him properly, her view was obstructed by the boxes and gym equipment, but all of a sudden his body fell like a sack of potatoes. She heard a sickening crack and her stomach lurched. Avery Richmond's body hung suspended by a rope around his neck, slowly rotating and revealing the red stains on his school shirt.

Sophia woke up screaming and she heard a commotion on the landing before her door was flung open by a wide-eyed Elias brandishing a baseball bat.

'Sophia?' Elias said. Sophia's body trembled as she recalled the nightmare, no, it had been a vision. She clutched her head as warm tears fell over her cheeks and she gulped and winced at the burning sandstorm in her throat. 'Sophia, what's wrong?' Elias asked, dropping his bat and reaching her in three long strides.

'I saw... I saw...' She gulped again, her sobs choking as she tried to supress them and breathe in shaking gasps which sounded like violent hiccups.

'Hey, hey, it's alright,' Elias said, hugging her tightly. Flo and Louise stepped into the room.

'What did she see, it wasn't..?' Flo said. Elias shook his head as he held his sister. Flo approached Sophia and placed a hand on her shoulder; immediately Sophia felt a gentle warmth emanating from her grandmother's palm. The calm warmth soaked into Sophia's skin and she felt her breathing become a little easier and her heart slowed its running pace. 'Too much Negative,' Flo said. Sophia straightened up and took several deep breaths before facing her family.

'I saw Avery Richmond. He's going to hang himself.'

'Explain what you saw and spare no details,' Flo said. Sophia nodded and rubbed the moisture from her eyes as Louise handed her a glass of water. She took a couple of sips and then recounted the nightmare and all the details she could remember. Flo perched on the edge of Sophia's bed in silence for some time, her eyes closed, her hands clasped and her forefingers pressed to her lips. She dropped her hands and opened her eyes.

'I don't like it. This complicates things. I think the collision and humiliation is Avery's tipping point,' she said.

'He's depressed, I would say clinical depression,' Louise said.

'Does he not have a professional psychiatrist?' Elias asked.

'Yes, most likely,' Louise said. 'But we don't know who or what they've done with Avery.'

'Bloody fools for sending him into school,' Flo said. 'They should have just home-schooled him.'

'I agree, but they were probably concerned that he would become too withdrawn from society,' Louise said.

'I just need to stop the collision then?' Sophia asked.

'Perhaps, but it might not be enough, Sophia, he might still…' Flo said.

'It's worth a try though, right? Can't we call someone? His dad? The school? Anybody?'

'They wouldn't believe the truth, but we could perhaps warn them and say that we're concerned,' Flo said.

'I'm not so sure that would work. He might resent his dad or anyone else who gets involved,' Elias said.

'Flo, we must do something, we can't let the boy die,' Louise said. 'If Sophia's vision comes to pass then it could seriously affect her soul and ours too.'

'Yes, I know. This has always been a problem for our family, we see too much.' Flo frowned. 'Let me think for a moment.' Sophia watched her grandma and no one said a word for several minutes until eventually Flo stirred. 'I think Sophia should go to school and try and stop the collision. Meanwhile, we will post watchers at Avery's address. Elias, will you watch over Avery's home tomorrow night, well actually, it would be today, wouldn't it?' Flo glanced at the clock on Sophia's nightstand with its digital numbers rising slowly up to two in the morning.

'Yeah, sure,' Elias said.

'We could do with a Deykashee to help. Do not attempt to talk to or communicate with Avery or his father unless you have to.'

'OK. I'll call Thomas, I reckon Oliver would help,' Elias said.

'Good idea,' Flo said. 'Sophia.' Flo turned her dark gaze on her granddaughter. 'I don't know why you keep seeing Avery but just stop the collision; don't interfere any further than is absolutely necessary.'

FOURTEEN

The night air had long robbed the ay of its last warmth and Ahrl watched as the old man lay beneath the bridge swaddled in rags, newspaper and bin bags.

'I've found something useful for you,' Ahrl said. The old man didn't stir. The visions that Ahrl had wrestled from the fountain disturbed him deeply. No matter how many times he felt sure something would go right, he could never relax until the events had actually come to pass. There had been countless times over the years where a single bad decision had drastically altered a critical Positive event. A loud splash sounded suddenly beside them as something fell from the bridge above into the river, swallowed completely into its murky depths. The old man jolted beside him, rolled and fell out of his manmade nest. Ahrl looked up to see a man stumbling along the bridge, staggering into and clutching the crumbling brick barrier every few steps. The man had a soul as dark as the starless night and flashed intermittently with fiery orange and sickly green hues. 'Negative,' Ahrl murmured.

'Whaddya want? Eh? Eh?' The old man leapt to his feet with his fists clenched and his knees bent as he surveyed the immediate area. He ground his teeth and then his shoulders slumped suddenly. The old man yawned, revealing a cavern of stained, broken teeth and stretched. 'Jus' great, jus' great, I was havin' a nice lil old nap too.'

'This way,' Ahrl said pointing up a steep muddy bank to the pavement on the roadside. The old man couldn't see or hear him but the suggestion of his words seemed to work this time.

'I guess I better move then,' the old man said, putting his hands on his hips and arching his lower back until it cracked. He scooped up armfuls of his bed and, with a piece of dirty rope, fashioned his meagre belongings into a bundle and secured it. He threw it over his back and made his way up the slippery muddy bank to the pavement above. Ahrl walked effortlessly beside him; not a single speck of dirt clung to his white robes nor did the softest breeze stir his long, straight, ebony hair. They continued in this fashion, one aware and the other oblivious, until Ahrl stopped suddenly and pointed down a little street lined by terraced houses. The old man paused at the end of the road, looked left and right, and then continued on past the street and towards the town centre. Ahrl felt a crease form between his brows. 'You're going the wrong way,' Ahrl said to the old man's back; his suggestion had no effect. Ahrl gently reached out with his mind and a thin tendril of Positive golden energy bloomed from his outstretched palm and nudged the old man's soul. The old man stopped sharply, straightened up and his features smoothed over for a moment as he tilted his chin up to the universe. The years seemed to melt from his skin and he gazed up at the sky as though he was searching for a hidden and unknown answer to a problem he had heard only in a passing mention decades before. He shook himself as one might try to throw off the clutches of sleep and Ahrl's influence waned. The lines of age etched their way back on to the old man's skin, he dropped his chin and his body sagged under his load. Ahrl felt his hold on the fountain wobble and he glanced down the street and saw his desired destination, a yellow skip on the road outside one of the houses. The old man continued onwards and all Ahrl could do was watch and wait.

FIFTEEN

'So she still doesn't know?' Thomas said. Elias shook his head. Thomas let out a low whistle. They were in William's car, watching the gates of the Richmond's imposing home. Sophia had been to school that day, but nothing had happened, so now they were waiting outside, just as a precaution.

'Flo thought she would see it by now, but it's been years and still, nothing.'

'Well, I can't say I'm totally surprised. I haven't seen it, and everyone who I've come into contact with over the years haven't seen it either,' Thomas said.

'It was just one rogue vision. I think we should tell her,' Elias said.

'You've always thought that,' Thomas said. 'But I have to agree with your grandma on this one. This is too important and we don't want to mess up, both for Alice and Kyle's sakes but also for Sophia's and our own sakes. If we time it wrong and Flo's right about certain circumstances that risk Sophia's soul becoming Negative, we could instigate the outcome. She needs to be ready.'

'I know, I know, it just feels wrong, that's all. If it was me, I would want to know. By being aware, I could contain that negativity inside me and understand it for what it is.'

'Would it really do any good?' Thomas said. 'We don't even know if the circumstances are likely to occur yet; lots of things could change between now and then. We know more than anyone how the future is never set in stone.'

'Only for so long,' Elias said. 'Until your options run out because so many pathways become impossible.'

'That will happen eventually for all humanity if we don't colonise space in the future.'

'You're thinking far ahead,' Elias said.

'Of course, our continued existence in the afterlife is tied to human life, if people realised that then I'm pretty sure everyone would be thinking further ahead.'

'I can't believe she actually saw one of her classmates commit suicide.' Elias shook his head and glanced at the clock as the numbers crept towards midnight; he knew they would be sat there for many more hours.

'I'm surprised she hasn't seen this sort of thing sooner to be totally honest,' Thomas said. 'Sure, she's seen a couple of bruises and broken bones, but I mean, come on, our gifts deal with the deceased and death. Also, this is Avery Richmond we're talking about here. His mother was murdered; it's not your usual set of circumstances. She's been lucky so far.'

'I wouldn't call it lucky,' Elias said. 'I know what you mean but you didn't hear her screaming. I thought she was being attacked.'

'I don't envy you.'

'Has Ollie been pulled across the divide recently?'

'Yes.'

'And?' Thomas raised a dark eyebrow at him.

'Same old, same old. He can't tell me very much, and the Thirteen don't tell him very much either. Though apparently Ahrl wasn't there. Ollie thinks he has been spending a lot of time studying their fountain recently.'

'That doesn't bode well, but neither does it help,' Elias said.

'You can't blame them. They're trying to protect their souls too at the end of the day. They're too afraid to interfere because they don't want to deal with the consequences of those decisions should they be bad. It could turn their souls Negative, and we both know what fate awaits them when that happens.'

'I know,' Elias said. 'It's just so frustrating.'

'They do the best they can,' Thomas said. 'Or at least, that's what Oliver says.'

'Do you think Ollie's OK?' Elias asked, his gaze flickering back to the Richmond's house.

'Oh, he'll be fine, up to no good, no doubt, and having a good nosey around. But he's done this kind of thing before. He'll tell us if Avery wakes up and starts behaving suspiciously.'

'What did you see the other day when you came to the house?' Elias asked. He yawned and stretched then reached for the flask of coffee from between the seats.

'I thought I saw something to do with Alice and Kyle that may have helped Flo and Sophia, but it turned out to be a false alarm.'

'Oh, right. How's business?' Elias gulped down some coffee and then put the flask back between the seats.

'Surprisingly easy when you can see people's souls and you have an invisible twin brother, who can walk through walls and eavesdrop on conversations between clients and potential business partners.'

'Ouch, I wouldn't want to be in a business meeting with you.'

'I didn't say it was fair, but you've got to use all the skills and gifts that you possess in the business world.'

'I can't argue with that; I just hope your conscience is OK with it.'

'Oh, I'm always careful there; I always try and make good decisions for both parties involved. I don't want my conscience to crucify me when I eventually crossover and Oliver is enough of a Jiminy Cricket for anybody.' Elias laughed.

'Yes, I can believe that.' They sat up, they both felt it, a rush of tingling energy. Elias let his vision switch and saw a golden, glowing ghostly form hurry over to the car. Oliver passed through the car door and sat down in the back.

'Nothing to report.'

'Then why are you back?' Thomas asked.

'Because I was bored, Teddy. The boy and his dad are asleep, though his dad doesn't half snore.'

'Please don't call me that, and Avery might wake up whilst you're gone.'

'I doubt it,' Oliver said.

'Do you see what I have to deal with?' Thomas said, gesturing to his twin. 'I can't even go on dates without him commenting in my ear.'

'I'm only looking out for you, brother,' Oliver said. 'Besides, you like having me around.' He grinned.

'I can see people's souls; I don't really need help in the romance department.'

'He's so grumpy,' Oliver said.

'How are your energy levels, Ollie? Do you think you can manage to keep an eye on Avery until he wakes up and goes to school?' Elias asked.

'Of course I can, I've got enough energy to last me a decade.'

'Don't overdo it, Oliver, last time was scary enough,' Thomas said.

'See, I told you he likes having me around.' Oliver got out of the car, waved and then dashed back through the gates to the Richmond's house.

'It's going to be a long night,' Thomas said.

'Thanks for doing this.'

'It's not a problem. After everything the Leto family have done for me and my brother, I would do pretty much anything for your family.'

SIXTEEN

Sophia felt as though her stomach had spent the morning at an amusement park. It cramped, dropped, squeezed and flipped its way through the hours to lunchtime. It had been two days, but still her vision hadn't come to pass. She couldn't concentrate on her lessons and if Avery shared her lesson, her gaze would inevitably find its way to his seat. Avery didn't notice her, though he never seemed to notice anyone. He behaved as he usually did and chose to stare out of the window at the rain or bury his head in his arms.

When the lunch bell rang, Annie joined Sophia and chatted happily about that morning's events, but her words hovered around the edges of Sophia's preoccupied mind. Occasionally Annie would pause, silent questions lurking in her eyes, but they stayed hidden behind sealed lips when it was clear that no answers were forthcoming.

Sophia's stomach turned as they joined the queue of students lining up for lunch. Avery stood before them, his hands in his pockets and his head bent towards the ground. His sandy-coloured hair hung forwards, veiling his eyes. Sophia clenched her fists. She wanted to flee from the room, but she knew that it wouldn't prevent the nightmare from becoming a reality. She bit down hard on her lower lip and willed herself to be calm.

'Sophia, are you alright? You've been really *off* all morning,' Annie said.

'Yeah, I'm fine.' Sophia smiled brightly. Annie folded her arms and raised an eyebrow. 'I'm just tired that's all,' Sophia said. The queue shuffled forwards and Sophia forced back bile as the lunch hall came into view. Annie clasped her hands together and began bouncing on the balls of her feet like a small child.

'Ooo, do you smell that?' she said. 'It's spicy tomato pasta!' Sophia paled, she could smell it too; the sweet tangy tomato aroma mixed with spices that tickled her nasal passages.

'So it is.' She smiled weakly. The queue shuffled forwards again and Sophia kept her eyes fixed on the back of Avery Richmond's head; there was no sign of his mother. Minutes later they passed through the open doorway and Sophia's heart dropped. Harry and several other boys were running around between the tables, hitting a paper ball as though they were playing makeshift volleyball.

'Sheesh, they act like a bunch of primary kids,' Annie said, bristling as she followed Sophia's gaze.

The queue rounded a corner and the students walked in single file, collecting trays from the side and then approaching a line of hot and cold food stands. The school's cooks stood behind the counters, serving up plates, and Annie eagerly pointed at the spicy pasta. Sophia kept an eye on Avery the whole time, barely mumbling a thank you to the cook who served her. The line moved down and she chewed on her lip, desperate to say something but not sure what to say. *Avery, you might want to watch where you're going? Avery, I hope you aren't thinking of hanging yourself tonight?* Sophia groaned inwardly as she followed him to the last counter where drinks were being served. Her knuckles whitened around her tray and she felt a warm breath of air by her ear.

'Do you like Avery or something?' Annie whispered. Sophia's spine straightened sharply and her nerves sparked as though she had been struck by lightning.

'No,' she said, pushing her words out of the side of her mouth.

'You've been staring at him for two days.'

'No I haven't,' Sophia said

'What did you dream then?' Annie said. Sophia hurriedly

picked up a drink and followed Avery with Annie close on her heels. She could hear Annie muttering but her gaze was fixed on Avery. It was all happening too quickly, not in slow motion like her dream vision. Sophia stole quick glances at the paper ball group, mentally calculating the distance between them and Avery in a vain attempt to predict their erratic movements. The boys were oblivious to all thoughts and notions that their actions could or would push someone over the line as they balanced on the fringes of the world. The group yelled and shouted to one another and Sophia caught sight of Harry up ahead. It was just like her dream, just like her vision. Avery walked with his head down, a man on a mission to avoid everyone, and Harry jumped around, swinging his limbs like a man perpetually caught in limbo before he fell off the edge of a cliff.

'No, no, no,' Sophia whispered to herself. She saw a table on her right with an empty spot, set her tray down with a clang and in three quick strides, reached Avery and placed a hand firmly on his shoulder. The reaction to their physical contact was both immediate and intense. A sharp cold pain shot into her hand and her legs buckled as though all her energy was being drained. Nausea consumed her, smothering her, and her hand turned numb as though the nerves had been severed. Somehow she managed to speak. 'Avery, stop,' she said clearly, loudly, maybe a little too loudly. It was enough. He paused and Harry sailed backwards right in front of him, hitting the paper ball with his elbow and sending it flying into the air.

'Watch it!' Avery snarled at Harry. He clutched his tray protectively to his stomach.

'Woah, sorry dude,' Harry said. A stupid grin split his face in two but dropped the second he registered Avery. Sophia prised her hand off Avery's shoulder and gasped; she couldn't feel her hand. Avery didn't even look at her, but every student in the near vicinity was watching them. Cradling her hand protectively to her chest,

Sophia glanced back to see an open-mouthed Annie staring back. *Oh god, what have I done?* Her gaze returned to the back of Avery's head; every nerve in her body was waiting for the refute she was sure she was going to get. Even the paper ball group had paused their game, tapping unaware students on the shoulder and pointing at the pair. Avery didn't turn around; he rolled his shoulders and then continued to walk as though nothing had happened. Her shoulders dropped and she sighed as she cradled her hand and tried to massage warmth back into the cool skin. Annie stopped by her shoulder.

'So that's what you dreamed, and that was just plain rude,' Annie said, scowling in Avery's direction.

SEVENTEEN

Sophia held back a sigh of relief when Avery walked into their classroom the following morning. She had spent the night hours staring into the gloom with Avery's suspended corpse rotating slowly in her mind like some sort of perverse ballerina in a musical box. The sleepless night, the worrying, had thankfully been for nothing. Dark semicircles cupped his eyes but he was alive. She let her body slump onto her desk. *I wish I could just sleep and never have visions or see souls ever again.* She sat up, leant on one elbow and glanced in Avery's direction. He didn't seem to notice her. It was as though he chose to live in a self-contained bubble that the real world couldn't penetrate. The bell sounded and she followed Annie as they were dismissed from registration. They headed to the maths classroom and commandeered two of the window seats before the rest of the students drifted in. Ten minutes into the lesson, Sophia found her gaze drawn to movement out of the corner of her eye. She glanced out of the window and saw Avery darting into the woods with a rucksack on his back. *Where's he going? I hope he's not going to do anything stupid.* She refocussed her attention on the class but every so often her gaze would wander and she would check to see if Avery had emerged or not. When the class ended an hour later, Avery still hadn't appeared.

'What's so interesting outside?' Annie asked as Sophia gazed at the treeline and packed away her things.

'Does Avery often skip class and disappear into the woods?' Sophia lowered her voice as her gaze darted to their maths teacher.

'Yeah, he does that a lot,' Annie said.

'How do you know, have you seen him?' Sophia slung her bag over her shoulder.

'He used to do it the first time he tried to come back to school; Joe knew about it.'

'Oh, right.'

'Did you dream something again?'

'No, not this time, just curious, that's all.' Annie pursed her lips for a moment then they turned around and walked to their locker room. A green sticky note with "witch" in black capitals was affixed to Sophia's locker. She sighed, and ripped it off. Annie plucked the note from Sophia's hand, crossed out the first letter and was about to add a new one before Sophia managed to wrestle it back again.

'Oh, come on, Sophia, she deserves it,' Annie said as she tried and failed to get a hold of the note.

'No,' Sophia said, ripping the sticky note into several pieces.

'Spoilsport,' Annie said, poking her tongue out at Sophia. Sophia's muscles locked into place as a warm, tingling sensation crawled up the back of her neck and over her scalp. She felt a pressure around her mind as though someone were poking her. Her vision switched and she turned instinctively to the source. Disappearing amongst the crowds of students she saw Avery with his rucksack and beside him, a faint, ethereal figure. Mrs Richmond turned, her pale blue gaze locked with Sophia's and the woman's jaw dropped. 'I guess he's back then,' Annie said. Mrs Richmond disappeared around the corner, her soul pulled along by her son. 'Hey, are you OK?' Annie asked. Sophia blinked and tore her gaze away from the spot where Mrs Richmond had vanished.

'I just saw Avery's mum.'

'What?' Annie's eye widened. Sophia bit her lip. 'Right, you definitely need to talk and we definitely need to go and get that ice cream,' Annie said.

* * *

'You've got to be kidding me.' Annie paused, digging her spoon in her ice cream sundae glass. 'Mrs Richmond is still around and you think you know who killed her?' Sophia cringed as she glanced around the virtually empty café. They sat in the furthest corner, away from the counter and any prying eyes or ears. The sun shone through the lattice windows, casting golden squares which glided slowly across the floor and furnishings. The light flickered as traffic passed by outside – it was as if the sun was taking snapshots of the café's interior

'Yes, but I've only seen her twice and only recently.'

'Wow,' Annie said, dropping back in her seat. 'It's been almost two years though.'

'I know,' Sophia said.

'And Avery was going to top himself?'

'I don't know for certain,' Sophia said. 'But yes, it's what I saw.'

'Jeez,' Annie said. 'You should have said something sooner.' Sophia sighed and twirled her spoon around in her half-eaten ice cream.

'It's been difficult,' Sophia said. 'I've never seen anything like this before.'

'Yeah, I know, but you could have told me.'

'Elias, Thomas and Ollie have been camped outside Avery's house for the last three nights, just to be on the safe side,' Sophia said.

'What would they do if Avery did… you know…'

'I guess they'd jump the gates somehow, or ring the buzzer, something to get Mr Richmond's attention or disrupt Avery, and if that failed… well, they would probably break into the house to save him.'

'Should they really be doing that? I mean, what would they even say?'

'I don't know, but I've seen it and my family now know about it thanks to me. Could you just stand by and let someone die?'

Annie's gaze dropped down to the table.

'No, I guess not. I see your predicament. They need to get him a psychiatrist or something. I'm sure Joe said that he had one for a while,' Annie said.

'He may still be seeing one, for all the good it's doing, but it's not that simple. Avery's counted as an adult now in the medical world; no one can force him to go to the doctor, or get help.'

'Maybe he wouldn't actually do it. Maybe it was just a fantasy he was playing out in his head?'

'Maybe, but to even fantasise something like that…'

'Well, it's hardly surprising,' Annie said. 'I mean, it's been no time at all really. He probably shouldn't be in school, and they still haven't actually caught the killer; it must be on his mind constantly. I'd hate to think what I'd be like in that situation, or anyone really.'

'I know.' Sophia nodded.

'So what's the plan?'

'Elias seems to think we're in the clear now and Grandma doesn't think that Avery's likely to be connected to Alice and Kyle's pathway.'

'Ugh, really?' Annie rolled her eyes and Sophia felt a sharp jolt shoot up her spine.

'What? What's wrong?' Sophia said. Annie sighed.

'Don't you ever get tired of talking about Alice and Kyle?'

'What do you mean?' Sophia asked. 'They're part of my future, part of humanity's future.'

'Yes, I know, but you've even said so yourself, your visions aren't always one hundred percent accurate. I mean, what if it doesn't happen? What if they never get together? What if you never actually meet them?'

'No, no.' Sophia shook her head. 'Alice and Kyle, they're different. My ancestors have seen their visions for centuries, there's no way that it won't happen.'

'But there's a chance, right? A chance that it might not happen or that it might work out differently?' Annie asked. 'They might make different choices, or something else might change the course of their lives?'

'I guess, but I don't understand why you're saying all of this. I thought you believed me?'

'I do believe you, Sophia, but your family seem obsessed with them. It's like all they ever do is worry about them, even if you don't have visions of them. I just wonder when you'll start to focus on you and your own life? I wonder what you'd be doing now had you never seen them.'

'I...' Sophia was flummoxed, she had never really thought about it before. Sure she had wished to never have visions, but she hadn't really considered what that meant for herself or her potential future.

'Besides, if Avery isn't important, then why do you keep seeing him?'

'I don't know, probably because I knocked into that Negative soul at the supermarket.' Sophia said, staring down at her ice cream. *What would I be doing now if I didn't know about Alice or Kyle? Would I still be studying for a future career in physics, even though I do love it?*

'Perhaps, but you saw him as an older person too,' Annie said. 'You think he's somewhere in London? What if there's a pathway for Avery where he'll eventually be involved with parliament? He would see the London Eye from there.'

'I didn't think about that.'

'Well, I'm only speculating. His father is a rich business man, he probably has contacts all over the place; it could just be linked to that.'

'I'm more worried about what Avery will do now.' Sophia sighed. 'He might be driven to suicide again at some point, something else might trigger it, and then what? What if I do see it and what if I don't?'

'Hmm,' Annie said, leaning on one elbow and placing a

spoonful of ice cream into her mouth. She gulped. 'Well, I know if I were Avery and I really wanted to die then there would be only one thing that would hold me back.'

'And that is?'

'Seeing the killer either dead or locked up.'

'Annie!'

'Yeah, I know you're not supposed to kill, it's bad for the soul, but I wouldn't want to actually kill them myself. I'm just saying I wouldn't lose any sleep if they were accidently run over by a bus.' Sophia frowned. 'I can't really imagine what Avery must be feeling right now, but if there is anything that would persuade him to live, even if it was only for a few extra days, then I'm certain the promise of finding his mother's murderer would make him pause.'

'I can't tell Avery about the man I saw, I don't even know if he really did it or not,' Sophia said.

'Avery doesn't need to know that,' Annie said. 'All Avery needs to know is that you might have information about his mother's death. You just need to dangle enough of a carrot so that he's tempted and takes a couple of steps back from the cliff edge.'

'But I'd be lying,' Sophia said.

'It's not an outright lie. And besides, if you have another vision where he tops himself again, what other choice do you have? It's either this or constantly worrying about when he might be tempted to do it again, and it's not like you're going to be near him forever. You can't possibly be Avery's secret guardian angel for the rest of your life and Elias can't camp outside of his house every night forever.'

'Hopefully it'll never get to that.'

'You said so yourself, he might be tempted or driven to it again.'

'What do I do then?'

'Write a note,' Annie said. 'If you see another vision where Avery commits suicide then you can put the note in his locker and ask him to meet you somewhere. You don't have to put your name on it, though meeting him outside of school would probably be best.'

'Then what?'

'Then you talk to him, tell him that you have information which might help him find the killer.'

Sophia inhaled deeply.

'It's too risky. What exactly do I say? That I think I know who the killer is and I ran into them at the supermarket?'

'No, don't say that, just make something up,' Annie said. 'The goal here is to delay him, if you can do that, then you've already won half the battle. The more believable it is and the more interested he is, the longer he might be put off from… you know. It could buy you some time and get you to talk him out of it for good.'

'And what if he doesn't believe me?'

'Then you can always say you know what he's been planning to do and that you'll tell his dad or someone about it if he still plans to go ahead with it.'

'My family won't be happy about this; they'll try to stop me if they find out,' Sophia said. She pushed her ice cream glass to the side and leant forwards on the table, massaging her temples. 'I sure hope they don't see any of this in their visions.'

'You don't need to worry about it now,' Annie said. 'Wait and see if you have another vision; if you don't and Avery still goes ahead with it and you can't stop it then it's not your fault. You've got gifts but you're not a freaking oracle for every single person on the planet. That would probably drive you insane.'

'I guess, I just… I don't know, maybe I should try and talk to him or something, be his friend?'

Annie snorted.

'Good luck with that one. Avery drove all of his old friends away. Joe messages him and calls him every few days, but he never gets a reply.'

'Your brother still does that?'

'Yeah,' Annie said. 'He's left voicemails saying that if Avery ever needs to talk then he just needs to call whenever and at any time. Joe would pick up a call from Avery even if it was three in the morning.'

'I didn't know he still did that.'

'He felt pretty bad about how things were left between them; they had an argument before he left for university but Joe doesn't hold that against Avery. He knows he's struggling.'

'Your brother's a good guy.'

Annie pulled out a piece of paper and a pen from her school bag. 'Here, I'll help you write a note. Let's just hope you won't ever need it.'

EIGHTEEN

There was a loud, wet, crack and his body, suspended by a rope at his neck, turned slowly to reveal a pristine white shirt. Sophia's eyelids flew apart and she sat up, catching the screams before they erupted from her throat. She clamped a hand over her mouth and squeezed her eyes shut as she took several steadying breaths. She pulled the fabric of her pyjama top away from her burning skin in an attempt to soothe her body as the light outside strained through the cracks in her curtains. She twisted and reached for the glass of water on her bedside table and gulped down the cool liquid as her gaze zeroed in on her alarm clock; it was twenty past five. She clutched her head and cursed. *I can't take this anymore. I'm going to have to do something. I can't just stand on the side-lines and watch.*

* * *

Shoppers and business people hurried around the square whilst the chinking sounds of waiters and waitresses serving and clearing tables outside quaint bars and cafés echoed under the din of steady traffic and conversations. Two days had passed since she'd dropped the note in Avery's locker. She had detailed her second vision of his suicide to her family, and Elias had agreed to keep watch on the Richmond's house for the rest of the week, but she hadn't told them about Annie's idea or the note. She knew they would disagree with her direct interference, but what choice did she have? *I can't keep having those visions of his suicide; I'll go crazy if I see him hang himself again.* Sophia's body felt as though it were shrinking in on itself as

Flo's voice echoed in her mind. '*I don't think you should be going about on your own anywhere for a while.*' Her gaze flickered to a café a few hundred yards away where Annie sat at an outside table, wearing retro circular sunglasses as she sipped coffee and kept watch.

'I'm not totally alone,' Sophia said quietly as she gazed down at the smooth stone by her feet. She let her vision sweep over the few weary and hungry people who had also descended upon the steps at the centre of Chiliad Square. Behind her was a large statue, depicting modern, reimaged versions of untaught ancient gods and goddesses, a recent instalment from the art museum just around the corner; though she had no idea which deity would be the most likely to have two cats.

She spotted Avery as he approached the statue and its steps and watched as he turned his head from left to right. She hadn't put her name on the bottom of the note and she hadn't given him any indication of who she was or what she looked like, just a couple of sentences, a time, a place and a date. She raised her hand to wave at him and his piercing blue gaze found her quickly.

'It was you?' he said, scowling at her. 'You wrote the note?' She blinked at him; it was a surprise to hear his voice.

'Yes.' Sophia nodded; she didn't need her otherworldly vision to tell her he was angry. He glanced around, let his shoulders drop and clasped his forehead briefly before drawing closer to her and folding his arms tightly across his middle.

'OK, you have my attention. What do you know?' Sophia bit her lip and resisted the urge to look at Annie.

'Well, I think, I might have some information about the person who…' Sophia looked up at him; god, it was hard to finish this sentence but thankfully she didn't have to.

'If you have information then why didn't you go to the police months ago?'

'Oh.' *Yes, that would have made sense.* 'Well, it's a bit difficult you see… I don't think they would believe me.' *Oh god, I'm screwing this up already.*

'Believe you? If you've got information then they have to listen.' Sophia bit the inside of her cheek. *What do I say now?* Avery frowned. 'Look, if you don't actually know anything then do me a favour and quit wasting my time.' He shook his head, turned and began to walk away from her, but all Sophia could think about was his body hanging by a rope. *No, he can't leave, I can't let him leave.*

'Wait, Avery! I'm not like you.' Avery paused and turned back to face her. 'I have certain, abilities.' She peeked up at him but his face was a mask of stone. 'I see things sometimes, visions,' she said as her gaze darted around at anyone who might be close enough to hear her. 'When I see visions, I usually see events from the future but sometimes I see things from the past too. I saw what you planned to do. I know you were planning to end your life and that's why I put a note in your locker.' She raised her eyes but he didn't say a word. He stood very still and then suddenly turned on his heel and marched away. Sophia jumped up, dashed down the steps and grasped his wrist.

'Wait,' she said. Avery yanked his arm away from her. 'Avery, please.' He turned to face her and she shrank away from his blistering gaze.

'Are you enjoying this?' he said. 'Do you get some weird kick out of emotionally torturing people?'

'No. I swear it's not like that. I'm telling the truth.' Avery snorted and rolled his eyes.

'Visions? You can't be serious.' Sophia didn't reply. 'That's the craziest thing I've heard anyone say, ever.' He turned away from her again.

'I'll prove it to you.' Avery kept walking. Sophia licked her lips and eyed the people in the square. 'You want to know who took your mother, don't you?' she said. Avery paused. 'You don't have to believe me right now, but I'll prove it to you, just please, trust me.' She stared at his back for several long moments and then, finally, his shoulders slumped and he turned back to face her.

'Oh really, and how are you going to do that?' Sophia held her tongue as a man walked by. She waited until he was safely out of earshot.

'I don't know right now.' Sophia scrambled quickly in her mind for an answer; this hadn't been part of the plan. Avery rolled his eyes and started to turn away again.

'Look! I care. I've seen good things for you that you can't see right now. If you really want to leave the world that badly then pick another date, a random date next week,' Sophia said. The idea seemed to form as she spoke. 'Don't tell me about it or when; I'll come to you. If I successfully come to you during the day, before you decide to do it, then will you listen to me?' *What am I saying? My visions don't work like that. I can't always predict the exact day!*

'Yeah, like you can actually do that.'

'I've already done it once before,' she said, steeling her nerves and gesturing at him. She had no idea if he had actually planned to do it today, but when Avery's pale blue eyes darkened to a deep cerulean blue, she knew she was right, lucky, but still right.

'You're mad. And what if you're not successful?'

'Then whatever, you can go ahead with your plans if you wish and I'll have to live with the consequences.' *I absolutely cannot live with the consequences. What am I going to do?* She would have to rely on luck again and that didn't sit comfortably with her. Avery worked his jaw from side to side as he thought about it for a few moments.

'If this is some kind of sick joke…'

'It's not,' Sophia said. 'I've been trying to talk to you for weeks.' She bit her bottom lip. 'I… I don't have answers right now, but I might be able to help you find the answers. I can't help you if you're dead though.' Avery exhaled loudly through his nose and turned his head to the side, gazing at a spot in the distance. He laughed but it was a short, humourless laugh and eventually he turned back to face her with narrowed eyes.

'I can't believe I'm actually saying this, but fine, I guess. I've got nothing left to lose; a few more days won't really make much difference. If you can do it, then I'll listen, but how will you come to me if I'm not at school?'

'I'll know, I'll find a way,' Sophia said.

'Sure,' Avery said, dragging out the word and arching an eyebrow at her.

'I will,' Sophia said, closing the gap between them. She stuck out her hand. 'Do we have a deal?' Avery clenched his teeth; his gaze bounced down to her outstretched hand and back up to her face. He gave her a stiff nod, turned and walked off and out of sight.

Sophia glanced at her outstretched hand and dropped her arm to her side. She caught sight of Annie hurrying over to her out of the corner of her eye.

'Is he gone?' Sophia said as soon as Annie reached her.

'Oh yeah, I don't think he'll be coming back,' Annie said. 'How was it?'

'Awful. I messed up and I told him about my gifts. I made a stupid deal and now I have to prove that my gifts are real by predicting when he next plans to commit suicide. I have to predict the exact day and I have no idea how I'm going to do it.' Tears welled in Sophia's eyes and Annie's eyes widened. 'My family are going to be so angry about this.'

'Can't you watch his soul or speak to Mrs Richmond? Maybe she can help?'

'Maybe, but his soul is grey, there's very little colour to go on, and Mrs Richmond's soul is weak, I haven't seen her since the locker room. God, Annie, what have I done?' Sophia covered her face with her hands and felt Annie's skinny arms wrap around her.

'It will be OK, we'll figure something out,' she said.

NINETEEN

Ahrl leant his imagined form against the side of a tall, pale sandstone building, the old man sitting on the floor next to him. They watched the world go by and the old man held up a stained paper coffee cup.

'Please can ye spare some change?' the old man said to all the people who walked by. The majority didn't even look at him; others glanced at him with fear; not fear of the old man, but fear of what he represented – and fear that they could quite easily end up the same way. They hurried by and adults tugged away young children who stared at the old man with an untainted mixture of innocence and curiosity; if they realised the truth at this age they would probably ask why nobody was helping. Occasionally someone would drop some loose change into the old man's cup and he would smile and thank them, but they didn't stop to chat or spare him any long looks. The town centre was alive with activity, noise, and the smothering ambience of engine fumes and trapped lives. It reminded him oddly of the districts from his home world, how they had been heavily overcrowded in the last few years. Ahrl gazed idly at the different souls as they passed by; the majority were weakly Positive souls, but every once in a while a soul would shine out from the crowds. Ahrl rarely caught glimpses of their faces and he couldn't direct the fountain at them without leaving the old man.

He looked up from their corner, across the square to where a stone statue commanded attention, raised up on several steps. Sophia sat there waving tentatively, and he watched as a young man with a familiar, yet enraged soul approached her. They spoke for only a few minutes, and the young man's soul flashed with an orange anger as though a person was pumping a small fire with bellows. The young man walked away from her but Sophia leapt up and caught his wrist. He didn't look happy about it; he yanked his arm away and walked off again but then she said something and he stopped. They seemed to reach some agreement and although Sophia offered her hand, the young man ignored it and walked away.

Ahrl frowned as he watched this scene, irrelevant to the majority and played out in plain sight yet completely overlooked and ignored, save for one individual. Ahrl felt the coldness of his presence before he registered the man. He had vivid green eyes and a grey hood covered his bald head as he stared at Sophia, his mouth open in a small stretched "O" shape. Green and purple bruises decorated his face but Ahrl recognised him from the visions; he was the man who had shaved his head, the same man who he had seen running through the woods. Ahrl glanced down at the man's soul. Green guilt and dark grey despair twisted in on itself, darkening his soul as icy blue fear flashed around the outer edges. Ahrl raised a hand and reached out with his mind, letting a faint tendril of golden light emanate from his palm towards the man, but darkness leapt out and annihilated Ahrl's Positive energy before it could even reach him.

'I pity your soul in this moment,' Ahrl said. 'You're sheltering Negative energy.' Ahrl lowered his arm and pulled his mind back. The man was trapped in spirals of self-loathing, guilt, anger, misery and frustration. He had had no support and no means to build support, and often these souls would fall so far that they would know only hopelessness and reach out for more Negativity. Bad decisions were often not the cause of hard lives, they came from hard lives. The man's lips moved and then he turned and hurried away from the square.

Ahrl watched silently as Sophia's friend joined her; Sophia

covered her face with her hands and her friend hugged her before they moved out of the square completely. He could see the green guilt growing within Sophia's soul.

The hours crept by and the sky turned from pale blue and grey to a burning orange and pink, eventually giving way to cooler shades of purple and navy. The crowds died down to the point where only one or two individuals would pass the old man every so often. The old man stood up, placed his hands on his lower back and pushed his hips forwards with a crack. He held his cup, which rattled with change, tightly in his hands and hefted his makeshift bundle onto his back. He made his way through the town, passing silent shops closed for the night and quiet weekday evenings in the bars.

Ahrl found himself gazing up at the sky, to the few stars he could see. *How things will change for this world in the next couple of decades,* he thought. It wouldn't look much different but at the same time he knew that these streets, and all the streets on Earth would be altered. One day, soon, Alice, Kyle and Sophia would make a great discovery and it would lead to great advancements in technology. These streets wouldn't be quiet as they were now. There would be machines that would look almost human, and they would walk about carrying out chores for humanity. They would help in so many areas but at the same time it would come at a cost; humans were about to do something no one had done before and Ahrl wasn't sure whether the outcome would be Positive or Negative.

The old man stopped suddenly and tilted his head. Ahrl paused and listened; he heard a faint scrabbling sound and a muffled cry. The old man dropped his bundle and sprang down the darkened street, paused briefly and then turned sharply into a narrow alleyway. Ahrl followed a few steps behind but the old man had already picked up an empty wine bottle from the floor and cracked it over another person's head.

'Ye bastard,' the old man shouted, pulling 'the' other man away from a wall. A woman slid down the wall and sobbed; the straps on her dress had been torn and she pulled the material up to cover herself. Ahrl looked down at the man who lay unconscious by the old man's feet; sweat shone over his pale complexion and greasy skin, and there was a large brown birthmark on his left cheek. The man's soul was as black as the bottom of the deepest pit, suffocating all colours which struggled beneath the Negative. 'Are ye alright?' the old man said to the woman. She nodded, fear and panic prevalent in her colours. 'Quick, call the police,' the old man said. The woman fumbled for her bag and drew out her phone whilst the old man glowered at his captive on the floor.

When the police were arriving, the old man said, 'I have to go. Ye take care of yourself, right?'

'OK. I understand. Thank you,' the woman said, her eyes on her assailant in case he moved before the police arrived. The old man hastily left the alleyway, picked up his bundle and watched from a shadowy corner as the police tended to the victim. The young woman was escorted away and the man placed in cuffs while they waited for paramedics to arrive. The old man nodded with a grim satisfaction and carried on his way.

TWENTY

She gazed at him from underneath her eyelashes on the other side of the lunch hall. He sat alone as always, pushing his food around his plate. She hadn't said a word to her family about her deal with Avery, and they hadn't asked. The last week had been tortuous; every night she had gone to bed with a feeling of dread but she had seen nothing, that was, until last night. She had seen his suicide again, but she couldn't be sure he was actually planning to do it that night, or even if he was planning to do it at all that week.

'What do you think?' Annie asked. Sophia tore her gaze away from Avery.

'I don't know,' she said. 'It's impossible to tell. Usually we try and figure out the time or the date of a vision by looking for a clock, or a calendar, or the weather outside, but there's nothing like that in his garage.'

'Is Elias still camping outside of Avery's house?'

'Yes. They know I saw the vision again last night so he will again tonight.'

'Well, at least you know Elias will be able to stop the worst from happening.'

'Yes, but for how long?' Sophia said. 'It's like you said, Elias can't camp outside of his house forever, he's already complaining about becoming nocturnal. And if Avery does do it tonight and Elias stops it, then what will stop Avery from telling him about our deal? My family will be furious if they find out.'

'Maybe it's for the best,' Annie said. 'You know, if Avery knows about you and your family then at least your family will have to explain it all to him, and maybe they'll even agree to help him.'

'I don't know, it's not like we think anyone will take us seriously,' Sophia said. 'They won't want to get involved with something like this, especially if it means talking to the police. They won't want to risk exposing the family or our gifts.' A warm tingling sensation caressed and spread across her left side; she let her vision switch and glanced up. A soul glowed beside her, its colours morphing into a brilliant golden light before stretching out into a bodily form. Mrs Richmond appeared, her body waning as she tried to gain purchase on the living world. Her hair was bound up behind her head and she wore a beautiful necklace, the type that Sophia had only ever seen as costume jewellery, and a black satin dress. Mrs Richmond opened her lips as her body flickered. Sophia could make out the other students and the lunch hall through her semi-transparent form.

'Please save him,' Mrs Richmond said. Her voice was weak and unsteady as she tried to get her words across. She pinched her lips into a thin line and clenched her gloved hands; she almost faded out and disappeared completely but then somehow found a sudden burst of energy, her body becoming more whole for a brief moment. 'Save him,' she said again, her voice stronger than before. She looked over at Avery, a sad smile lighting her face and then she dimmed, her body and soul slowly dissolving into thin air. Sophia whirled round and watched as Avery stood up. He dumped his tray, but just before he left the hall, Mrs Richmond flickered briefly into existence beside him and stared at Sophia.

'Sophia?' Annie said. Sophia stood up.

'He's going to do it tonight.'

'How do you know?'

'I just saw Mrs Richmond,' Sophia said. She dumped her tray and followed him out of the hall.

Mrs Richmond appeared in brief flashes up ahead, and Sophia

followed her down the corridors like a trail of twinkling stars. She stepped out of a side door on the westerly side of the school and saw Avery disappearing into the treeline. Mrs Richmond appeared briefly again, her body stuttering in and out of the living world. Sophia took a deep breath and followed them into the woods.

TWENTY-ONE

He had noticed how his silence was often mistaken for indifference, but it had its uses. He kept a careful eye on Sophia, the girl who had plagued his waking and sleeping hours and who had so deliberately ruined his plans to escape from this world. She didn't seem to be like the rest of them, offering pointless, nescient condolences, claiming to understand his feelings when he knew they never could. The sheer audacity of her claims was laughable, and he now understood why someone had put a post-it note with "witch" written on it on her locker. She was clearly unhinged, grabbing his shoulder in the lunch hall and claiming to have visions – though since their meeting at Chiliad Square she hadn't approached him. He rubbed his shoulder; he could remember the burning, tingling sensation that had seized his skin when she touched him and he thought about that moment more often than he was willing to admit.

The day finally arrived for his delayed plan to be set into action and he was almost sad that the strange girl hadn't bothered him. Her so-called gifts were fake after all. He thought he would give her half a chance by picking a school day; she hadn't approached him but he knew she was watching him, she watched him all the time. He decided he would give her the slip at lunchtime; she wouldn't be able to follow him, no one knew about his hideout in the woods. He quickly dumped his tray, grabbed his belongings and stole himself away into the woods for one last time. He felt the weight of his rucksack on his back and his violin case pressing between his shoulders as the trees grew denser and denser, and then, after twenty minutes or so, he came out into a clearing where an abandoned building stood. It was a tall structure, three storeys high, an old timber factory, rotting and falling apart as its wooden victims closed in around it, eagerly watching its slow demise. Sanctuary was what Avery called it. He squeezed through a gap in the flimsy chain-link fence meant for keeping trespassers out and walked through a broken doorway and into the heart of the building; it was empty, caked in dust, grime, broken glass and bricks. He headed up the rusty metal stairs hugging the corner of the building, and then onto walkways lining the walls. At one time, people would have been able to look down from these walkways and see the timber cutting process in action. Avery took another flight of dilapidated stairs up to the top floor to a separate, smaller room and made his way over loose and broken floorboards to the open window where the brickwork crumbled around the edges. He looked out over the treetops as the light faded behind a sea of wispy clouds and he sighed as a cool breeze grazed his cheeks, nose and lips. He pulled out Sophia's note from his trouser pocket. He smoothed the creases out of the paper on the top of his thigh and reread the cursive handwriting.

I may have information about your mother's death. Meet me on Saturday, 11 o'clock, Chiliad Square, beneath the statue. She had picked an awful spot to meet, it was barely a block away from where his mother had died and the museum was just around the corner. He dropped the note out the window, watching as it fell down to the ground in big, swooping arcs. He put his rucksack on the floor and pulled his violin out of its case. The polished dark wooden curves caught the sunlight as he placed the violin gently on his shoulder and under his chin. *One last time.* He moved his fingers into position and pulled the bow delicately across the strings. A sweet, sorrowful sound reverberated through the air. He closed his eyes and let his mind become lost in the music. His arms and fingers moved easily into well-practised movements and the violin sang a beautiful, sad tune. When the last note faded he opened his eyes and lowered his instrument. He heard one of the floorboards creak, crack and groan behind him. His head whipped towards the sound and he felt his jaw slacken. *How did she find me?* Sophia stood in the doorway to his sanctuary, the one place he'd reserved for himself.

'How long have you been there?'

'A while. You play beautifully.' Avery exhaled loudly and then packed away his violin.

'You must practise a lot,' Sophia said.

'Why are you here?'

'You know why I'm here,' Sophia said. Avery's guts twisted as he snapped the clasps shut on the case.

'How did you find me?'

'Oh, I followed you. I used another one of my gifts.' She shifted on her feet, touched the cracked and mouldy doorframe and then snatched her hand back.

'OK,' Avery said, standing up. He slowly turned to face her. *There's no way she has gifts, this is insane.* 'Perhaps you were just lucky.'

Sophia sighed.

'We can do this again but I'd rather not,' Sophia said. 'I deal with death a lot with my gifts but this is the first time I've seen murder or suicide; you know most people just pass away at home or in the hospital. What I can't understand is why you would want to do it; it's not what your mother would want.' Avery's nostrils flared.

'You never knew my mother,' Avery said.

'No,' she lowered her gaze to the floor, 'but then again I have my own mother and I can imagine having my own children one day, and I know she loved you, and you love her, otherwise you wouldn't be feeling this way.'

'Do you know what it feels like to lose someone unexpectedly? Someone you love, someone who is a cornerstone of your life, someone who you just couldn't imagine living without?' He didn't wait for her response as he turned his back on her and stood by the window. 'You know that everyone will die eventually, and even when they're old and have lived a full life you'll feel sad when they're gone, but it's different when it's someone who's been taken before their time, when someone else decides that they can just take another person's life. Even prison seems too sweet for people like that. Who made them god? Who gave them the right to decide who lives and who dies?' Avery tightened his hands into fists as he felt rage barrelling down his nerves like bullet trains rocketing through tunnels. 'And you think when something terrible like that happens that it would be the depression that hits you the hardest, and yeah, it hurts, it's like falling into a well that leads straight to the centre of the earth. But it's not the sadness that's the real killer; it's the injustice that really gets you. You know they should be alive, that they should have been allowed to live, you know their life was unfairly cut short and there's nothing you can do about it. My mother should be here and that animal who killed her should be dead instead, yet he's out there roaming free, and you ask me why?' His whole body shook as he turned his gaze on her.

'No. No, I don't,' Sophia said. 'I don't know how it feels, and my imaginings would only be a faint echo; I can never know how you truly feel.' Avery waited for her to say the dreaded *but* word but she said nothing more. She had been sincere, he could give her that much, and she hadn't tried to combat his feelings or compare his tragedy to anyone else's. He took several deep breaths as his emotions ebbed away. 'OK, how did you know?'

'It's a gift I have, or a curse, depends on how you want to see it.'

'Is this why you had a witch note on your locker?' He glanced in Sophia's direction; her cheeks flushed pink beneath her downcast eyelashes.

'Yes, I guess so,' she said. 'It's like I told you before, I see visions sometimes, visions of the future. I usually have visions in my dreams but I have some when I'm awake too.'

'So you're psychic?'

'Not exactly, though I'm not sure what to call it. I have several gifts; I can see emotions and their corresponding energies, and I can see souls.'

'Souls?'

'Yes, even you have a soul; it appears to me as a small bubble at the centre of every person, and within that bubble there are multiple colours which correspond to emotions.'

'OK...'

'I also see things from the past sometimes,' Sophia said. 'They're like extreme imprinted memories but that only appears to happen under certain circumstances.'

'My mother?'

'Yes, I saw some of your mother's final moments.' Avery felt the urge to launch himself across the room but he sat down on the edge of the window and gripped the sill instead.

'They caught him, you know,' Avery said as he gazed down at the floor. 'They had the killer and then they let him go because apparently having blood on your clothes isn't enough evidence.' Avery turned his face and glowered across the treeline.

'Are you sure it was him? There were other suspects.'

'Then do you know who did it? Do you know who killed her? What they look like?'

'No.' Sophia avoided his gaze. 'I only saw parts and the person had their face covered.'

Avery's shoulders slumped. 'OK, say I believe you for a minute, could you potentially see more from the past?'

Sophia hesitated.

'Depends on the circumstances and conditions.'

'What circumstances and conditions do you need?'

'Hard to tell. I think my mind is more in tune with certain aspects of the human consciousness but most events in life aren't extreme. You can have extreme good and extreme bad, and they have energies; I call them Positive and Negative. I would have to be near to someone or go somewhere where something extreme had happened, but there's no guarantee that my mind would actually pick up on anything.' Avery frowned and watched a spider dash from one crack in the brickwork and disappear into another whilst he mulled over his thoughts.

'If we went to the place where my mother died, would that work?'

'Possibly,' Sophia said. 'I won't know until I try, and I haven't tried yet.'

'What else have you apparently seen?'

'Many things,' Sophia said. 'For instance, I saw that you would be paired with Beth and that she would forget to remove the cork from her conical flask before it happened. I often see a boy and a girl named Kyle and Alice, but I've seen them for a while; they're set to do some great things in the future.'

'Do you know them?'

'No, I haven't actually met them.'

'Then how do you know they're real people and not just a figment of your imagination?'

'Visions are different, they feel different. It's almost like I'm there with the people in my visions, all my senses are active and they have more clarity than ordinary dreams. I also wake up with a warm, electric, tingly feeling on my skin from the Positive energy or a cold numbness if the vision was Negative.'

'What is this Positive and Negative?'

'It's hard to explain; they're energies that are tied to human emotions and consciousness, but it often depends on how the emotions are coupled or grouped together and what circumstances those emotions are responding to. Positive feeds off of positive emotions and Negative feeds off of negative emotions. It's like... have you ever had days when everything just seems to go right? Or when everything just seems to go wrong? Or have you ever been introduced to someone and you just hit it off straight away? Or you just don't like them and you don't really know why?'

'I guess so.'

'It's more complicated than that but that's when Positive and Negative are most at work. There are people out there who have what I call Negative or dark souls; they have almost no colour and their souls are mostly black. These are the sorts of people you want to stay away from. They've held on to negative emotions and allowed them to grow inside them. Sometimes they're not easy to spot, other times they're blindingly obvious.'

'What? Like Hitler?'

'Yes,' she said. 'The sad thing is, no child is ever born Negative; it's something that people gain as they grow.'

'So the thing that killed my mother, they'll have a Negative soul?'

'Yes, it's most likely.'

'But not always?'

'Like I said, it depends on circumstances, but there is a difference between having a choice and having no choice; some people fail to recognise that and their souls turn Negative as a result.'

'OK, say I do believe everything you've just said, would you come with me to the alleyway where my mother was killed and try and see something from the past?' Sophia bit her lip and gazed everywhere but at Avery. 'Please?' She looked up.

'Only if you promise not to kill yourself, but I can't guarantee that I'll see anything.' Avery groaned and drew his hands down his face.

'You better not be screwing me around. If I find out you're lying then there'll be nothing you can say or do that will make me stay here.'

'I get it, and no, I'm not,' Sophia said. Avery stared at her long and hard and then he nodded, stood up and picked up his violin case and rucksack. He offered a hand to Sophia as he approached her in the doorway. She glanced down at his outstretched palm and then clasped it lightly. He shook her hand.

'I guess we have another deal, Sophia Leto. You help me and I'll stay on this planet for a little longer.'

'I hope you stay for a long time yet.'

TWENTY-TWO

There were no sounds, no light, no senses at all. She tried to reach out, tried to move, but she felt nothing. She couldn't feel her body, or a single hair on her head; it was as though she had no body yet she was aware, she was somewhere. The darkness seemed to close in around her on all sides, or perhaps she was the darkness and there was no beginning or end. She panicked but she felt no bodily reaction, her heart didn't race and her body didn't sweat. She felt a piercing coldness grip her and somehow it burned as her awareness dimmed and faded. Her voice made no sound yet she imagined that she screamed into this void, and no answer came back. Not even an echo.

* * *

'I dreamt of nothing, Grandma, but I was aware. I was aware of the nothingness.'

'What do you mean, Sophia?'

'It was just dark; it was as though I was blind, deaf, mute and bodiless.'

'That is strange,' Flo said.

'It hurt too, Grandma. I remember this icy coldness; it felt like… like Negative.' Flo frowned. 'It felt like the hell-state that you once described, that state of temporary existence for Negative souls before they cease to exist. It can't happen to living people? Can it?'

'No.'

'I've never seen anything like it before. I'm not going crazy like some of our ancestors, am I?'

'No, no, of course not. I think your visions must still be jumbled with everything that has been happening with Avery and his mother; it's thrown off your extended senses, that's all. Tell me if it happens again, but don't worry about it for now, OK?'

The conversation had done nothing to ease Sophia's mind. She stood waiting for Avery by the statue in Chiliad Square. *This is stupid, you lied to him; you have no idea if you'll actually be able to see anything.* She studied the statue, the flowing shapes of the unpainted marble. *Well, I guess he's still alive.*

'Sophia,' Avery said. She turned and saw him approach; he didn't smile, he rarely smiled, but at least he wasn't scowling at her.

'Hi,' she said.

'Hi.' He fidgeted on the spot. 'Let's just get this over with.' Avery turned and led the way out of the square and she followed him to the less busy side streets. They walked in silence and, after a minute or so, his pace slowed as they approached the mouth of a narrow alleyway. His eyes were wide, he looked genuinely scared. Sophia realised how brave this was of him and how he must be fighting to keep the pain from his face, yet the corners of his mouth pressed downwards. He stopped and stared down the alleyway. *So this is where it happened then, down here.*

'We don't have to do this,' Sophia said softly. Avery curled his fingers into his palms and straightened his shoulders.

'No, I have to do this. Whoever killed her pulled her in at the other end of this alleyway.' He stepped forwards and led the way. Sophia followed and let her gaze wander over the brick walls and backdoors. Bins lined the alleyway and it wasn't big enough to drive down. The stench of rotting garbage and damp infiltrated her airways. She glanced up at the drainpipes and the narrow strip of sky above. They walked for a short while and came to a larger part of the alleyway which then bent around a ninety-degree angle into a narrower section. 'It was here,' Avery said, gesturing to a corner of the larger section. He paced up and down, his gaze roaming everywhere and nowhere all at once.

'OK. Are you alright?' Sophia asked.

'No, not really.' Avery gulped and blinked back tears. 'It's just hard. I never thought I would actually come here. Do you sense anything?'

'Give me a minute,' Sophia said. She closed her eyes and took a deep breath as she tried to focus her mind. She tried to imagine the evening when Mrs Richmond had been killed, the cold winter air, the rapidly fading daylight, the flurry of half-melted snow falling from the sky. When she sensed nothing, she tried to put herself into Mrs Richmond's shoes, the quiet contentment of shopping for her family at Christmas time followed by the overwhelming fear and anxiety as someone grabbed her and threatened her life. She felt a pressure around her mind and then a cold numbness which seeped down to her toes. Sophia's vision wavered and the alleyway began to fade from her sight. She blinked heavily a couple of times and the alleyway disappeared. Sophia found herself on a street lined with a few shops, their decorative lights twinkling in darkened windows. She saw it then, across the road from where she stood, a figure clad in black glanced up and down the street. She followed the line of his gaze and further down the same street. The figure clad in black moved, crossed over the road and hurried after Mrs Richmond with an unnatural silence and stealth. The cladded figure's head whipped up and down the street one last time and then in one quick movement, he grabbed Mrs Richmond by the waist, clamped a hand over her mouth and pulled her into an alleyway.

Sophia didn't have time to scream as the scene jolted forwards suddenly, like skipping video frames and resting on the moment when the supermarket man gripped Mrs Richmond with his knife wedged deep into her stomach. Sophia saw the blood trickling down the hilt of the knife and dripping onto the floor. Mrs Richmond's bright blue irises faded into a pale ashy blue, her dying screams muffled by a gloved hand as her body slipped backwards towards the wet slushy ground.

The vision faded and Sophia opened her eyes. Her head spun and she felt bile churning up the back of her throat.

'Did you see something?'

'Yes. Yes, I saw.' She blinked hard several times and leant against a wall for support.

'Well… what did you see?' Avery said, stepping to her.

'Can we… just get out of here first?'

'Yeah, sure.' Sophia followed Avery back out the way they had come into the alleyway. They stopped just outside, and the light-headedness started to fade.

'I saw… I saw her last moments again,' Sophia said.

'Any idea who…' Avery licked his lips. 'Who…'

'No,' Sophia said. 'I don't know who he was.'

'It was definitely a man then?'

'Yes.'

'What else did you see? How big is he? What colour were his eyes?'

'It's hard to say,' Sophia said. 'He was probably a little taller than you, skinny and his eyes are green, almost close to a bright apple green.'

'Green?' Avery said. 'His eyes can't be green, they must be brown.'

'No, they're definitely green,' Sophia said. 'It's the most vivid detail I saw.'

'But the man who killed her, the suspect they let go, his eyes were brown, I'm sure of it.'

'Why are you so fixated on that one suspect?' Sophia said. Avery said nothing and looked away from her.

'Did you see him take anything from her?'

'No, I don't think so.'

'What about her necklace?'

Sophia's brow tightened.

'I didn't see a necklace.'

Avery bit the inside of his cheek and glowered at the ground.

'Let's go, I don't want to hang around here any longer. I don't feel like I'm in control of myself.'

Sophia nodded as she rubbed the sides of her aching head.

TWENTY-THREE

'No, you can't be here,' Den said as he tried to shut his front door. There was a *thunk* sound as his father wedged his foot in the door.

'Den, please, that's not a very nice way to treat your father now, is it?' Jack said.

'What the hell do you want?'

'I just wanted to talk to you, that's all.'

'You're lying already,' Den said. 'You haven't spoken to me since it happened and now you show up out of nowhere and just expect me to let you in because you want to talk?'

'Den. Look. Don't cause a scene, just let me in.' Jack glanced up and down the street. 'Who knows who might be watching right now?' Den cursed and let go of the door. His father smiled, stepped in and closed the door behind him.

'I want you gone,' Den said, standing barely inches from his father's face.

'It's a bit cramped down here, Den, let's go upstairs, shall we?' Jack pushed past Den and headed up the narrow stairwell. Den followed his father up to his small lounge. 'I like what you've done with the place,' Jack said. 'Real nice. Simple.'

'Why are you here?' Den asked, folding his arms.

'Did you know they caught that man, you know, the one who ran away?' Jack said.

'No, I didn't.'

'It was quite funny actually; he got hit over the head by a tramp.'

Jack laughed. 'Oh, come now, Den, why the long face? I thought you'd be pleased they caught that monster.'

'You know why, it doesn't change anything.'

'No, I suppose it doesn't,' Jack said.

'Why are you really here?'

'Well, I thought my son could help me out,'

'No. Get out, you're beyond help.'

'Oh come on, Den, don't be like that.'

'No. The last time I believed anything you said, a woman ended up dead. You're going to leave, right now.'

'Ended up dead?' Jack said as a cruel smile split his face. 'You make it sound like it happened by magic. That's not really what happened, Den, now was it?' Den gripped his hands into fists and bristled with rage.

'Get the hell out of my flat,' he said. 'We both know it was your fault, if you hadn't been there…'

'Don't go trying to pin the blame on me, I didn't do it,' Jack said. He sat down on Den's battered sofa and smiled.

'If you don't get out, I'll… I'll…'

'You'll what?' Jack said. 'Kill me too? I don't think so.'

'Just get out of my house,' Den said as his body shook. The smile dropped from Jack's face.

'I will, I just need a little help first.' Jack stood up.

'What do you want?'

'Money, Den. Let me have your debit card and I'll be on my way.'

'You've got to be kidding me! Why should I?'

'Oh, Den, don't make me threaten you; we both know what happened that night.'

'No,' Den said. 'There's hardly anything in my account and you won't give my card back.'

'Of course I will; you'll be coming with me to a hole in the wall.'

'No way. If Cooper finds out I've been with you, he'll kill me.'

'Oh, is he still around?'

'How do you think I got these?' Den said, pointing to the bruises on his face. Jack frowned.

'I'm truly sorry about that, Den. Look, you give me some money and I'll go talk to him and sort things out, how does that sound?'

'You said you'd smoothed things over with Cooper last time.'

'I know, but I mean it this time. I'll really go and talk to him but I'll need some money first, otherwise we could both end up dead.' Den frowned at his father. They stared at each other and then Den's shoulders slumped.

'Fine, whatever, but this is the last time I help you.' His father smiled and stood up.

'Of course, my boy.' He pulled Den into a hug. 'Of course.'

* * *

Den watched his father disappear with nearly every penny that had been in his bank account. He swore and pushed his card back into his wallet and walked in the opposite direction. The disappointment stung, triggering uncomfortable childhood memories and awaking the demons lingering at the back of his mind. *He can still make you feel like this after all these years.*

'I'll bloody starve to death by the end of the month.' He headed towards the bus stop. He'd finally got a new job at a gym in town, but he was still cleaning, only now the disinfectant actually worked. He kept his head down and caught the bus, using the last of the loose change in his pockets. *I'll have to walk to work for the rest of the month now. Damn my father. I never want to see him again.* Den stared out of the window and twenty minutes later stepped off the bus. He felt his nerves firing up all over his body as he walked down the street. *Why does the gym have to be so close to where she died?* Den froze on the spot at the sight before him. Up ahead, on the other side of the road, he could see the girl from the supermarket with the Richmond boy, standing at the mouth of the alleyway where the unspeakable had happened.

They disappeared down the alleyway and Den watched as his vision started to sway and the blood vessels beat furiously around his brain. He inhaled deeply and crossed the road. *This is the second time I've seen them together, how do they even know each other?* He remembered her burning eyes and the way she had looked at him, staring right into the depths of his mind as though she were holding a magnifying glass up to everything he had said and done in his life. Her words echoed around his mind. *It was you, you killed her.* Den squeezed his eyes shut as a pitiful moan escaped his lips. He stared down the alleyway and could just make out two figures disappearing around a sharp bend, the very spot where Mrs Richmond had died. *Why is she here? Does she know? Is she digging for information?* Den cursed and moved to his left behind a decorative garden screen which belonged to a little café and bar. He hid there and waited, unsure if they would return as there were two ends to the alleyway. Eventually they appeared, and they paused by the wall on the opposite side. He could just about make out their words.

"No, they're definitely green,' the girl said. *Green? What does she mean green? Is she describing my eyes?* A car went by and drowned out their conversation as Den pressed his ear as close to the screen as he dared.

'Did you see him take anything from her?'

'No, I don't think so.'

'What about her necklace?'

'I didn't see a necklace.'

'Would you like a table sir?' a voice asked. Den jumped and whirled round. A waiter stood before him, waiting for his response. Den's mouth opened and closed and he glanced back at the girl and the Richmond boy and saw them walking down the street in the opposite direction.

'No, sorry. I'll be going now,' Den said. He stepped around the waiter and hurried off towards the gym. *Shit, I've got to do something about that girl.*

TWENTY-FOUR

The old man held his cup tightly in his hands and hefted his makeshift bundle onto his back. He continued along the pavement, pausing briefly at a small shop to buy a loaf of bread and a bottle of water. The cashier behind the counter wrinkled her nose as the old man approached, but accepted his money, leaving him with one shiny penny.

'This way,' Ahrl said, pointing down the road that would lead them out of the town centre, but the old man ignored him again. Ahrl followed him through the town, past many big, luxurious homes and buildings. He eventually stopped beside the gates of one and, with a quick glance up and down the street, he slipped around the back. He came across a gate which came off at its hinges as he opened it and entered a tarmacked area at the back. One of the back doors was open and he stepped inside into a large, tiled room. Three individuals huddled around an old fashioned fireplace where a small fire crackled and spat sparks across the floor. A deep growl reverberated down the room and two eyes flashed beside the flames. A shaggy dog emerged from the gloom with its teeth bared and one of the figures stood up.

'Who are you?'

'Nobody, jus' lookin' for a place to settle tonight, that's all,' the old man said. 'I don't mean no 'arm. I've been told about this place.' The dog's growl deepened.

'Oh, that's enough, Hope, it's no one dangerous,' the male voice said. The old man drew nearer and, from the glow of the fire, Ahrl could see another man with long matted hair and a beard streaked with silver, a middle-aged woman whose face seemed almost hollow, and a young teenage boy who wore a dirty hooded top pulled up over his head, shadowing his face.

'May I join ye'?' the old man said.

'Do as you like,' the man said. 'My name's Ralph, that's Mary, the young one is Sam and my dog's called Hope. And you are?'

'An old man,' the old man said. Ralph raised his eyebrows but didn't comment. Ahrl gazed at the souls before them; none were Negative but all had high levels of sadness, fear and guilt. Their hazy colours spoke of ill health, but Mary's were by far the worst out of the three. 'Since yer being so kind, I 'ave got some food and water if you'd like some,' the old man said. He set down his bag and pulled out the bottle of water and the loaf of bread. 'It's not much but it'll fill the hole for a while.' The old man opened the bread and offered slices to Ralph, Mary and Sam.

'Thank you,' Ralph said. 'We've eaten some but there wasn't much.' The old man smiled and nodded. They ate quickly in silence and shared the water between them. Mary trembled, clenched her eyes shut, gripped her arms tightly and muttered under her breath.

'Don't worry about her, she does that sometimes, used to do drugs to block out her past but now she gets the shakes and pain from her cravings,' Ralph said.

'What happened?' the old man said.

'Abusive family. Raped when she was young, left home pregnant but lost the baby, took drugs and ended up on the streets. It's an all too familiar story.' The old man grimaced.

'What about you?' he asked.

'Me? I lost my wife, my job and then my house. She died suddenly and I couldn't do my job properly anymore. I had some time off but it wasn't long enough to come to terms with it. I was renting a place but once I lost my job they said they didn't accept tenants on housing benefits; it just got worse from there.'

Mary rubbed her arms and opened her eyes.

'Everyone has got a story,' she said. 'You try to get help but no one listens and forms are too long and confusing, and there's so many of us; the homeless aid centres do what they can but they can't cope and can't get you a place.'

The old man looked at the young boy, obviously still a teen.

'I'm gay,' Sam said, lifting his gaze from the fire. 'Where I'm from that's illegal. It's dangerous. A friend helped me to get here to the UK. My family have disowned me, and I can't get a job when I'm not supposed to be here.' Sam lowered his gaze back down to the flames.

'We're all just lost souls, not all of us are bad,' Ralph said.

'No, you don't 'ave that meanness in your eyes that the bad ones 'ave.'

'What about you? What's your story?' Ralph said.

'My story? I don't remember, I don't even know my name or how I got here, I jus' try to stay alive,' the old man said, suddenly looking lost. Ralph didn't press any more questions on him but Ahrl stood silently at the side, absorbing all of their stories. *I wonder what happened to you, my friend* he thought as he gazed down at the old man.

TWENTY-FIVE

She was alone with the darkness, and the darkness was alone with her. If any other soul existed in this hellish state, then she knew nothing of them and they knew nothing of her.

* * *

'Sometimes when I see things, I think I'm going crazy,' Sophia said.

'Aren't you concerned about your grades?' Avery asked. Sophia bit the inside of her cheek.

'Yes and no.'

'I'm surprised the teachers haven't called you out for it yet, skipping classes isn't good for the school's reputation,' Avery said, reaching into his rucksack on the floor.

'The teachers don't bother you, do they?' Sophia said.

'No, they're afraid of me,' Avery said, pulling out a bag of birdseed. 'I just have to look at them and they go silent.' A weary chuckle picked up the corners of his lips and barely made itself known on the end of his breath. 'My eyes must be real scary.'

'Sometimes.'

'So then, since my plans are on hold, who else do you see?' He poured some of the birdseed into his left hand, held his hand still across the windowsill and then leant back against what was left of the window frame.

'All sorts of people,' Sophia said. 'Though I'm not sure how much I can say. There are big changes up ahead for humanity, advances in technology, though I suppose anyone would be able to

125

predict that. I've seen both friends and strangers. I saw Mr Gilliam being loaded into the back of an ambulance just hours before he was taken into hospital.'

'Who's Mr Gilliam?'

'He's Sarah's grandfather.'

'Oh, Kirsty's friend,' Avery said.

'Yes. I've seen many things, trivial things really. I've avoided accidents like dropping plates and glasses, or taken a different route to somewhere to avoid traffic…'

'The travel news does that,' Avery said.

'I see these incidents before they happen and way before the news reports them. I grabbed your shoulder in the lunch hall so you wouldn't collide with Harry because I saw it happen the night before.'

'I was wondering why you did that.' Avery tilted his head and his gaze seemed to stare at a point in the distance for a moment before refocussing again. 'You can say that but it could just be that you saw Harry flailing around like an idiot and you calculated at the time that he would knock into me.'

'Yes, that could also be true.'

'You're not denying it?'

'Why would I? I know there's no easy way to prove to anyone that I can see what I see, and at best it's sporadic, it's not like I can control it. I hope one day that I'll be able to explain it scientifically, but until then I'm going to do my best to become a physicist.'

'You're not in my physics class.'

'No.' Sophia smiled. 'I'm a year ahead with physics. Already doing A Level.' There was a loud cackling sound and a magpie descended upon the windowsill. It chatted again as if it were talking then greedily pecked at the seeds in Avery's palm.

'You've got a pet?' Sophia said, noting the claw mark on the side of the magpie's beak and the fact that it only had one leg.

'I wouldn't call Bob a pet,' Avery said, as he watched the magpie.

'You gave him a name?'

'Of course,' Avery said. *Was that a smile?* 'He kept bothering me when I was up here playing my violin and when I was trying to eat my lunch, so I fed him bits of my sandwiches, and now he turns up nearly every time I come here. He doesn't seem to be afraid of me and he even lets me stroke him, sometimes.'

'How do you know Bob's a boy?'

'Do you see the white patch on the back of his neck?' Avery said. 'It's called a hood and its pure white; females tend to have a greyish coloured hood towards the bottom.'

'So you're a magpie expert?' A smile tugged at the side of Avery's mouth.

'No, I just did some research.'

'How long have you known Bob then?'

'Just over a year now,' Avery said. 'He started turning up several months after my mum died; he was in pretty bad shape back then.' Warmth rushed over Sophia's cold limbs, a tingling sensation sparked through her veins and her vision switched as a faint glow appeared on the windowsill beside Avery. The glow began to take on the loose form and features of a person as Avery continued to talk. 'I like that he knows me. I don't know how he got the mark on the side of his beak but he's always had a missing leg. I think he used to struggle to feed himself, so once I started feeding him there was no getting rid of him.' The features became more coherent and recognisable as a semi-transparent Mrs Richmond appeared. She wore a black dress with black gloves and her hair was swept back behind her head. A pretty and expensive-looking diamond and sapphire necklace hung about her neck. Sophia sat perfectly still; afraid that if she blinked then Mrs Richmond would disappear again, and afraid that any sudden movement would scare Bob away. 'My mum would probably love Bob; she was more of an animal person. She always wanted a cat but Dad's allergic to them.' Mrs Richmond's form waned and flickered as she turned her face towards her son and a small, sad smile appeared on her lips. Sophia could see both of their souls; grey hues obscured all the other colours in Avery's soul, with black streaks pulsing throughout like lightning strikes. Mrs Richmond's soul was considerably brighter and more colourful, yet there was a deep layer of grey circling around her core. The grey suddenly splurged out from Avery's soul and Avery tilted his head back and blinked hard. Mrs Richmond shook her head gently as she faded from Sophia's vision.

'How long have you been playing the violin?' Sophia asked.

'A couple of years.'

'You sound like you've been playing for longer than that.'

'I practised a lot after my mother died; it helped to distract me, though I almost gave up on it completely. When you're distraught and grieving, the last thing you want to do is do anything that used to make you happy. But my mother bought me my violin, it was delivered to me, it's the reason why she was walking to the museum the night she was…' Avery gulped and licked his lips. 'It was one of the last things she touched; I couldn't bring myself to return it to the shop.'

'Did your mum work at the museum?'

'Yes, she was on the board of directors and helped the curators from time to time. My family also donated a lot to the museum. She had just managed to acquire a valuable piece for a new art exhibition and we were invited to the opening night. My father and I were already at the museum, my mother had been out of town that day so was travelling separately. She stopped off on route to look in a music store, then she walked to the museum, but she never made it.' Sophia remained quiet and lowered her gaze. 'Anyways,' Avery cleared his throat, 'I've been thinking about what you saw in that alleyway. The events you see are emotionally charged.'

'Yes, I mean it's possible I might see something, say if I were to go to your house,' Sophia said.

'Hmm,'

'But I'm not sure anything at your home would help you find answers.'

'I guess not.' He exhaled deeply. 'It's just so frustrating; it's like you have information but not enough, and it's just out of reach.'

'It's often the way with the visions we see.'

'We?' Avery said. Sophia clamped a hand over her mouth.

'I probably shouldn't have said that.' She lowered her hand. 'We as in people like me. Some of my ancestors have been known to share my gifts.'

'There are more psychics then?'

'We're not psychics; people who call themselves that are usually fake and give people like me a bad name.'

'That must be annoying.'

'Yes and no, it helps sometimes. If people don't believe then they're less likely to ask questions or keep an eye open for anything unusual, though we're usually pretty careful.' Avery nodded and their conversation lulled into a semi-comfortable silence. 'You mentioned a necklace the other day when we came out of the alleyway; was it something that was stolen?' Avery kept his gaze fixed on the treetops as he clenched his jaw.

'Yes, my mother was wearing a diamond and sapphire necklace on the night she died; it was taken by her killer. No one has found it since then; the police think it was the most likely reason she was targeted. It was my fault.' He rubbed tears from his eyes.

'No, don't think that,' Sophia said.

'It was,' Avery said. His lower lip trembled and tears began to fall down his cheeks. 'I picked that necklace, and I chose to play the violin; if it hadn't been for me then she wouldn't have even been there.' Sophia frowned. *She definitely wasn't wearing a necklace in my vision, but she was wearing it when I just saw her then.* Bob spoke in his way at them, interrupting their thoughts, and then flew off into the trees. Avery emptied the remaining seeds from his hand, and stood abruptly with his back to Sophia. 'We should go.'

TWENTY-SIX

Ahrl gazed into the fountain and let the images flash across its surface. He felt a muted nudge on his mind and tore his gaze away from the pool, straightened up, closed his eyes and nudged back before opening his eyes.

'Ahrl, what are you doing?' Ioel said. 'You've been gazing into the fountain nonstop for weeks now.'

'It's nothing compared to what others have done in the past,' Ahrl said.

'We know you've been up to something, we've felt the disturbance rippling through the timelines.' Ioel frowned.

'There are outlying pathways which feed directly into Alice and Kyle's pathway, other factors and lives to consider,' Ahrl said. 'Some of them have only just come to light, though that's probably because we weren't concentrating on them sooner.'

'And can't you let things follow their natural progression?' Ioel said. 'We all agreed after the last time that it was better not to interfere if possible.'

'It's too important,' Ahrl said. 'The Negative pathways for both Alice and Kyle are becoming more frequent, one in particular. I'm placing suggestions with souls on outlying, smaller pathways. However, my main concern is Alice's health; I'm not sure what we can do about it, if anything, should that pathway arise.'

'It depends on what the ailment is,' Ioel said. 'We may be able to prevent an accident, but I don't think what has been seen is an accident.'

'No, which means it's most likely down to a disease or illness.'

'There's a chance it's treatable then.'

'There's also a chance that it's not, and we both know Negative energy will attack her because of her Positive soul.'

'Her energy should be able to cancel it out,' Ioel said.

'Not all the time; she just needs a moment of uncertainty or a bad day and then it could strike.'

'Ahrl, you're worrying over a vision that occurs relatively infrequently in comparison to the Positive visions we've seen.'

'I'm concerned because its frequency is growing, even if it is only slight. Every time I see it I feel…' Ahrl pinched his lips together and shook his head.

'I shall mention it to the rest of the Thirteen and ask for more Positive focus on the pair,' Ioel said.

'Ask everyone. Everyone who is willing.'

'I shall pass the message on, my friend, in the meantime you should rest,' Ioel said. 'You're not totally immortal in this state of our existence, please remember that.' Ahrl inclined his head and Ioel began to fade, disappearing completely from the garden. Ahrl turned his attention back to the fountain and let his mind dive into the depths of its memories of the present and future.

The old man walked away from the town centre with his bundle on his back and Ahrl walked beside him as the world around them shimmered into his mind. Nature appeared first, the green shoots of grass and weeds growing in gardens, plant pots, or out from the cracks in the road and pavements. The odd tree appeared next, followed by the cars, the lampposts and the buildings. The sky appeared last, colouring itself into Ahrl's vision in overlapping shades of midnight blue. The old man spotted an abandoned shopping trolley and quickly commandeered it, gratefully dumping his meagre belongings within its sturdy frame. The front right wheel squeaked in protest as the old man pushed it along and they walked for a long time before they came to familiar roads lined with little terraced houses. Ahrl spotted the street he wanted the old man to find and he once again reached out with his mind and energy to nudge at the old man's soul. The old man paused, raised his chin up to the sky and then he turned to gaze down the street and a slow grin spread across his chapped lips. He pushed his trolley and moved with a surprising fluidity towards the skip up ahead.

'Treasure,' the old man whispered under his breath. He shuffled over to the yellow, rusty skip and peered inside. 'Aha!' he said, his voice echoing around the metal container. He clamped a hand over his mouth and glanced up and down the street. Then he rubbed his hands together and reached inside, hefting out a battered looking, single-sized futon. 'This will do jus' nicely,' he said to himself as he rolled up the futon and squeezed it into his trolley.

'I'm glad you found it,' Ahrl said as he watched the old man wheel his treasure off down the street. *Perhaps there is hope for the boy yet.*

TWENTY-SEVEN

Sophia, Kyle, Alice and another young man she had never seen before stood around a computer screen, pointing excitedly at little clusters of neon colours and numbers. She glanced around the nondescript room; it was large and filled with dozens of monitors and cables wired up to boxy machines. It looked like an office but felt more like a lab; she knew from the positioning of chairs, desks and the lack of telephones that this grey-carpeted room was for research, not sales calls. She turned to the others. Kyle and Alice were beaming at one another and the other young man with glasses and caramel hair grinned too.

'We did it,' Kyle said.

'We should send this off straight away,' Alice said.

'No, we should recheck these results first and rerun the experiment,' the other man said.

'Cameron's right,' Sophia heard herself say. She gasped silently in her mind and tried to cover her mouth with her hand but her body and mouth moved without her. 'We need to rerun the experiments one last time and see if we get the same results.' Kyle and Alice nodded in agreement. 'If we're correct, this will be huge; we may have discovered new particles and have the evidence to back it up,' Sophia said. She could feel her own excitement bubbling up like a volcano from her guts. The four of them in her dream couldn't keep their faces straight; they smiled unconsciously and when they realised, they would try to quell their excitement, straighten their smiles, and maintain an air of sceptical professionalism. It was no use though, they knew they were onto something big and the smiles broke out again. Alice's eyes flickered to Kyle, conveying a silent thought that only two lovers could share, then she spoke.

'I knew you would do great things, Kyle, those tough years studying have been worth it.'

'It wasn't just me, it was all of us,' Kyle said.

'Maybe, but you sparked the idea when you drew the timelines,' Alice said. *So there is another dimension of time*, Sophia thought.

'The four of us.' He motioned to himself, Alice, Cameron and Sophia. 'This would have never worked without all of our input; I needed Sophia's knowledge, Cameron's ridiculous maths brain, and you.' He looked at Alice and a slow smile spread across his face. 'I needed your support and imagination to create our theories. This, if we are correct,' he pointed at the screen, 'could change the world.' The four could hardly contain their excitement; they laughed as lifelong friends would do and discussed their next move.

A persistent and monotonous beeping sound pulled Sophia from her dreams. She stretched sleepily, a big smile on her face, and then reached out for her alarm clock and hit the off button. She gazed up at the ceiling, the dream vision still vividly playing in her mind. Her smile stretched even wider when she realised it was Friday. She got out of bed, showered and then dressed before heading downstairs.

Louise stood by the kettle; the smell of coffee flooded the kitchen with its rich aroma.

'I thought I could hear you,' she said and handed a mug of coffee to Sophia.

'I saw Alice and Kyle again, I saw us working in a lab; there was another young man with us too. His name's Cameron.'

'You need to write it down,' Louise said.

'I know, I know, I'll do it after school.' Sophia grinned.

'Flo said you had a strange dream a couple of nights ago, a dream that was just nothingness. She said it frightened you because you thought it was the Negative hell-state. You haven't dreamt about that again, have you?'

'No, thankfully,' Sophia said supressing a shudder. 'What do you think it is?'

'I don't know,' Louise said. 'I don't think I've ever heard of anyone dreaming something like that before, only...' She stopped herself.

'Only what?'

'Nothing.' She shook her head and smiled. 'I was just thinking out loud and got caught in my own mind rambles. How has school been lately?'

'Great,' Sophia said.

'And Avery, is he OK?'

'Seems to be,' Sophia said, though she couldn't meet her mother's gaze. 'I haven't had any more disturbing dreams of his suicide. So that's something.'

'Is everything OK, Sophia?'

'Yes.'

'Well, I had a call from your headmaster yesterday.' Sophia held her breath.

'Oh, why?' Sophia said.

'He said that some of your teachers have been concerned, apparently you've missed a couple of classes.' Louise's gaze dropped to Sophia's soul. 'I can see the guilt in your soul, Sophia, what's going on?' Louise frowned. Sophia froze, she couldn't tell her about her strange and fragile friendship with Avery; the family thought she was just watching him from a distance. *Quick, think of something, think of something that will hide the guilt.* Kirsty's face flashed in her mind.

'I'm sorry, Mum, I should have told you sooner,' Sophia said, adopting what she hoped was a sincere and sad expression. 'Kirsty was giving me a hard time for a few weeks and I just needed to get away from her.'

'Oh, sweetie, why didn't you say anything?'

'I know, I feel terrible. I didn't want to make a big deal out of it, I just needed to get away from her for a bit. It's OK now.' Sophia could feel her guilt stabbing at her stomach, everyone hid things from their parents sometimes but with the Leto's gifts, it wasn't something that happened often. Unlike her grandma and the older members of Sophia's family, Sophia hadn't mastered her emotions completely yet and she couldn't control the fluctuations in her soul.

'Oh, you don't need to feel bad about it, but you should have said something.' Louise hugged her tightly.

'I know, I know.'

'If anything happens I want you to let me know, OK? No more skipping classes.'

'OK.'

* * *

'So you seem happy today,' Annie said.

'I dreamt about Alice and Kyle again.'

'That figures,' Annie said. 'I've hardly seen you lately.'

'Aw, Annie, you know that isn't true,' Sophia said. 'I'm in most of your classes and I'm sat eating lunch with you now.'

'Yeah, I guess. Though Avery sure does take up a lot of your time, though at least he's not going to top himself anymore.'

'For the moment, but he's preoccupied now by my gifts and finding answers,' Sophia said. 'It's difficult, on one hand I'm happy he isn't considering suicide but on the other hand I'm worried that he'll get frustrated with my lack of information and end up going back to those thoughts.'

'You haven't told him about seeing deceased souls, have you?'

'No,' Sophia said. 'That's a Schrödinger-like box that I do not want to open.' The right side of Annie's mouth quirked upwards.

'I'm assuming you haven't told him about running into the man at the supermarket yet either?'

'No.' Sophia shook her head. 'I carefully avoided that one.'

'Does he know that I know about your gifts too?'

'He hasn't asked yet, but probably suspects it.'

'Has he mentioned anything about Joe?'

'No. I haven't managed to bring him up into conversation yet. He's too busy trying to think of other places and objects that might spark visions of the past and lead him to more clues about his mother's killer.'

'Yeah, I should have realised he wouldn't be satisfied with vague answers,' Annie said. 'Now I have to share my best friend and I don't like it. It's a strange feeling.' She pouted at her lunch.

'I'm hoping this won't go on for much longer but I don't know what to do,' Sophia said. 'I can't tell him that I think I know who killed his mother, I don't even know where the man lives.'

'No, and you don't have evidence either. He could still avoid the courts and prison if the police can't find any incriminating evidence against him.'

'Yes, and that would be two suspects that the police let go in Avery's eyes, two potential killers.'

'Hmm,' Annie said tapping a finger against her lips. 'I guess there's not much you can do now except bide your time and celebrate every day that Avery doesn't think about suicide.'

'I think we're becoming friends, I'm hoping that might help to change his mindset. I don't know though, I've never been suicidal before.'

'You're finally melting the glacier?' Annie asked.

'He's quite nice and interesting when you get to know him.'

'Yeah, I know. He always used to be, he's just been so cold and distant for so long, I didn't think he would ever make any friends again. Joe will be pleased for him. He does have a scary look on his face; it's as if he's seen every terrible thing on this planet and it's been imprinted onto the lenses of his eyes. If ever anyone wanted to peer into the gates of hell, then I could point them in Avery's direction.'

* * *

'Do you sense anything?' Avery asked. Sophia clasped the slim book between her hands and desperately tried to concentrate but she felt nothing. She looked up at Avery and shook her head.

'I'm sorry, Avery, I can't sense anything from this book.' She handed it back to him.

'It's OK, I just thought you might see something, even if it was Positive rather than Negative,' Avery said. They sat at opposite corners of the large open window, gazing out across the treetops.

'What is the book?' Sophia asked.

'It's an old poetry book, it belonged to my mother.'

'Oh, wow. Did your mother read a lot of poetry?'

'She loved all the arts,' Avery said. 'She used to love going to the art exhibitions at the museum, and one of her favourite pieces was the statue in Chiliad Square.' Avery stood, placed the book in his rucksack and then lifted his violin from its case.

'How about this?' he said. 'It was the last thing she touched.' Avery handed the violin to Sophia. She ran her fingers over the smooth polished wood; she had never held a violin before, or any instrument. She felt a sense of regret and a pang in the bottom of her stomach; it was a well-known fact that her favourite physicist, Albert Einstein, had played the violin. She felt the murmur of Positive energy beneath her fingers; warmth seeped up into her hands and tingled through her arms up into her head. She tried to imagine being Mrs Richmond and holding this violin, she tried to imagine the love Mrs Richmond must have felt when she decided to get this violin for Avery. The tingling sensation grew and Sophia's vision wavered as the world began to fade around her. Sophia closed her eyes, cast all thoughts aside and let the vision take over.

A bell chimed and Sophia watched as Mrs Richmond entered the music shop. A taxi pulled away from the kerb and carried on down the street as the door shut behind her. She wore a black fur coat, buttoned up tightly to her chin.

'What can I do for you, Miss?' an elderly man behind the counter asked.

'I'm in a bit of a rush, but I was just passing by when I noticed the violin in your window, may I take a closer look at it?' Mrs Richmond said.

'Ah yes, beautiful workmanship on that one and a solid tune,' the man said as he moved around the counter and carefully picked up the violin from out of the display window. He carried it back to the counter and set it down on a thin piece of velvet. 'It's a Stentor Conservatoire Two, it has a solid maple back and neck, and a carved spruce front, varnished with shellac which gives it this warm amber colour,' the man said.

'It's beautiful,' Mrs Richmond said. She touched the violin's smooth curves.

'Is it for yourself?'

'No, no,' Mrs Richmond said. 'It's for my son, he's been having lessons for a while now but he's been using his teacher's spare violin and hasn't got one of his own yet.'

'Well, if he's a beginner I'd usually recommend Stentor's student violin, but this violin does have a superior sound and if he is serious about playing, then this one's good value for money.' Sophia's attention snagged on a man standing outside the shop; he gazed in through the window staring directly at Mrs Richmond with a hungry look in his eyes which made Sophia shiver. He wore black from head to toe, and she caught sight of a birthmark on his left cheek, just before he moved a black scarf up and over his mouth. *Wait, that's not the man from the supermarket.* He slunk away from the window, his gaze lingering on Mrs Richmond.

'It comes with a bow and case of course,' the man said.

'I'll take it,' Mrs Richmond said. 'I'll pay for it now but I'll have to collect it later,' She glanced at the clock hanging behind the counter.

'Of course, or I can deliver it to you if you would like?'

'Actually, that may be easier,' Mrs Richmond said. The corners of Sophia's vision began to darken and the scene shuddered.

'I'll just need to take some details,' the man said as the vision slipped from Sophia's mind.

Sophia blinked several times as Avery and his sanctuary returned to her field of view.

'That's pretty freaky, you know,' Avery said as he peered into Sophia's eyes.

'What is?'

'You sort of space out when you do, whatever it is you do,' Avery said. 'Plus you're going to snap my violin if you're not careful.' Sophia glanced down at the violin in her grasp; her knuckles and fingers were white.

'Sorry,' she said loosening her grip and handing the violin back.

'So, did you see something?' Avery asked. Sophia massaged the sides of her head.

'Yes, there was a man, a man I didn't recognise.'

'What do you mean? What did he look like?' Avery said, putting the violin back into its case.

'When your mum was in the music shop, there was a man staring at her through the window, it could be totally unrelated but...'

'But?'

'I don't think it is; I didn't like the way he looked at her.' Avery's mouth pinched into a hard thin line and his fingers curled into fists. He let out a deep breath and began to pace up and down the room.

'Did you get a good look at him?'

'Yes,' Sophia said. 'He's tall, and he had brown hair and I think he had brown eyes too, but I can't be sure.'

'No green eyes then?' Avery said.

'No, it was a different man, I'm sure of it,' Sophia said.

'Sounds like the guy they caught and let go.'

'No,' Sophia said. 'This man was Caucasian.' Avery paused in his pacing and stared at her with an open mouth. 'There was one other thing too,' Sophia said. 'He had a large birthmark on his left cheek which he hid underneath a scarf.'

'This doesn't make any sense,' Avery said. 'The man they caught, he had my mother's blood on his clothes. How could he have her blood on his clothes if he wasn't the one who did it?'

'What was his story?'

'He said he was running because he was late for his son's school play, they were doing Aladdin or something. He said he had run past all sorts of people without really paying attention to them.'

'It's possible he passed the person who did it then,' Sophia said.

'I guess, he did say there were a few groups he had to squeeze through but I thought he was just saying anything to save his own skin.'

'Perhaps he was just unlucky and just happened to be in the wrong place at the wrong time?' Sophia said. Avery glowered out of the window and worked his jaw from side to side.

'Yeah. Yeah, I guess you could be right. My mother… was she… did she seem happy in that shop, before it…' He blinked hard.

'She seemed very happy, Avery,' Sophia said. 'She loved you a lot, I could hear it in her words and I could feel it from your violin.' Avery gave a stiff, short nod and then reached into his bag and drew out Bob's birdseed. 'Here, hold out your hand.' She cupped her hand and he poured a little of the birdseed into her palm.

'How has your father been, since, well, it all happened?' Sophia asked.

'Up and down, mainly down,' Avery said. 'He drinks himself unconscious most nights.'

'Oh.'

'Yeah, it's why I've been reluctant about inviting you to the house. The lounge is a bottle and can haven at the moment.'

'How have you been lately?'

'If you mean, have I been thinking suicidal thoughts lately then the answer is yes, but I don't plan to act on them, not at the moment anyways,' Avery said.

'I wish you didn't think like that.'

'I've found it's not something you can just switch on and off,' Avery said. 'But when it does happen I usually come here, play my violin, and wait until it passes.'

'Why do you come here? I mean, why this place in particular?'

'I found it one day when I'd had a hard day at school. I got angry and I…'

'Is this the day you flipped the desk over?'

'So you heard about it then?'

'Yes, I think everyone heard about it before the day was out.'

'Figures,' Avery muttered under his breath. 'Well, I escaped into the woods and was walking around for a while when I stumbled across this place. I shouldn't have really attempted coming back to school last year, or even this year, it was too soon. It's just… I can't shake the trauma, or the injustice… and the guilt.' Avery gulped and Sophia noticed the tears welling in his eyes.

'It takes years to come to terms with someone's passing, probably longer when it's sudden and unexpected,' Sophia said.

'Yes but society and the education system doesn't really allow for that. Anyways,' Avery cleared his throat. 'I just liked it here, it was quiet, peaceful, and then Bob started turning up and keeping me company too. I found it was easier to speak to the wind, the trees and Bob, than it was trying to speak to people. You probably don't know what it's like but people ask questions and when you give difficult, honest answers, they don't know what to say so they say sorry, look at you with pity and then try to give you advice. It's irritating. I didn't even understand what I was feeling for a long time. I couldn't ever explain my emotions or my thoughts to people, and when I did they cut me up with their empty advice. My father and psychiatrist were the ones who thought going back to school this year would be a good idea.'

'And was it?'

'I don't think so,' Avery said. 'But I'm finding it easier talking to you than most people. I don't know, maybe I was just ready to talk now and I didn't realise it before.'

'Well, if you feel like talking to people then you know you can always talk to me and Annie,' Sophia said.

'Joe's sister?'

'Yeah.'

'I don't know if that's such a good idea. Joe and I fell out pretty badly. I was awful to him actually.'

'What happened?'

Avery rubbed his brow and sighed.

'He kept trying to talk to me and make me do normal things after my mother died, as if nothing was wrong and all was right with the world. I found it frustrating at the time and felt that he was pestering me. He was probably just trying to take my mind off of it all.' A faint smile flickered briefly across his lips. 'I let my anger and sadness turn nasty and I directed it at him, and all my friends really. We ended up having a fight one evening before he went off to university and I said some pretty awful things to him. I've not spoken to him since. I guess I'm too afraid to. He texts and calls from time to time, but I can't bring myself to reply or pick up.'

'It doesn't seem like Joe holds any grudges against you.'

'That makes it worse though, doesn't it?' Avery said. 'He's one of the nice guys, and he's never mean and he rarely gets angry and I was horrible to him, no, evil really.'

'You should cut yourself some slack; you were going through a terrible time. If Joe still makes the effort to try and speak to you now it's probably safe to say that he's forgiven you, so you should forgive yourself too.'

Avery bit the inside of his lip.

'I'll think about it.' A flapping sound drew their attention; it was followed by a familiar cackle as Bob descended onto the windowsill. Sophia's muscles tensed as she held herself perfectly still. Bob hopped closer to her hand and then pecked at the seeds and hopped away from her slightly. He hopped to her hand again, pecked at the seeds and then hopped back again and kept this pattern up for a while before finally deciding that Sophia wasn't a threat and hopping right onto her fingertips. 'I think he trusts me,' she said quietly.

'Yes, he's a big fan of food,' Avery said. Sophia narrowed her eyes at him and poked out her tongue. 'So did you and Kirsty fall out too?' Avery asked.

'We used to be friends a long time ago,' Sophia said. 'We met at primary school and she caught me using one of my gifts and was totally fascinated by it. She thought that one day I would be super famous and that we'd all travel the world in a private jet sort of thing. I had been warned not to tell anyone about my gifts but I just felt so alone and I wanted to fit in with people. I just wanted somebody my own age who would understand me and who was outside the family. It was good for a few years; me, Kirsty, Bianca and Sarah got along really well and if I had a vision I would tell them and we would go and,' Sophia raised her free hand and mimicked quotation marks with her fingers, 'investigate. I don't know what happened really but at some point they stopped believing me. Kirsty decided we were getting too old for make-believe games and that if I didn't stop then we couldn't be friends anymore. I should have just walked away then but I tried too hard to get them to believe me, to see what I see, and that's when the name calling and bullying started. At first it was just the odd shove and hair pulling, childish things really, but then I had a vision and I saw Bianca falling from a roundabout at the park and breaking her arm. I tried to stop her but she wouldn't listen and the others wouldn't let me get near her. When I did finally manage to reach her, she slipped and fell.' Sophia grimaced and blinked hard as she took a deep breath. 'Her arm was bent at an unnatural angle and her screams were so loud and piercing. All three of them swore it was my fault; they said that I'd caused it to happen because I was a witch, of course. After that I avoided them completely, but the name calling was already routine by that point and it hasn't stopped since.'

'I always knew that Kirsty was mean, but to keep something like that up for all this time is just cruel. It was an accident. She should grow up, it's not like you're still ten,' Avery said.

'They didn't see it that way. I shouldn't have interfered really, I should have just ignored it,' Sophia said.

'Maybe,' Avery said. 'You'll never know if your actions or absence of actions would have led to the same results though, and you probably would have felt bad about it either way.' Sophia slowly and gently moved her free hand to stroke the back of Bob's head. Avery raised an eyebrow when Bob nudged Sophia's hand affectionately with his beak and then went back to eating more seeds.

'Do you regret interfering with my life?' Avery asked.

'No, do you?' Sophia said. Avery snorted.

'No offence, but sometimes,' Avery said. 'It's not like you live in the normal world, it's a bit hard to get your head around sometimes.'

Sophia nodded.

'Have you ever seen visions that are more like a hundred years into the future?'

'I haven't personally, but some of my ancestors did.'

'What did they see?'

'Alice and Kyle.'

'You've mentioned them before, who are they?'

'They're important, or rather we think they're going to be important. They're supposed to make a big discovery at some point in the near future.'

'What? Like a lost tomb or something?'

'No, a scientific discovery, physics to be exact. It will change all our understanding of science and the future of technology as we know it.'

'Oh, so they're like a genius power couple then?'

'I guess,' Sophia said. 'My ancestors have seen them and recorded their visions for hundreds of years, though the older visions are amusing to read.'

'How so?'

Bob squawked and hopped in an awkward, jerky fashion over to Avery.

'Because they didn't understand what televisions were, or computers; one of my ancestors wrote that there was a box with little people trapped inside.'

'Oh yeah, that would be entertaining to read.'

'It is but it can make translating it all difficult.'

'Since you see me in your visions, does that mean I'm important?'

'I don't know,' Sophia said. 'It's possible.' Bob cackled again and pecked at the shiny face of Avery's wristwatch.

'Hey!' Avery scooted his arm away from Bob who tilted his head, protested loudly and then launched himself into the air and flew off. 'He's always doing that,' Avery said, checking his watch.

'I'll have to bring him something shiny next time.' Sophia brushed the remaining seeds from her hands.

'He won't leave you alone if you do that.'

'I'm sorry I couldn't be more helpful this time,' Sophia said.

'Well you've given me more to think about, and a headache.'

'I hope that's a good thing, and sorry about the headache.'

'It's my fault and it's fine,' Avery said. 'I asked for more information, it's just not as simple as I thought it would be.'

TWENTY-EIGHT

Slap, thunk and *splash* were the only sounds Den heard as he ran the mop over the tiles of the changing room at the sports centre. The tightness in his chest had somewhat abated since he had left his job at the King's Cockerel, but every now and then his heart would seize up as though someone was clutching it tightly and he would whip his gaze around for any sign of Mr Cooper and his thugs – or was it the police? He stopped and put the mop back into the bucket with a splash and wiped his forehead with the back of his hand as he surveyed his work. The men's changing rooms weren't exactly sparkling but they were clean and fresh. He glanced at the clock hanging above the doors to the gym; its hands were approaching midnight rapidly. He called it a night and packed away his cleaning equipment into a store cupboard. He gave the security guard on the front desk a curt nod as he left the premises.

The cold night air stung the back of his throat as he pushed his hands into his pockets and hunched his shoulders. A few stars tried in vain to shine through the clouds, but they were mere specks of dust upon the dark cloth of the night sky. Den walked quickly along the pavements, avoiding the busy bars and pubs on the way, their customers staggering outside. He tried to concentrate on his footsteps and ignore the squeals and fluctuating laughter that seemed both too high and too low. His heartbeat thudded in his ears; his breathing seemed too quick and loud.

It was always the same when he was in this area of the town; he was too close to the location of his nightmares, too close to bear it, like holding his hands too close to a flame. He could always remember the rotting stench of rubbish, the coldness in the air that promised to turn to ice if only the temperature dropped by another degree, and the face of a beautiful woman wearing a sleek, fur coat. He shook his head in an attempt to dislodge the memories from his mind. *Don't think about it. Den, it's over, there's nothing you can do about it now.* The demons in his head chuckled. Den gritted his teeth and blinked hard as he tried to think of anything but that one evening. He bent his head and kept his gaze on the ground. *I need to be careful; the CCTV footage they managed to get of me is blurry, but even so.* He sped up and passed the alleyway and hurried out of town.

Half an hour later a fire engine tore past him with its lights flashing and siren blaring. *The girl, she knows, she knows,* Den's demons cried. *She knows. Remember how she looked at you and what she said in the supermarket. She knows the Richmond boy, and they went to the place where you…* He clutched his head and stumbled towards a low brick wall. He gripped onto it and looked over the side of the barrier at the river a few metres below. He could hardly see a thing, though the lampposts cast a dirty, faded glow upon the water.

'Shut up!' Den said. He clamped a hand over his mouth, his gaze darting from side to side. He could hear more sirens in the distance, getting louder with every step and his head pulsed as though his veins had become tangled and knotted. He drew nearer to his home and he could see the flashes of red and blue lights just a little further ahead. He could hear voices getting louder and saw people peering out of windows or standing outside their doors. His legs felt like concrete pillars as he arrive at the end of the field. A fire engine and a couple of police cars were parked outside as thick black smoke rose from Den's home. A group of people, including the elderly lady who lived beneath him, had congregated outside and stood staring at what was left of Den's charcoaled flat. Mr Cooper's voice sounded hollow in Den's ears. *Where's your father,*

Den? I wonder what would happen if someone set fire to that little flat of yours, Den. Den cursed under his breath and backed away, then he turned on his heel and fled.

TWENTY-NINE

Alice and Kyle clung to each other with tears streaming down their faces. Every line, every twitching muscle and every ragged breath sang sorrow in such a sweet and painful tone. Sophia could feel their emotions in waves crashing from their bodies. The colours of their souls twisted with grey, orange and every Negative hue possible, suffocating the brilliance of their souls and the golden Positivity that had once been so radiant within. Kyle lightly kissed the side of Alice's head, his hands rubbing her back as she sobbed into his t-shirt. Sophia reached out for them and on the horizon she saw a black fog rolling towards them. It engulfed Alice and Kyle within seconds and then it surrounded Sophia completely.

Sophia opened her eyes and felt the dampness on her cheeks and her pillow. Something was seriously wrong. She sat up in the gloom of her bedroom and held her arms across her stomach. *Why were they crying? Why were they so sad?* She brushed the tears from her eyes. She felt as though all the emotion in her dream had been dumped on top of her usual emotions and she couldn't tell which feelings belonged to her and which didn't. She glanced at her bedside clock and watched as the digits changed from four twenty-nine to four thirty. She groaned and lay back down again, desperate to catch a few more hours of sleep before she had to get up for school.

Her alarm roused her from her light slumber two hours later and she begrudgingly got out of bed and headed for the shower. Once washed and dressed she went downstairs.

'Grandma, Grandma Flo, are you up?' Sophia called out. She found Flo preparing some breakfast and Elias sitting at the table at the other end of the kitchen.

'Good morning, Sophia,' Flo said.

'Morning, Grandma.' Sophia yawned and flicked on the kettle.

'Someone looks like they've had a disturbed night, did you dream again?' Sophia felt her guts twist and her bottom lip trembled as she turned to her grandma. The smile on Flo's face vanished. 'What's wrong, Sophia?' Flo gently held Sophia's shoulders. Sophia's vision blurred as her eyes welled up.

'I saw Alice and Kyle, they were crying. They were crying so much.' Sophia felt the tears slide down her cheeks and pressed the heel of her palm to her forehead.

'Crying? Why were they crying? Are they alright?'

'I don't know, Grandma, I don't know.' Sophia's voice broke and she choked on a sob as Flo pulled her tightly to her chest and wrapped her arms around her.

'Tell me what you saw, tell me all that you can remember,' Flo said as she stroked the back of Sophia's head. Sophia recounted her vision, trying her best to describe every detail she could remember.

'They were just so sad. It felt like something bad is going to happen or is happening.'

'But you didn't see anything bad happen?'

'No.' Sophia shook her head. Flo held Sophia by the shoulders again and peered into her eyes.

'I'll call our friends and family this afternoon and ask if anyone has seen anything.' Flo sighed. 'You should get some breakfast and calm down for a few minutes.' Sophia nodded and turned back to the kettle.

* * *

'What's wrong?' Avery asked. Sophia jumped at the sound of his voice. 'You haven't said a word for ten minutes, are you OK?'

'Sorry,' Sophia said, shifting in her spot to relieve her numb legs. The old timber factory creaked and groaned beneath them. 'I saw a vision of Alice and Kyle last night; it's been bothering me.'

'What did you see?'

'They were crying, I've never seen them cry before.' Sophia brought her legs up on the narrow window frame and wrapped her arms around her knees.

'What, like happy tears?'

'No, these were definitely sad tears, very sad tears. I'm worried that something bad might happen, that it might affect the discovery they're supposed to make.'

'You put a lot of pressure on two people you don't even know exist,' Avery said. 'Besides, they can't be the only important people on the planet.'

'No, no they're not. The current Dalai Lama is pretty important, and there's a man in America who was a presidential nominee, unfortunately he never made it into the White House though.'

'Neither of those are surprising.'

'There are ordinary people too. All over the world. Everyone is important really; the majority might have little influence alone, but together they have a huge influence on what happens in the world.'

'Then I don't understand why you get so hung up on this Alice and Kyle? Surely it won't be a disaster if they don't make their discovery.'

'It's what my ancestors have seen, what I've seen,' Sophia said.

'But the future is constantly changing, I should know that better than anyone. One moment your life seems great and as if nothing could go wrong, and the next it's like someone turned the whole world upside down.'

'Maybe. I guess it's possible that someone we haven't seen yet, someone good, might make the discovery instead. It's just that my ancestors have seen them for so long, I guess it would almost feel like we failed if something bad happened which stopped Alice and

Kyle.'

'I think you should cut yourself some slack; there are billions of people on the planet today. There's no way you could see visions of them all.'

'No, I know, but…'

'But you don't know,' Avery said. 'You don't know what else may happen or who else may be out there who will help humanity.' Sophia bit her lip. Perhaps Avery was right, perhaps there were others out there who would, if needed, replace Alice and Kyle, but it wasn't what her ancestors had seen.

Avery stood, picked up his violin, raised his bow to the strings and paused.

'What are they supposed to discover anyways?'

'They're supposed to discover a new level of particle physics and put together an important hypothesis,' Sophia said.

'Can't any physicist do that?'

'Potentially, but it's what happens in the aftermath that is important.'

'Why?'

'It'll change the world,' Sophia said. 'The advancements in technology are both great and numerous. It will help with medical equipment, space exploration, electronic devices, climate change and even virtual realities.'

'Sounds cool.'

'Yes, but it's also dangerous. With so much advancement, the things that could go wrong are terrifying. You know what humans can be like; not everyone will want to use this new technology for good.'

'I see what you mean.'

They were silent for a few moments and then Avery began to play, producing deep, sombre sounds from his violin. Sophia listened for a little while and then turned to her bag on the floor and drew out a slim book. She called it her journal, and she often used it to write down her thoughts and ideas. She flipped through the pages of diagrams and notes, glancing over the fragments of her half-formed ideas. Avery stopped playing.

'What's the book for?'

'It's where I write all of my future science ideas.'

'You really do want to be a scientist.'

'I think so.'

'You think so?'

'Well, my father is a physicist, he's currently at CERN.'

'Just because your father is a physicist, doesn't mean that you have to be.'

'I know. I know. I've just been thinking about it a lot lately. I love physics, I'm good at it, but Annie asked me what I would be doing if I knew nothing of Alice and Kyle, and when she asked, I didn't know what to say. I think I would still be doing physics, but I'm not completely sure.'

'If you enjoy doing it then you should do it,' Avery said. Sophia smiled.

'What about you?' Avery gave her a pointed look. 'OK, what did you want to do?'

'I haven't wanted to do anything for the last two years,' Avery said. 'But before that I just assumed I would work for my father and eventually take over the company.'

'Is that what you wanted to do?' Avery shrugged.

'It wasn't a bad plan for the future. Hey, what's that?' Avery pointed with his bow at the page Sophia's hands had paused on. She looked down and saw a sketch she had drawn of a robot with a metal head and limbs like a human, but its face was a screen with a simple, blue smiley face.

'That's not supposed to be in here.' She tore out the page and shoved it into her pocket.

'Look, I was thinking about what you said, about your visions and how they only happen under certain circumstances, and I know that we talked about it before but…' Avery rubbed the back of his neck and gazed off to the side. 'Do you mind… would you like to… would you come over to my house?'

'Like now?'

'Yeah, I just thought that maybe, you might see something.'

'OK, I mean, I can try, but only if you're sure.'

'Yeah, I'm sure.' Avery packed his violin away and picked up his things.

'What about your dad?'

'He will probably be asleep on the sofa; I did try to tidy up a little before school.'

'Oh, does that mean you were planning to ask me?'

'Yes.' She followed him out of the old timber factory and back through the woods to school. A couple of cars were still in the car park, teachers marking homework and reports before heading home for the evening. The lights on a black hatchback flashed and Avery dumped his belongings on the backseat before getting in behind the wheel. Sophia sidled into the passenger seat and held her bag on her lap.

Avery drove them to his house and Sophia was grateful that Elias wasn't camping outside that night. Her family thought she was at Annie's house and Annie was covering for her.

'My dad is probably asleep so try and be quiet when we get in,' Avery said.

'Sure.' Sophia followed him to the front door, and watched as he carefully opened the door and ushered her inside. She noted the tension which had settled over Avery's features but it was the immediate heaviness in the air which hit her like a wave when they stepped inside. She felt the warmth fade from her skin but the heat from a nearby radiator told her the house was warm. She let her vision switch and glanced up to see vast amounts of Negative energy hanging in the air like thunderous clouds. She shuddered and kept a wary eye on it as Avery reached for a light switch. Two lights on the wall lit up the hallway they were standing in, but Sophia could see the room at the far end was dark and glowing with its own dim light. Avery motioned silently to her and she followed him down the hallway and into a darkened lounge area. The television was on, casting its muted glow across the room and she saw Mr Richmond asleep on the sofa in a dressing gown. She could see his soul, it was almost identical to Avery's but the grey was somewhat contained by a deep red band, love. They had almost crossed the room when Mr Richmond coughed and stirred.

'Avery? Avery, is that you?' Mr Richmond said. He groaned and sat up, clutching his head. Avery shook his head and stopped.

'Yeah, it's me.' Mr Richmond grunted and switched on a light beside him.

'Oh.' He blinked at them. 'Oh, I'm sorry. I didn't realise there was someone with you.' He glanced down at his dressing grown and pulled it tighter around him.

'This is Sophia, Dad, she's a friend from school.' *Friend?* Sophia supressed a smile.

'A friend?' Mr Richmond raised his eyebrows. He stood with a groan and smiled politely. 'It's nice to meet you, Sophia, excuse the mess…' he held out a hand and surveyed the tidy room with a frown. Sophia shook his hand.

'Sorry for disturbing you, Mr Richmond,' Sophia said. She noted the sharp lines on his face and the dark circles under his eyes; he looked like a man who had hardly slept or eaten for weeks.

'No, no, not at all. We don't get guests very often,' Mr Richmond said. He smiled more cheerfully now and glanced at his son. The grey in Mr Richmond's soul seemed to lift a little, and a yellow band of colour emerged.

'I can't tell you how pleased I am to see that Avery has brought a friend home.'

'Dad…'

'Would you kids like some pizza? I fancy a pizza.'

'Dad, you really don't…' Avery said.

'That would be great,' Sophia said.

'Great, I'll order some,' Mr Richmond said. 'I'll just grab a shower and get dressed first.' He rubbed the stubble on his jaw almost as an afterthought. 'I could do with a shave too. Sorry.' He smiled sheepishly but Sophia felt the coldness she had felt earlier melt away. She glanced up at the Negative clouds above them; they didn't seem quite as big or numerous as they had done before. Mr Richmond hurried out of the lounge and disappeared into another room.

'I'm sorry about that,' Avery said.

'No, don't be,' Sophia said. 'Your dad seems nice.'

'He is. He seemed… different.'

'Different?'

'A good different. Come on, I'll take you to our library. It was my mum's favourite room.' He led her down to another hallway and opened the first door they came to. Beyond was a large room with a fireplace on the far wall framed by two big windows. Bookshelves lined the walls on either side and a large white rug dominated the wooden floor. Two cushioned chairs were positioned near to the fire; on one was a blanket as though someone had been sleeping there and there was a stack of books beside it. As the door closed behind them Sophia detected a change in this room; the Negative clouds which permeated the heart of the house were nowhere to be found here. Instead, little bands of golden energy danced around as though ghostly fireflies were leaving trails of light. The cold, numb feeling on her skin lifted completely, but just before her otherworldly vision faded she felt a rush of warm energy surround her. The room wobbled out of focus and as it readjusted, Sophia saw Mrs Richmond sitting in the other chair with a young Avery on her lap. Mrs Richmond held a book in her hands and she was reading aloud to her son.

'But now I am six, I'm as clever as clever, so I think I'll be six now for ever and ever,' Mrs Richmond said.

'I'm six.' Avery grinned.

'I know, and you're very clever.' She tickled him and Avery laughed.

'I like this poem. Who wrote it?'

'Ah, this one was written by A. A. Milne; do you remember who he is?' Avery shook his head. 'Yes, you do.' Mrs Richmond smiled. 'He wrote Winnie-the-Pooh.'

'Oh, I know who that is.'

'I know you do.' Sophia's vision wobbled again and when it refocused, Mrs Richmond and the young Avery had disappeared. Tears welled in Sophia's eyes and from the tingle of Positive energy rushing across her skin, she could tell there had been many happy moments within this room.

'Sophia?' Avery said.

'This room is amazing,' Sophia said.

'It's the best room in the house.'

'The energy in here is Positive,' Sophia said. She bit her lip as she wondered whether or not to tell Avery about the vision; it had been a private moment between them, one she probably shouldn't have seen, but she wondered if he remembered it. She walked over to the bookshelves on the left and gazed over the titles. She found the book she was looking for and plucked it gently from the shelf.

'Ah, A. A. Milne, I love that book, my mother read it a lot to me when I was a younger,' Avery said. Sophia handed the book to Avery and he smiled sadly at it before putting it back on the shelf. 'I guess we should try a different room?'

They left the library and Sophia soon learnt that Negative energy had claimed all the other rooms and no matter how hard she tried to will another vision, there was nothing to see.

Eventually, after an awkward meal with Avery and Mr Richmond, Avery agreed to drive Sophia to where she was supposed to be, Annie's house.

'I'm sorry that I couldn't help you,' Sophia said.

'It's OK. It was a long shot,' Avery said.

'There just weren't any Negative extremes to pick up on.' *Apart from the Negativity caused by the sadness you and your father are feeling.*

'I suppose it makes sense. It's not like anything bad happened at my house. Sure my parent's argued occasionally, but they were never violent or extreme.'

'I'm not keen on the idea, but we could always try going back to the alleyway?' Sophia said. Avery shook his head.

'I'd rather not.' Sophia nodded and turned her gaze to the road ahead. The hum of the engine was the only sound. 'You know you said you see souls and that everyone has one?'

'Yes?'

'What does mine look like?'

'Your soul is mainly grey.'

'Grey? What does that mean?'

'It means you're sad.'

'Oh. I shouldn't be surprised, anyone would be able to guess that.'

'Yeah, they probably would.'

'Where do they come from? Souls, I mean?'

'Where do souls come from?'

'Yeah, how are they made? Where do they go? Does my mum still…?'

'No one knows how they're made,' Sophia said. 'We think they come from what we call Positive energy, and it's more that we, as humans, have the capacity for a soul, so therefore one forms just before we are born. Animals and other creatures, as far as we know, don't have souls.' Sophia bit her lip, so far she had avoided the topic of Mrs Richmond's soul but now she had to say something and she had to be careful about it. 'When we die our souls cross over to the afterlife; there is a continued existence.'

'Is it like heaven? Is there a god or something?' Avery said.

'No, there's no gods or deities, but there is something like a heaven and a hell. Your soul is you, and whatever you do and think in life affects your conscience, which in turn affects your soul. Generally speaking, if you're a good and kind person and you don't cause harm to others then your soul will be OK on the other side.'

'What about if you're not a good or a kind person?' Avery asked.

'It's complicated, a lot comes down to circumstances and the choices you make, but yes, the truly evil people and those who are selfish to the extreme expense of others, they end up in an existence which is worse than death.'

'Worse than death?'

'Yes, I believe it is like being buried alive for all eternity.' Avery winced and shook his head.

'And I thought going to hell and meeting a devil would be bad. How do you know all this? Is this stuff your ancestors have seen in visions?' Sophia nodded. She didn't trust herself to speak; Avery still didn't know that Deykashee souls existed and that his mother was one of them. 'So, if there really is an afterlife, why don't people know about it? What's to stop people from just giving up on life and crossing over?'

'You can't see it, or touch it, so it's not real for most people. There's also religion, it's done a really good job at twisting things, and I've already told you, the soul is complicated and fragile, it's affected by your emotions, you can't just, you know...' Sophia glanced at him but Avery was staring straight ahead at the road.

'So my mother, I guess she would have crossed over to the afterlife by now?'

'Yes.'

'I hope she's happy.' Sophia nodded and then turned to look out of the passenger side window. Life was a fragile thing, and people's lives were like meandering paths on one giant mountain, intersecting one another and curving in all sorts of twisted directions. You couldn't have something happen on one side of the mountain without it having some sort of effect on the other side. Some of these paths were big and strong, others were short and weak, some were sturdy and safe, others were flimsy and chaotic. Some of these paths had barely started whilst others were mere impressions, overgrown and virtually forgotten. Some were easy whilst others were extremely difficult, and if you weren't careful, you could step on someone else's path and lose your way altogether.

THIRTY

Den jumped over the garden wall and spotted his mum in her kitchen window, washing dishes, framed by yellow and green curtains. He ran across the garden, dodging a swing and slide, and opened the back door.

'Lucian!' Linda said, dropping a plate into the sink.

'Don't call me that, Mum, it's Den.'

She hugged him fiercely.

'Oh, thank god, where have you been? Molly told me your flat had been set on fire, but that no one could find you.'

'I crashed at a friend's house last night. Mum, my flat…'

'Lucian, you can't be here. If Pete sees you…'

'Yes, I know, he'll beat me to a pulp, but I need help, Mum.'

Linda moved to the kitchen door, peered into the hallway and then shut it quickly. 'Dad's been back around and he emptied out my account.'

'Oh Den, you didn't let him do it again, did you?' Den hung his head. 'Oh Den, why?'

'Yeah, I know, I'm an idiot.'

'Your dad was always lying and stealing money; it's why I left him for Pete.'

'I don't know why you're with that monster either,' Den said.

'Pete's good with the kids,'

'Only his own…'

His mother smiled, sadly.

'Why would someone burn down your flat, Den?'

'It was Cooper, I think. He was looking for Dad. I saw him recently. He threatened to do it.' Den watched his mum's face turn white.

'If I see your bloody father I'll wring his neck.' Linda began to pace up and down across the orange linoleum floor. She pressed the heel of one hand to her head and placed the other on her hip. 'Jesus Christ, Den, what do you need?'

'I need some money.'

'Den, you need to go back to that flat and you need to go to the police and the council,' Linda said.

'I don't think that's a good idea.'

'You have to, Den. You need to get another place. The authorities will be looking for you and you can't stay here.'

'I know that,' Den said. 'I just need a bit of money; I'll pay you back as soon as I can. I'm working now, at the leisure centre.'

Linda stopped pacing.

'I can't, Den. Pete will know.'

'Mum, anything would be good right now,' Den said as he peered into his mother's green eyes. They heard a sound coming from the hallway.

'Hello?' Pete's voice boomed.

'Oh no, he's back. Den, you've got to go.' She pulled a ten pound note from her pocket and pushed it into her son's hand as she urged him towards the back door. Den cursed and ran into the garden just as the kitchen door opened. He vaulted over the garden wall and kept running until he realised he was heading back towards his flat. He stopped, placed his hands on his thighs and bent over to catch his breath. *You can't go back* his demons said. *What choice do I have?* Den turned and headed towards the nearest police station. The brick building sat on a corner, a big blue sign hanging above its doors. Den gulped past the raw lump in his throat. *Don't do it* his demons said. He knocked his thoughts aside and walked up to the door and pushed it open.

THIRTY-ONE

A frail teenager lay on the bed before her. Despite the harsh lines and thin skin drawn taunt over her skeleton, Sophia recognised her. *Alice.* Her pale lips were tinged a bluish purple and deep shadows hung under her blue eyes; her skin seemed to sag into every dip and hollow of her body. She wore a beanie hat but Sophia could tell that she'd lost her hair. A narrow tube fed into her arm and various machines were hooked up to her body. Sophia drew nearer to the bed, her gaze scanning the four white walls and shiny floor. One window looked out upon what seemed like a fantasy, mythical world that was too far away from the stark realities of the hospital. Alice's lips moved but no sound came out and her soul cast a lilac aura onto her body and around the room; sometimes a flash of yellow, pink, red and blue would shine through too. Sophia gazed down at Alice's soul sitting beneath her trembling ribcage; her bright, Positive colours still remained but they were shrouded by sickly grey and brown hues. *What happened to you, Alice?*

Alice's face twisted into lines reflecting excruciating pain and her body arched slightly away from the bed. The machines beside her erupted into a frenzy and all of a sudden, nurses and doctors rushed into the room. Sophia stood back and watched the horror unfold before her. Alice's body fell limp, her chest stopped rising and the doctors tried to resuscitate her. Sophia watched as they pushed at Alice's body with their hands and then they brought out two metal pads and placed them on Alice's chest. Her body jumped a few times but then fell limp again. The doctors and nurses stepped back from the bed and looked at each other; their faces faltered slightly, the years of professionalism not enough to hide their emotions. Their souls, varying in colours and intensity, were all encased in grey and one by one they shook their heads. Alice was gone.

Sophia's eyes flew open; her whole body felt as though it had crashed into full consciousness. She threw back the covers and ran out of her bedroom without checking the time. She arrived at the bottom of the stairs in a couple of heartbeats and pushed open the door to Flo's study.

'Grandma! Are you here?' The study was empty but the lamp on the desk was on, casting its yellow halo across the room. Sophia stepped into the room; a folder lay open on top of Flo's desk. Sophia felt drawn to it. There were notes there, letters and, most intriguingly, hand-drawn sketches and pictures. She had seen these pencilled pictures before, sketches drawn by their ancestors to help remember and preserve important visions. She saw depictions of Kyle and Alice standing together holding hands. Alice wore a pretty, knee-length dress with spaghetti straps whilst Kyle wore a t-shirt with a pair of jeans. She stared at the picture, her fingers tracing the lines through the plastic wallet. It was them, there was no doubt about it. She turned the plastic wallets over; there were more drawings, more scenes that Sophia recognised from her own visions. Her eyes snagged on an unfamiliar notebook which lay open, peeking out beneath the folder. She moved the folder aside and picked up the notebook; she recognised her grandma's flowing handwriting but it was the date at the top of the page that held her attention. *December 20ᵗʰ 1988.* A few months before Sophia had been born. Her gaze dropped down to the first line of her grandma's graceful handwriting.

Important Negative vision. Alice's Death. Alice appeared in a hospital bed, deathly pale and sickly at the beginning of my vision, she then perishes due to what I believe is a heart attack. Illness/disease is probably cancer. The vision leapt quickly through the following events, showing Kyle abandoning the physics path to university, and showing Sophia in a lab with other individuals. These individuals do not share the same morals or ethics as Alice and Kyle. Cracking open the secrets to the foundations of the afterlife solving the theory of everything. Despite the group making the same discoveries, the consequences are disastrous for humanity. I saw a blackened world, wars, poverty, and advanced technology, more dangerous than the world can imagine. Sophia feels the guilt of her actions and those of her fellow colleagues, her soul becomes weighed down with abundant sadness and guilt and becomes Negative. She eventually crosses over, unhappy in old age and her soul is too Negative. She will be confined to the Negative hell state and eventually cease to exist. Must discuss!

Sophia's vision started to blur and then she felt tears spilling from her eyes. She heard the door creak and looked up.

'Sophia? What are you doing? Why are you up so early?' Flo said. She held a cup of coffee in one hand and her gaze travelled down from Sophia's face to the book in her hands.

'What is this?' Sophia said.

'Sophia…'

'Did you see this?'

Flo stepped into the study and shut the door behind her. She tried to meet Sophia's gaze but was unable to maintain eye contact. 'I saw her,' Sophia said, her voice barely above a whisper. She looked back down at the book in her hands as her tears splattered across the pages and the desk below. 'I saw her, she… she…' Sophia looked up at Flo. 'She died, Grandma, I saw her, but she died – just as you've written here, just like your vision.' Sophia's throat let out a tortured sound and she felt as though her body was breaking. Flo set down her coffee and gently wrapped her arms around Sophia, surrounding her granddaughter's senses with warmth and the overwhelming fragrance of sweet floral perfume mixed with the sharp bitter notes of coffee.

'I'm so sorry, Sophia,' Flo said. 'I'm so sorry we've had to be careful with you. We've had no choice but to keep this hidden from you for so long.'

Sophia drew back and looked at her grandma.

'Why? I don't understand. Why would you keep this from me? Is my soul doomed if Alice dies?' She sat down.

'We were planning to tell you. Now that you've seen my vision I might as well tell you everything.' She pulled up her chair and sat down behind her desk and sipped at her coffee. 'When did you see this vision? Tell me exactly what you saw.'

'I saw it just minutes ago,' Sophia said and explained all the painful details she could remember. 'I came down here to look for you so that I could tell you about it, but you weren't in here and then I found your notebook.'

'This all began in the year before you were born, in December actually, a couple of months before you were born. The whole family had arrived to celebrate Christmas here, and some of our friends too. I awoke during the early hours on the twentieth. My screams woke up the entire household. I had just seen the very vision you saw and then some, it had frightened me to the core. I told everyone, but my brother, George, was very stubborn about it, questioning me about my vision from every possible angle, but he was right to do it. No one had ever seen a vision with one of the pair dying before. Sure, we had seen the consequences on the world if they failed to make the discovery, but no one had realised that it might affect you too, Sophia. It was the worst possible vision to see; not only did we lose the last hope for the future of humanity, but I would also potentially lose my granddaughter.' Flo gazed down at her coffee. 'George was quick to point out that I had only seen this vision once and that I was the only person who had seen it; normally a major vision like that would have been seen by several members of our friends and family at the same time, and would crop up frequently over the years, but no, it was just me. He also pointed out that we would need some unbiased proof to weigh up my vision against the centuries of unchanged visions seen by our ancestors, and since everyone in the room had heard my account of the vision, there was only one person who would count.' Flo gazed at her granddaughter.

'Me,' Sophia said, 'because I hadn't been born yet.'

'Yes, precisely. Your dad wasn't happy about it, the family argued about it all over the Christmas period and everyone was waiting for me to see the vision again but it never happened. Eventually it was decided that we would keep only the knowledge of my vision from you and nothing else. Your mum and dad agreed reluctantly, because there was a chance my vision could be correct and they didn't want that to burden their consciences. It seems like a very selfish thing but you must understand, Sophia, the family want the best for the world, humanity, but we also want to survive ourselves, for our own sakes and for the sakes of our loved ones. It was hoped you would see my vision relatively quickly or that we would stumble across an outsider with our gifts who had also seen the vision, but this never happened, and no one else in our circle has ever had the same vision. So it seemed unlikely that it would happen after all. So the decision not to tell you seemed justified.'

'I thought that we only saw the most likely scenarios the most frequently,' Sophia said.

'Yes, for major visions that affect a lot of people all at once, but that is because there's more emotional energy involved in those types of visions, it causes extreme surges in Positive and Negative which are easier to pick up on. That's not always strictly true for minor visions which only affect a few people. You've had minor visions yourself that happen only moments or days before they actually occur.'

Sophia nodded.

'You're supposed to help the pair with their physics research, although if Alice dies, then Kyle is unlikely to follow the pathway which would lead him to their discovery.'

'Is it really cancer?' Sophia asked.

'We're not one hundred percent sure but it looks like it,' Flo said. 'Alice doesn't die because of an accident in the vision. She's very, very sick, Sophia, and if that is the case then she probably already has it but doesn't know it yet.'

Sophia's body froze and her heart stuttered.

'We need to find her. We need to warn her; she needs to get to a hospital as soon as possible.'

'We're trying to find her, Sophia, but we may still be too late,' Flo said. 'The visions are quick and limited in detail. We rarely see place names or landmarks that we can recognise. She may not even be in Britain; she could be in the United States, Australia or New Zealand, even though we think she's in Britain based on her accent.'

Sophia stared at her grandma; she opened her mouth and then closed it again as the enormity of the situation struck her. How did they find one girl in a country with over sixty million individuals, when they only knew her first name and had no idea where she might be living?

'We think she's somewhere in the south of England; your aunt and uncle are currently trying to track her down but it's been a process of elimination, greatly aided by the recent advances in technology and the internet.'

'Yes,' Sophia said. 'I can see why, you didn't even have mobile phones when I was born.'

'Exactly, it's been hard, even harder for our ancestors,' Flo said. 'We believe Alice and Kyle were only born shortly after you.'

'What if Alice really does die, what will happen to me?'

'I don't know for sure,' Flo said. 'It seems that the guilt caused by being part of the discovery without Alice and Kyle could potentially turn your soul Negative.'

'I guess if that ever happens then I need to stop them from making the discovery,' Sophia said.

'Perhaps, but someone else will probably make the discovery

instead.'

'Then what can we do?'

'We don't know what will happen yet; there are so many different pathways and so many different circumstances that could arise. The future could completely change again tomorrow. We were left facing a paradox in the end because no one else had or has seen my vision, though we've all tried to. If we told you and you never saw the vision then we wouldn't know either way if the possibility was more likely or not. Yet if we did tell you and you saw the vision then it would hardly be unbiased and wouldn't have much weight against the visions of our ancestors.'

'So, now what?' Sophia asked.

'Your saving grace is that you did find out this way; it may just be enough to set up the right circumstances, whatever they may be. We'll wait until the rest of the family wake up and then I'll call George, your cousins and some friends. We need a meeting to discuss what we do next, especially now you've validated my vision.'

'How could they not believe you, Grandma?' Sophia asked, gripping the chair's armrests, but she knew, she knew that one vision wouldn't have been enough.

'Because our ancestors have seen both Alice and Kyle frequently for hundreds of years, and every vision they saw ended happily with Alice and Kyle making the discovery that they needed to make. One vision from one person wasn't enough to persuade part of our family that something was wrong, though we didn't want to take any chances.'

'Is this why Elias and George always argue?'

'Your brother and my brother have disagreed about withholding this information from you since the very beginning; your brother never liked the fact that you were kept in the dark.'

Sophia lowered her gaze.

'I understand why, I just wish there had been another way,' she said.

Flo nodded.

'You should get some more rest; there are still a couple of hours before the rest of the house wakes up.'

'Can I look at that folder later?' Sophia asked.

'Yes, of course. I'll tell you everything we know.'

'We will find them, Grandma, won't we?' Sophia asked, rising from her chair.

'I hope so, Sophia. If we lose Alice though, we may have no choice but to look elsewhere for answers.'

'I hope it doesn't come to that,' Sophia said, pausing in the doorway.

'Me too,' Flo said. 'But we've got to be prepared for that possibility; I will not lose my granddaughter over this too, no matter how far humanity falls.'

'Your conscience wouldn't forgive you for that,' Sophia said.

'My conscience wouldn't forgive me if we lost you either,' Flo said with a wry smile. Sophia stared at her grandma and held her emotions in check as a sudden wave of determination rushed through her body.

'I understand, but I'll never give up on them.'

THIRTY-TWO

Ahrl watched as the wheels of the old man's trolley kicked up little clouds of dust as they rolled down the dirt tracks of an old, forgotten road. Trees flanked them and grass leapt up at the sides like long green fingers trying to claw back the edges of the road. The trolley rattled as its wheels were pushed over the uneven ground and it squeaked in protest at the movement.

'Shame about that nice place, a real shame,' the old man said to himself, shaking his head. He looked up. 'I 'ope ye find a new place, Ralph and Mary… and Sam, was it? Aye, Sam. Nice people. Real shame.' The nice house had been reclaimed and builders had settled in to fix the place up. It helped Ahrl, but he felt sadness for the troubled three; they were nice people.

The old man hummed to himself and kept a watchful eye on the rolled-up futon as it wobbled within its metal confines. Ahrl gazed up at the trees, their branches becoming more exposed as their fiery adornments fell to the ground. He thought back to the plant life from his home planet and sighed at the loss of the beautiful rainbow fields, not too dissimilar from the English wheat fields or the lavender fields of Provence, and the majestic butterfly-like creatures that had made their homes there. The memory was tantalising, he could see the fields stretching across the feet of mountains under a blushing sky.

The old man suddenly shouted in glee. Up ahead, a weary building hid behind the trees.

'So, we've arrived,' Ahrl said to himself. The old man pushed the trolley with renewed vigour towards the building. He was blocked by a chain-linked gated fence for a while but Ahrl strolled through the metal wiring unblemished and unhindered. He gazed up at the building whilst the old man followed the fence. 'This building has seen better days,' Ahrl said. He heard a *chink* followed by a *thud* and a grating metal sound as the old man pushed open a rotting gate and wheeled his trolley inside.

'It's falling down,' the old man said as he shaded his eyes with his hand and peered up at the building. Much of the brickwork had peeled away from the building and collapsed into small clumps of rubble.

'It is,' Ahrl said.

'Well, at least it'll be warmer 'ere than under that bridge when winter kicks in,' the old man said. He wheeled his trolley round to the front of the building and looked up to the second floor with its gaping, glassless window. Underneath the window the brickwork had mostly fallen away and had left holes in the walls. The old man bent down to pull up a rusty iron bar that pointed out of the ground. *Good, that solves one issue,* Ahrl thought. Then the old man began clearing some of the bricks and rubble away before finally hefting the futon out of the trolley and laying it flat on the ground. He wandered off, collecting broken boards and bits of wood and putting them into a pile near his futon. Ahrl stood by the tatty futon and gazed up at the open window and then back down to the futon and up again. He felt his lips pinch into a tight line and his brow tighten.

'I don't like the odds,' Ahrl said. He watched as the sky darkened and the old man lit a small fire a few yards away from his newly acquired home. He pulled out all the rags and ends from his trolley and piled them around him in a heap, like a mouse in a nest. He gazed up at the clear night sky and stared at the millions of stars, twinkling like jewels. Ahrl stood beside the old man and wondered how he had come to be in this state. The old man lay down on his side and his snores soon echoed through the air. Ahrl watched his soul for a moment and realised that the flashes of lilac and aqua across the old man's soul meant that he was dreaming.

'Who are you, my old friend?' Ahrl said. He reached out a hand and let his positive energy flow from his fingertips and delve into the deepest recesses of the old man's memories. Ahrl's vision exploded into colours around him; he saw a wife, a daughter and a younger version of the old man smiling and laughing in a clean and comfortable, two-bedroomed flat. The scene changed and the man wore green army uniform as he ran through a dusty village where the dry, bleached earth swept into the streets and broken homes. Sweat dripped down into his eyes as he fired bullets at people who fired back. He ran into a building with its roof blown off and found a man and a woman dead, lying side by side. They were just civilians, they had no weapons and bore no emblems or flags; the man stared down at their bodies as green, grey, orange and pale blue hues all fought for dominance over his outer soul colours. He surveyed the room and his gaze caught on a small body, sat up against the wall with bullet holes in its chest and blood splattered against the wall. Orange fired up around his soul; the boy was just an innocent child.

The scene shifted and Ahrl could see the man back at home again but this time the smiles and laughter were all gone; his wife argued with him and it was obvious their marriage was falling apart. She was drinking, and she screamed in his face and clawed at his cheeks. Ahrl watched him push her away and she stumbled, catching her arm on the side of the kitchen counter. She accused him of physically abusing her. Neighbours and good friends turned on him and sided with his wife, delivering their testimonies of fights and arguments that had never happened. Lies. His wife left with his child and all of his savings. Ahrl could see the man's mother and grandmother die shortly afterwards. The man couldn't cope anymore; he suffered a mental breakdown. He didn't turn up for work and he lost his flat when he couldn't afford to pay the bills.

He was turfed out of his home with nothing but the clothes he was wearing.

The scene changed again and Ahrl watched as the man aged before him, sleeping rough in doorways, bus stops, on park benches and under bridges. A few bought food and gave it to the old man, whilst other men yelled 'Get a job' and beat him when he tried to sleep. He passed hundreds of similar faces in homeless shelters, all with similar fates, fighting for survival, physically, emotionally and often mentally.

'Have you seen my daughter?' the old man asked anyone and everyone who would listen. 'Have you seen her?' Ahrl watched the question fall from the old man's lips as the seasons turned around him. Finally, he found her, and he watched her from afar as she attended university. She stood tall and proud as she graduated and had a sparkle in her eyes and a beautiful smile. He took one step towards her and stopped; tears rolled down his cheeks and he turned and walked away without making his presence known to her.

The university faded and gave way to the bustling streets of the town. 'Can ye spare any change?' the old man asked as people passed by. Ahrl followed the old man as he walked down the streets, sometimes eating and sometimes not. He passed the few books he had collected on to the young and homeless. The sky shifted from dawn to night and back again dozens of times with the same cycles of begging, eating and sleeping, until eventually Ahrl recognised a familiar spot. The old man found his way to his place under the bridge, and he camped there most nights, begging in the town centre and then returning to his squalid home by the river.

Ahrl pulled his mind from the old man's subconscious and could feel the drain on his energy; the detachment he felt between his mind and soul was like trying to play unstrung chords. *Life can be cruel to good people,* he thought. Hours passed. The fire had died out long ago and daylight finally roused the old man from his slumber. He stretched and began to busy himself. After relieving himself in the woods he came back and pulled a dingy cloth bag out of the trolley. He sat down on the futon and removed a dirty paper cup from the bag which rattled as he shook it. The old man frowned and emptied the cup into his fingerless-gloved hand. A coin fell out and the old man held it up to the sky; it was a penny, and it glinted in the sunlight. Ahrl looked up to the nearest tree where a magpie sat. It dived from its perch, swooping towards the old man and plucking the penny from his fingers.

'Why ye!' The old man yelled and jumped to his feet. 'That's mine.' The magpie took off through the trees and the old man chased after it. Ahrl smiled, and then he felt his mind slip as he was pulled back across the divide. He sagged against the fountain and slowly lowered himself to his knees.

'There's nothing more I can do now, but hope,' Ahrl said. 'I will see you again soon, old man. I'm sure under happier circumstances.'

THIRTY-THREE

Den left the police station with little more than a confirmation that he was indeed still alive. His fingers still shook from the brief ordeal and he felt cold. He retraced his actions and words hoping he hadn't given away anything which would lead them to his past.

'We're also going to need your fingerprints for elimination,' the officer said.

'What?' *Don't give her fingerprints* his demons screeched.

'If it was arson like you think then we need to take your fingerprints so we can eliminate yours and find other fingerprints, if there's anything left to go on.'

'Right.' Den gulped but reluctantly agreed.

He wandered aimlessly around the town, the hustle and bustle of everyday life succeeding slightly in drowning out the demons in his mind. *Did the police have any fingerprints from the killing? Would they now recognise him from the grainy CCTV footage they had captured? Would they come for him?* He found himself heading down a route he hadn't taken in a while; he passed through a council estate, over a sloping strip of grass and entered a large swathe of woodland. He didn't know if it was nostalgia or paranoia governing his actions but he remembered the path he was treading. He remembered clasping the cardboard box in his hands and ducking into the trees during the dying evening hours. He walked for ages in an almost perfectly straight line until he came to the spot. Beside a large uprooted tree stood another large tree with a small mark in the form of a tear shape near the bottom of its trunk. He remembered the trowel he had bought with him and how he had dug a small hole at the base of this tree, then placed the box inside and covered the hole again. He stood staring at the spot, now littered with leaves. Nobody would ever know, he reassured himself.

He heard the crunching of twigs and looked up. *No way!* He quickly hid behind the tree and peeked out from around the side to see the girl from the supermarket walking through the woodland. *That damned girl is here! Does she know? Is she searching for the weapon too? How can she know? Follow her! Follow her!* his demons yelled. He dropped to his knees and raked up the soil by the foot of the tree with his hands.

THIRTY-FOUR

She felt the wind rushing past them, grabbing at her hair and clothes, and she screamed as the ground rushed up to meet them.

* * *

Sophia trudged through the woods with her heart beating furiously against her chest. *He promised me he wasn't going to do it.* Her stomach lurched as she recalled her vision and she picked up her pace. *I thought things were going well, he even asked Annie about Joe. Why would he kill himself now? Did he think no one would find him out here?* Sophia had made her excuses to get out on her own for the morning; the rest of the family weren't due to arrive until later that afternoon. She had managed to stave off questions about her dream and said she was simply worried about Alice, Kyle and her soul, which she was, but it was secondary to her concerns now. She headed towards Avery's sanctuary. The rusty stairs creaked, clanged and groaned as she climbed them. Then she entered the little room, which she supposed had once been an office, on the second floor. There was no sign of Avery. She sat in the window, leant back against the frame and looked out across the treetops. *He's not here yet, thank god. I should be able to stop him.*

The creaking of a floorboard drew her attention and then she froze, wishing she could hide herself or meld into the brickwork. *He* stood there before her, his trainers in one dirty hand and a rusty knife in the other. She glanced down at his feet where his big toe poked out of his right sock and then back up to his burning green eyes. Sophia's thoughts scrambled in her mind. *Why is he here? How did he find me? What does he want?*

'Are… are you lost?'

'Lost?' the supermarket man said. 'No, I followed you.' Sophia licked her lips as her mouth ran dry.

'Followed me? Why?'

'Oh, you know why,' the supermarket man said. 'See, I've been watching you and I know you've been talking to that Richmond boy about his mum's death. I've seen you.'

'Seen me?'

The supermarket man frowned.

'Yes, but it doesn't matter,' he said, waving the knife at her. She thought she recognised the hilt of the knife; was it the same knife that had been used to kill Mrs Richmond? *If I can get that knife, I'll have proof and Avery will finally have some justice.* 'Do you remember me? You were acting all weird when you knocked into me at the supermarket. I thought you were having some sort of seizure but then you said those three little words and it really shook me up. So I thought to myself, this girl knows something, she knows something she shouldn't, and I want to know how and why, and you're going to tell me the truth.'

Oh please, Avery, don't come here today.

'What did I say?' Sophia gripped the window ledge. 'You're mistaken; I don't know what you're talking about.'

'Don't lie to me!' the supermarket man shouted. 'I've had a really bad week and a really shit life, I know when someone is lying to me. You said, *you did it, you killed her.* Remember?'

'I think you're mistaken…'

'I know what I heard. Stop lying.' The knife trembled in his hand; she realised that denying it was making him angrier, was it already too late? 'Who did I kill? What do you know?' Sophia clamped her mouth shut and stared at the approaching blade. He drew nearer and Sophia leant back and felt her stomach heave. She caught herself and eyed the drop below her; it was a long way down. *Oh, the irony, I'm going to die in exactly the same way Avery has now planned for himself. You've got to move, Sophia, do something!* The supermarket man was barely a metre away from her when she suddenly leapt up. He swore, his eyes almost popping out of his head as he hesitated, as if he didn't know whether to come towards her or swerve from her advance. Sophia grabbed onto his wrist, almost out of reflex, and tried to wrestle the knife away from his grasp. A cold numbing sensation spread through her fingers and up into her arm, and a sharp electric energy tore through her mind and burned beneath her skin. She screamed and was barely aware of the supermarket man also screaming beside her before her vision switched and she saw black clouds of Negativity rising from the man and swallowing the room. She felt as though her mind was trying to peel away from itself and suddenly the pain and cold numbness lifted.

She blinked and found herself not in the dilapidated room at the old timber factory, but on a street following two men, wrapped up for the cold in dark clothes.

'Ah, Den, it's good to be back for Christmas,' the slightly bigger and older man said. They walked past shops with their twinkling festive displays closing up for the night.

'I'm just glad you've cleaned yourself up, Dad,' Den said. He pulled his hood up over his blond hair as snow tried to fall, only to collect in lumps and melt into puddles. 'A few drinks and spending time with you will be the best Christmas I've had in a long time.'

'You're not wrong there, son,' Jack said. They passed market stalls that lined the centre of the street. Jack froze suddenly, bending his knees and holding his arms out wide with his gaze fixed firmly ahead.

'What is it?' Den said, following his line of sight. Three men who Sophia didn't recognise stood around the end of the Christmas market, talking to one of the stall owners. 'Oh no, it's Cooper…'

'Quick, down here,' Jack said, darting into the mouth of an alleyway.

'Wait. I thought you said everything was OK between you two now,' Den said, following his father.

'Well… I'd just rather not bump into them tonight.'

'I can't believe this. You've not sorted out anything, have you?'

'It's difficult, Den.'

'You lied to me,' Den said. 'You said that everything was sorted, that you were a changed man and that there was nothing to worry about anymore.'

Jack opened his mouth to reply but a muffled shriek and a loud crack echoed down the alleyway.

'What the?' Jack moved quickly towards the noise.

'Hey,' Den said, chasing after him. Jack stopped suddenly at a bend in the alleyway. A man had pinned a woman up against the grime-covered walls.

'What do you think you're doing?' Jack said. The man whirled around; he was pale with protruding yellow teeth and a large brown birthmark on his left cheek. He glanced between both men and then ran off out of the alleyway. Sophia recognised Mrs Richmond, her coat had been torn open at the top and her lipstick was smudged against her face. She held her hand up to her heaving chest.

'Thank you, thank you, you saved me,' she said, her eyes welling. Strands of dark hair hung wildly about her face. She was beautiful, there was no doubt about that, and wealthy from the look of her clothes.

'No problem, sweetheart,' Jack said. He eyed the woman, his gaze falling on the necklace around her slender neck. 'Now why don't you be a darling and hand over your bag and necklace, you know, as repayment.'

'What the hell?' Den said, looking at his father with disgust.

'Shut it, you,' Jack said. Mrs Richmond stared at them and Jack reached into his pocket and drew out a knife.

'This isn't right,' Den said. 'Leave her alone, we should be calling the police.'

'I said, shut up.' Jack glared at him. 'OK sweetheart, now give us your bag and necklace and we won't trouble you anymore.' Mrs Richmond threw her bag at them but covered her necklace with a gloved hand and sank back against the wall. 'Good, now the necklace, sweetheart,' Jack said. Mrs Richmond shook her head.

'Leave it,' Den hissed.

'No. This should be more than enough to pay back what I owe. I'm not leaving it and besides, she owes us.' Jack approached Mrs Richmond. She glanced from side to side, pushed herself off the wall and tried to run, but Jack caught her by the arm.

'No,' Den said, closing the distance to his father.

'Help, someone, please help me,' Mrs Richmond cried.

'Christ, shut her up,' Jack said. Den panicked and reluctantly obeyed, pressing a gloved hand over Mrs Richmond's mouth, but he held firmly onto his dad with the other.

'Stop it, drop the knife!' Den said. The three struggled, crashing back into the wall and then Jack grasped Mrs Richmond's necklace with his free hand and yanked it sharply, breaking it from her neck as Den pried the knife from his father's grasp. It all happened so quickly then. Mrs Richmond lurched forward, tugged by the necklace, slipping on the slushy ground, and crashing straight into Den. Den still held one hand over her mouth; his gaze dropped down to where his arm was bent at a sharp angle, grasping a knife he could no longer see. She struggled but her cries became faint whispers and her eyes dulled.

'No, no, no, no,' Den said as he felt her body sag. He gazed at the knife as he felt a warm wetness trickle down the handle, the blade buried in the folds of her coat. He lowered her gently to the ground as a small pool of crimson blood spread out beneath her.

'Jeez, what have you done, Den?' Jack said, grasping Mrs

Richmond's necklace in one hand. Tears erupted from Den's eyes and flowed like rivers down his cheeks.

'I didn't mean to… I didn't…'

'You've killed her.'

'You… No, I… I was just trying to make you stop, why wouldn't you stop?' Den stared down at Mrs Richmond as her glassy eyes stared up at the night above. 'It was an accident,' Den said. 'We've got to turn ourselves in, we need to call the police and explain…'

'No way,' Jack said. 'No way am I going back inside for this.' He looked down at his son, shook his head then turned and fled down the alleyway and out of sight. Den trembled. He pulled the knife from the body with a slick wet sound and ran in the opposite direction to his dad. He lifted his scarf across his face and put the knife in his pocket, cradling the blade with a gloved hand. He walked as quickly as he dared down the street, and threaded his way through a large group of people. Someone knocked into him, a man with dark hair and coffee-coloured skin, a man later to be identified as Dr Asim Umar.

'Sorry,' Asim said as he pushed his way through the rest of the group and carried on at a hurried pace down the street and out of sight.

The corners of Sophia's vision began to blur and fade; the colour ran like paints on a tilted canvas. She blinked several times and found herself face to face with the supermarket man, no, Den. He blinked too, his green eyes brightening with awareness.

'What was that?' Den asked.

'I don't know.'

'Did you just see that? Did you just… It was like I was there again.'

'Sophia!' Avery yelled. He charged into the room, his gaze fixed on Den and the knife in his hand.

'Avery, no!' Sophia cried but Avery lunged forwards, pushing Sophia aside and slamming Den back into the brick wall beside the window. A cloud of dust enveloped them and the knife fell from Den's grasp, clanging against the floor. Den's face twisted into a hideous snarl and Sophia let her vision switch to see orange rage exploding from his dark soul. Avery and Den coughed and choked and then grappled as the dust cleared, each trying to throw the other onto the floor and gain leverage. Sophia heard the building groan and she edged back towards the doorway. 'Avery, stop!' she yelled.

There was a loud cracking sound and half of the room, the half where Avery and Den stood, fell at a sharp angle. Their bodies fought against gravity and the steep slope of the floor for a moment but Sophia could only watch in horror as they fell straight through the open window. She caught a glimpse of both of their faces as they twisted through the air and then they were gone. 'Avery!' she screamed. She turned on her heels and ran straight into someone.

'Sophia!' Elias said. He pulled her sharply from the room as it continued to creak and groan, the floorboards ripping and brickwork shattering on the ground below. Elias cursed. 'I didn't make it in time.'

'Elias?' Sophia said.

'Flo saw, she saw everything. Dad, Mum and I all ran out to get you; they're not far behind me.'

Sophia pushed away from her brother and started running down the stairs.

'Quick, we need to call an ambulance,' Sophia said. 'Avery and that man fell out the window.'

THIRTY-FIVE

It had been nearly a week since the accident, and Sophia hadn't been allowed to see Avery, despite turning up at the hospital every day. For the sixth day in a row, she sat on the uncomfortable foam-padded chair, her hands clasped between her knees.

Elias reached out and caught her hands. She looked up at him with bleary eyes.

'It's my fault, Elias.'

'No, it's not.'

'I feel terrible.'

'It's not your fault, Sophia, you didn't know, you couldn't have known,' Elias said.

'But we see the future, Elias, and I saw it, I saw him fall.'

'You didn't see enough,' Elias said. 'That has always been our curse, we never see enough.' He wrapped an arm around her and hugged her gently as her tears fell. The door to waiting room opened and a nurse appeared.

'Sophia?' the nurse said. 'Avery is asking for you, you can see him now.' Sophia glanced at Elias and nodded; she stood up and wiped the tears from her face with the cuff of her sleeve and took a deep breath.

'OK, I'm ready.'

'Follow me,' the nurse said. Sophia followed her down a corridor and they paused outside a door. Sophia could see Avery lying on a bed inside the room through a window partially obscured by vertical blinds. The nurse knocked on the door and then held it open for Sophia. She rubbed her eyes again and stepped into the room.

'Sophia.' Avery smiled. He was sitting up but he appeared to be sliding down his bed as though weights pulled at his feet.

'I'm so sorry, Avery,' Sophia said.

'Hey, no, it's not your fault,' Avery said. 'I'm just glad that you're alright.'

Sophia sat down in the vacant chair by Avery's bed.

'Avery, I'm so sorry, I heard about your legs…' Sophia glanced down at his bedsheets.

'Yeah,' Avery said, his smile faltering for a second. 'It sort of sucks being paralysed from the waist down but at least no one can ask me to participate in sports day.'

Sophia eyes welled up.

'How can you joke about it?' she said as the tears tumbled from her eyes.

'Hey, it's a miracle I'm alive,' Avery said, his voice still little more than a whisper. 'I know that ever since my mum died that I've wanted to die, and I really believed I did.' He took a breath. 'But when I was up there and the floor just tipped suddenly like a slide, in that split second as we were falling, I suddenly thought to myself, I don't actually want it to end this way.' As Avery smiled, Sophia noticed that the iciness in his gaze had disappeared, his eyes were warm. 'It was weird, because I'd been so sure in my choice up until that moment, but when the choice was taken away from me, I wasn't sure at all. It happened so fast. We were up in that room and then suddenly we were down on the ground and all I remember is this excruciating pain but feeling relieved that I was still alive.'

Sophia clasped his hand. 'It's a good job you landed on that futon, otherwise you probably would have died.'

'I know, the doctors said it was a miracle."

'Yes, apparently a homeless man had been sleeping there. He was interviewed on the news and won the hearts of people;

someone has started an online campaign to raise money for him on social media. They've already raised twenty thousand pounds and it's still rising.'

'Amazing.' Avery smiled. 'Dad will probably want to help too.' Sophia could feel the tears welling in her eyes again.

'I'm so sorry, Avery. It was my fault that Den was at the old timber factory, he followed me there.'

'It seems weird now that he actually has a name.'

'His actual name is Lucian,' Sophia said. 'But people know him as Den.'

'Lucian?' Avery let out a humourless snort.

'Lucian Denys Boothe,' Sophia said. 'It sounds so posh.'

'Do you know what the name Lucian means?'

'No.'

'It means light,' Avery said. 'It's a bit ironic, don't you think?'

'Avery, if I hadn't led him straight to…'

'Then we would have probably both fallen,' Avery said. 'I was heading there anyway and you were already there; we probably would have both been sat on that window ledge and the building would probably still have given out beneath us and we might not have been so lucky, both of us might not have made it.' Sophia blinked back her tears and wiped her eyes. 'So don't blame yourself, it wasn't your fault.'

'I thought you were going to jump.' Sophia sniffled. 'I saw you falling in a vision and I thought…'

'You thought I was going to commit suicide again?' Avery managed a faint laugh.

'Don't laugh; I just saw you falling in my vision, I didn't see anything else.'

'I told you I wasn't going to do it.'

'You might have changed your mind.'

'You got the falling part right at least,' Avery said. He gazed down at his bedsheets. 'Just before I came in though, when you were fighting Den, you saw something else, didn't you? What really happened, you know, before I fell out of the window?'

'I've not been totally honest with you, Avery.' Sophia bit her lip. 'I've known about Den for a while, or I knew he was possibly responsible for your mother's death.' Avery raised his eyebrows but let her continue. 'I saw him at the supermarket, I bumped into him actually and that's why I saw the original vision of your mother's death. Only I messed it up because I accused him of murder right then and there, and he knew it. It made him wary and paranoid of me, which only got worse when he saw the two of us together.'

'Why didn't you tell me?' Avery leant his head back on his pillow and closed his eyes.

'I didn't know for sure. I thought I knew but I wasn't one hundred percent sure. But I was right not to say, I was wrong about him.'

'What do you mean, wrong?'

'Just before you turned up, when I touched Den and the knife, I had another vision and I saw the truth. He didn't mean to kill your mother, Avery, it was an accident,' Sophia said. 'Another man pulled your mother into the alleyway. Den and his dad were out together and happened to come across them. They chased the man away but Den's dad decided to threaten your mother with a knife and demand her belongings as payback. Den didn't agree and things got out of hand. Den tried to get the knife away from his dad but there was a struggle and she slipped...' Sophia cast her gaze to the ground. Avery didn't say anything for a long time and Sophia glanced up to see his chest steadily rising and falling. Finally, he exhaled deeply and opened his eyes.

'It's OK, at least we know the truth now. You could have told me, you know.'

'I was afraid that you would kill yourself; I was trying to buy your time,' Sophia said. 'I thought that if I kept your mind interested in the possibility of catching your mother's killer then it would delay you. Only now…' She gazed down at his legs. 'I'm sorry, Avery.'

'He's still alive. Has he already confessed?'

'Yes, I think so. I saw him briefly when they wheeled him to a private room with police guards. He's broken several bones, including his collar bone and pelvis. He was rambling on about seeing the darkness and facing the consequences head on, I think he was spaced out from the pain relief. He spotted me though and seemed to have a brief moment of awareness. He called over to me and asked me to tell you that he was sorry, even though he knew that sorry couldn't change anything.'

Avery pinched his mouth into a tight line and gave a curt nod. He gazed up at the ceiling, as if he was unable to look Sophia in the eye again.

'Why do I have a feeling there's more?'

'I suppose there is,' Sophia said quietly; he could read her and he didn't even have her gifts. 'This one is the hardest. I have another gift that I haven't told you about. I can see deceased souls sometimes. They're always attached to a living soul and we call them Deykashee souls. I saw your mother.'

Avery continued to stare up at the ceiling. Eventually he stirred and cleared his throat.

'You see ghosts?'

'No, they're not ghosts,' Sophia said. 'They're souls, but yes I suppose ghost is the nearest accurate description we have.'

'Can you talk to these souls?'

'Sometimes,' Sophia said.

'Did my mother, did she speak to you?' Avery said.

Sophia nodded.

'She asked me to save you.'

'Is she here now?'

'I can't see her now. Each Deykashee has different energy levels, it usually depends on the bond between the deceased and living person. Generally the more Positive memories you recall about a deceased soul, the stronger they will be, but they don't last forever.'

'What do you mean?'

'Deykashee souls usually fade over time as their living counterpart recovers from the cycle of grief and moves on with their lives; they enter a temporary sort of slumber for the rest of the living person's natural lifespan and then both souls cross over together to the other side completely.'

'Why are you telling me this now?'

'I guess because you asked, and I want you to know the truth,' Sophia said. 'The whole truth. I need to for my own conscience.'

'Was my mother OK?'

'She seemed to be sad if anything, as you can imagine, but yes, otherwise OK.'

Avery tilted his chin up to the ceiling as his eyes glistened with unshed tears. They turned to the sound of the door opening and Mr Richmond walked in.

'Hey, how are you feeling?' Mr Richmond's skin was grey and dark circles hugged his eyes.

'I'm OK,' Avery said. He wiped his eyes and struggled to sit up again. Mr Richmond rushed to his side to help him. 'There you go, easy does it. Do you need anything? Some water?'

'No I'm fine, Dad, really.'

'I'll leave you two to it,' Sophia said, rising from her chair.

'Thank you, Sophia,' Mr Richmond said.

Sophia made her way to the door.

'Sophia,' Avery said. 'You will visit again, won't you?'

'Avery, she visits every day,' Mr Richmond said.

'Of course, I'll be back again tomorrow,' Sophia said. She opened the door and felt a warm tingling sensation caressing her skin. She paused and let her gaze be drawn to the source. A bright glowing pocket of Positive energy was beside Avery's bed, like a star. It transformed into the form of Mrs Richmond. Her body was more substantial and appeared more solid than it had ever been before, and her soul shone brightly at her core in deep red and blue hues of love and compassion. She smiled at her son and husband, and then turned her gaze to Sophia, mouthing the words *Thank you* before her bodily form flashed and disappeared for good.

'Are you OK, Sophia?' Mr Richmond asked.

Sophia blinked.

'Yes.' She smiled. 'Yes, I'm good. I'll see you later.' She shut the door behind her.

THIRTY-SIX

Ahrl stood beside them, silent and invisible as he watched them from the fountain. They stood beside a grave, apart from Avery who was seated in a wheelchair. Ahrl gazed down at Avery's legs, it was devastating that the boy would never walk again, but it was still better for him and his soul than being dead.

'It's so sad he's gone,' Avery said.

'He had many health complications, Avery, the doctors were amazed he had lasted this long,' Mr Richmond said. 'I'm glad I got to meet him before he died, in an indirect way, he saved your life, I can't thank him enough for that.'

'What will happen to all the money that was raised for him?' Sophia said.

'We hope it will be given to a homeless charity,' Mr Richmond said. Sophia nodded.

'Dad, may I have a word with Sophia?' Avery said.

'Sure, just call me if you need me.' Mr Richmond walked away and left Sophia and Avery alone beside the grave.

'I didn't even get to thank him properly,' Avery said. 'Do you think he'll be alright on the other side?'

'Yes, I'm sure of it,' Sophia said.

'Who could have known that a homeless man, with a tatty old futon, would save my life?' Avery laughed. 'Now that's an ironic twist of fate isn't it?'

'I guess it is. I'm glad we found his daughter. It would have been sad if there had been no relatives at his funeral.'

'Yes. She said she hadn't seen her father in over forty years; she thought he'd been dead all this time. It was sad, but she said she was happy that he had done something good.' They remained silent for a while, staring down at the grave that now named the old man as Steven Shepherd. A large bouquet of white roses had been set on the grave.

'What are you going to do now? You're not still planning to…' Sophia bit her lip and stared down at her feet.

'I don't know, it's a bit difficult to carry out a suicide in a wheelchair.' Avery grinned. 'I think I might try staying alive for a while, now that I can't use my legs anymore perhaps I'll start using my brain instead.'

Sophia smiled.

'I'm going to give Joe a call and sort things out with him. It wasn't fair for me to lash out at him the way that I did; I need to apologise.'

'I'm sure he'll forgive you,' Sophia said.

'I know. I know. There's one other thing, my mother? Is she still around?'

'She will always be around in some way or another, you've got to remember the good times and cherish your happy memories of her. She will be waiting for you and watching over you.'

'I guess I best not let her down then, besides, I can't hide anything from you, can I?' Sophia smiled and shook her head.

The fountain hummed with energy as images from the past, the present and the future flickered across the pool. Ahrl followed Avery and Sophia's pathways once more, the two spiralling around each other like a double helix. He saw Avery sitting behind a large desk in an office that looked more like the inside of a stately home than a workplace. He watched as Avery shuffled papers and sorted them into two piles. There was a knock at the door and a young man in a suit stepped in, holding more papers.

'Mr Richmond, I'm afraid there are more reports to go through, oh and there's a letter.'

'Thank you, Christopher,' Avery said. Christopher placed the letter and the reports on Avery's desk and left. Avery sighed and picked up the letter. The envelope was small and white with his name and address handwritten on the front. He opened it and pulled out a small piece of paper; he turned it over and raised his eyebrows. There was a picture, a drawing that he recognised of a metal, human-looking robot with a blue smiley face. Underneath, a certain someone had written, *I'm glad I met you. I guess you are important after all. Let's meet for dinner?'* There was a phone number written underneath followed by the initials S.L. He dropped the picture on his desk and hurried to pick up the first report, accidently sending the others sliding across his desk.

'Damn it,' he said as he moved to stack them up again. His gaze snagged on one of the reports as a name leapt out from its pristine white surface. He paused and lifted the report from his desk. *Dr Sophia Leto.* He scanned the report and understood the general gist of it within a few moments. They were proposing an experiment which might prove the existence of a secondary timeline; an experiment which could open up a new level of particle physics, and potentially give a definitive theory of everything. They were requesting parliamentary funding and international funding with the proposed experiment to take place at CERN. Avery's hands trembled and he felt a slow smile stretch across his lips.

'I'll be damned, Dr Leto.' He placed the report back on his desk, picked up the picture and then wheeled himself over to one of the long windows. He gazed out across the River Thames and watched the London Eye rotate slowly in the afternoon sunshine. He pulled a smartphone from his jacket pocket and responded quickly to a text from Joseph White, and then he entered in the number under the picture and hit the call button.

I guess that's one problem solved. Ahrl let the vision fade away and turned his attention to a closer point in the future and watched again as the outer edge of the pool lost all colour and turned dark with Negative energy. The garden gleamed in the sunlight from the corner of his eye and a fresh breeze stroked his angular features. The visions for the future remained the same, bleak at best. He felt his brow crease as he gripped the crenulated edges of the fountain. *There must be something else I can do. There has to be something, anything?*

He searched through all the probable and improbable scenarios and just as he reached one of the last possibilities, the edges of the fountain flashed with a brilliant golden burst of Positive energy. He focused on the image and saw a sickly Alice in a hospital bed, writing and sketching in a black, hard-backed notebook. The fountain zoomed in on this notebook and he caught a flash of delicate silver curves and lines adorning the front cover. The vision faded and vanished and the pool fell silent once more. Ahrl blinked and gazed out across the garden; its grassy hills stretched into the distance as far as the eye could see. Little purple and golden flowers appeared like stars twinkling on an emerald sky. It was a long shot, a rogue variable, and it was going to require a lot of time, patience, energy and hope, but hope was a powerful thing.

Ahrl gazed once again into the fountain and called forth the vision before letting his mind travel along its pathway. It was an anomaly, but sometimes, that's all that was needed.

* * *_* * *

PAGES FROM SOPHIA'S JOURNAL

23rd September 2011

If aliens were watching Earth now and they were 100 million light years away, they would be seeing our past. They would see the dinosaurs roaming the Earth, something which we humans could never observe. Their observation of us now is 100 million years in our past, yet to humans living on Earth right now, this obviously isn't the present state of Earth. It can take millions of years for light to travel across large distances, so the question is, what is now? In fact, what is instantaneous? If I run for 20 minutes at 10mph and burn off 200 calories, I could in theory burn off the same calories in 5 minutes if I could run at 40mph instead. If I wanted to burn off those calories in zero seconds I would have to reach a point of infinite speed.

Are infinity and zero really the opposite ends of a numerical spectrum, or are their properties the same? Perhaps there is some sort of numerical circle? The mathematics breaks down but in theory I could burn off those calories instantaneously, and if I did, allowing for the first law of thermal dynamics, where would all the energy go? Would it disappear into time itself? Did time absorb the energy? Is time, energy?

6th October 2011

If we say that everything in the universe is information, this would include all matter, people, and even thought. Where did all the information in the universe come from? Was it all there before the Big Bang? What will happen to it all when the universe ends?

10th October 2011

What is time?
What is now?
What would happen if a Photon could observe itself?

11th October 2011

There are theories which discuss the idea of multiverses. Alternative or parallel universes are all stacked up on top of each other like sheets of paper. There could be an infinite number of universes with different versions of 'us' all leading slightly different or vastly different lives. These multiverses hold all possibilities and everything that exists.

I wonder if this could be simplified? Some string theories dabble with the idea of a separate dimension of time but they don't quite fit properly. If we have one possibility which is a physical reality then all other possibilities are simply just possibilities.

14th November 2011

If the centre of the circle is the birth of a person and the outer edge of the circle is their death. Then a person's path through life would not be a straight line, it would look more like this. The rare and strange events will have the biggest impact on a person's life, such as winning the lottery or the death of a loved one. It is all like quantum tunnelling in the end.

3rd December 2011

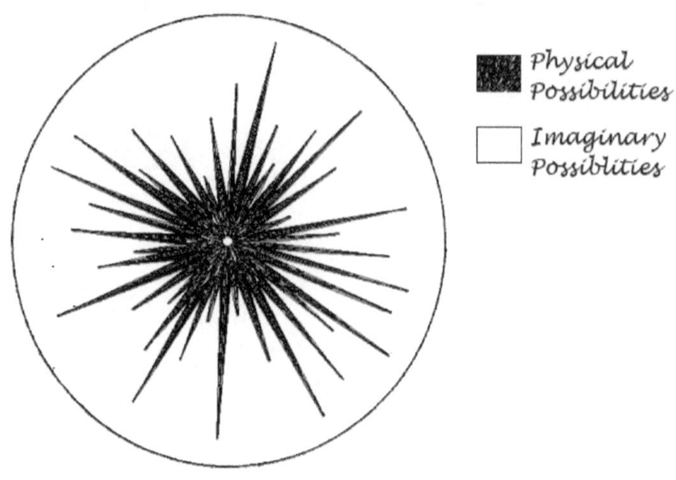

This circle is a slice through time and represents NOW. The shaded area displays all the thousands of physical possibilities open to a person in any given moment of time. The unshaded areas are all the imaginary possibilities, such as thought, that a person may have or decisions they didn't make, and they are infinite. Some possibilities are more remote than others so stretch further away from the centre dot. Others are more likely so are only a short distance from the centre dot. In its simplest form, if you were to imagine a person standing in a flat field, they could choose to walk in any direction and think any thought; all possibilities are open to them just before they make their decision, although historical, personal and outside factors will make certain possibilities more likely than others. If the universe is 'aware' of all possibilities, even the most remote ones, then it would also know the most likely possibilities too. The passing of time would turn a possibility into fact, but then if this is the case, time must interact with all the knowledge of the universe. Does the universe observe itself?

February 25th 2012

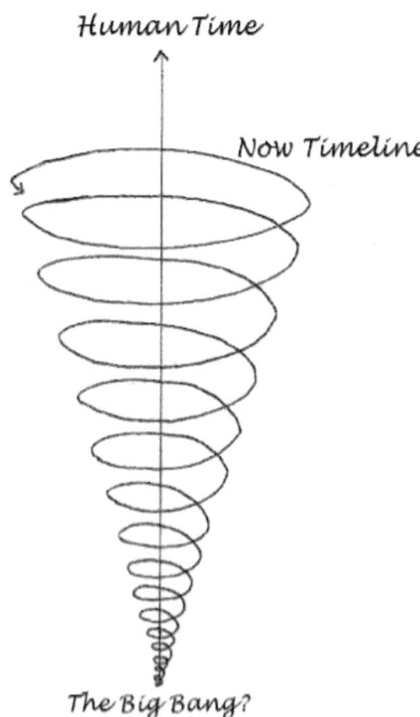

Kyle Hunter came up with the idea of two timelines. One is human time as we know it, past, present and future. The other is a secondary timeline which spirals around human time and contains every possibility and everything in the universe. We have decided to call this timeline the Now Timeline. If he is right, then all information, all energy must exist within the Now Timeline. Everything created and every possibility must be entangled somehow into the fabric of space itself. Time must hold or store energy; perhaps this could be dark energy? The real nature of time has to be independent of space time and relativity as we know it. The Now Timeline must have its own properties.

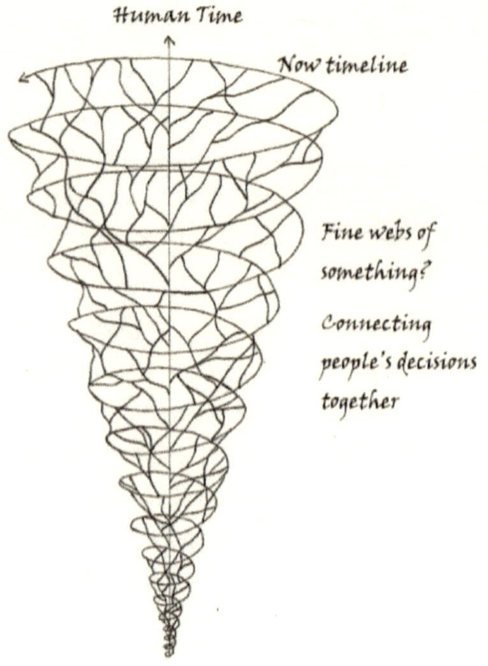

We would have to find a way of proving the existence of the Now Timeline by measuring something which interacts with it. This would most likely be a new type of particle. The only way to do this would be with something like the Large Hadron Collider.

18th March 2012

I spoke to Cameron today; he knows about the Now Timeline idea through Kyle. We talked about the maths and why it would probably break down. Cameron suggested that in order for the Now Timeline to work, there must be a field of some sort connecting the Now Timeline to human time. We wondered if this would be the same as the quantum field or if it would be a different field. Cameron suggested that virtual particles might hold part of the answer as they appear to pop in and out of existence. If a new particle were to be discovered and found to interact with the Now Timeline, then maybe it too would appear to pop in and out of existence. I think it might decay instantly and it could have other unusual properties. Perhaps if we were able to find more about the nature of virtual particles and understand why the Casimir Effect can exist, then maybe we would be able to start a hypothesis for the Now Timeline and any associated field.

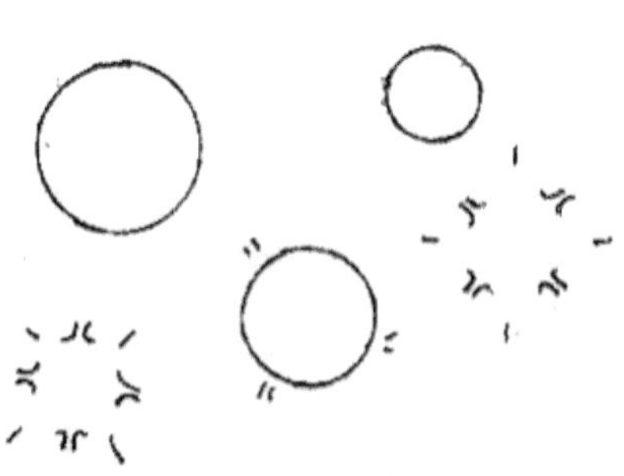

Virtual particles pop in and out of existence. The Casimir Effect is a small attractive force which acts in a vacuum between two, close, parallel, uncharged, conducting plates. A vacuum is not empty - it is full of fluctuating electromagnetic waves. Their presence creates the small attractive force and tells us that an apparently empty space contains energy.

Scientists can predict the movement and orbits of planets, and work out assessments for when objects in space might collide. What they can't do is predict the scattering of matter across the universe after the collision. The chaos is probably even more unpredictable on a scale beyond the quantum world; this would potentially explain the behaviour of virtual particles.

March 20th 2012

My dad called. I told him everything about the Now Timeline idea. He said that it is possible that the ATLAS experiment might detect an energy shift and that maybe the energy would not be lost to another universe, but actually lost to time. He said, 'If you could take a snapshot of a moment in time that is always now, does this mean that time is fluid? Space time is fluid but what about the Now Timeline? This moment in time that is always now, are all moments like a camera with an infinitely small frame rate? Your measurements would have to include Planck's constant.'

March 23rd 2012

Hey Sophia, Cameron here. This is a visual representation of the energy that would be scattered by the Now Timeline. If you take the pieces of a jigsaw and scatter them all over the country, then stop time and retrieve all of those pieces. If you restart time again after you have collected the pieces, then the energy you used to travel, eat, and breathe would technically be energy absorbed by time. If it is dark energy, we can't detect it, we can only see the effects of it in the expansion of the universe.

Are we visualising the universe wrong? Was Einstein right with the cosmological constant after all?

ANOMALY

PROLOGUE

Two years earlier…

Imagine if you could see glimpses of the past, present and future. Random, unconnected points in time, converging on your senses alongside your daily routine. Now imagine the thoughts of a stranger, perhaps that homeless man you pass on your way to work every morning or maybe the striking blonde who gets on your train. Imagine the thoughts of an elderly person, strolling along by the seaside as they enjoy their winter years. Or perhaps the thoughts of someone who has recently passed away…

Sophia had a busy mind, a very busy mind. Just like the rest of her family and the generations before. They had thoughts, emotions and memories, like any other person, but they also experienced thoughts, emotions and memories that were not their own. They saw visions; fragments of the past, present and the future. It felt divine, like a god hearing thousands of prayers or a radio tuned in to every station on Earth. Sophia Leto's mind was saturated with the thoughts, memories and emotions of other people, those alive, and those who were already dead.

Sophia and her family had these abilities. Gifts they could never speak about. Every Leto had been born with these gifts, and every Leto had learnt to recognise and control them. Some would consider them a curse, but the Letos had recognised the importance of these other voices, thoughts and memories long ago. There was no other family alive on Earth who understood the afterlife as well as the Letos did. Their gifts had led them into lines of research that only they could carry out and every member had played their part. Generations of Letos had kept meticulous notes, descriptions and drawings of everything significant they saw with their own eyes, and things they saw within their minds.

It was dangerous, yet it was necessary; the Letos had never been wrong. They had followed the strongest images, the most desperate voices and emotions; they had found the strangers who flashed in their minds like images in an old movie reel. They had helped these people whenever they could, poor and rich, young and old, male and female. The Letos had watched like guardian angels, guiding from the side-lines. They knew of the hidden energies and science which governed the minds of man, of life and of what lies beyond. They could see these energies working in the very air, swaying humanity like a pendulum. These energies were called Positive and Negative by the Letos, and by every deceased soul. There had always been a struggle between these forces, or between good and bad, but the truth was far beyond what had already been written.

The swinging pendulum was never easy to predict - you never knew how long Positive would reign, or Negative. So when Florence Leto cried out from the kitchen and the sound of shattering glass pierced the air, it should have been of little surprise to Sophia and the rest of her family that the pendulum had swayed again. The images that had shocked Flo crashed down on the rest of the family only seconds later; forcing their way through, consuming every other thought and painting pictures none of the Letos had ever wanted to see. Sophia's mother gasped, her aunt let out a small squeak, the colour drained from her brother's face and then the phone rang and silence descended upon the household. Sophia's father picked up the phone and slowly raised it to his ear. They all knew Sophia's uncle was at the other end, and they all knew what he was going to say.

'Hello?' Her father's voice cracked; he listened and his hand shook. Flo appeared under the archway between their dining room and lounge; her wrinkled face was ghastly pale and her lips were slightly parted as she reached out a hand to steady herself against the wall. They knew, even before Sophia's father had put down the phone. The two people they had been watching, the pair their ancestors had been waiting for all these years, had now become one. *Alice* was gone.

ONE

It was night in the garden and Ahrl stood by the fountain like a white marbled angel. He did not move, he did not breathe, and his sapphire blue eyes did not blink. A faint breeze whispered through his white robes and picked at the midnight strands of his long hair, and every few seconds the underside of his pointed jaw, nose, cheeks and brow would be awash with a warm glow. The fountain of memories wasn't much to look at; it was a simple, grey, crenulated column of stone, with a bronzed bowl holding a small pool of water, yet it contained all the clues to the mysterious future. It was the only guide The Thirteen had. He gazed into the fountain, but his soul felt heavy and weak. After all this time, after all their careful planning, after every life they had managed to save, it still wasn't enough.

Images painted themselves across the surface, sometimes highlighted by a Positive golden glow and at other times a Negative void-like darkness. The fountain showed every critical thought, emotion, decision and event taking place all over the Earth. Ahrl could see the past, the present, and every possible pathway for the future. The most likely scenarios flashed across the pool's surface frequently whereas the less likely appeared less often. Ahrl knew everything and felt everything; he could see individuals of the human species and he knew which ones would have important decisions and choices to make that would affect the planet's future. However, the future was constantly changing, humanity had freewill and they did not always make Positive decisions. There was also nature to add in to the chaos; for it was nature which had the power to ruin everything.

The images changed again. There were so many people, so many lives and decisions tangled together in great webs of energy; it was a specialist task to study the fountain. Yet Ahrl continued to search, for what else could he do? The answers had to be in here somewhere, there had to be something? They had made it so far, surely their existence couldn't rely on the life of one human soul? But he knew the answer, of course it could, they had only made it so far because of one particular soul. He and the rest of the Thirteen knew better than anyone how one life could save or destroy an entire future. They had seen the good effects of Positive decisions, lives saved, laws passed, freedom and equality for all. And they had seen the disastrous effects of Negative decisions; lives taken, wars started, futures reduced to despair. It was a continuous battle between the two forces, one that had been there from the very beginning and one that would continue and evolve to the very end, and it didn't care if they continued to exist or not.

Images of a burning world flashed across the fountain, it appeared to be a devastating battle, but it was actually an annihilation. A metallic face peered up at him and was quickly swept away, replaced by a man on a stage speaking to a crowd of people. This too, faded and different people, scientists in laboratories, were shown, all of them racing to one major discovery, but it wasn't the right mix of people. There were only certain individuals who could handle this discovery with the correct care and caution. Now there was a catastrophe just waiting to happen, he saw Sophia in some of these groups, but the others were absent.

The burning world appeared again for a moment but then the fountain fell silent. It did this every so often. The images would fade, the water would become still and the stars above would reflect upon its smooth surface. Ahrl blinked once as his mind digested everything he had learnt. He had seen it all before, seen the chaos which was coming but he still searched, he still hoped there would be another path. A tiny depression formed in the centre of the pool. The water dipped down sharply and then jumped back into place. A small drop broke away from the pool and flew a couple of inches up into the air, then fell back down again with a soft *plop*.

And so it began, like a rare raindrop heading for a cosmic ocean – an ocean swelling with uncertainty. A seemingly insignificant event charged into the chaos of the universe, creating a ripple in the dimensions of time. Its energy was small, but it would expand outwards, swinging life's pendulum into the Positive force. It had happened before and it would happen again. This single moment would change everything.

Ahrl's ancient consciousness prickled, jolting his seven senses. He felt the murmur of Positive energy as it danced across his illusive synapses. Each shock and tiny vibration, each pulse and movement, was amplified along the Positive scale. This was new and unexpected, yet desperately needed. The pool's surface rippled and shone brightly; he let his thoughts slow down with the patience of a well-practised Buddhist. Images formed and passed over the fountain, imparting their knowledge. *Her sister, a book.* Understanding dawned on him in the way only hindsight could, but this was potentially dangerous. There had been books before – words from the wise, fatally misconstrued. However, the smallest decisions were often the foundations for the biggest changes. He felt the tremors of clarity, shaking through the core of his soul. An anomaly was about to shake the Earth. He stepped back from the fountain and gazed upwards at the universe. He realised it would take all of his will and a lot of suggestion in order for certain events to align, but would they come to pass? And would it be enough?

TWO

The present day

'Next please,' Kyle shouted into the throngs of fresher students on the other side of the bar, their faces highlighted in a cold blue from the neon sign above them. He looked expectantly at a girl with a towering mass of blonde hair piled on top of her head. She leant forward and he mirrored her actions - it was the only way to hear her over the loud, blaring bass.

'I'd like a vodka and Coke, please,' she said, trying hard to pronounce her words correctly and then bursting into a fit of intoxicated giggles. Kyle nodded and turned around to the back wall, quickly scooping up a shot measure and a large plastic glass. 'Make that a double!' he heard her yell and reluctantly he poured another shot. He'd been working all week; freshers' week was the most popular week of the year for the first year students. For most of them, it was the first time they'd left home for any considerable period, and they liked to spread their new wings of freedom by bathing their throats, livers and stomachs in alcohol. He glanced towards the other end of the bar. His flatmate and team leader, Dani, was pummelling a cash register and shouting orders to a couple of newbies. They hadn't been given the staff uniform yet, an oversized black t-shirt with a red oak tree emblazoned on the front. He swiped his work identification card over the cash register and then swung back round, placing the drink on the bar.

'That will be three p…' The girl's face had changed, her blonde hair had fallen down and somehow morphed into soft, brown waves, and her eyes had changed to a deep, startling blue, it was a face he hadn't seen in what felt like forever, a face he thought he would never see again. His heart squeezed and he felt tears pricking his eyes. She couldn't be here, she couldn't be…

'What?' the girl said cupping her ear. Kyle blinked and the blonde girl's face snapped back into focus, her giant hair wobbled precariously. He shook his head, leant on the bar and took a deep breath. He pushed his thoughts and feelings aside, they would come back to haunt him, they always did. He straightened up and glanced at her drink.

'That will be three pounds eighty,' he yelled over the noise and then he turned his face to the side and coughed into the back of his hand; his throat was killing him already. The girl raised an eyebrow at him as she handed over the money. She disappeared with her drink, squeezing back out of the crowd. Kyle stepped back from the bar and pinched the bridge of his nose. How could he have ever mistaken her for someone else? They looking nothing alike.

'Kyle, are you alright?' Dani yelled. Her words cut right through his thoughts and he could see her poised at the other end of the bar, ready to leap over to him should he need the slightest assistance. Kyle smiled weakly at her and gave her a thumbs up. There was no time to soothe his mind or calm his frayed nerves. He stepped back up to the bar where the next student was staring expectantly at him, and the next, and the next.

He poured drink after drink and the thought of the end of his shift teased his stiff body; he could sleep in tomorrow, although he mustn't forget to read up on the module content for the new semester. He could almost imagine his father, Matthew, nodding in agreement. He had drilled into Kyle at an early age the importance of work and study. *'There's nothing wrong with a little extra work,'* he would say. *'Employers these days want more than just a first class degree, though you must aim for a first class degree.'* He lowered his gaze to the floor. His father encouraged him to climb a career ladder to a managerial position in a big, global company, any major company would do, so long as he reached the top and earned a fat pay check. It was what his father had been trying to do all his life, and the only way, he believed, to be successful in life.

Eventually, the drunken students drifted back to their accommodation blocks, their legs wobbling like new-born fawns. Dani hefted two black sacks; the tell-tale clinking sound of glass bottles told him where she was heading. He picked up the remaining two sacks and followed her towards a fire exit and down a flight of gridded metal stairs.

'God, what a night,' she said in her soft northern accent. 'My feet are killing me.'

'It was busy,' Kyle said.

'I don't think I've ever seen it that busy before,' Dani said. Kyle nodded in silence, their footsteps echoing heavily as they reached the bottom step. Six large plastic bins were positioned against the brick walls, enclosed in a tall wooden fence, right next to the now vacant beer garden. They emptied the sacks one by one into the nearest bin. Dani sat down at the bottom of the stairs and stretched out her long legs in front of her. 'I'm really sorry I kept you on, you must be tired.'

'It's OK,' he said, turning to face her. He didn't mind staying on and he didn't want Dani to walk back to their flat alone. As he moved, something glinted like a flame in the corner of his eye. He turned back to the bin. There, half hidden behind one of the bin's giant wheels, was a coin. The red lighting of the exit sign above them bounced off its metallic surface. He scooped it up, and ran the curve between his thumb and forefinger; it was a penny, with the date, 1991, stamped on the side.

'I still don't know why you collect discarded pennies,' Dani said, watching as he straightened up and slipped the penny into one of his pockets. 'Oh!' she interrupted herself, a devilish grin breaking onto her face. She fished out a piece of paper from the pocket of her jeans. 'I believe,' she said, offering him the paper, 'that this is the third phone number this week, Mr Hot Stuff.' She winked at him. Kyle groaned as he accepted the small scrap of torn paper.

'Please don't call me that,' he said as he unfolded the note. Whoever had written this had been more artistic than the others - they had dotted their number with little hearts. He sighed and crumpled the number into a ball before tossing it in the bin.

'Why don't you call any of them?' Dani asked, her eyes boring into him as he rocked uncomfortably on his heels. The doors in his mind had been shut long ago, but he still felt the whisperings of old memories pressing against them. He lifted his shoulders, and felt the muscles in his chest tighten. He couldn't explain to Dani the thoughts or feelings in his mind, hell, he didn't even want to feel them. Kyle grimaced as one of his mental doors opened and he forcefully pushed it shut again; his memories had ambushed him once tonight already. He looked upwards to clear his thoughts and regain his control; he thought about work and his upcoming modules and the studying he would have to do. He recited a handful of facts, and slowly he felt strength returning to his system. If he isolated the memories, if he separated the reality and detached the emotions, he could speak about *her* again, even if it was only for a few risky moments.

'I...'

'Don't,' Dani said sharply though not unkindly, holding out her hand. She gave him a weak smile. 'It's OK, I know that look; sorry, you don't have to speak about her if you don't want to. I get it.' Kyle nodded as he tried his best to hide his relief.

'Come on, let's get out of here,' she said.

He followed her back up to Blue Bar, her heavy boots clanging against the stairs. They finished tidying up just after four, and then brought down the shutters over the bar. They left the SU, and headed towards the library. Their flat was situated at the top of campus and their route took them up a slowly rising path, framed by the academic buildings. They passed in front of the chapel and over a public concourse then turned right up the hill. It was a steady incline; the bottom half was a wide path and the top half was a narrow tarmacked road. It was the most central point on campus, with easy access to all the buildings the students would ever need.

'God I hate this hill,' Dani said. 'It feels like it goes on forever.' She hunched her shoulders in her leather jacket. They fell silent but it wasn't the easy, calming silence Kyle was used to. He felt her eyes flickering to the side of his face as she chewed her bottom lip. Kyle slipped his hand into his pocket, he could feel the curve of the penny between his finger and thumb. His friends knew about his past, Cameron had made sure of that. Kyle wasn't sure whether he hated him or was grateful. They had been friends for years and Cameron knew all about *her*, he had attended the same secondary school after all, but there were some secrets which Kyle preferred to keep private.

'I think there's someone in those bushes,' Dani said, drawing him out of his thoughts. He had heard the confusion in her tone and his dark eyes followed her line of sight.

'You're right,' Kyle said. He broke out into a fast jog, crossing onto the tarmacked half of the slope, angling towards the physics building. A pair of canvas shoes could be seen sticking out of one of the bushes.

'Oh my god, it's Cameron!' Dani said in alarm, her footsteps echoing behind him. Kyle frowned. Cameron's arms were badly scratched, his glasses at an angle, and twigs decorated his caramel hair.

'Hey guys,' Cameron said, his words slurring. 'What you doing?'

'What are *we* doing?' Dani scowled crossly. 'What the heck are you doing, more like? Jesus, Cameron.'

'Yes,' he said, as he tried to put a finger to his lips, missing and touching his chin instead. He tried to pull a thoughtful expression which would have been comical at any other time. 'Yes, I am the son of God,' he slurred.

'Right, get up,' she said. 'Kyle, help.' She moved to the left side of Cameron's body and put an arm around his back.

'Man, you're not even a fresher,' Kyle said, going to his right side and supporting most of his weight as they hoisted him out of the bushes. Cameron's grey beanie fell off in the process and Kyle scooped it up, stuffing it into his back pocket.

'Re-fresher's!' Cameron said loudly. 'Woo!' He jumped on the spot for a few seconds.

'You're such a child,' Dani said crossly.

'No, no, Dani! Children can't drink.' He turned sharply to Kyle. 'Kyle? Do you remember when me, you and Alice…' His left leg gave way and he stumbled heavily into Dani. Kyle gripped him tightly, pulling him upright again despite the spasm of pain in his chest. *Alice, Alice, Alice,* her name reverberated cruelly through Kyle's skull.

'Whoa, take it easy; just concentrate on your feet, OK?' Kyle said, batting away his thoughts and letting out a little huff as he adjusted Cameron's weight once more. Cameron dutifully looked down at his feet, and his face broke into a tired, alcohol-induced grin.

'Kyle,' he said with difficulty, 'we don't have any feet.'

THREE

She didn't know why she was here, she just knew that it was important for her to be here, and quite frankly she didn't have much to lose. A red oak tree had flashed through her mind when she had browsed through the university booklets, and then it had invaded her dreams whilst she had slept, so she had applied to do her Master's Degree at Red Oak University. It was logical to her, that's what her visions had shown so that was what she was going to do. Great Uncle George hadn't been too happy about it, but the family couldn't argue with her or her visions, they had grown complacent once before and it hadn't ended well. Normal people would rightfully advise you to take no stock in feelings or dreams, but Sophia and her family were different. They had been watching the future with growing concern for a while now. Their visions of the future had been a mess ever since Alice's death, and they felt that nothing was certain anymore, it was almost like being as naïve and as blind as any regular human, something which unsettled them all deeply. New people and new futures had appeared to them, but these new pathways were flimsy and fragile. There was no way to know if the future would be Positive or Negative, but the latter had shown itself to them more frequently, and that was never a good sign.

Sophia hurried up to the physics building, smoothing her wavy dark hair as she crossed into the reception. *This should be a piece of cake*, she thought. She had rehearsed her presentation hundreds of times and the audience would only be a couple of professors, some elderly people and a handful of physics students. She went up a flight of stairs and hurried down a corridor; she could hear the idle chatter of a dozen voices coming from the lecture theatre, so she straightened her shoulders and pulled a friendly smile.

Professor Green's face lit up with relief as she entered and a hushed silence fell over the room. She put down her bag and shrugged out of her coat.

'I'm sorry I'm late, though I hope you've had plenty of time to enjoy the tea and coffee,' she said with a grin; that drew a couple of chuckles from her audience. *Good,* she thought. At twenty-two she was young in the physics world and that often drew confusion from the older professors, however her reputation and papers exceeded her years and she was considered something of a child genius. She fished out a memory stick from her trouser pocket and stuck it into the computer. Her files were all there. She brought up her presentation on the overhead projector and her opening slide appeared on the screen above and behind her. *Virtual Particles and Time* appeared at the centre of the blue screen. She smiled and clasped her hands together as she turned to face her audience.

'Ladies and gentlemen, professors and students,' she said in a loud clear voice, her dark eyes scanning the faces.

'I'm here to…' her eyes locked onto a young man sitting at the back. *It was him, he was here!* Her thoughts stopped and her mouth became dry as her eyes flickered to the person seated on his right, a *Deykashee* soul, the brightest soul Sophia had ever seen. *They… are here.* She blinked and caught other members of her audience turning their heads and muttering under their breaths. They were *all* here, but not in the way the Letos had once hoped. *The red oak tree* she thought as giddiness threatened to overtake her senses, her intuition had been right! Kyle shifted uncomfortably under her gaze and she recognised Cameron Goodchild on his left; she had met Cameron, along with his peers, only a few days ago, but never realised Kyle was here. Cameron leant towards Kyle and muttered something into his ear. The Deykashee soul stared at Sophia with her vivid blue eyes and Professor Green looked stricken. Sophia coughed.

'Sorry,' she croaked bringing the audience's attention back to her. She sipped some water. 'I've just got a tickle in my throat.' She muffled a cough for show and then smiled pleasantly, her audience relaxed and she did her best not to stare at Kyle and his Deykashee soul.

'What are virtual particles?' she began, launching effortlessly into her presentation. She could see Professor Green smiling now and she quickly moved on. 'And what is time for that matter?' She sighed dramatically. 'How do we even explain time? It always seems so slow when anyone else does a presentation doesn't it?' A ripple of laughter made its way through the front rows. *Good, I'm winning them back.* 'How can you observe something that is constantly popping in and out of existence?' she asked. She clicked a button on a small handheld device and her second slide appeared. She stole a glance towards the Deykashee soul and supressed a frown. *She shouldn't be here, not like this.* A tingling sensation spread through her body, her stomach fluttered, and she could feel the Positive energy charging through the air. *Oh Alice,* she thought as she glanced at the Deykashee soul, *why would you come back?* Her chest tightened and she resisted the urge to shake her head. *But of course you would,* she thought, *of course you would.*

FOUR

She waited for that moment, that first moment, just as he opened his eyes. The first blink before realisation hit and the truth consumed him. Every morning was the same, it was the one moment she could always count on, when she would see a fleeting shadow of the old Kyle. It gave her the smallest measure of hope, but it was still hope. His body moved restlessly, as his mind swayed over the lines between fiction and reality. Alice stepped closer to his bed, whilst his eyelids fluttered tauntingly. He opened them slowly, and as the sleep haze lifted, golden amber speckles seemed to ignite, like stardust floating around the edges of his chocolate eyes. It lasted mere seconds, then those speckles died out, their light vanishing. It came from remembering his loss, a death that had corrupted his eyes, and turned them dark. *Her* death.

Alice stepped back as he came to. He had been dreaming again and, with every dream, whether it was good or bad, his expression was always pained. He stumbled out of bed and took three long strides to the mirror above his wash basin. He patted down the odd tufts of bed hair and adopted his mild stoic look, a mask that would help him to make it through the day. He dressed quickly into simple sweats and worn trainers, before picking up his keys and mobile. He selected a playlist and plugged in a pair of black earphones, securing his belongings in a zipped pocket.

He jogged out of the block and into crisp morning air, like he did nearly every morning. Alice followed. She had no choice, she was a Deykashee soul, and her soul was bound to his. It wasn't a common occurrence; she had been vehemently stubborn. Her death had stolen everything from her and she had refused to fully move on. The few hours after she had passed away had felt like years; it had been a shock to say the least. Alice had always been scientific and analytical, she had never believed in anything beyond death. She had presumed people just ceased to exist – she had been very wrong. The afterlife was complicated; there were forces and energies that the living weren't even aware of. There were rules, universal rules that couldn't be ignored or changed, rules that separated out the souls and determined their states within eternity – and not all of those states were good.

Alice focussed on Kyle, keeping pace with him easily as they ran along the edges of the sports fields. It was one of the perks of being deceased, no bodily limitations. She had been watching him for just over two years and his routine since starting university had barely changed. They looped around the sports fields and then down through the centre of campus, where the old buildings loomed with windows like vacant eyes, no sign of movement from the living. Kyle increased the pace, unaware of her presence as they passed the library and rounded a corner. He took a narrow road through the trees and up to the old, red-bricked, manor house, which was hidden from view, but was still part of the university. Kyle ran past the old manor and alongside the first of nine lakes dotted between large patches of woodland. She fell behind him as he darted off into the trees.

Alice heard the steady beat of his trainers hitting the path, his laboured breathing and the muffled rhythm of his music. Her vision was better than it had ever been when she had been alive; she saw colours with perfect clarity and her senses were sharper too. Death had literally opened her eyes; she could see things that the living wouldn't see and she could feel things that the living wouldn't feel. Death had allowed her to see the souls of the living and the dead.

She gazed at Kyle's back, his soul appeared at the centre of his body as a ghostly ball, definitely there, but not physical. It was about the size of a grapefruit and the colours contained within were far from typical for a young man. She could see layers of colours, like the layers of the earth, moving around in patterns. Some of the layers were moving faster than others, but all were shrouded by a layer of grey. It was dense and thick, choking the other colours as it suffocated his emotions. A wave of sadness and compassion washed over her. She had hoped that time would help heal the wounds she had left behind, but there hadn't been enough time, and she wasn't sure there would ever be enough time. She wished he had taken more time off from his studies, to try and rediscover his passions, a reason to live, or at least to try and figure out what he wanted to do with the rest of his life. Her death was reflected in his soul as though it was a testament to her short-lived life; his soul was more of a tombstone than her actual grave.

Alice felt a sudden heat accompanied by a fluttering sensation, and then an image forced its way behind her eyes. She saw Kyle running ahead of her, just as he was now. A root from a large tree protruded out of the path like a curved handlebar. He caught his left foot on it and his ankle twisted sharply; she heard him cry out in pain as he stumbled forward and hit the ground, grazing his palms. Alice let out an involuntary gasp, and the image faded as quickly as it had arrived. She felt her energy levels falter, and watched as her arms began to fade in and out. Deykashee souls didn't need to sleep but they did need to rest sometimes; they were very much like rechargeable batteries. If they used too much energy it would weaken them, and if they pushed it too far they would fade out completely. She calmed her thoughts and focussed on her arms, willing back their solidity, and then she searched the path ahead. Her mind had jumped the timelines again, showing her a vision of a possible future scenario. Ahrl had told her that all Deykashee souls could see things that humans couldn't see, a soul wasn't bound to one timeline like the living were. It was a defence mechanism all

Deykashee souls had due to their bond with their living counterpart. If the person they were attached to was in danger, then the minds of the Deykashee souls would sometimes jump forwards and reveal certain scenarios. Ahrl believed it was linked back to the Thirteen's old world, and to the fountain, the result of an ancient mind who had seen too much.

Alice spotted the root up ahead, and focussed on an ability that the deceased used all the time. She could place suggestions into the minds of the living. It wasn't an accurate ability as she couldn't override freewill, but it did help provide choices to the unsuspecting living, good choices. It didn't work all the time, but her chances were better when her target was more relaxed, and right now Kyle was both distracted and relaxed. Her eyes narrowed in on Kyle's soul, and she felt what could only be described as a bolt of electricity, shooting across their invisible bond. She pushed away her fears and concerns as she repeated a silent mantra in her mind - *Move to the right Kyle, just a little to the right.* She repeated this over and over, as she followed him in a sort of meditative trance. She felt her energy drain, and was just about to pull back, when he moved a few inches to the right. She smiled, and retracted her mind as she came up beside him. He noticed the root as they passed it, a quick flash of relief crossing his features, and a shake of his head as he berated himself for not noticing it earlier. Suggestions were useful sometimes, but Deykashee souls had to think carefully before they tried to place one. Sometimes it was better to conserve energy.

He stopped suddenly, breathing hard, sweat spreading in dark patches through his clothing. Alice stopped beside him and focussed on her fading body; she appeared more ghostly now and she didn't like it. She watched him as he put his hands on his hips, taking deep, steadying breaths. He had a lean, strong frame, and broad shoulders, his muscles were defined, but not overbearing. His skin was clear, with a healthy light tan, and his dark brown hair fell in jagged layers against his forehead. He closed his eyes and inhaled deeply; his thoughts were miles away, and a hint of a smile graced his lips. She stared, mesmerised for a short while. She wondered desperately what his thoughts were about, and envied them for making him smile. He opened his eyes again and carried on.

Finally, once he had looped round most of the campus, he headed back to his block. He shrugged out of his outer layer and dried his face with it as he opened the front door. Two more doors stood to the left and right, and a central staircase led up to the upper floors. Grey, coarse carpet scratched under his trainers as he turned left and entered a narrow hallway, just as Stuart stumbled out of his bedroom. The hallway had three doors on either side. One was a bathroom and another was their communal kitchen, the four remaining doors were the bedrooms. Stuart groggily ran a pale hand through deep burgundy hair; he was small and slim, with blue eyes and a black lip ring.

'Morning,' Kyle said. Stuart grunted in reply, trudging off down to the bathroom as though he had just come out of hibernation. Cameron appeared from the kitchen then, his hair poking out from underneath his grey beanie. He smiled as Stuart went past and rubbed his knuckles into the top of his head.

'You alright, Stuart?'

'Yeah,' Stuart mumbled knocking Cameron's hand away, and then he disappeared from view.

'I don't even know how he manages to get up sometimes,' Cameron said. His gaze turned to Kyle and a cheesy grin erupted over his features, the same grin he had worn when Sophia Leto had finished her presentation last night.

'Knock it off,' Kyle said, shaking his head.

'She was so staring at you,' Cameron pointed out for the hundredth time and Alice had to agree. Sophia had stared at Kyle, but she had appeared to have been staring at Alice too. That wasn't supposed to happen; the living weren't supposed to see the dead. It was unsettling.

'No she wasn't, she had a cough that's all.' Kyle tried to convince himself, but his soul spoke otherwise, *he knew.* He pushed past Cameron and opened his door.

'Sure and that's the oldest trick in the book,' Cameron called as Kyle disappeared into his bedroom. He gathered a towel and a wash bag from his room, and slowly made his way down the hallway to the bathroom. Alice remained behind, collecting her energy, and staring at the familiar four walls of Kyle's temporary bedroom.

Every wall had been painted an off-white colour and remained bare; there were no photos or posters. There was nothing in Kyle's bedroom that hinted at his personality or interests, and there was certainly very little that would remind him of her. She knew he had done it on purpose; it had been a cleansing mission for him, a way to avoid painful memories. In fact, there was only one object in Kyle's bedroom that Alice could associate with herself. A clear jam jar, containing a few dozen or so pennies, sat neatly in the corner of his windowsill. It had been her childhood collection, and she had watched as Kyle had added to it, slowly, over the last couple of years. She realised it was the one thing that he could do to ease his conscience and honour her life, without having to remember too much. It brought on a strange mix of contradictory emotions for her, but overall, she was happy, perhaps selfishly happy, that he had kept at least one small part of her past with him.

A short while later Kyle returned, hair wet and a towel around his waist. He pulled out some clothes and Alice looked away as he dressed. He shaved, sorted his hair, and then ate some breakfast, before collecting his things for that morning's lecture. Kyle left the block alone and headed straight for the centre of campus. He passed the physics building and the bush he had pulled Cameron out of a couple of days ago, and he made his way down the slope to the business building. Alice braced herself for what was sure to be another long and boring hour. She hadn't lived long enough to study at university but she was certain that she would prefer sitting in Cameron's physics lectures, and she was almost certain Kyle would prefer it too.

Kyle was as diligent as ever at carrying out his dad's wishes, but Alice saw more in Kyle than he would have ever liked to believe. There was a reason he was drawn to physics, and why he attended the evening guest presentations in the physics building. Alice saw the way Kyle listened and how his eyes sparkled as though they contained the stars in the universe. She saw the creative and imaginative hues colouring the outer layers of his soul in aqua and lilac. She saw the interest in his gaze, his mind working silently behind his eyes, and the notes he kept in the subject he had given up on. Then she saw the way he worked for his business degree; the spark wasn't there. He took everything in, did all the work and carried out his revision, but it wasn't the same, there was no passion. He wasn't the Kyle she had once known; in these lectures, he was a lifeless zombie.

She took a seat next to him, hoping that no one would try to sit through her today. She was aware of the girls whose eyes followed Kyle subtly and she could see their pink souls. She tried to keep calm; she wasn't around anymore and she couldn't expect Kyle to remain single for the rest of his days, but even so, the pink souls annoyed her. She scanned the room lazily; the souls were all typical of their age and only a couple of Negative souls had shown up today. Their souls were almost entirely black, and Negative energy hung in dark clouds around their bodies, invisible to the living world, but completely visible and dangerous to Alice.

She leant back in her chair as a female professor entered and began busying herself behind the large desk at the front of the room. Alice could feel Positive energy tingling through her imagined body. There had been a disturbance recently, throwing a static type of energy up into the air, very much like the feeling before a thunder storm. Alice had felt it, and she was certain all of the deceased had felt it too. It made her wonder what Ahrl and the

Thirteen were up to.

The lecture began and Alice tuned out, her thoughts kept returning to Sophia Leto. A sudden feeling of déjà-vu had hit Alice when Sophia had looked at her last night and Alice couldn't shake off the nagging feeling that Sophia had truly seen her. The young woman seemed way ahead of her years, her knowledge was overwhelming and her soul blindingly Positive, brighter than any soul Alice had ever seen. It almost hid the rest of her colours, but not quite - there was grey within Sophia's soul, though it was faint. She also displayed dark blue for compassion and deep red for love and the tell-tale hues for imagination and creativity. Sophia's soul was almost a perfect example of everything that was good and positive in this world, yet... there was something unusual about her.

Alice frowned. She felt like she should know Sophia, as though they should have been friends, but she couldn't explain why. If her déjà-vu feelings had any grounding at all, why hadn't Ahrl mentioned anything? As a Deykashee soul she wasn't allowed to see the fountain directly, but Ahrl had shown her important memories before, and sometimes Alice saw things when they involved Kyle. Ahrl could pull Alice across the divide for a discussion, albeit temporarily, at any time. Surely someone with a Positive soul like Sophia's would be important? She didn't know and that troubled her. A disturbance and a very Positive soul, here, with Kyle, at Red Oak? That couldn't be a coincidence? Could it?

FIVE

Hailey Hunter was nose deep into her book. She was sat on a bench at the local park, Fairhaven, the skate park to her left, a large grassy field to her right and a big man-made lake in front of her. She had a rating system for every book she read. If it could distract her from Tank for a few minutes it was a good book. If it could distract her from Tank for more than ten minutes, it was an extremely good book. If it failed to divert her attention from Tank for less than a minute, then it was a bad book. Her current book fell into the extremely good category; so much so, she barely noticed when Tank approached her.

Tank was two years her senior; his real name was Robert Smith but everyone called him Tank. It had nothing to do with his strength or size, Tank was slim and lean, but it had been the nickname his mother had given him, purely because he had loved Thomas the Tank Engine as a kid, not that his friends knew. His shadow fell across her book and Hailey glanced up at him, supressing the blush that fought its way into her cheeks.

'So what are you reading today then?' He flashed pearly white teeth at her as he sat down next to her. She glanced around and noticed that the kids he had been coaching were all leaving the park; football practice was over.

'The Invisible Crown.' She closed the book and showed him the cover. It was a fantasy book about a young girl with an evil stepfather, set in medieval times where lords governed the land. The young girl had run away, and was winning the hearts of the common people.

'Bad? Good? Or extremely good?' Tank grinned; he knew about her ratings, but not how she did it. Hailey blushed.

'Extremely good.'

'You read more books than anyone I know,' Tank said. 'I swear you have a different book every day.'

'Sometimes.' Hailey shrugged. She wanted to be a writer and the best way she could learn to write was by reading other authors' books and to practise. Tank smiled and massaged his right shin.

'How's your leg?' Hailey asked anxiously. Tank had broken his leg a couple of years ago and it sometimes ached when he practised for too long. In the earlier days she had watched him hobble around on crutches and, when he had taken up coaching, he had sometimes grimaced in pain.

'It's OK, just a little stiff,' Tank said. She felt her heart fluttering in her chest as he caught her gaze. 'How's Kyle?' he asked and Hailey's heart stopped. She didn't talk about her brother often; they hardly spoke so there wasn't much to say.

'He's...' she searched desperately for the right words. *Emotionless? Stubborn? Depressed?* 'He's not coming back for his twenty-first birthday.' She sighed, suddenly remembering the tense conversation that had taken place between Kyle and their mother Stacy, during a phone call earlier that week.

'Oh?' Tank didn't seem too surprised. 'Still hates coming back then?' He stretched out his long limbs, the muscles in his legs shifting under his dark skin. Their mother had tried her best to contain her disappointment whilst she had been on the phone, but as soon as Kyle had hung up she had been tearful.

'More than ever,' Hailey replied bleakly, remembering their mother's crushed features. Tank's dark eyes softened and he leaned towards her, causing Hailey's heartrate to skyrocket.

'It will get better with time, Hailey.' She felt her shoulders and heart melt; she loved the way his father's Caribbean accent had worked its way into Tank's and how it caught on her name.

'I hope you're right,' she said glancing away from him. Tank had lost his mother and he had lost his dreams too with his accident, but he hadn't just given up on everything like Kyle had. Alice's death had destroyed the old Kyle and Hailey didn't think he would ever come back.

'It will,' Tank said.

'I know. I just wonder how long it will take.'

'All people are different; it might take months or it could take several years.'

'I hope it won't be much longer.' She stared down at her feet. There had once been a time when the rattle of skateboard wheels and laughter would have filled the air, when Kyle and his friends had still been around, when Alice had been alive, but those days seemed long gone now and those memories had lost their warmth.

'Why don't you suggest that he comes back for Bonfire Night?' Tank said. 'We all used to go as a group every year. If he's not coming back for his birthday he could at least come back for Bonfire Night.'

'I don't know…' Hailey began as she worried her bottom lip.

'You can only try,' Tank said and he nudged her playfully with his shoulder. 'Come on, be that demanding little teenage girl I remember.' She felt her cheeks grow hot and Tank laughed at her. 'Call him,' he said, and stood up.

'OK.' Tank nodded and strode off to collect his cones and footballs.

SIX

Kyle waved as he spied Cameron speaking directly into a suspended microphone, huge, neon green headphones clamped over his ears. Two large computers and a mixing deck were in front of him, along with pages of scribbled down notes. Cameron raised a finger and pushed a number of buttons and sliders, before removing his headphones and opening the door to let Kyle in.

'Hey, how's it going? Want some headphones?' he asked, dashing back to his chair.

'Na, I'll leave the geek channel to you I think,' Kyle replied, taking one of the three vacant chairs.

'You're just jealous.' Cameron placed his bright headphones around his neck. 'The whole nerd community is huge. You're missing out.'

'Yeah, I'm sure.' Kyle smiled and looked around the small office room situated at the back of the Students' Union on the second floor. There was a large window and one of the pale yellow walls was covered in photos of previous student presenters. 'Busy today?' Kyle asked, glancing at the computer screens.

'A few people have been talking, fairly quiet though.' Cameron shrugged. 'Everyone is busy sleeping or they're actually doing work. What have you been up to?'

'Revising.'

'Good God, you're not revising for exams already are you?'

'Yes, so should you,' Kyle said, knowing full well that Cameron had a brilliant memory. He had always aced every exam with the minimum amount of revision, even at school.

'Yes, but I'm in my third and final year, you're only a second year.'

'Second year is harder than first year,' Kyle said. Cameron grinned and placed his headphones back over his ears. He flicked a switch and then spoke directly into his microphone.

'That was Chasing Demons by Imagination. For all of those who have just tuned in, we have a discussion about virtual particles on our web page. For all those who are interested we also have another vlog debate from the usual culprits. If you want to find out more, visit our website at www, dot, n show, slash, red oak, dot, ac, dot, uk, or you can search us up on social media, or text in to six five three, five eight nine. Don't go anywhere; we have a new band coming up, Pretty Girls' Whispers.' Cameron flicked a number of buttons again to play the various jingles and looped them on to adverts before muting the mic and placing his headphones back around his neck. 'How were Dani and Stuart when you left? Still arguing?' Kyle grimaced; he had seen them briefly at lunchtime and they were arguing about Halloween decorations. Dani wanted to go all out and Stuart was complaining that it would be a fire hazard.

'I think she just likes winding him up to be honest. I mean, Halloween's still weeks away,' Kyle replied.

'I guess you guys will be working?' Cameron said, rooting in a rucksack on the floor and taking out a flask and a couple of paper cups.

'Yeah, it's going to be a busy night,' Kyle replied dismally; he hated his job but it was even worse when the university hosted major events.

'I don't know why you do it; you're not really a socialite,' Cameron said, pouring himself and Kyle a cup of coffee.

'Money, CV, the usual reasons why people get jobs.'

'Yeah, but you hate it.'

'Doesn't everyone?' Kyle asked; the coffee was barely warm

so he gulped it down quickly. Cameron raised a finger again and placed his headphones back on, hitting buttons and sliders before speaking into his mic.

'Welcome back to the N Show. If you've just tuned in, that's too bad, we only have about six minutes left, but don't worry, we're here every week, on Thursday afternoons, one till two. We have a couple of awesome last minute songs lined up so without further ado, this is Pretty Girls' Whispers.' Cameron flicked off the mic and fiddled around before turning to face Kyle again. 'Maybe you should try doing something you enjoy.'

'No one does what they enjoy.'

'That's not true.'

'OK, only if you're stupidly rich or famous, the rest of the world has to do whatever they can to get by.'

'You're very cynical, you know that, right?'

'I call myself realistic.'

'What are you going to do when you get your degree?' Cameron asked.

'Get a job somewhere, work my way up the career ladder. The usual.' Kyle shrugged. Cameron's stare made him uneasy.

'That seems so odd coming from you. I remember when you wanted to be a physicist. God, Alice would be...' Kyle gave him a cold stare. 'Come on man, don't be like that, you know what I'm saying.'

'Where did you get these cups from, by the way?' Kyle asked, motioning to the design adorning the side of the paper cup. It was a quirky advertisement for the Halloween event at the SU, a black print on a rustic orange background. Cameron sighed but let their conversation go.

'I got them from downstairs; the staff let me have them.'

'Oh, I've not seen them...'

'It's something Dani designed apparently; she wanted to make sure we had extra advertising this year.' Cameron shrugged. 'She's even got me playing advertisements alongside my jingles.'

'Oh, she's gone all out this year as team leader then.' Kyle was pleased that Dani loved her job and took it so seriously, but the extra advertisement would probably make their night harder.

'Dani was pining for the position last year; I'm not surprised she got it this year.'

Cameron placed his headphones back on again, one of the few things he hadn't unplugged, and then flicked another couple of switches. 'What's up, listeners, that was Pretty Girls' Whispers and I See Lions.' Cameron smirked, his eyes darting to Kyle. 'Here's one last song for you, Vortex by Dead Souls. I'll be back tomorrow, same time.' Kyle cast him an irritated glare and Cameron ignored him as he whizzed about on his chair, flicking off switches, shutting down his laptop and logging out the main computer. Kyle could hear the song, muffled but still audible through Cameron's headphones. The first verse was just starting with, '*Look for possibilities, you're the vortex surrounding me. Burning pathways in my mind, we must have travelled a thousand times. And when the storm is crashing down, you're the lightning I'm the sound. You have to open up the doors, to see something more…*' Kyle grimaced and Cameron unplugged his headphones, and packed away the rest of his belongings into a rucksack.

'Why did you have to play that song?' Kyle asked, more than a little annoyed.

'But it's your favourite song,' Cameron said.

'I hate that song.'

'Well, that's a lie, you never used to hate it,' Cameron said as he walked out the door with Kyle close behind him. He handed over the room to a confident-looking girl with wild brown hair.

'Don't be an arse, you know why I hate that song.'

'No, you hate what has happened with your life and associate it with the song, you don't hate the song. No one can hate the Dead Souls.'

'I happen to hate the name of the band too.' He scowled at Cameron but he couldn't stay mad at him for long, the lanky idiot meant well. Cameron always felt the need to bring up the past; he believed they should remember the happier times, but every time Kyle remembered, he felt as though more of himself was slipping away, carried off by some invisible ocean tide.

* * *

A few hours later, after another business lecture, Kyle returned to his block with a couple of library books weighing down his bag. His stomach growled as he dumped his things in his room and he ventured into the kitchen. He opened the fridge just as his mobile began to ring loudly in his pocket. He groaned and slid his mobile out and shut the fridge door again. His sister's face flashed up on the screen.

'Hey, Hailey.'

'Hey, Kyle, how are you?' She seemed happy and bubbly, suspiciously so.

'I'm fine,' Kyle replied warily. 'You?'

'Good, good. I'm good.' *Too many goods* Kyle thought. He heard the door swoosh open behind him and he turned to see Cameron.

'What are you up to?'

'Ah, just reading,' Hailey replied. *Of course.* His sister was always reading, she had often swapped books with… he shut the thought out of his mind. 'I was wondering if you were coming back for Bonfire Night?' Hailey asked quickly. 'You know, the one they do with the firework display, in the field next to the old cathedral.'

Gold, red and green fireworks flashed through his mind; he remembered the cold air and the warmth of the fire. The idle chatter and laughter, the odd squeal from an excitable child, and *her* face, *her* smile… he pinched the bridge of his nose and squeezed his eyes shut as he cut the memory from his mind.

'I think that's a week day, Hailey.'

'No it's not, it's a Saturday,' she said. 'Kyle, you have to come back for either your birthday or Bonfire Night, I'm not letting you duck out of both of them. Besides, Mum will be really happy to see you.'

'I'm coming back for Christmas and New Year. Isn't that enough?'

'No, choose one.'

'I'll think about it.' He sighed, he felt tired all of a sudden; her persistence was exhausting and he was all too aware of Cameron lingering.

'You have to choose one.'

'OK, OK,' Kyle said as he tried to stave her off.

'Great. I'll let Mum know you're coming back,' Hailey said, backing Kyle firmly into a corner.

'Fine. Bonfire Night.'

'Good,' she said happily. 'Speak to you later, bro.' She hung up. Kyle glared at his mobile as he pocketed it.

'Man, you really don't like going back home, do you?' Cameron said.

'It's…' Kyle searched for the right term, 'hassle.'

'Sure, I mean, I know parents and siblings are annoying, but I think going to the bonfire event is a great idea.' *Oh Christ, not you too* Kyle thought. 'We should both go. I know a bunch of our old school friends will be there. It'll be like old times.' *No it won't be, it will never be like old times*, Kyle thought.

'I don't know… I haven't really spoken to anyone in a long while.' He couldn't even remember the last time he had hung out with any of his old school friends apart from Cameron.

'The more reason you should go. They were our friends, they still are, and they understand, they won't hold your absence against you.' Kyle didn't reply. Cameron stared at him.

'Fine, I'll go.'

SEVEN

Kyle had spent nearly every available hour in front of his laptop for days now; he had an assignment and an essay to write, which involved searching through papers and books. Alice was glad Kyle was going back to Elbridge. Though she knew he hated it there, it would be nice to see her old home again. Despite the repetitive nature of Kyle's days, the forces had been restless and so Alice was restless too. She propped herself up on her elbow and pondered this for a moment, poking her slender forefinger at the dark blue sheets, and watching as it made no mark or indentation on the bed. She felt a tingle of Positive energy, centred at her soul and spreading out in little sparks through her limbs. *Interesting.* She knew that Positive had the edge, and the disturbance she had felt earlier in the semester was close, very close. She sat up straight and her gaze was drawn upwards to where faint, wispy ribbons of golden light swirled through the air above their heads.

'Positive,' Alice whispered. The living couldn't see it, but it was the Positive force and energy which maintained Alice's strange existence. It had an opposing twin, just like matter and antimatter, which the Thirteen called Negative. Both Positive and Negative could interact with the human soul, or more importantly, with emotions. Negative gained from destructive emotions, whereas Positive gained from the happier and peaceful emotions. It was a subtle exchange, but the effects of these two forces were seen everywhere. The living put it down to a bad or good feeling, a lucky guess or hunch, but there were accepted properties like the placebo effect or the home advantage or form in sports. Some scientists dismissed its importance but most could agree that these strange things happened – and couldn't always be explained.

Alice stood up and travelled through Kyle's door with ease. She walked down the hallway and came to a stop outside one of the doors in the middle. There was a glass panel through which she could see Dani and Cameron inside the kitchen. They were whispering loudly, struggling to keep their voices down, whilst thin bands of Positive energy shimmered in the air above their heads.

'But we have to get a cake.' Dani pouted, disappointment staining the outer edges of her soul with a murky brown and green.

'I honestly don't think that's a good idea,' Cameron replied. 'You know what he was like last year. Kyle doesn't do birthdays.'

'Yeah, but it's only a cake. Surely he would accept a cake?'

'Seriously, I wouldn't, Dani,' Cameron said, shooting her a stern look. 'He hates it when I remind him about Alice as it is, what do you think will go through his head if we make a big deal about his birthday?' The outer edges of Dani's soul flashed grey and her face seemed to crumple in on itself.

'He won't see the celebration; he'll just see that Alice isn't there.'

'Exactly, that's why I don't think it's a good idea. I'm already pushing it by inviting our old school friends for a get together on Bonfire Night, I know he isn't happy about it. I wouldn't even mention his birthday at all right now.'

'OK, OK,' Dani groaned, letting her shoulders slump.

Cameron put a hand on Dani's shoulder, gave her an affectionate squeeze and then left the kitchen. Alice followed him, feeling empty. She knew she was the reason Kyle would not, or could not, enjoy his life. Everything reminded him of her in some small way or another. The guilt she felt was consistent but pointless; there was nothing anyone could do, there would always be reminders, everywhere. She could put up with not being able to touch, taste or even be heard. She never had to worry about feeling pain, or hunger, and her body would never age unless she willed it to. There were pros and cons to being dead, but it was hard to watch your loved ones mourn you. Being dead wasn't the problem, it was being invisible.

Cameron flopped onto his bed, placed his giant headphones over his ears and started to play music through them from his iPod. He put his hands behind his head, closed his eyes, and it wasn't long before his left foot was bouncing up and down in time with the music. Alice ignored him and let her eyes wander around his bedroom. His walls were covered in posters of bands and various famous people. A woman with very little clothing was stuck to the ceiling above his bed, and there were clothes strewn about the floor. Physics books occupied his nightstand and desk, along with a couple of dirty plates and a laptop buried under a pile of notes. A couple of photos were stuck to his wardrobe, mainly of friends and family, along with the ticket stubs from the many gigs he'd attended. Alice saw a photo of their old friendship group; she was there next to Kyle, they were both smiling. It had been taken at the skate park just over three years ago, and Alice recognised all of the faces. Adam, Imo, Jamie, Lara, Jess, her younger sister Talia, and Tank and Hailey. They all looked so young, so happy. She wished that they could go back to that time, back to that place, and stay there forever.

She felt as though her soul had grown heavy; she stepped back out of Cameron's room and across the hall to Kyle's. He was standing up now, and logging out of his laptop, whilst simultaneously packing a few items into a rucksack. He picked up his bag and crossed over the hallway to Cameron's room, locking his bedroom door behind him. Cameron greeted him and they set off for their afternoon lectures.

'Hey, don't forget there's another guest presentation tonight about Quantum computers,' Cameron reminded him.

'I haven't forgotten. Are you going?' Kyle asked.

'Yeah, Professor Green likes it when his students attend extra lectures. It's a pain.'

'Cool.'

'Sophia will be there too,' Cameron said, the corners of his lips twitching. Kyle rolled his eyes. He said goodbye to Cameron at the physics building and then made his way down the slope to the business building.

* * *

Kyle's lectures finished hours later and, as he headed back up the slope, he drew out his mobile from a side pocket in his rucksack. Alice eyed the air nervously as her skin tingled and crackled with Positive energy. He had three missed calls, all from his mother. He hit the call back button, she answered on the second ring. 'Hey, Mum…' she interrupted him quickly and he listened to a torrent of words. Alice stepped closer but could only catch the odd word of their conversation. 'No, I haven't been…' he was interrupted again, and his dark brows knitted together. 'But I'm almost back at the flat…' Kyle's mother unleashed another string of words which Alice couldn't decipher. 'OK, OK, I'll go and get it,' Kyle said, annoyance flashing over his soul. 'Right,' he said softly. 'Bye, Mum.' He hung up and shook his head. He turned sharply and headed back down the slope.

Alice hurried after him, each step sending a jolt of static energy though her. She felt the familiar flutter of intuition in her soul. She saw Kyle disappearing ahead of her and pushed the weird sensations aside and sped up to catch him. He passed the main entrance and sharply rounded the bottom corner of the physics building, colliding with someone.

'Sorry!' Both of them apologised in unison. Alice caught up and peered curiously over his shoulder - it was Sophia. She smiled awkwardly at him, and then a flash of recognition passed through her dark eyes.

'You're Kyle, right? Kyle Hunter?'

'Yes.' Kyle nodded. *How does she know his name?* Alice wondered.

'Nice to meet you,' she said. 'I'm Sophia Leto.' She extended a slender hand and he shook it briefly.

'Nice to meet you too.' He looked flustered, caught by the shock of the unexpected interaction. 'Sorry I can't chat, I'm in a bit of a hurry.'

'No worries.' She smiled brightly at him, stepping to the side to let him pass. He hurried down the path and Alice followed close on his heels. 'I hope you make it in time,' Sophia called back. Alice paused and glanced back over her shoulder. Sophia stood watching them, her eyes locking with Alice's for a split second, and an amused smile creeping over her lips. She turned away and disappeared around the corner, leaving Alice with no choice but to chase after Kyle.

Alice felt little sparks of Positive energy move through her. It was a pleasant sensation, difficult to describe, but she felt excited; it was like a long forgotten boost of adrenaline. Kyle weaved his way through more buildings until he arrived at a small car park. On the opposite side of the car park were two long, temporary, shed-like buildings, painted white and lined up side by side. The building on the left had a sign above the door with black lettering which read, "Students' Post Office". Kyle crossed over the car park and a bell tinkled as he pushed open the door. He glanced briefly at the opening times, then at his watch - he had made it with five minutes to spare.

There wasn't much room inside the post office and the air was laced with the smell of freshly cut wood. A noticeboard hung on the wall to the left, and below this a shelf protruded, lined with pens and trays with paper forms. Behind the counter was a longer room, taking up the remaining space. A young man with a Negative soul was arguing with a female staff member; her hands were planted on wide hips and a stern expression wrinkled her face. Alice kept a wary eye on the Negative soul, but so far his Negativity appeared to be small and contained. She glanced upwards to see thin bands of Positive, golden energy dancing though the air, only slightly hampered by the presence of the Negative soul. The door behind them opened again and a young girl with pale skin and tightly curled red hair joined the queue behind Kyle and Alice.

Alice felt as though a thundercloud of static energy was hovering above her head; the tingling sensation continued to grow and it began to spark furiously through her. The colours in her soul thrashed violently within their sphere, spilling out into her body and casting a strange lilac aura about her. She let her consciousness branch out with its invisible fingers, as it searched through the souls of the living and into the sorting room beyond. She felt a sudden cold slap, as if someone had dunked a towel into an icy bucket and thrown it at her. It wrapped around her, and she felt the warmth of her Positive energy dull beneath its destructive nature. Negative.

Alice's eyes narrowed on the boy and she watched as his soul churned with a dark, smog-like cloud, which seeped through his pores and clung to his skin like oil. The boy started to shout at the woman opposite him as his Negativity grew exponentially with his anger, and his emotions spiralled out of control. The cloud was blacker than obsidian, thick and cold, as it plumed outwards, brushing against Kyle's grey soul and quickly surrounding Alice. The golden bands above them disappeared and Alice glared at the dark cloud, stepping backwards out of its clutches. She cleared her mind and focussed inwardly on her soul as she recalled happier memories, generating their associated emotions. It was like lighting paper with a match for Positive; it jumped at the chance, and she felt a sudden rush of warmth through her limbs.

Alice wouldn't allow Negative to worm its way into her thoughts. She had to push aside her anger and hatred towards Negative because it didn't do anything to help; it just allowed the destructive energy to grow. She saw Kyle's soul dim even more under the Negative atmosphere in the small room and she glanced back at the red-head, to see her soul dimming too. The living were irrational sometimes, they often got upset or angry over the smallest of things, unknowingly feeding this destructive force. Energies didn't have a consciousness, they didn't make decisions, they just were. They existed, and they either grew or they were cancelled out, they had no controls or restrictions. Only Positive souls like Alice could help to influence things, but unfortunately not everyone ended up Positive. She felt her soul swell and forced her energy out and away from her; it appeared directly like a fine vapour, where the light from each Positive spark bounced around the tiny, mini droplets and split into thousands of tiny rainbows. She pushed it out with her consciousness towards the Negative void-like cloud, and as soon as it came into contact, the two began to annihilate each other.

She took another step backwards, her arm brushing against the red-headed girl behind her. The red-head let out a little gasp and jumped, swinging a large brown bag and knocking over a tray full of paper forms onto the floor. Alice cursed in surprise, and turned around instinctively to help her; she knelt on the floor and then paused. She blinked, she couldn't do anything, she couldn't help; her imagined, projected body couldn't alter the physical world. She cursed again as she felt the icy taint of Negative brushed over her shoulders, and then she saw a pair of legs and feet disappearing as the front door slammed shut. The Negative source was gone. Alice was about to get up when she felt a familiar, warm presence beside her. Kyle had bent down, his body brushing against hers. He reached out a hand through Alice's frozen one, and picked up the forms from the floor. Alice stared in bewilderment as she saw Kyle's arm and hand pass through hers; it was as though she'd been knocked on the head and was suffering from double vision. Little sparks jumped from her skin, invisible to Kyle, but very real to her. She stood up quickly and snatched her arm back, clutching it to her chest in alarm. Her energy had never reacted so violently with Kyle before.

'I swear I didn't touch it,' the red-head said in a soft Irish accent, as she scrambled across the floor.

'It's OK; your bag must have knocked it or something,' Kyle said, as he piled together some of the forms.

'I didn't touch it!' she said, staring him straight in the eye.

'OK. OK.' Kyle got to his feet, holding his palms up in surrender. He offered her the forms and she snatched them from him quickly.

'Next, please,' the woman at the counter said, looking at the students with disapproval.

Alice watched as Kyle stepped up to the counter and handed over a white identification card. The woman scrutinised his card before slapping it down on the counter and hurrying off to the store room. Kyle returned the card to his wallet and the woman appeared moments later with a few letters and a larger padded, red and white envelope. Alice's eyes were drawn to the padded envelope; it glowed with positive energy and the fluttering sensation pounded like a drum inside her. She let her mind stretch out and brush curiously against the package and it sent bursts of warmth straight into Alice's soul. The woman thrust Kyle's post to him aggressively. He thanked her quickly, tucking his post into his rucksack. As he left he glanced at the nervous red-head, who was having difficulty unzipping her bag. Alice kept close, rubbing her arms as her energy continued to spark furiously. The disturbance she had felt was inside the envelope, she was sure of it, but if that was true, then why hadn't Ahrl mentioned it?

EIGHT

Sophia made her way up a bricked path to the glass front of her modern accommodation block. It was new, expensive, and the carefully manicured lawns and garden areas were a bonus; they even had their own carpark. Most of the students here were wealthy; a lot of them were studying medicine and were in their final years. As a postgraduate student, Sophia had been given the choice between her current accommodation and a house which she would have shared with other postgraduates. However, Sophia liked her space and time alone; she couldn't always explain the strange occurrences that happened around her so she preferred to be as isolated as possible. It was safer and less hassle.

She grinned and put her key in the lock to her bedroom; she hadn't felt this giddy or excited in years. She could feel Positive energy sparking in the air; its warmth swept gently over her coffee-coloured skin, and its peaceful nature overwhelmed her senses. She had been careful so far. She was sure Alice had noticed her but the Deykashee soul hadn't tried to communicate with her yet. Sophia had kept her distance, and even though she had attended most of the guest presentations, and Kyle had been present at them all, she had avoided eye contact with both him and Alice. Kyle didn't have a clue; he showed no reaction to Alice whatsoever and Sophia had informed the rest of the family of their current predicament. Visions and dreams containing the pair were slowly inching back into the Leto's minds but no one could make any sense of them. She stepped into her room and past her little bathroom as she shrugged out of her coat. She pulled the hairband out of her hair and let out a sigh of relief as her dark tresses fell about her shoulders.

'Well, hello Sophia,' said a jovial voice and then she appeared – the Deykashee soul Mabel, who had frequented Sophia's room ever since she had arrived. She was the nosey, deceased, grandmother of a girl on the floor above Sophia's. Mabel floated down through the ceiling and sat on the corner of Sophia's bed. She had dark grey hair twisted behind her head and she wore a long skirt with a cream top and pretty shawl.

'Mabel,' Sophia said, folding her arms. Usually she would have frowned at the soul's sudden intrusion but today she felt nothing but hope, and hope was a powerful thing.

'You seem in good spirits,' Mabel said staring directly at Sophia's soul. Mabel was semi-transparent which often happened with Deykashee souls; they didn't usually hang around for more than a few years because the bond that sustained their existence weakened as the living person moved on with their lives. It's what made Alice's soul even more unusual; she had been completely opaque. If the rest of the living world could see her, their eyes wouldn't have picked up on anything strange. Unfortunately for Sophia, Mabel was only a year old in soul terms and it didn't look like she would be fading out any time soon.

'She's definitely here,' Sophia said as she moved over to her desk in the corner and began to pull out folders and notebooks.

'Oh?' Mabel brightened up, her imagined body becoming more solid as her positive energy charged through her system in one burst. Sophia opened a battered old folder and started flipping through its contents.

'It's confusing, though. Alice shouldn't be a Deykashee and Kyle... well he's studying for a business degree, not physics. He's on the wrong path, but it's almost as though it's running twisted and parallel to the original path,' she said, her fingers paused on one of the pages. On the page was a hand drawn sketch by her own great, great grandmother; the faded pencil drawing showed a young man with Kyle's attributes holding hands with a young woman who looked remarkably like Alice. The sketched version of Alice wore the same knee-length dress with thin straps over the shoulders and her feet were bare. She was slightly behind Kyle as they held hands, frozen as sketches in mid-stride, and in Kyle's other hand was a small, slim, book with what looked like a spiral pattern on the front cover. Sophia's eyes sparkled; her ability to see deceased souls was not a common ability and many who claimed to have the same ability were either very good liars or ended up in care. It was another gift, passed down through the generations in her family. Many Letos had proposed that it was something deep within their genetics which made them more sensitive to certain frequencies, where others were not. Sophia and her family were very careful about the subject and kept their mouths shut; they didn't want to draw unwanted attention and they didn't want people to fear them.

'Is that the pair?' Mabel asked. She had silently moved beside Sophia and was peering down at the folder.

'Yes. My great, great grandmother drew this picture years ago and every Leto has had dreams and visions where these two appear, or at least, that used to be the case.'

'So now what are you going to do?' Mabel asked.

'I don't know,' Sophia replied. 'Kyle and Alice were different; together they were meant to be the catalyst for change, destined to nudge humanity in a certain direction, to help guide the world,' Sophia said. 'They were... how do I explain?' A faint smile crossed her face. 'You know when you see a couple and you just know they were meant to be, without really knowing why you know it.'

'Yes, I guess I do,' Mabel said.

'That's what it was like when we had visions of Kyle and Alice; every Leto said exactly the same thing, they were simply meant to be.'

'I don't see how one couple can be so important,' Mabel said.

'It's not just them.' Sophia sighed as she shut the folder. 'Whatever they talked about together, whatever they did, wherever they went, whoever they met, whatever ideas and thoughts they were supposed to have together… something, somewhere, was supposed to spark the idea which would then lead to a discovery.' Sophia placed the folder back on the shelf.

'A discovery?'

'Yes. Kyle, Alice, Cameron and I were supposed to discover a new level of particle physics, an important paradigm shift in our understanding of science, the universe and our role in it. Probably the discovery of a new particle which behaves like a virtual particle but is not a virtual particle. This discovery would open up the ideas for well, everything.' Sophia gestured vaguely. 'Every Leto saw it, felt it, understood it, but we couldn't just go about telling people that we had seen a vision of a future discovery, no one would believe us.' Mabel's eyes had become distant with thought as she placed a hand under her chin.

'I only saw the Thirteen once, when I died, but they did mention something about an important discovery, something that would change humanity. That was before I came back as a Deykashee soul to my dear little Bethany,' Mabel said.

'The four of us were supposed to work together; we made up the right minds, but the timing is also crucial.' She paused as a frown marred her features. 'If someone else discovers it, much later, they may not think in the same way and that could have disastrous consequences. This knowledge is vital for the direction of mankind.'

'But you said that Alice and Kyle were supposed to be together for this to happen. How can that be if she's a Deykashee soul? Does Kyle have your gifts?'

'No,' Sophia said with a shake of her head. 'I don't think he can see her, and his soul is very grey.'

'How grey?' Mabel asked.

'It covers his entire soul and virtually blocks out all of his other colours,' Sophia replied.

'He's been nurturing it for a while then.'

'It's not surprising but that's what I've been afraid of,' Sophia said. 'Mourning isn't a crime but the extent of his despair will draw Negative energy to him.' Sophia shuddered; the mere mention of Negative energy always made her anxious. She strived to avoid it; the energy was unpredictable and manipulative, it would creep into your thoughts and emotions, make you uncomfortable by reminding you of a bad memory, and then disappear just as quickly. When it succeeded in pulling a person into a Negative spiral, reminding them constantly of their mistakes, or refuelling their hatred, pain, and anger, then it could cause relentless problems. Sophia already accepted her mistakes; she didn't need Negative to remind her. 'He already attracts it because of who he is, but he will make it stronger and he doesn't even realise...'

'None of the living realise,' Mabel interrupted. 'If the living believed the truth about the afterlife then most of the problems in the world would have been sorted out by now.'

'That's why we needed Alice and Kyle,' Sophia said. 'Something has changed recently, just after I moved in to my room actually. There was a disturbance, did you feel it?'

'Yes, I did.'

'I saw Alice and Kyle, and a book, just like this picture...' Sophia said, pointing to the sketch. 'I'm not sure what it means anymore, and my grandma, Flo, wasn't sure either when I spoke to her on the phone yesterday, but we think a remote possibility has been thrown into the mix, something that might be able to steer humanity onto a better path.'

'And what do you plan to do about it?' Mabel asked. 'Don't you think sometimes it would be better not to intervene?' Sophia grimaced as one of her memories flashed behind her eyes, a boy with vacant eyes and a strangled smile. She had asked herself that question many times before; she had misunderstood her visions before, and it had left its mark on her soul.

'I'm not planning to do anything right now. I'll watch and see.'

NINE

Kyle let out a sharp hiss as he suffered another mild static shock. He'd been getting them ever since he'd returned from the post office yesterday, and his hair refused to stay down unless it was heavily gelled. He shook his right hand and sucked the end of his forefinger; almost everything he touched was making him spark like a faulty plug socket. It was the twenty second of October, a Saturday evening, and Kyle was up late reading one of the books he had borrowed from the library. It discussed and explained quantum entanglement - a strange phenomenon where two particles or a pairs of particles could be observed independently in their opposing quantum states, instantly, regardless of distance. It was one of the most complicated and weirdest features of quantum physics; Albert Einstein had famously referred to it as *'Spooky action at a distance'*.

He had borrowed business books too, for his assignments, all about finance, management, and marketing, but they didn't hold his attention for more than a paragraph at a time. His phone buzzed on the desk beside him, and he tore his eyes away from the book. It was a text from Hailey; *Happy Birthday brother!* it read. *Now you're an old fart. Love, Hailey.* She had ended it with a line of kisses. He glanced at the time; it was a minute past midnight, so technically she was right, it was his birthday, his twenty-first birthday. He was surprised and relieved that Cameron hadn't insisted on going out, and he felt a little guilty about not going home too. He hated upsetting his mum, but she didn't understand; he just wanted to be left alone. He sighed as his gaze settled on the small collection of unopened post at the foot of his bed. *I guess I should open them now*, he thought.

He opened all the cards first, putting them into a drawer under his desk as he finished reading them. Most of his relatives had sent him cash or gift cards; Hailey had included a bracelet with her card. It was elasticated and made out of alternating black matted and silver metal rectangles. He slipped it over his right wrist and placed her card into the drawer with the others.

Finally his hands settled on the larger envelope. It was about the size of an A4 piece of paper and it had a red, blue and white plastic covering. It was padded, and he could feel a solid, rectangular object inside. He scrutinised the outside. It had been delivered by Air Mail and had *'Registered Post International'* printed on it in big white letters. He couldn't think of anyone who lived abroad. His gaze caught a line of much smaller letters in the top right corner, printed in white italics, *'Postage Paid, Australia'*. The air suddenly felt like grit as it passed down the back of his throat, robbing the moisture from his tissues. *Australia?* He knew of only one person who could have possibly sent him post from Australia - Alice's sister, Talia.

Kyle's grip tightened around the envelope, his fingers almost ripping into the plastic. Why would she send something now? They had moved to get away, to cut all ties, to start again, that was the whole point, wasn't it? He let out a deep breath as he tore open the end of the envelope. He reached inside quickly and fished out the object. It slipped from his shaky grasp and tumbled to the floor in two parts. It was a black notebook, he realised, and one of its pages had fallen out. He cursed and swooped up the items, mixed emotions overwhelming his frustration. His eyes automatically scanned the single page. There was a pencil sketch on the page and one of its longest edges had been torn; he wondered if it had ripped as the book fell or if it had been ripped out deliberately. Under the sketch there was a single line of handwritten words. His heart spluttered, choking, his neurons failing to relay the correct messages. This was *her* handwriting, *her* curved and rounded words, the lines of ink worked from *her* hand. He recognised it instantly, but he had never thought it would ambush his eyes like this. He glanced at the notebook, his gaze running over the cover where she had taken a silver pen and drawn delicate patterns, interweaving webs of endless turns and pointed edges. At the centre there was a small untouched bubble, containing one word, one name, *Kyle.*

Kyle's eyes flickered between his silver name and the torn page, clenched in separate hands. Thoughts and questions wouldn't even form in his bewildered mind. She had always doodled in notebooks, especially when she had been passing the time in hospital, but he didn't remember this notebook. His eyes scanned over the sketch; it showed two houses, their houses, with a big removals van parked on the road outside. The words underneath read: *The day we first met.* There was also a date written in the top right corner, *21ˢᵗ January, 2009* - Alice's eighteenth birthday. A little under five months before she had died. The blood drained from his face. Several doors in his mind flew open with such force, their nerve-encrusted frames splintered. Memories forced their way through the cracks in his mind, random and unconnected. He dropped the book and page, pressing the heels of his hands into his eyes as he tried to force them back. He let out a moan and began to whisper to himself over and over.

'Just forget, Kyle, just forget. Please just forget.' He let out a low inaudible moan as he rocked back and forth in his chair. A memory pushed its way to the forefront of his mind and he shook his head, trying desperately hard not to remember. *Just forget, just for…*

He had been fifteen years old and it was the summer of 2006. Kyle was lying on his bed at home, listening to his favourite band, Dead Souls, through his earphones. It was warm outside and his room was golden in the afternoon sunshine. Posters of various rock bands adorned the pale walls, along with articles cut from his favourite music magazines. He was wearing a black band t-shirt with jeans and a studded belt looped through the belt loops. His skateboard lay on the laminated floor, alongside his school books, CDs and magazines. He had both an acoustic and an electric guitar, propped up in stands, along with a box amp. Physics posters were stuck to his ceiling, but he wasn't looking at anything, he was just concentrating on the music, tuning into the chords of the guitarist. His bedroom door swung inwards and his father appeared; he looked flustered. He motioned to Kyle to take out his earphones and Kyle reluctantly did as he was told.

'Can we have your help, Kyle? The new neighbours have arrived,' his father said.

'What?' Kyle groaned as he sat up.

'The removals van is outside. Come on.' He left Kyle's door open as he headed back outside. Kyle got to his feet and quickly laced on a pair of Converse before heading down the stairs. They lived on a narrow street called Angel Drove, lined with detached houses, all a couple of metres apart. The houses mostly had four bedrooms, with front and back lawns, and neat little fences or walls to separate their gardens from their neighbours. Kyle opened the front door, immediately blinded by the summer sun as he stepped onto the porch. As his eyes adjusted he saw the van parked up outside the house on the left; the house had been empty for months while the previous owners had tried to sell it. Now there was a blue Jaguar parked in the driveway. He heard someone letting out a huff and the hollow footsteps of someone moving inside the van. Then she appeared and he felt a strange spasm in his chest. His thoughts meshed together into one mighty, congealed mess. He watched her as she walked towards the end of the van and placed the heavy cardboard box she was carrying down on the edge before jumping down to the ground. She wore a white vest with blue ripped jeans; her bronze-brown hair hung straight to her shoulder blades. Her skin was fresh and fair, her eyes blue and her lips a pale rose; she was beyond beautiful. She must have been his age, maybe younger, but as his heart began to thunder and his guts began to flutter, he already longed to be near her. She picked up the box again awkwardly with her slender arms and tried to manoeuvre it towards the house. Her grip began to slip and Kyle ran down the path without a thought, vaulting over their iron gate like an Olympian and catching the box before it could completely slip from her grasp. His arms brushed against hers and they froze there on the pavement.

Her eyes locked with his; they were a deep, ocean blue and he was already drowning. Her cheeks flushed as she moved her hands into a better position. Kyle knew he had to speak.

'It's OK, I've got it,' he said, trying to offer her a smile. She gawked at him as though he were some alien life form, then loosened her grip.

'Thank you,' she said quietly, letting go of the box. She lowered her gaze and brushed the hair from her face. He noticed then that the back of her hand was covered in ink. He readjusted his grip; the box was really heavy, he was surprised she'd even managed to lift it.

'This is heavy, what have you got in here?' he asked.

'Books and dreams,' she said. Her eyes widened and her lips parted. 'I mean pennies! Books and pennies.'

'I see you've met Alice, Kyle,' his father said as he walked over and placed a hand on Kyle's shoulder. 'She's going to be in your year at Queen's.' Matthew made his way to the back of the van and helped another man with some of the furniture - Alice's father, Kyle presumed.

'Where would you like this?' Kyle asked, glancing down at the box.

'Upstairs, third door on your right,' she said, lowering her hand and letting her hair cascade back over her pink cheeks.

'OK,' Kyle said, turning towards the house.

'Be...' She faltered as he glanced back at her. She was looking directly at him, her right hand outstretched. 'Careful,' she said, dropping her hand.

'It's OK, Alice.' He savoured the feeling of her name rolling gently off his tongue. 'I'll look after your dreams,' he added, suddenly feeling bold. He headed off before she could reply, but not before he caught the look of surprise that had danced across her face.

Tears leaked from behind his palms and flowed over his cheeks as he forced the memory back to the past. He knew he had failed, he hadn't looked after her dreams, no, their dreams. He felt the breath had been stolen from his lungs, the heavy beat of his heart hammered around his skull, and his veins were pinched. Each muscle was aching for sustenance, as his organs cried out for more oxygen. He inhaled unsteadily. No matter how hard he crammed his hands into his eyes, he could not stop the tears. He gave up, his eye sockets aching and tender. Her book and page still lay on the floor where he had dropped them, but he couldn't muster the energy to care. He stood up, flicking off all the lights, and then he got into bed and brought the duvet over his head. The darkness wasn't comforting, it was hot and suffocating, but he focussed on it anyway. His mind was fragile. It had been too long since he had opened his little box of memories, too long since he had confronted his emotions, those angry demons. They had grown vicious in their waiting and were now revelling in his moment of weakness, rearing their little ugly heads and squeezing their way through the cracks in his resolve.

Just forget Kyle, just forget. Just forget Kyle, just forget, he chanted silently in his mind. He curled up tighter and squeezed his eyes shut, he didn't want to remember, remembering was cruel. He thought he was stronger than this, but nothing, nothing, could block out Alice. He cried silently for hours, his head aching as he closed the doors on his past one by one. Eventually he succumbed to pure exhaustion; his body and mind could no longer function, and he fell willingly into a deep, dreamless sleep, hoping and praying that this time, he might not wake up again.

TEN

'A writer?' Hailey heard her father as she sat at the top of the stairs listening in on her parents' conversation as though she were a small child again. They had just returned from her last ever parents' evening at school and her father wasn't happy.

'Well, she is predicted an A in English,' her mother replied.

'Yes, an A in English, a C in maths and a C in business! Even the English teacher said she would have to get B's in her other subjects if she wants to be considered for an English degree at a good university.' Hailey winced. She wasn't even sure she wanted to go to university and she had told her father as much.

'Perhaps she doesn't have to go to university,' her mother said.

'She's going to university. I haven't worked hard all these years so she can flush her education down the drain and be a writer! How is she going to support herself as a writer?'

'Matthew, keep your voice down. There are other options besides university you know. I didn't go.'

'I know, I know,' her father said. 'It's just,' he paused. 'I want the best for our children. I want them to do well and be successful. I want them to have a better life than the one I had. We couldn't even afford to feed ourselves sometimes, and Christmas never happened. I don't want Hailey, or Kyle, to struggle like that…'

'They won't.'

'Writing isn't a sensible career, Stacy, only the lucky ones make it.'

'You could say that about being a musician too,' her mother argued. 'I've done OK.'

'I know and we were lucky. And you were lucky that you managed to make a career doing what you love. I had to work hard to put food on the table.'

'Perhaps you could have done what you loved too.'

'I needed stability. We needed stability. I needed a job I knew would pay me every month. We couldn't afford a drum kit back then anyway.'

'You don't know that; it might have worked out OK.'

'Might have, those are uncertain words.'

'You could buy one now.'

'I don't have the time to play; I've got far too much work to do at the office.'

'Yes and you work yourself ragged every evening. Even the doctor said you need to take a break. You'll end up ill if you don't.'

'The doctor fusses. I'm fine,' her father insisted. 'We're supposed to be talking about our kids here, not me. I want them to be safe, secure and happy.'

'Well, I'm not so sure Kyle is happy at the moment.'

'He's OK. He's on track for an upper second class degree in business studies, and he's got a plan.'

'That's only part of it, Matthew.'

'He's had a little hiccup in his life…'

'It was more than a hiccup. Alice's death has scarred him in more ways than you know. Matthew, he's miserable; it's not study that stopped him coming back for his birthday. He struggles all the time with his memories and reminders of Alice. He doesn't like coming home.'

'He's OK, it will take time, but he's OK. He's smart. He knew it was sensible to stay.'

'Matthew…' Hailey recognised the disapproval and concern in her mother's tone.

'He has to move on Stacy, time moves forwards not backwards. It's sad and it's horrible, but he'll have to move on eventually.'

Hailey had heard enough. She tiptoed back to her room and shut her door quietly behind her. She felt for her father; he had lost his own father at fourteen and had had to help provide for his family. He had worked hard and deserved his success but he wasn't Kyle and he wasn't her. She loved him, and she didn't want to let him down, but she knew she wasn't a business woman, and it irked her that Kyle had given up on his dreams so easily. Perhaps dad was proud and relieved that Kyle was planning to step into the world of business, but it wasn't Kyle, it wasn't really his choice. Her brother had done a good job at putting up walls and distancing himself from everything and everyone, but she wondered if, behind those layers, he felt the same way too.

ELEVEN

Alice was sat on his desk in his university bedroom. Now that she no longer had a biological body and had both lost and gained senses, she was much more aware of the elaborate layout inside her mind. The living paid little attention to the grand map inside their own heads; they were naturally concerned about their bodies, the people around them and the materialistic objects that defined them. They lived life on autopilot allowing their minds to take the shortest routes, not bothering to understand, just following blindly and avoiding the scenery while society guided their opinions. Alice's mind was more powerful than a supercomputer and she was aware of it in its complete entirety; she knew about the routes less travelled and she understood them. There were no shortcuts in the afterlife; eternity was a long time to become familiar with one's mind.

Even now, as she sat on the desk, a small part of her mind was devoting itself to keeping on Kyle's physical plane. Her thoughts had branched down hundreds of different avenues. Some of them were quite terrifying; others were too beautiful for the living to comprehend. She was thinking about Positive, Negative, forces, energy, the world, Kyle, her notebook, the Thirteen, maths, physics, education, politics, cultures, religions and so on; the list was long.

She glanced briefly at Kyle as he slept, and then she turned to look over her shoulder; the campus had aged overnight and the sports fields were now white with frost. She reached out her right hand through the gap in Kyle's curtains and touched the window.

Frost had claimed all four corners and she tilted her head upwards at the sky. The night was fading but grey clouds loomed ominously above. She shivered; the temperatures had dropped quickly through October, a cold winter was on its way.

Kyle moaned and shifted and Alice spun back to face him, ready to leap off the desk. The springs in his mattress creaked as he turned over onto his side and resettled under his duvet. Alice frowned; she was troubled by the arrival of her notebook. Her grandmother, Paula, had given her the notebook when she had been in hospital as a means to pass the time and to stop her from drawing all over her hands; a childhood habit that didn't sit well with the doctors. She remembered the day clearly though and Paula's words, *'Don't worry about university and grades just now; you need to get better first. Do what you enjoy, we encourage children to play not work. But we tell adults to work and we don't encourage them to play. However, if you enjoy your work, is it really work? Or is it play?'* Alice smiled fondly at the memory, old people always seemed to be able to baffle the younger generations with their words of wisdom. Kyle had shut her notebook and the page in a drawer beneath his desk without looking at the rest of it; it was as though the mere sight of it sickened him, and his soul colours were a mess. She didn't know why the notebook had arrived now, or even how the page had been torn; she couldn't remember tearing it out herself. It was a mystery, and it had upset Kyle. She didn't like that; she had never wanted to cause Kyle more misery and pain.

She knew the notebook had a role in the disturbance she had felt now, but not why. This was going to be hard for them both. Her notebook was somewhere between a diary and a scrapbook. She had meant to give it to Kyle for his nineteenth birthday, but she hadn't survived that long. Inside were photos, drawings, quotes, everything that she thought related to the pair of them. It was supposed to have been a nice reminder, a *look what we've done already and look how much we can do in the future*, sort of thing. Alice hadn't banked on her crappy heart spontaneously combusting.

Kyle's breathing suddenly shifted from its usual pattern and Alice sat up straighter. She listened intently and then he groaned and she leapt off the desk gracefully. Her silent footfalls reached him within a second and she leant over him, seating herself on the edge of his bed.

'Alice,' he groaned, even though his eyes were clamped tightly shut. She saw the tell-tale lines deepening in his face. He twisted sharply, almost knocking her senses sideways as she placed a hand on top of his forehead. A bright orange flare illuminated his soul and then rolled over into a dark cloud of Negativity. She cursed and unhooked her mind, like a fisherman unhooking a net. She felt her thoughts slip through the gaps and into her body form. She directed her mind towards her soul and felt the Positive energy pulsing from her core as it rippled outwards. She guided her mind towards Kyle and willed her energy to curve around his soul. Kyle's soul bristled and unknowingly knocked her away; it attacked her as though she were a foreign antibody invading his immune system. She felt her energy stutter and her body trembled as she continued to will her energy around his. It was like a great cosmic hug, a blanket of Positive thoughts.

Alice willed him to be calm, she willed the nightmares away, and she willed the pain to stop. Kyle's body tossed and turned violently, and a thin layer of sweat coated his skin. The subconscious existed closer to Alice's current state, even her suggestions were placed within the subconscious mind. When Kyle was asleep his consciousness was temporarily silent, and his subconscious took over, giving him, beautiful, weird, and sometimes distressing dreams. Sometimes, when the emotions were extreme, Alice could tune in and see Kyle's dreams. Negative emotions and their colours flashed within his soul and Alice gave one last shove with her mind and dove straight in…

There was a doorway with a closed, but the constantly changing door. One minute it was a wooden, double door with slender, glass panes, the next it was a single, white door with a large glass window. The doorway switched back and forth between the two and a younger Kyle stood next to it with a younger version of Cameron, both of them dressed in grey suits, the Queen's sixth form's uniform. Alice peered curiously at the doors but even Kyle's dream self didn't appear to register her. There were other people waiting outside this doorway but their faces were fuzzy and held no details. They were just bodies, figures that were there but not there. She recognised the double doors with the glass panes immediately; it was the doorway to the Queen's school hall, where the assemblies, drama productions and examinations had taken place. She could see rows of single desks lined up through the glass, and she could see the big stage at the back with its green velvet curtains.

The door switched again and she gasped as she peered through the window. It was her hospital room, a sparse, white cube with a single bed and one big window on the far side. She could see herself in the bed, though she scarcely recognised herself. The Alice lying in the bed was deathly pale and sickly thin. She had no hair or eyebrows and her skin appeared taut and stretched over her bones. *Why are you dreaming about this, Kyle?* She hated seeing herself like this, she hated what had happened to her, this Alice was a shadow of the girl she had once been. She looked back at Kyle and saw that he was crying, his tears making translucent pathways down his cheeks. *This is wrong, Kyle, you shouldn't have to see this, you shouldn't have to relive this, even in your dreams.*

* * *

'You look exhausted,' Cameron said as he and Kyle walked back up the slope to their flat.

'I didn't sleep very well last night,' Kyle replied. Alice walked beside them; Kyle's eyes were bloodshot and shadowed. He had been struggling to keep awake through his lectures all afternoon.

'Are you really that worried about going back home?' Cameron asked. Kyle rolled his eyes.

'No, that's just annoying.'

'Oh, it will be fun,' Cameron said, putting his arm around Kyle's shoulders and giving him a squeeze. 'Lara will be there too.' Kyle shrugged him off. Alice stopped. Lara had been a girl at their secondary school; she had never been particularly fond of Alice but the two of them had been civil with each other. Alice had always suspected that Lara secretly liked Kyle; the thought did nothing to calm her nerves now though. *You're being stupid, Alice; he can go out with whoever he wants.* A stab of pain hit her and her soul flashed with both sadness and guilt. It was so hard watching the ones you loved move on with their lives, Ahrl had warned her. She caught up with the two boys as they entered their flat.

'What has she done?' Cameron said in dismay, his eyes darting between fake cobwebs and spiders hanging down from the ceiling to plastic miniature skeletons and ghosts. 'You guys aren't even going out tonight, hell, you're not even pre-drinking here with us.'

'Do you like it?' Dani called cheerfully, appearing from the kitchen. 'Ta da!'

'Tell her it's a fire hazard,' Stuart yelled from the kitchen. Dani shot a scowl in his direction.

'It looks great, Dani. Are you sure it's really all necessary though?' Cameron asked.

'Yes,' she said, her gaze travelling to Kyle. 'Are you alright?' she asked. 'You look shattered.'

'I'm fine.' Dani frowned.

'Well, get some caffeine in you or something, we've got to be at work soon, it's going to be super busy.' Kyle nodded resignedly.

A couple of hours later Alice had positioned herself in the back corner of the bar, closest to where Kyle was stationed. She watched as he darted back and forth from the drinks on the back wall to the cash register. The crowds were so thick you could barely see the people three feet behind you. Most of the students were dressed up in bright and elaborate costumes, ranging from the traditional witches and ghosts to the not so traditional crayons and traffic cones. With alcohol kindling in their veins, students squeezed past each other in the narrow gaps, making their way to the bar and then back through the bodies to the dance floor. The bar provided a small but substantial barrier between the sober and intoxicated souls, and Alice gazed in fascinated horror at the students on the other side.

Alcohol was a Negative tool. It clouded the emotions and blurred the lines, meaning that anyone, even after a couple of drinks, had less control over their mind than they would have had otherwise. It seemed obvious, yet it was one of mankind's biggest mistakes; drinking had become a cultural norm, and with drink, the living unknowingly opened their souls to Negative energy. This was the reason so much violence and hatred occurred around intoxicated people, and why so many gave in to primitive desires. Alcohol also blurred the soul and Alice struggled to pick out the individual emotions. She could see huge splurges of colours throughout the masses, yet she couldn't tell which emotions belonged to which person.

Alice's eyes caught a spectacular golden flash from somewhere at the very back of the ballroom and then it was sucked underneath the sea of emotions. Someone positive was amongst the envious, the lustful, the tired, and the angry. Alice narrowed her eyes as she searched for the source; it was like being an astronaut in space and searching for a single burst of aether. Movement distracted her search, as Dani ran over to Kyle with a panicked expression and a desperate look in her eyes.

'Kyle!' she shouted over the loud blaring music. 'We're running out of glasses!'

'I'm on it,' Kyle replied as he picked up a couple of plastic baskets and made his way out of the bar. Alice followed unwillingly; she kept close on his heels as Kyle weaved his way through the crowds with surprising agility. He swiped up empty glasses from the sides, chairs, and floors. He made several trips into the main room and back to the bar, swapping his baskets for empty ones. Then he descended down a flight of stairs into the little beer garden outside.

Just as Alice's bare feet hit the bottom step she felt a sudden heat in her torso accompanied by an all too familiar fluttering sensation. She felt an overwhelming pressure surrounding her mind and then the colours merged into one cinematic image. She saw Kyle, or at least a future version of him, as he picked up glasses from a low wall. A chill shot through her as, seconds later, a man with a Negative soul entered her vision. It was as though a mighty black hole was centred at his torso, overwhelming every other emotion. He was tall, broad and muscular; he held a drink in his right hand and had his back to Kyle as he talked to a young woman who was dressed as some sort of animal. Kyle moved along the wall, collecting the empty glasses and heading closer to the Negative soul. The vision distorted slightly, stuttering like a scratched disc and causing Alice to wobble as it struggled to correct itself. *What the?* Her question echoed around her mind, just as another man, dressed as the Mad Hatter, ran by. He tripped over his own feet and stumbled straight into Kyle, who then fell like a domino, straight into the man with the Negative soul.

It happened quickly then. The Negative soul spun round. Orange fire surged up at the centre of his soul and blackened quickly like the mushroom cloud of a nuclear explosion. His anger fuelled and intensified the Negative energy inside him. It obscured his torso and most of his face, moving like a swarm of blurry mosquitos around his skin. He lashed out and punched Kyle in the jaw with a resounding crack. Kyle's body twisted awkwardly to his left and he fell, his head catching the sharp edge of the brick wall and sounding another gut-wrenching crack. Alice cried out as his body slumped to the floor and Kyle, conscious but disorientated, touched the side of his temple. Bright red blood painted the tips of his fingers and then he passed out.

The vision faded, slipping from her mind. Her ears popped and she was greeted with the low mismatched chorus of drunken conversations. She blinked and clutched the sides of her head as it pulsed painfully. She tried not to panic as person after person passed through her on their way down the stairs, jarring her senses. She stepped out of their way and almost fell through the fencing. She bent over with her hands on her knees and closed her eyes, willing the dizziness to end.

As soon as she could, she straightened up and scanned her surroundings. She spotted Kyle collecting empty glasses from a table, and then she spotted the low wall and the Negative soul, just metres behind him. She cursed and made her way over, dodging the bodies and flailing limbs as best as she could. She approached the wall cautiously. The Negative energy around the man's soul bloomed like a dark, twisted rose. It stretched out with fog-like, thorny tendrils, reaching towards her as it tried to cancel out her Positive energy. The man, who was completely unaware of the Negativity in his soul, seemed relaxed; he had a charming face and an easy-going smile. He would have seemed normal and friendly enough by any living person's standards. Alice felt the chilling bite of Negativity even before the repulsive energy brushed against her body. She grimaced as the glow from her skin faded. She ignored it and focussed all of her attention on the plastic pint glass before her and then she tried to grab it. She blinked in surprise as her fingers curled straight through the plastic. She panicked and tried to grab it again and again.

'No, no, no,' she said, as every attempt at moving the glass failed. She swiped at it and watched as her hand and wrist sailed right through it. 'Damn it!' she yelled in frustration. Kyle's bloody fingers and ashen face flashed through her mind and she felt hot tears erupting from her eyes. She swiped at the glass again as Negative energy seeped into her skin and entangled itself within her. 'Move. You. Stupid. Cup!' she hissed through clenched teeth. She glanced backwards over her shoulder and saw Kyle approaching the wall. 'No!' she cried. She glanced around desperately; there was no way she could use suggestion here; the souls were either Negative or blurred from alcohol. It would be like trying to penetrate a glacier with a bendy straw.

She tried to grab at the cup again, tried to will her fingers to feel its organic polymer dimensions. Despair washed over her and she felt a burst of icy pain deep in her soul. She stared down at her right arm in horror as Negative energy swirled around her form. Its smoke-like appearance made it appear weak and harmless, but Alice knew better; it was burning pathways into her soul. She felt her energy levels drop and her awareness and intuition became slow and fuzzy. She cursed herself for losing her head; she had panicked when she should have remained calm. She had opened the door to Negative energy without even realising it herself. The Thirteen had warned her so many times about this; there was a skill to controlling the emotional balance in one's soul, but that took time and she didn't have time. Fear threatened to overtake her emotions as she clutched her burning arm. She had to remain calm; she had to focus on Positive. She shut her eyes tight, as wrinkles of pain etched their way on to her face.

The Negative energy began to recede, its grip loosening as it withdrew from her soul. Alice opened her eyes as warmth cascaded through her. It was gentle but powerful, like the sun's rays melting the early morning frost. She could sense and see this Positive energy; it was a misty, golden cloud, with colours that refracted as though the cloud were made of fine prisms. She felt contentment and let out a sigh of relief; Positive always brought an overwhelming quality of peace with it. Alice turned to her left, her eyes locking briefly with Sophia's as the Positive energy radiated from her living core. Sophia was dressed as Wonder Woman, and her hair was held back by a shiny red headband. Sophia's red painted lips smiled as she reached for the problematic cup. Her tanned arm brushed against Alice's, sending shockwaves through Alice's soul. She felt the flickering vibrations, the spikes and surges; this was one exceptionally powerful soul. Sophia's energy was evolving on its own momentum, growing in intensity and flowing with purpose. It knocked away the last remnants of Negative energy in one sweeping, fluid movement. Sophia picked up the empty glass without a word and turned away from the oblivious, dark soul. She strode off in the opposite direction, stacking all the empty glasses along the wall. Alice stared after her, her mouth forming a small 'o' as she watched the positive soul go.

TWELVE

Thoughts were funny things, Kyle realised. They weren't always logical or linked to one another. Halloween had been a busy night; the staff had been kept on their feet. Though this wasn't the thought that troubled him; he remembered Sophia being there amongst the crowds, she had been acting strangely. He had been sent out several times to collect the glasses and on one particular occasion, Sophia had decided to cut across him and stack glasses too. Maybe she was drunk; everybody else was.

If he was honest, he didn't know what possessed most drunk people to do half the things they did, but helping stack glasses along a wall was a new one for him. He also wasn't sure why the insignificant memory had resurfaced in the first place. He was standing on a strip of grass with strangers, friends and family. It was cold and dark, and they were all facing in one direction as though they were about to pay homage to one God. The cathedral stood behind them and a large, controlled bonfire crackled to the left. He was trying to relax and enjoy himself for the sake of his family and friends. There was no reason for Sophia's erratic drunken behaviour to enter his thoughts. If thoughts were a game of chess, he decided they were goddamned knights and queens. They either veered off sharply or went wherever they pleased.

'Hey, Kyle!' he heard Cameron call. He turned and saw Cameron and a couple of old school friends approaching him. Guilt twisted his insides as he recognised the faces. Along with Cameron there was Jamie and his girlfriend Imo, Adam, Lara and Cameron's younger sister Jess. Kyle stared at them; they were the same people but somehow changed, two years had altered them. Jess was still at the sixth form but the others had gone to university; they looked different, older. All of their lives had changed direction. He wasn't sure if they were more strangers now than the friends he had once known.

'Hey, Kyle.' Imo was the first to greet him, her white-blonde hair pinned behind her head. She held Jamie's arm but she smiled and Kyle immediately felt his unease slip away. Alice had always liked Imo.

'Hey, Kyle, it's been too long,' Jamie said. He was tall and dark compared to Imo and he clasped Kyle's wrist in greeting.

'Hi.'

'Kyle!' Lara said and she hugged him tightly. He felt her arms crushing his ribs and he could smell her sweet shampoo wafting up from her dark hair. Lara had been the popular, loud girl at school. 'Oh my god, it's been ages, how are you?' she asked, releasing him.

'I'm fine,' Kyle said, forcing a smile.

'Oh, look who it is.' Adam had always been the arrogant and charming type; a trail of broken hearts had followed him wherever he went. 'You're looking a bit rough,' he said, as he clasped Kyle's wrist and patted him on the back. It was true; Kyle was looking a little rough. His sleep had been plagued by nightmares he couldn't properly recall; he only knew that he woke up frequently with his heart thundering in his chest. His disrupted nights had been getting steadily worse ever since Alice's notebook had arrived, and he didn't think it was an ill-timed coincidence.

'You're not looking too good yourself,' Kyle replied. He could feel himself sliding back into the same routines again, the same old conversations and friendly insults. It was easy but it was different.

'What are you doing with yourself these days?' Jamie asked.

'I'm studying business at Red Oak,' Kyle replied. 'What about you?'

'Me and Imo are at Bath,' Jamie said. 'I'm doing business too but Imo's studying Spanish, and French… and German…' He wrapped an arm around Imo's small shoulders. 'She's the real brains, we can go anywhere in the world.' Imo blushed.

'Well, I think everyone is here,' Cameron said as he glanced around. 'Who wants a drink?' He was answered by a chorus of yesses.

'I'll help you carry them,' Adam said.

'I'll go too.' Jess said and the three of them disappeared. Kyle gazed around; he could see his parents a little way off to his right and closer still, Hailey and Tank. They were both laughing. *They look good together* he thought and he wasn't the only one who had noticed the pair; Kyle could see their father keeping a watchful eye over Hailey. He had noticed that the atmosphere at home had been a little tense between his father and sister; he wondered if Tank had something to do with that.

'So,' Lara said, jolting him from his thoughts. Somehow he had ended up alone with her as Jamie and Imo were cuddling a couple of metres away.

'Where are you these days?' Kyle asked. He couldn't think of anything else to say.

'Oh, I study drama at Warwick,' she said. *Of course she does,* Kyle thought. Lara had always loved drama at school, and she had been the leading lady in most of the school's productions.

'I should have guessed that,' he said. He noticed then that her face was slimmer and her hair was slightly longer too; she had always had a short bob at school.

'Well, you have been out of it for a while.' Lara smiled. *You could say it like that.* Her face dropped slightly with concern. 'How are you keeping?' she asked gently, leaning in close, too close.

'Fine.' Kyle coughed into his fist and stepped away. 'I'm fine.' She narrowed her hazel eyes at him but didn't press him further.

'I've missed you,' she said as she toed the grass with her boot.

That threw Kyle; he didn't know what to say to that but Lara kept talking. 'It's not been the same since you left the group. I mean I know we've all sort of gone our separate ways now with university and everything but…' A firework suddenly screeched up into the air and exploded, followed by another and then another. Red, green, pink, gold, blue and purple; they were rainbow flurries of colours decorating the smoky night sky.

Cameron and the others returned with the drinks and Lara dropped the conversation. Kyle almost relaxed as the warm coffee soothed his insides. It was getting colder, and most people were wrapped up in coats and scarves. He stood there in a daze watching the fireworks, listening to the music, the crowd, enjoying the faint smell of heated candy mixed with filter coffee, and the sharp, pungent tinge as sparklers were lit. Memories of Alice began to taunt the edges of his mind and he felt his face tighten.

'Kyle,' Lara said drawing his attention again. The light from the bonfire gave her jacket a metallic shine and highlighted her face; she was speaking, he realised, but no words were reaching his ears. He blinked and it wasn't Lara standing beside him anymore, it was fifteen-year-old Alice. Kyle's eyes shot around and he saw Talia, Cameron, Adam, Lara, Jess, Jamie, Imo, Tank, Hailey and others dotted around the field in little clusters, but they were all younger, all from a different time.

'Are you alright, Kyle?' he heard Alice ask. He whipped his head back round and stared at her. She tucked her hair behind her left ear as she watched him.

'I'm great. What are all those doodles?' he heard himself ask, but he was sure he hadn't said a word. Alice paused and glanced at the back of her hand.

'Oh, nothing, it's just a little quirk of mine,' she said, embarrassed. 'It drives Mum mad. She's forever buying me notebooks in the hope I'll stop.' He laughed.

'A quirk?'

'I guess. I think everyone has some quirks. I bet you have little quirks.' She smiled and he felt his heartrate speed up.

'I don't think so.' They fell silent and he cast his gaze around the field. 'Would you like to go out for a coffee? Or something? Maybe?' Kyle asked. Alice glanced at him warily. 'I mean, I know we walk to school together but you haven't been here that long.' He rubbed the back of his neck. 'I could give you a tour of the city? There's a really cool science museum and, well, you've seen the cathedral...' She watched him silently and he felt his cheeks grow hot.

'Sure,' she said. Her eyes lit up and she smiled. He could feel the pounding in his chest, travelling up to his head. 'It'll be fun.'

'Kyle?' Lara's voice brought him back to the present and she waved a hand in front of his face. He blinked a couple of times but Alice was gone. 'Are you OK?' His head was throbbing and his throat burned.

'Sorry.'

'Sorry for what?' Confusion clouded Lara's eyes. 'Did you hear anything I was saying?' Alice flashed through his mind again and he gripped his coffee too tightly, splitting the flimsy polystyrene cup and then dropping it on the floor. 'Kyle, what's wrong?'

'I'm sorry.' He backed away from her. He could see Alice again, standing next to him as colours erupted in the sky, each glowing burst highlighting the soft curves of her face. Her eyes sparkled as she tilted her head towards him and she smiled, a full-blown, heart-stopping, blood-warming smile. It was as though the earth no longer had gravity; he was in love with her, and she didn't know it...

Kyle shook his head. *NO!* he told himself forcefully. He gritted his teeth. His head continued to throb. He felt a pressure in his skull and behind his eyes as little circular voids started to obscure his vision.

'Kyle?' Lara's voice had risen by a couple of octaves.

'I'm alright, I'm just going to get some,' he winced again at a particularly painful throb, 'space.' He turned around quickly, not bothering to check if he was being followed as he slipped through the crowds.

He didn't slow down until he had passed the entrance and was out onto the main road, heading away from the cathedral. It dawned upon him quickly that he was running away from his memories, running away from any potential trigger, of which there were many in this pathetically small city. There was no escape in Elbridge. Alice had only been here for a few short years and yet Kyle's memories of her had rooted themselves firmly into everything, even the bricks and mortar. He could hear the *pop, pop, pop,* of fireworks and the grating *screech-bang* becoming fainter as he headed back to the house.

The dull pain in his brain pulsed with every heartbeat, as though the blood in his veins had congealed and now struggled to circulate. He pressed his palm to his forehead; his skin was hot and slightly wet. He let out a deep, shaky, breath. He wanted to scream, kick something, throw a chair, anything, but he knew he wouldn't. He quickened his pace and kept his head down, avoiding people as they milled around the pavements and outside the pubs and restaurants. The further away he headed from the cathedral, the quieter it became. The ache in his brain became a dim echo. He walked down the main street in Elbridge, passing the shops, the science museum, and Elbridge's only shopping mall. He reached the outer edges of the small city, passed Tank's little terrace house and then finally made it to the top of his street.

He gazed down at the familiar houses that lined either side. Cars were parked by the pavements and on the driveways, and lampposts lit up the street at regular intervals. Everything was quiet, peaceful; the road itself was its own little bubble. He squared his shoulders and pushed his hands into his pockets as he made his way down the street. He kept his head down and counted each step, a game he had played as a child. He knew exactly when he was standing outside Alice's old house. He winced and shot a passing glance at the door he had once so eagerly knocked on. A new family lived there now, a young family with young children, but that fact did little to console his memories.

Kyle stopped. He didn't know why but his feet were unwilling to move, or perhaps his brain had given up completely. There were so many thoughts going through his mind, so many memories drifting like ghosts around his neural passageways. He sighed and looked back at Alice's old house. It was the same as it had always been; a pretty red-bricked cube with large bay windows. The front lawn was a patch of damp grass lined by bare rose bushes, enclosed by a low brick wall. There had been so many mornings where he had sat on the wall outside her house with Hailey, waiting for Talia and Alice, before they had all headed to school. They had spent many hours after school finishing homework or revising for exams together. Every weekend they would knock on each other's doors and go out into Elbridge if the weather was fine, or down to the skate park. Or if it was miserable and cold, they would stay inside and watch TV, play games, or Kyle would play guitar alongside Alice's piano.

He stared up at the dark windows; he could almost pretend that she was still living there, still alive. He inhaled a deep breath. What could he do when the person who had become his oxygen was no longer around? It was as though every molecule of air had been coated with invisible barbed wire. He felt moisture budding behind his eyes again and he dropped his gaze back down to the wall. He rubbed his eyes, blinked a couple of times and took a deep breath, and then he frowned. There, in the dim glow of a lamppost, was a black mark against one of the bricks. He bent down to it and noticed the letters K and H written in black marker pen in the corner of the brick. They had been written in a shaky hand and the K was backwards. He poked it, confused. It was loose. An almost forgotten memory surfaced from the back of his mind. The sky brightened impossibly and he saw a younger version of himself sitting on the wall next to a young Alice. He held a skateboard in his lap and they were both in their school uniforms. Alice glanced back at her house but Talia hadn't come out yet and they were waiting on Hailey too.

'Are you ok?' Kyle said. Alice gripped the edge of the wall with her hands and swung her legs, knocking her heels against the wall.

'Yeah, it's just weird starting at a new school again,' Alice said.

'Queen's is OK, the teachers are pretty cool and most of the students are nice too.'

'Yeah, but I don't know anyone yet.' Alice worried her bottom lip with her teeth.

'You already know me and Hailey,' Kyle said. 'I won't leave you on your own. I'll introduce you to everybody and after school you and Talia should come with us all to the skate park. It's what we usually do when the weather is dry like this.' She blushed and smiled.

'I'm not much of a skateboarder.'

'You don't have to be, the girls just tend to sit and talk on the ramps anyways.'

'Oh.' A flash of disappointment crossed over her features.

'But I'll teach you if you'd like, I mean I can teach you how to skateboard.'

'Really?'

'Yeah, it's easy once you get the hang of it.'

'I don't want to do it if everyone will be watching.' Her cheeks glowed pink and she let her hair fall down and obscure her face. Her heels thudded harder against the wall.

'Well, we can go when no one else will be there. Sometimes I get up early and go there on the weekends, just because I know no one else will be around. It's when I practise most of my tricks and… when I fall a lot.' Kyle glanced away from her. Alice laughed.

'Yeah, OK. You can teach me then and I'll watch you fall a lot.' He looked up at her and saw her smiling and as her heel hit the wall again one of the bricks fell out and clattered to the ground.

'Shoot,' Alice said jumping up, and then the sky darkened and the young Kyle and Alice were gone.

Kyle blinked. His heart thudded in his chest and he gulped. How could he have forgotten that memory? How could he have forgotten the very first day she had started at school?

'Alice…' he whispered.

'There he is! Kyle!' he heard his sister call. His head whipped round and he saw his family along with several other neighbours walking down the street. He glanced at the brick one last time and saw the shaky letters of his initials, he hadn't imagined it, they were there. 'Kyle,' Hailey called to him. He looked back up and saw her waving, so he forced a smile and waved back.

THIRTEEN

Alice watched over him as he slept. She figured that this would be considered creepy or at least strange by most people, but she didn't have anywhere else to go, or anything else to do. She had been on edge ever since Halloween and Bonfire Night hadn't been much better. Her gaze was drawn to the second drawer under his desk. Kyle had shut her notebook with its single torn page in there and he hadn't opened it since. She had seen the letters on the brick wall outside her home but she hadn't written them, and she was sure it wasn't Talia. Kyle had stared at the wall with a tortured expression, but it had reminded Alice of the time she had sat there with him before their first day of school. She smiled fondly at the memory.

Kyle let out a low moan and she saw him twist under his duvet. His grey soul darkened and Alice jumped down from the desk. This was becoming a regular occurrence now. She sat down beside him and placed one hand over his chest and the other on his forehead. He winced but his eyes remained firmly closed. She reached out to him through her mind and soul. She willed him to be calm, she willed the nightmares away, and she willed the pain to stop.

'Alice,' he groaned and his soul lit up like fire - orange and crimson twisting around one another. He began to toss and turn violently; his legs shifted under the duvet as though he were trying to run. 'Alice,' he groaned again. 'Alice, don't… Alice… don't… leave me.' Alice grimaced and drove her mind straight into his dream.

He was running, running down a long white hallway and she

chased after him. He was wearing his sixth form suit again, but he wasn't at Queen's, he was at the hospital. She recognised the place and the distinctive smell of sick people and cleaning agents. The white hallway began to glow with a dim red glow and she turned her head to look out of the windows. She gasped and dread flowed into her hollow veins. Elbridge wasn't even recognisable anymore, the Earth wasn't recognisable. What greeted her eyes was a charred and blackened Earth with a blood red sky. She had seen this before. Ahrl had shown her this memory; it was the end of all humanity, life, and the afterlife. She gazed back at Kyle; he too was looking at the ruins of the planet but then he looked ahead again.

'Alice,' he yelled desperately down the hallway. Alice frowned and looked past him and then she understood. A single white door with a window stood slightly ajar at the very end.

* * *

'Wait for me!' Cameron called. Kyle paused and Cameron appeared.

'Why?' Kyle looked perplexed.

'I'm going to study too,' Cameron replied.

'You're going to study?' Kyle said, raising an eyebrow.

'Yes, don't give me that look,' Cameron said and then he darted into his bedroom and returned seconds later with his rucksack and coat. 'Let's go.' He grinned. Kyle shook his head and the two boys left the flat.

The last few days of November had brought snow and ice. Snow showers had fallen over the campus, the layers of snow partially melting during the day and then freezing again at night. This constant pattern of melting, refreezing and build up had made the walkways treacherous. Red Oak's staff and security had spent longs hours spreading salt and grit, and in some cases shovelling the hardened snow, but it was of little use. Alice could feel the drop in the air temperature, though she was in no danger of frostbite or hypothermia now.

'It's bloody freezing,' Cameron said, shoving his hands deep into the pockets of his coat and tucking his chin beneath his scarf. They passed some of the staff's cars parked on the sides of the slope; all of them were covered in a couple of inches of snow.

'Yeah, it's cold.'

'I've been meaning to ask…' Cameron paused and glanced at Kyle. 'What happened with you and Lara on Bonfire Night?'

'Really, you've waited this long to ask?' Kyle raised an eyebrow.

'Well, there's not been a good time to ask you about it. Lara said you freaked out and disappeared.'

'Nothing happened; I had a headache that's all,' Kyle replied. Cameron stared at him for a long moment but said nothing.

Cameron made a pile of physics books whilst Kyle searched through the business shelves. They found a table on the first floor and sat by one of the library's floor to ceiling windows. They worked pretty much in silence for the next few hours and then Cameron left and Kyle continued to study. As the evening wore on, the snow began to fall again and a niggling of unease crept into Alice's soul. She felt anxious about something but couldn't put her finger on it. She reached out tentatively with her mind; there was no Positive energy here at the moment, but there were two Negative souls somewhere within the lower levels of the library.

She looked at Kyle's soul; the colours around his core were dim and shrouded by his grey hues but they were moving sluggishly. He was exhausted and a faint orangey-brown told her that he was experiencing some mild pain, probably a headache. He yawned into the back of his hand and eventually stirred just after one in the morning. His eyes were glazed and bloodshot, and the shadows under them seemed deeper and darker. He picked up a stack of books and headed into the main belly of the library where rows of metal bookshelves stood and shelved them into their correct places.

As he picked up the last stack he noticed that Cameron had left his headphones and iPod behind. Kyle shook his head and returned the last of his books back to their original places and then packed up his belongings and wrapped himself up in a scarf and coat. He slipped Cameron's headphones over his ears and hit play. He put the slim iPod into his front pocket and headed out of the library with his rucksack slung over one shoulder. The stone steps outside the library were covered in fresh snow and Kyle gripped the icy handrail as he walked down them. The solid ground was treacherous so he chose to walk across the snow-caked grass rather than the slippery pathways.

Alice frowned as she watched him pick his way over the snow and ice, his feet slipping into little hollows. Music blared through Cameron's headphones and Kyle frowned as he held the iPod and flicked through the selection of songs. Alice grimaced at the wailing din and let her eyes wander nervously over the campus. The frosty cold air barely affected her but she recognised a cold, rotten, numbness. It was a heavy and crushing feeling, like earth being thrown into a grave. She looked up and squinted at the sky and her eyes widened. Hidden amongst the darkness of clouds she saw a miasma of Negative energy. Her gaze snapped back to Kyle, his footsteps crunched over the frozen ground and his face was lit from the dim glow of Cameron's iPod. He headed towards the bottom of the big sloping path which would take him back up to his flat.

A small cloud of Negative energy descended on Kyle, poking at his soul with wisp-like fingers and feeding off of his sadness. Kyle paused for a moment, shuddered and rolled his shoulders. *Oh no you don't.* Alice hurried over to him and recalled the laughter and the smiles, the many *I love yous* and past embraces; she could feel a tingling sensation firing through her, warming her soul. As soon as she was beside him the Negative energy around him shrank away from her presence. She kept close to him, eyeing the area and glancing upwards until she turned her head and caught something strange in her peripheral vision.

It was a blurry smudge at first, hardly noticeable against the shadowy background of night, but the more she focussed the more she saw. A black cloud of Negative energy revealed itself near the top half of the slope. It spilled out underneath a white van which had been parked on the side and was covered in a thick layer of snow. She watched as she heard something metallic crack and then the van shifted forwards a couple of inches at a time, like the shopping on a conveyor belt. She saw the Negative cloud swell as it grew and spiralled outwards; it traced a deadly straight line down the slope. Alice gasped in horror, Kyle was heading straight for its path. Out of habit she tried to grab hold of Kyle's arm, but her hand passed straight through him.

'Kyle, stop,' she said. She jogged in front of him and tried to push him back but he walked straight through her. Her head spun and her body flickered. She could hear the van grating along the snow, picking up speed and momentum. She chased after Kyle who was still frowning at Cameron's iPod. Music roared through the headphones and Alice waved her arms and hands frantically in front of Kyle's face. 'Kyle, stop. Look up. You need to stop. Look up for god's sake!' She stepped into the path of the van and threw a hasty glance in its direction. The van was moving faster now, too fast; it had closed half the distance and would finish the rest in less than half the time still. 'Kyle, stop!' she shouted. 'Stop, stop, stop!' Her voice grew more hysterical and panic overrode her emotions. She didn't care whether it was Negative or Positive, or some other unknown energy, but she reached out for something, anything that would give her the power to make him stop. She felt the sharp stab of a thousand needles as Negative energy began to flood its way into her soul. A flash of surprise crossed over Kyle's features. His jaw fell open and his eyes widened.

'Alice?' Kyle said. Alice thrust her hands out with all her might.

'Kyle!' she shrieked as a shocking burst of energy erupted from her hands and he stumbled backwards. He collided with someone in a tangled mess of limbs, and they both fell over onto the snowy verge.

Pain and peace, hurt and happiness, anger and love claimed her soul all at once. She saw the shock on his face as his eyes locked with hers. The van's bumper crumpled impossibly as it started to pass through her. Kyle's dark eyes were locked on hers and his face portrayed a thousand different thoughts. Alice's energy drained out of her suddenly. Her vision blurred with lethargy and an intense, high-pitched *ping* vibrated through her soul. She glanced down at her arms as they stuttered in and out of existence.

'Alice!' Kyle yelled. He leapt to his feet and Alice caught a glimpse of Sophia struggling in the snow behind him. Alice looked up at him and tried to offer him a smile, but she felt so weak and so tired. She had wanted this, she had been waiting for so long, hoping that one day he might see her, even though Ahrl had said it wouldn't happen. She lost all feeling, and then she couldn't hear, she couldn't see, she couldn't sense the energies, and every soul disappeared from her focus. Kyle's soul was the last to vanish from her mind, and then she felt nothing at all.

FOURTEEN

Sophia's eyes flew open. She threw herself out of bed, hitting on the light before she pulled on a pair of wellies. She was still in her pyjamas and she grabbed her coat and keys as she ran out. Her feet crunched and slipped on the snow but that didn't stop her. The vision had rudely roused her from her sleep; she had seen the van, and she had seen Kyle's body fly up and over its front bumper. *Is it going to happen now? Is it going to happen today? Has it already happened?* She didn't know, but what she did know, was it had been dark and the ground had been covered in snow, just as it was now. She struggled into her coat and the cold air pinched the back of her throat and cheeks as she hurried over to the library. She could feel the weight of Negative energy and she glanced up to see its dark clouds looming above. She approached from the back of the library, rounded a corner and then she saw them. She saw Kyle walking across the grass with his head bent over a small screen, she saw Alice before him shouting and waving frantically, and she saw the van sliding down the path, grating across the ice and snow.

'Kyle!' Sophia yelled. Her gaze fell on the headphones encasing his ears and she realised he couldn't hear her. She hurried over to him as fast as she could. She could see Alice panicking, they were almost at the path, almost directly in line with the van as it raced down the slope. Sophia pushed herself forwards, ignoring the cold bite of the snow as she used her hands to catch herself every time she fell. She saw Alice close her eyes and saw thin branches of Negative energy worm its way into Alice's soul. *What is she doing?*

No! Stop! Sophia was almost there, she reached for Kyle's shoulder and a flash of a memory passed through her mind, she remembered grabbing another young man's shoulder. Kyle stopped and he looked up, but then a blast of energy erupted from Alice and he staggered backwards. Sophia couldn't stop in time and both of them fell to the ground.

'Alice?' he said. *Wait? He can see her?* Sophia pulled him backwards just as the van tore up the ground inches before him. She heard a loud *thump* and the sound of cracking metal and glass as the van passed through Alice. There was a loud crash and Kyle was up on his feet. At the bottom of the slope the van had come to a stop by crashing into the university's strange, metal statue. Sophia felt a burst of cold Negative energy shoot outwards in all directions like a mini explosion. Alice knelt on the ground as Negative and Positive energy raged around her like a mini lightning storm. Her body stuttered as her soul tried to gain purchase on the living world and then she was gone.

'Alice!' Kyle shouted, his voice hoarse. The headphones had slipped around his neck. 'Alice!' He screamed her name so loudly and with so much passion. He scrambled to his feet and he half-ran and half-slid across the ground, wheezing heavily as he reached the van. It was a wreck, its inner workings spilling out through jagged cracks in its exterior. 'Alice!' he yelled as he ran round the van. 'Alice, can you hear me?' He gripped the sides of his head. Sophia heard the shouts of other voices and she saw the librarian and security staff hurrying across to them from the library and the Student's Union. She cursed again, she needed to get Kyle away from here, and she needed to process what had just happened. Sophia caught up to Kyle and grabbed him by his arms.

'Kyle, stop!' she said. 'There's no one else here, there's only you and me.'

'Alice!'

'Kyle. Look at me!' Sophia said as she forced him to turn

around. Kyle stared back at her with a wild and desperate look and then realisation hit him quickly and cruelly. He stared down at his hands, his chest heaving as his lungs begged for air.

'I'm sorry, I'm so sorry.' He gazed down at the ground. His eyes were wide but Sophia knew he wasn't really taking anything in.

'It's OK. It's going to be OK,' Sophia said. He looked down at her and his face twisted with confusion.

'Are you wearing pyjamas?'

'Never mind about that, just keep quiet and let me do the talking.' His eyes roamed blankly over the wreckage of the van and then landed back on Sophia. He nodded, turned off the iPod and slipped it into a pocket. Sophia zipped up the front of her coat and turned to face the approaching staff.

'Are you alright? Is anyone hurt?' one of the security men said as he reached them.

'We're fine, no one's hurt,' Sophia said.

'Jesus Christ,' a second security man said as he stopped beside them and surveyed the van. 'The heads of the university are not going to be happy about this, this statue cost them a fortune.'

'What happened?' the first security man said.

'I don't know,' Sophia said, she came up with a story on the spot. 'I was walking back to my accommodation and I heard this weird noise so I went to check it out. I noticed Kyle walking across to the chapel but he was looking at his iPod and the van was just sliding down the path all on its own. No one driving.' Sophia pointed to where the van had been parked. The librarian arrived with more security staff and asked the same questions. Sophia evaded them all and gave only the basic details.

'Did you see what happened to the van?' the first security man said looking at Kyle. Sophia saw the blank, dazed expression on Kyle's face and stepped in.

'He's still in shock,' Sophia said. 'Can we please go? There isn't really anything we can do now.'

'I guess, but hang on a sec. I better take your names and details, just in case the university want to get in touch with you,' the first security man said.

'Sure,' Sophia said. The librarian offered her a pen and Sophia, with a few gentle questioned directed at Kyle, wrote their details on a small scrap of paper. She handed it over, linked her arm with Kyle's and quickly marched him away before the security staff could change their minds. Sophia guided Kyle back towards her accommodation block and kept an eye out for Alice, but there was no sign of the Deykashee soul anywhere. *What the hell do I tell him? What does he even think he saw?* She glanced up at his face but he just looked lost and confused. She got him inside and sat him down in her bedroom.

'Just wait here, I'll be back in a minute,' Sophia said. She hurried down to the kitchen and boiled the kettle. Old Mabel appeared, sinking down through the ceiling.

'Why have you got one of the pair in your room?'

'I saw a vision and I stopped it from happening, that's why he's here,' Sophia said.

'He doesn't look so good.'

'Please don't go in there, he's a little unhinged at the moment.'

'He can't see me,' Old Mabel said. 'I was standing right in front of him and he didn't see me.'

'Well, I don't want to risk it,' Sophia said. 'He already thinks he's seen one ghost tonight.'

'We're not ghosts.' Old Mabel frowned but she vanished back up through the ceiling. Sophia found a tray, made two cups of tea and grabbed a packet of chocolate biscuits before she headed back to her room.

Kyle was sitting on the end of her bed with his hands clasped beneath his chin. He was still wearing his coat and rucksack and he still had the ridiculously huge pair of headphones around his neck. Sophia put down the tray, kicked off her wellies, removed her coat and replaced it with her dressing gown.

'Here,' she said offering one of the cups of tea, laden with sugar, to Kyle. Kyle looked up at her as though he were seeing her for the first time. 'It will help.' He stared at her and took the cup, sipped and supressed a gagging reflex; she guessed he didn't like sweet tea. She glanced around quickly, but there was still no sign of Alice; she had a really bad feeling about that.

'Thanks.' He coughed, wrinkled his nose and then took a deep gulp. Her phone buzzed on her desk with another incoming call, but she turned it on silent and ignored it; the family would have to wait for answers.

'Are you OK?' Sophia asked. Kyle shrugged. 'What happened out there? Who's Alice?' She knew the question was mean but she needed answers. *How much does he know? What could he see? Had this happened before?* Kyle winced as though she had stabbed him and stared down at his tea.

'I thought she was there. I thought…' Kyle shook his head. 'It's impossible. I'm sorry, I don't know what happened.' The cup of tea trembled in his hands. Sophia caught sight of her reflection in the mirror on her desk. She put down her tea and attempted to smooth down her frizzy bed hair. She picked up the biscuits and turned back to Kyle.

'Here, eat one of these,' she said. He took a biscuit and bit into it as he stared across the room. Sophia could still feel Negative's cold taint. It was different from the cold she felt during winter; it was a numbness that burrowed deep into your bones and seemed to suck all colour out of your thoughts. She gazed at his soul; the ghostly sphere revealed itself but it was impossibly grey. She struggled to see any of the other colours. 'You look tired,' Sophia said. There were dark circles like half-moons under his eyes. He glanced up at her briefly, his eyes sad and distant, and then he looked back down again.

'I've not been sleeping much lately. Nightmares keep waking

me and I can't get back to sleep again,' Kyle said. She knew what it was like to wake up from nightmares, only her nightmares were often reality and not fuzzy pictures formed by her imagination. He ate the biscuit and started to look around at her room. His gaze was drawn to the large pin board on the wall where she had put a couple of photographs, important things to remember and upcoming events. 'Are they your friends from back home?' Kyle gestured to one of the photographs.

'Yes,' Sophia said moving towards the board. The photograph was a picture of her best friend Annie, Annie's brother, and a young man in a wheelchair called Avery. Beside this photo was another photo of her entire family from a Christmas get-together a couple of years ago.

'Was he in an accident?' Kyle said, gazing at Avery.

'Yes,' Sophia said. She felt guilt pinch at her nerves; it was a memory which weighed heavily on her soul. She saw Kyle wrinkle his brow and wondered if he was thinking the same as she was, what would have happened to him had the van hit him?

'What's that?' Kyle said.

'What's what?'The bed creaked as he stood up, and he unpinned a piece of paper from the board. It contained some of her thoughts and notes on time, but she had been thinking about time from a deceased soul's perspective. Thankfully she had been careful not to mention deceased souls, but she had been meaning to do some more work on it. She was about to take it from him but then she stared at his soul, the grey was easing slightly, it was almost as if....

'This is interesting,' Kyle said.

'It's just some notes,' Sophia said. 'I've been trying to think of an alternative to the multiverse theory by using time.'

'You've written non-physical universes with a question mark, what does that mean?'

'Well, you'll probably think it's a little silly.' She wracked her brain for a suitable answer which didn't involve mentioning dead people, but she realised she could explain the mechanics of a soul, at least in part. 'It's to do with how we think. The way our minds have thoughts and can recall memories, and the way we can imagine things that don't actually exist. I wondered how the properties of the mind would fit in with time and if time itself was a bit like a super mind. I guess it would be a little like if humans were computers but we were all linked to the universe which was like a giant quantum computer. I want to try and explain it, solely from a time perspective.'

'You would have to include time as we know it, or rather space time into a combined theory,' Kyle said. The grey subsided almost entirely for a moment and all of his colours emerged in so many different shades and hues. His inner soul was so Positive, so pure, there was very little in the way of Negative energy.

'Yes, a theory would still have to encompass that, naturally. Imaginary time too,' Sophia replied, her eyes fixed on his soul.

'You think about these sorts of questions in your free time?'

'Yes.' Sophia nodded. 'I'm always asking questions, especially when there are indefinite answers.'

'Well, the string theory does explain the multiverse theory.'

'Theories,' Sophia corrected. 'There's more than one string theory, a lot more. I think it could be simplified, but I can't figure it out or make the maths work in my head yet.'

'True, though in any case, you would have to have some way of proving that your hypothesis was correct.' His soul dimmed again and the grey swarmed back over his colours.

'Perhaps someone might come up with a theory and prove it one day, someone totally unexpected.' She cast a sideways glance in his direction as the silence stretched between them. 'But for now it is the beginnings of a thought experiment at best.' Kyle nodded but she knew he had lost him, his soul was grey again, his mind sucked into his own thoughts. His soul had been so bright for a few moments, she realised then that Kyle still had a genuine interest in the unknown aspects of science. 'You seem very interested in physics for a business student, is that why you come to the guest presentations?' He looked at her, but the distance was back in his eyes.

'I should get going,' he said.

'Will you be OK? You can stay as long as you like,' Sophia said.

'No, I'm OK. I should go. Thanks for… well, you know.' He gave her an uneasy smile.

'No problem, I'm just glad I could help.' He paused and frowned.

'Why were you there, by the way? It was late.'

'Oh, I was leaving a friend's block. We…' Sophia glanced at the ground as she tried to come up with a believable story. 'We had a pyjama party and ate snacks and watched movies. I was on my way back to my block when I saw you outside the library.'

'Oh, do people still do that?'

'The younger students do, sometimes,' Sophia said. Kyle nodded but looked unconvinced as he headed towards her door.

'Hey wait, you might be interested in this.' Sophia pulled a slim book from one of her drawers. 'Here, you can borrow this.' She knew that her family wouldn't necessarily be happy about this, but it felt right.

'What is it?' Kyle said as Sophia pushed the book into his hands.

'It's a journal of sorts, it's where I write down all my crazy ideas and notes on physics, I just thought you might want to look at it.'

'Oh. OK. Thanks,' he said awkwardly. He shifted his rucksack on his shoulders.

'I can walk you back if you'd like…' Sophia bit her lip, he looked extremely pale.

'No, no-no, I'll be fine,' Kyle said. 'Er, here.' He picked up a pen from her desk and wrote his number on a sticky note. 'You can call me if security or whoever wants to talk to me about the van.'

'Sure.'

'Thanks for the tea and biscuits, and, err, thanks for the book.'

He gave her an awkward wave with her journal in his hand and then the door slid shut behind him as he left. Sophia moved over to her window and peeked out from behind her curtains. She watched as Kyle appeared in front of her accommodation and then he followed the path and disappeared out of sight. Her eyes darted up to the sky; she could see black shadows moving against the night sky. Her feeling of relief that Kyle had survived was overshadowed by a new concern. *What had happened to Alice?*

FIFTEEN

She felt heavy, as though she was falling. The cold darkness was lifting and she saw strange spots of lights floating randomly in her vision. Were her senses returning or was this an illusion? She tried to feel something but there was nothing, she was nothing. She still didn't know where she was or how she'd gotten here.

Little fragments of knowledge pieced themselves together in some distant corner of her mind as she recalled emotions. Then she remembered, living souls and deceased souls, and she was dimly aware that the living would feel fear if they were falling, as she was now, at great speeds into the unknown, but was she afraid? She remembered laughter and the warm, bubbling sensation the living felt somewhere in the middle. Living? Deceased? Which side did she belong to again? No it wasn't a side; it was a state of transition. Had she made that transition? Her mind was delirious, as though consciously aware of being asleep as she searched for her senses. She just felt peace, peace and warmth, and a familiar tingling sensation. Her eyes focussed on the darkness around her and she could see distant bright sparks, twinkling like little lights in the distance. No, not lights she realised, but stars, she could see stars, but… *I'm in space amongst the stars, that's not possible.* She gazed down at her body; there was nothing protecting her from space, her clothing was thin, it was a dress she realised, but dresses weren't suitable in space, you needed something much more substantial, something much more important. She felt something overpowering and warm seeping its way into her body form. Knowledge and memories all rushed at once to their lost places in her mind. She let out a gasp as images flashed behind her eyes. Suddenly all the answers appeared and she knew… she knew everything.

Kyle appeared in her mind and she saw his life, split into many lines, sprouting upwards like a huge tree. She saw all of the decisions and possibilities weave back and forth like webs and all of his potential future pathways. She saw futures where Kyle wore a suit and tie and sat in an office with hundreds of others, bent over computers and telephones. She saw distressing futures where Kyle wandered aimlessly with a sickness of the mind; in these possibilities he found doorways to death that Alice hadn't even considered. She shuddered involuntarily at the desperate look in his faded eyes before he threw himself in front of a train, off a bridge, onto the motorway. She saw futures where he lived alone, where he had partners, where he even had a family.

She saw futures where he travelled and futures where he became a recluse and withdrew from society. There were futures where the unbelievable happened - winning the lottery, gaining a massive inheritance. However, she noticed that he was never happy in any of these visions. She saw lots of empty glass bottles, and needles and pills for god knows what. She saw yachts, fast cars, and gadgets, shiny and new but cold, emotionless and largely unused. She saw women and men with greed and envy in their souls, dressed in fine garments but ultimately unhappy and unsatisfied with their lives.

There were so many possible outcomes, so many decisions for Kyle to make and for others to make around him, friends, family, strangers. Thin webs, which were fine and flexible but could never be broken, even by death. The dead left their marks on all paths. They were there and they always would be, as if woven into a tapestry of time and endless possibilities. She felt her heart sink into despair; in every future, even the ones where Kyle lived out a relatively normal life, there was no joy behind his eyes, no excitement in his actions, no happiness in his smiles. He was a machine, a robot, a zombie that lived a routine of the same hours every day, every week, every year.

She felt the flow of energy slackening; the futures were coming to an end and she was reaching the fragile end of the furthest branch. Kyle appeared for her again just as she had left him and she felt her face relax into a smile. He was sat by the lake at Fairhaven Park. A breeze tousled his hair, and she could almost feel the gentle air splitting against the hairs on her arms. He had a rucksack beside him, with his legs bent up and his elbows resting forwards on his knees. He seemed calm but he had drawn the inside of his left cheek between his teeth and his eyes were far away. She could tell that he was mulling over a big decision.

Alice wondered where his thoughts were as she glanced around at the familiar surroundings. She remembered sneaking out of the house one evening, long ago, and stargazing with Kyle. She wasn't sure why this spot was important now but it seemed to be the focal point for this particular future. Kyle looked at her then and smiled brightly. She clearly saw herself on the grass next to him; she was wearing the same creamy dress she had worn since her death, and she could see the pale golden hues of positive energy shimmering faintly over her skin. She saw both of their mouths moving but no sounds reached her shell-shocked state. The vision jumped forwards and she saw the rest of his future from this single branch; he could be happy she realised, he could change the world from this moment. She saw Sophia and Cameron, she saw labs and conferences, she saw scientists and high-tech equipment, she saw articles and news reports. She saw the face of a boy with blonde hair and blue eyes kneeling by a grave and gazing up at the sky.

The future disappeared from her mind too soon and her thoughts puzzled over all the knowledge she had been given. She felt her shoulders turn downwards, or was it upwards? Her whole body seemed to curve. Was she falling? Or flying? She could have been sailing on a cosmic ocean. She felt the invisible lines of time ripple around her, bending, bulging and compressing as she passed by. She felt the warmth of Positive energy coating her with its golden rays, glowing and pulsating over her pale skin. She wasn't alive, but she existed, and that was all she needed.

SIXTEEN

On the last day of the first semester, Kyle boarded an early afternoon train home to Elbridge. He sat at a table with four seats, with his holdall and rucksack occupying the seat next to him. A middle-aged man in business attire sat opposite. The train rattled relentlessly over the tracks and the other passengers in the carriage were going to great lengths to dutifully ignore one another. Last night's shift at Blue Bar had ended just after five in the morning and he had been woken again by another nightmare that he couldn't properly recall. It was infuriating; his memory teased him with fragments but nothing actually made any sense.

He caught his haggard reflection in the train window. Raw pink and charcoal smudges curved under his dark, bloodshot eyes. He looked away and tried not to think about the incident with the van, but by trying to avoid it, he inevitably found his thoughts caught up in it. *Did I really see her? Was she really there?* It had been so real, she had seemed so real. He shook his head. *Don't be so stupid Kyle, she's gone.*

Kyle's gaze wandered to his rucksack; it had been a last minute decision, but he had wedged Alice's book and Sophia's journal between a couple of business tomes from the library. His eyes kept travelling back to the bag, like an itch that couldn't be ignored. He closed his eyes and massaged the bridge of his nose as his head thudded dully. Sophia Leto entered his thoughts and he remembered the strange burning intensity in her dark eyes. *'Who's Alice?'* Her voice rang out loudly in the back of his mind. He stifled a groan and his eyelids fluttered open. He reached towards his rucksack and unzipped the main compartment. He hesitated for a moment, his fingers hanging uselessly above Alice's book as he debated the logic of looking at it.

The man opposite him coughed to clear his throat and shifted in his seat. Kyle glanced up at him and saw that he'd opened a large newspaper. Kyle's sub-consciousness made the decision for him and he plucked Alice's book from the bag and then set it down on the table in front of him. The silver artwork stared up at him, and he traced his fingers along one of the curving lines. She had drawn a maze, he realised, a circular maze, with his name at the centre, but the lines were not blocked, she had added her artistic flare to the curves and angles. There were dots and stars and little squiggles and pictures, some of the lines trailed off into thin slender points whilst others were more solid. His heart suddenly jumped from its ambling pace into a full out sprint as he turned to the front page. In Alice's delicate handwriting was written, *'For Kyle, on your 19th Birthday, love Alice x'*. Kyle stared at the blue-inked words. *My birthday? This was meant to be for my birthday?* His brain didn't even need to do the maths, he knew why he hadn't received this notebook. Alice had died four months before his nineteenth birthday. He felt his throat tighten and he blinked back the moisture smarting in his eyes.

He turned to the next page before his emotions could get the better of him but the page had been torn out. He frowned; the following page had the date the *20th January 2009* written in the top right corner and a photo stuck to the centre of him and Alice. The younger versions of themselves in the photo were sat close together on the ramps at their local skate park. They were smiling and their youthful skin glowed with healthy tans. Their eyes sparkled with uncontained happiness and contentment, an expression that was alien to Kyle now. He frowned as he fingered the remnants of the torn page. He flipped quickly through; there were more photos and lots of writing, quotes and hand-drawn sketches. He pulled out the loose page he had stuffed inside her book. There was a date in its top corner, *21st January 2009*. He flipped to the front of the book and let out a low breath, the date fitted perfectly before the following page. He lined up the torn edges, it almost fitted exactly.

His fingers trembled as he gazed between the photograph and the hand drawn sketch of their houses with a removals van outside. A droplet splattered onto the page, followed quickly by another and another. He sat up straighter and dabbed the moisture away from the sketch with his sleeve, then he dabbed his eyes and lifted his head as though gravity would roll the tears back into his eyes.

'Are you alright?' Kyle's eyes found the man sat across from him, peering at him from over the top of his newspaper. Kyle's face grew hot and he shut Alice's book quickly.

'Sorry, I'm OK,' Kyle said. He barely glanced at the man as he switched Alice's book for Sophia's journal and set it down on the table in front of him. *I don't even know why she bothered giving this to me, she should have given it to someone like Cameron.* Kyle frowned as he opened it. He flipped through the pages and found that Sophia's notes were all to do with time and how humans observe the universe. She had written notes on some of the basics of quantum physics; Space Time, Virtual Particles, Time Dilation, Dark Matter, String Theory and so on. In between these notes she had written questions to herself, *What is time? What is now? What would happen if a Photon could observe itself?* Sometimes she had stopped completely and started a new page in order to explore what seemed to be unrelated ideas from science fiction. She had drawn small diagrams of virtual particles popping in and out of existence and decaying particles splitting from one particle into two smaller, paired, particles.

He stopped on a page where Sophia had drawn a circle with a dot at its centre overlapped by what looked like a shaded star with numerous points, covering the dot and extending outwards into the circle but never reaching the outer edge. Some of the star's arms reached far from the dot, others were much closer. Beside this diagram she had written; *The circle is a slice through time and represents now. The shaded area displays all the thousands of physical possibilities open to any person in any given moment of time. The unshaded areas display all the imaginary possibilities, such as thought, that a person may have in any given moment of time. Some possibilities are more remote than others so stretch further away from the centre dot. Others are more likely so are only a short distance from the centre dot. In its simplest form, if you were to imagine a person standing in a flat field, they may choose to walk in any direction and think any thought, all possibilities are open to them just before they make their decision, though historical, personal and outside factors will make certain possibilities more likely than others. If the universe is aware of all possibilities, even the most remote ones, then it would also know the most likely possibility too. The passing of time would turn a possibility into fact, but then if this is the case, time must interact with all the knowledge of the universe. Does the universe observe itself?*

Kyle thought it through, he could imagine it. He could imagine himself standing in a field with the choice of walking in any direction and thinking any thought. In some ways the possibilities were endless, and he realised that it could be applied to any situation and moment in life. The physical body and world had limitations but what intrigued him was the idea of thinking any thought; thoughts could be limitless and infinite, and thoughts could change instantly from one moment to the next. Whereas walking would take time to get from one point to another, thoughts were almost free from time entirely. He thought back to what Sophia had said to him in her room on the night of the van incident but he couldn't remember it clearly. She had said something about simplifying the theories around multiple universes and the way the mind worked, *but what did she say?* He stifled a groan as he wracked his brain but that night was a blur to him. He studied her notes, absorbing every word she had written and examining every picture she had drawn.

He arrived at the small train station in Elbridge three hours later. He stepped onto the platform and groaned as he saw the thick layer of snow and ice; the winter weather had coated Elbridge too. His breath fogged up in front of his face as he made his way carefully out of the station and towards the main road. His home wasn't far from the station so he walked slowly along the snow-pocked pavements. He passed by the skate park he had frequented with his school friends and Alice, and paused on the path. The skate park was next to a lake, and further along there were tennis courts and a children's park. The lake was manmade and a sanctuary for waterfowl; there were a couple of walking routes around its shorelines. Today however, the edges of the lake were covered with a thin layer of ice and the ground was laden with several inches of snow. The waterfowl had all flown away or taken cover for the winter.

He felt a madness take over him, a sudden urge to go down to the ramps. He headed down some concrete steps and entered the skate park through a wire gate that had been pushed aside. The snow and ice had covered most of the grey surfaces, turning the dull and graffiti-heavy concrete into clean, cloud-like sculptures. He had always joked as a teenager that his heaven would feature a skate park. The cold air had already navigated the barrier through his jeans and claimed the skin beneath, and the snowmelt seeped its way up his legs and through his shoes. He headed over to the back corner and stared up at the ramp he had used for most of his tricks. It was the U-shaped ramp from his memories, and was almost as tall as Kyle; its smooth upper surface was framed by iron railings. He could remember many days skating up and down the curves of this ramp whilst his friends leant against the railings and sat on the edges.

A dull aching buzz grew in his brain and a low rumbling sound like the beginning of a storm was accompanied by the frantic rattle of a locked door. He gripped his hands into fists and bit down hard on his lower lip. New and vibrant images began to paint themselves over the featureless skate park, peeling back the layers of snow as though it had never fallen. He felt as though the images were reaching out for him, sucking him into a distant reality, and suddenly he was there, caught like a fly in the timeless webs of the past. Whatever nerves had surrounded and quelled this memory were suddenly overwhelmed and beaten back, the door flew open…

They were sat on the edge of a ramp in the back corner of the park, the sun was slowly making its way down to the horizon and sixteen-year-old Kyle still hadn't worked up the nerve to ask her out. Alice sat next to him as they spoke about their favourite bands; they had been listening to Vortex by Dead Souls as they discussed their dreamt-up explanations for the world and the universe, like they regularly did. He had been studying her closely all afternoon, the relaxed slope of her shoulders, the way the light made her brown hair shine like bronze wildfire, the consistent upwards curve of her mouth as she spoke to him and they laughed. He was amazed by her constantly, every second of every minute they spent together, and the other remaining time he spent wondering why she made him feel this way. Love was one of those things young guys pretended not to care about, even if they did, but Kyle found that love wasn't properly defined or explained. Most people were floundering after ideals when really the ideals were flawed. Love wasn't something you went out to find; if you were lucky enough, it found you.

'Alice…' he said. She stopped talking and looked up at him. 'I… would…I mean…' he stuttered horribly, and he felt his cheeks grow hot. Her deep blue eyes had captured his mind and he couldn't find the words he wanted to say. *No, it wasn't supposed to sound like this,* his thoughts scrambled frantically. 'Would you..? I mean… I'd like to…' His tongue tripped and fell as though his teeth were insurmountable hurdles. 'I've been meaning to ask…' His voice pitched awkwardly and he cursed his stupid voice box.

'Yes?' she said, confusion filtering into her eyes.

'Would you..?' He bottled it. 'Why do you keep a penny

collection?' he asked quickly. She raised her eyebrows. 'I've been meaning to ask you that for a while.' He turned his face away from her; he felt as though his cheeks were hot enough to cook with.

'It was my granddad's fault,' she said slowly. *Was that disappointment in her tone?* He glanced at her; she had her head down and her hands clasped between her knees as she spoke. 'He told me when I was young that lost pennies signified the dreams that people had abandoned. He said that I should collect them if I saw them on the floor and look after their dreams for them. Though never if they were in a wishing well or other such place.' She tilted her head towards him and smiled.

'Oh. That's pretty. Why did he tell you that?' Kyle asked, steeling his nerves.

'I found a penny in my grandparent's garden when I was really young; I thought it was treasure so I showed it to him.' She grinned. 'My granddad was silly, he liked to tease us and tell us things that weren't true and he used to make up stories for fun.' Kyle relaxed slightly and smiled back at her. 'He told us things like jam and jelly are actually slug slime, or snails could race, or that our crumpets had wormholes in them, and stupid things like that.' She chuckled and suddenly her eyes crinkled with sadness. 'He passed away a couple of years ago. Cancer.'

'I'm sorry,' Kyle replied. He reached out a hand to her and then snatched it back quickly before she could see. He didn't know what else to say, there was nothing else anyone could say.

'It's alright,' Alice said, visibly brightening. 'I had lots of good years with him and he even let me ride on the back of his motorbikes.' The heat vanished from Kyle's cheeks then; he didn't like the idea of her riding on a motorbike, they were dangerous. 'My grandma Jenny still lives in their house on the Isle of Arran. It's really pretty up there, though it can rain quite a bit.'

'Isn't that in Scotland?' Kyle asked.

'Yes, both my grandmas live in Scotland now. My Scottish

grandma lives near Larrick, that's half way between Glasgow and Edinburgh,' she said. 'My English grandma moved up to Arran with my granddad several years ago; most of the family live up north now.'

'Uh huh,' Kyle said, trying his best to keep up with all of Alice's family members; there were so many of them. He realised the daylight hours were fading and he still hadn't done what he had set out to do. He needed to ask her now or he feared he never would.

'Anyway, I just like to collect them,' she said. 'If I see a penny on the floor and I don't know who's dropped it then I'll pick it up and keep it. Most people think I just like to collect coins and save them up… and maybe I should save them up for my own dreams…' She looked distant then as she gazed out across the park, over the lake and to the trees on the far side. 'But it's just a piece of metal at the end of the day. The true value of money is when you can use it to help those less fortunate than you. I don't have that sort of money, but maybe I'll help someone else with their dreams.' She turned to him and smiled, her lips curving up and revealing her straight white teeth. In that moment he swore he could see the purest form of Alice then, the honest and caring Alice that was the foundation of her very being. She blushed and looked away from him. 'Would you… do you mind if…' she bit her bottom lip.

'What is it?' Kyle said. 'You know you can ask me anything.' He realised he was somewhat of a hypocrite; he couldn't even ask her the one question he had been wanting to ask for weeks now, but he reasoned that her question couldn't be as scary or as embarrassing as his. She turned her face away from him.

'Would you mind if I kissed you?' she said. He was staring at her, but he didn't realise it until she stole a glance in his direction and then gripped the side of the ramp to stop her shoulders from shaking. 'I'm sorry. I've ruined everything. I didn't mean to…' her words came out in a tumble as though a great dam had just burst in her mind.

'No,' Kyle said, reaching for her hand. 'No, I wouldn't mind.' He leaned towards her but then she closed the distance between them and kissed him. Surprise didn't even register with him completely until she pulled away a second later. Her cheeks were a deep crimson as she looked away from him and down at her shaking palms. He put his fingertips to his lips in a daze; he could feel the slight tingle of electricity, as though all of his nerve endings were sparking and his blood pumped furiously through his veins. He held both her hands, her eyes were wide and her face was glowing like a stop light. He didn't think about it, he returned her kiss. His lips moved softly over hers, their fleshy curves and angles gliding perfectly like liquid puzzle pieces. It was a sweet, conservative kiss, neither one dared to move too fast and deepen it further. He felt her fingers lace gently through his…

Kyle blinked back the tears threatening to spill from the corners of his eyes as the frozen skate park came back to him. That memory had been so real this time, almost as though he had been right there, reliving every moment of it. He felt as if he was living somewhere between consciousness and sub-consciousness, his mind hovering in the thick haze before sleep. He remembered that day at the skate park; of course he remembered that day. That moment had been one of the most important moments in his life; it had left an irreplaceable mark on his heart. *I shouldn't have come here.* He dug his hands into the pockets of his jeans. Time was cruel; the skate park would remain for many seasons to come unless it was purposefully removed from the site, yet Alice, Kyle, their family and friends, they would all pass by in a blink of an eye. The concrete would remain and it would hold a thousand secrets, new friends, conversations, falls and tumbles, tricks accomplished and… first kisses. These ramps had seen it all already and would watch silently for many years to come. He gazed sadly at the ramps and turned slowly as he headed back out; maybe his mind could chase the past, but he couldn't.

SEVENTEEN

Kyle's father worked in a large office on the other side of Elbridge. He was one of the managers of a successful company which sold tracking systems and devices to other companies. However, the competition was fierce and the company had a small army of employees who spent hours travelling up and down the country to various appointments. His father had asked him for help with some admin, and Kyle had found it difficult to refuse.

Kyle immediately recognised most of the faces as they entered the office. He had spent some of his holidays as a teenager and a year before university working with his father. Zack Smith, Tank's father, was the first to greet him.

'Hey, Kyle!' He smiled. 'Your father isn't making you study and work, is he?'

'Hey, Zack, no, I'm only helping for today.' He watched his father head to the back of the long office and into a smaller private office. Kyle settled down at a vacant desk next to Zack.

'How are you? How's Tank?'

'Oh, we're good. Tank's leg has been giving him a bit more trouble lately, it's never been quite the same since the accident but he's pushing through it like he always does.' Zack said. Kyle nodded, he knew about Tank's accident. It had been a bad tackle on a wet pitch. It had cost Tank his future as a professional footballer, and he had been on crutches for months. 'He coaches for a big sports group at Fairhaven Park now; the pay isn't great but he enjoys it.'

'You couldn't keep Tank away from football if you tried,' Kyle said. Tank had been the best footballer in the school; everyone had wanted him on their team.

'No, that's true,' Zack said. 'How's Hailey doing?' Kyle paused; his father wanted him to talk to Hailey about her future. Her grades were not as good as Kyle's and she had told him that she wanted to be a writer. Kyle was surprised; he had always known Hailey liked books but he had always considered it a hobby. Their father wasn't happy; he was concerned that it would be a bad career choice. Publishing contracts were hard to get and the costs of self-publishing mounted up; Hailey didn't have those kinds of savings.

'She's OK. She's confused about her career, but strong-minded,' Kyle said.

'Well, I know from Tank that she's been working hard.' Zack smiled and then the phone on his desk began to ring and he quickly answered it. Kyle logged onto the computer and opened up a spreadsheet containing the sales stats for the employees. It was easy and mind-numbing stuff; he just had to make sure the figures were correct and up to date. He left his desk to collect the relevant files from the storage rooms and passed his father's office on the way back. He could hear his father yelling at someone on the phone. He winced; it didn't sound good for whoever the other person was. He returned to his desk and saw that Zack was shaking his head. 'He'll give himself a heart attack at this rate.'

'What's going on?'

'Ah, there were a couple of big orders last week and a major mix up with fifty or so units. There are some angry customers, rude ones too. It's been stressing your father out.' Kyle saw that his father's face was red as he slammed down the phone. He watched him pick up a bottle of pills and swallow a couple with water. Kyle frowned.

He spent the rest of the day going through the data sheets and logging all the relevant pieces of information. He made many trips back and forth to the scanner and photocopier, and he passed a number of people working at their desks. Everyone seemed tired, their faces drained and their bodies stooped; he wondered how anyone survived long in sales positions.

Kyle's father stayed on after office hours and they didn't end up driving back home until later that evening. Kyle was exhausted and his brain was fogged up with figures and orders.

'Matthew, you can't keep doing this to yourself,' Stacy said as they came in through the door. 'And you dragged poor Kyle with you this time.'

'It's fine, Mum,' Kyle said as he loosened his tie and kicked off his shoes.

'It is not fine.' Stacy frowned 'And you're supposed to be taking it easy, Matthew, all this late night working is not good for your blood pressure; remember what the doctor said.'

'I'm fine, stop fussing,' Matthew said.

'Hey Kyle, Dad,' Hailey called as she came downstairs. 'Can we eat now? I'm starving.'

'You should have started without us,' Matthew said. Stacy shook her head.

Kyle helped his mum bring all the plates through from the kitchen and they sat down at the dining room table to eat.

'So Hailey, have you looked at any universities?' Matthew asked. Silence descended over the table, even the clinking of their metal cutlery on the china plates ceased for a moment.

'I've had a little look,' Hailey said.

'And?'

'There are some creative writing courses I could take…'

'Creative writing? What an earth are you going to do with that?' Kyle watched them wordlessly.

'Well, I'm going to write books,' Hailey said, gazing down at her food.

'Books?' Kyle noticed the cold disbelief in their father's tone.

'Dad,' Hailey said.

'I think you need to be a little more realistic, Hailey.' Kyle caught Hailey's gaze and a flash of anger sparked through her eyes.

'You didn't complain when Kyle decided to do physics rather than business like you wanted him to,' Hailey said. Kyle winced.

'Hailey,' Stacy said. Hailey cast a guilty glance at Kyle.

'Physics is very different from taking a creative writing course and writing books. It's science, you can get real jobs with science, and besides, Kyle decided against Physics in the end,' Matthew said.

'You can get real jobs with writing,' Hailey said.

'Like?'

'I could work for a publishing company. I could write articles. I could be a journalist.' Matthew shook his head.

'There are very few jobs in those fields; it would be incredibly difficult and the pay wouldn't be very good. Why don't you focus on getting a career elsewhere and then you can write in your spare time?'

'But I want to write books, I want a career in writing,' Hailey said.

'Hailey.' Matthew sighed. 'You need to be more realistic, you're not a kid anymore. You can't just publish a book and expect it to sell overnight. How many authors do you think actually make it?'

'I know it's hard but…'

'Don't you want to have a house? Go on holiday? Maybe even have kids one day?' Hailey wrinkled her nose.

'You need money, Hailey. It's the sad truth of the world but you need money so you can put food on the table and a roof over your head.'

'Dear, please, let's talk about this tomorrow,' Stacy said.

'I'm not hungry,' Hailey said. She stood up abruptly and left.

EIGHTEEN

Nightmares plagued his sleep and Christmas passed by quickly. On the day after Boxing Day Kyle sat revising at his desk in his bedroom at home. One of his large library books was open in front of him and he was scribbling away on a notepad. Not only did he need to learn and recite facts that he could find in books, he also needed to memorise references so he could use them in the essay question at the end of his exam. He lifted his arm and yawned into the back of his hand just as his bedroom door swung open. Hailey plonked herself down on his bed and then she was up on her feet again. It took him a few moments to realise that she was holding a book in her hands, no, Alice's book.

'Hailey, give that back,' Kyle said, standing and knocking his chair back.

'Why? What is it?' Hailey said jumping onto his bed and holding the book high in the air.

'Hailey, just give it back,' Kyle said tightly. He felt all of the muscles coil and twist between his shoulder blades and his heart stuttered uncomfortably in his chest.

'Is it a diary?' Hailey grinned and opened the book before Kyle could snatch it from her hands. The look on her face as he placed the book behind him on the desk told him that she had seen enough. 'That's Alice's book,' she whispered, her face frozen in disbelief. Her eyes flickered to his wardrobe, where she knew a box was hidden, containing some of Alice's belongings the Lynams had given to him.

'Yes, it's Alice's book,' Kyle said quietly. 'I think Talia sent it to me.'

'Oh.' Hailey's eyes widened. 'Oh, I'm so sorry, I should have said something. Talia emailed me weeks ago and asked me for your address. I thought she was going to send you a card or something, I didn't know she would send you this…'

'Hails, it's OK,' he said. 'It's not what you think. I haven't even looked at it all yet.' He frowned. 'Here, you can look at it if you want to.' He picked up the book and handed it over to her. Hailey accepted it cautiously, staring at him as he paced around awkwardly. He couldn't decide whether to sit or stand.

'Are you sure?' Kyle met her gaze and gave her a jerky nod as he settled back in his chair. Hailey sat down on the bed; she studied the front cover for a brief moment and then opened the book carefully. 'I thought you kept all of Alice's things in a box.'

'Most things,' Kyle said. He watched his sister and saw her smile as she slowly flipped through the pages.

'This is cute, Kyle,' she said, 'but why is this page torn?'

'I don't know, it came that way.'

'You should really finish looking at this, you know, it's beautiful.'

'I will, I just haven't gotten around to it.' Kyle avoided her gaze.

'You do know that there's another page that's missing, don't you?'

'What? What do you mean?' Kyle said. Hailey let him take the book. She was right, there was another missing page, it was the last page Alice had touched. After this missing page there were at least half, if not more, blank pages that hadn't been decorated or filled in any way. The book was incomplete. He ran his finger along the torn edge with its sharp angles and feathery curves as a question ran through his mind. *Where is this page? And why had it been torn out? Had she simply messed up here? Or was this page somewhere else?* The date on the page before was the eighth of June, just over a week before she had passed away. There was a sketched drawing of him on this page; he was sat down with his knees bent up gazing off across the creamy page. He had no idea what his sketched eyes were supposed to have been looking at, only Alice would have known the answer to that.

'She was a good artist,' Hailey said.

'I know.'

'What do you think happened to that other page?'

'She probably just made a mistake and threw it away,' Kyle said.

'But then why did she keep the other page she tore out?'

'I don't know.' Kyle sighed. 'Maybe she changed her mind?' He shut the book and turned away from her.

'Aren't you curious?'

'Curious about what?'

'Curious about what she put on that missing page?' Hailey said. Kyle paused. He craved anything from Alice, anything that he hadn't seen or heard with his own eyes and ears that had been born from her. All of the things she had owned that were now his, all the things she had written and drawn, they were all little connections to her, the only connections he had left. Of course he was curious, but no amount of curiosity would find the missing page.

'It hardly matters now, does it? It's probably in a landfill somewhere,' Kyle said.

'Kyle, that's cold,' Hailey said.

'Why are you so fixated on it?'

'I'm not, it's just…' Hailey bit her lip.

'Just what?'

'What if she left it somewhere?'

'Left it somewhere?' Hailey's imagination was already creating a stories.

'Yes, what if she left it somewhere and wanted you to find it?'

'Why would she do that?' He stopped, his eyes widened, he remembered the wall outside and his initials on the brick. *It couldn't be? Could it?* He put her book down and hurried out of his room.

'Hey, where are you going?' Hailey said as she followed him to the door. Kyle stopped to put his shoes on and Hailey slipped into a pair of wellies.

'Just…' he didn't finish his sentence. He marched out into the snow and stopped by next door's garden wall. The letter's 'K' and 'H' were still there, albeit a little faded now. He crouched down and poked the brick and sure enough it was the loose brick Alice had kicked all those years ago.

'Kyle, what are you doing?' Hailey said. He pulled the brick out and looked in the gap which had been left behind. He felt his fragile hopes deflate, there was nothing but dirt. He pushed the brick back into the wall and stepped back as Hailey crouched down to inspect the brick. He shoved his hands under his armpits and hopped from foot to foot. Neither of them had bothered to put on a coat, and the cold cut right through his t-shirt.

'K… H… Your initials,' Hailey said with a slight frown. She prodded at the brick and pulled it out to inspect it some more. 'These letters must be recent.'

'Huh?'

'It looks like it's been drawn by a child, or maybe someone who was really sick…' Kyle caught Hailey looking at him and he fought to keep any emotion from showing on his face. There was nothing there, he had just pulled it out and checked. 'Though I would have noticed this.' Hailey gestured at the brick and she too checked the gap before she slotted the brick back into its place.

'It's been there since Bonfire Night at least,' Kyle said as he watched his breath fog up in front of his face. His arms had turned pink.

'How do you know that?'

'That's when I first noticed it. I was thinking about… stuff.'

'OK, maybe I didn't notice it straight away, but I would have noticed if it had been there for years,' Hailey said.

'Sure,' Kyle replied. It was his turn to be sceptical. 'We should go back inside.'

'Yes, but these are your initials, I can see why you thought it could be.'

'There's nothing there. It's obviously just a coincidence.' Kyle began to walk away and Hailey looked back again.

'A coincidence, yeah, but your bloody initials are on this brick. How weird is the universe?'

'Bloody, bloody, bloody,' a small child's voice said cheerfully. Hailey's face paled as she stared back at Kyle; he had a feeling that her shocked features mirrored his own. They turned towards the sound to see a young boy, no older than five, in Alice's doorway.

'Kevin, I told you not to say that word,' an older voice scolded and then the door opened wider to reveal Kevin's younger sister and their exhausted-looking mother. The children were dressed in puffy jackets, wellies, gloves, scarfs and hats, ready for a day in the snow.

'Oh, hello Hailey and Kyle,' their mother said.

'Hello Mrs Holt,' Hailey replied with a bright smile. *Holt? Kevin?* It didn't take long for Kyle to piece the information together. *Kevin Holt, K H.*

'Aren't you two cold like that?' Mrs Holt asked as Kevin jumped out into their front garden with his sister tottering close behind.

'It's a little bit cold,' Hailey said. Kevin scooped up a pile of snow and turned towards his sister.

'Kevin, don't…' Mrs Holt cried, but it was too late. The boy flung the snow at his sister's face, and she began to cry, loudly. 'Kevin!' Mrs Holt said angrily as she marched out into the snow. She picked up the girl, scolded her son and forced him to apologise.

'We were just wondering who drew these lovely letters on your wall,' Hailey said, casting a sneaky glance at Kyle, once Kevin's sister had calmed down. Mrs Holt smiled and rolled her eyes.

'Yes, Kevin learnt his letters a few months ago, and he also took a fancy to drawing on the walls.'

'Oh,' Hailey said.

'Yes, oh,' Mrs Holt replied. 'He drew all over the walls in the dining room, and he even drew on the wall behind the sofa in the lounge.' She shook her head as Kevin's sister squirmed in her arms. 'Heaven knows where he got a marker pen from, his father probably left it out.' She tutted and set Kevin's sister down. 'I'm glad I was able to stop him before he added the entire alphabet.' She looked at Kevin with a friendly scowl.

'My wall,' Kevin said proudly with his hands on his hips. Hailey laughed and Kyle forced a small smile.

'We've been talking about rebuilding this wall for years now, but we never seem to have any time anymore.' She sighed again and glanced quickly at her children. 'You'll catch a cold stood out here like that,' Mrs Holt said as she looked at Kyle.

'Ah, my brother is not well known for his sense,' Hailey said. Kyle shot her a scowl and turned to head inside. 'I hope you had a good Christmas,' Hailey added as she followed her brother and waved.

'Yes, you too, Hailey, say hello to your mother for me,' Mrs Holt said and waved back.

'Will do,' Hailey replied as she stepped into their house and shut the front door. Kyle kicked off his shoes and headed up the stairs in silence. He felt so silly for thinking that Alice would have left him a page to find, and for thinking that it would be in a wall of all places. 'Kyle?' Hailey said, he could hear her following him up the stairs. 'Kyle, are you OK?'

'I'm fine. It was just Kevin.'

'I know that but…'

'There is no but. Kevin wrote his initials on the wall, that's all there is to it.'

'But the page is still missing.' Kyle didn't reply, he just needed to be alone. He reached for his bedroom door handle. 'I'm going to email Talia, maybe she knows something,' Hailey said.

'OK, sure.' He opened the door and turned to face her.

'Are you sure you're OK?'

'Yeah. I'm fine, don't worry.' Kyle shrugged and then smiled.

'OK.' Hailey didn't look convinced but she left him and disappeared into her bedroom. Kyle kept the smile fixed to his face until he heard her door shut and then he let it drop and he slowly closed the door to his bedroom. He leant his head against the doorframe, closed his eyes and took a deep breath.

NINETEEN

Ahrl stood within the garden again; his ancient mind had selected memories and thoughts in order to create this reality. He could erase it and construct a completely different reality instantly if he wanted to. Soft, grassy hills stretched out around him towards the horizon where they broke against a deep blue sky. Tiny golden and purple flowers dotted the ground and he stooped down to pluck one from the grass. The garden was more like an infinite meadow, though no animals roamed here and they never would. Ahrl straightened up; Alice had vanished and the rest of the Thirteen had reluctantly deemed their plans void. There was nothing they could do now. One minute she had been there, the next minute she was gone and he couldn't sense her soul anywhere. It had been unlikely that Kyle would have found the correct path in the first place, but now it was surely impossible.

He sighed. Everyone had many paths through life; doors opened and closed all the time, from the moment you were born to the moment you died. The only difference was that some people were highlighted in the fountain, and others were not. Ahrl's sapphire eyes darkened as they flickered to his left and gazed upon a small rise in the distance. The fountain stood there, their only guide for the future of mankind.

The soul who had created the fountain had been lost long ago, along with billions of others from their world. The creator's mind had been great, powerful beyond anything their species had ever known or seen and, because of this, no one had listened to him.

No one had paid any attention to the creator's warnings; they had written the soul off as a crank, a crazy person, a person whose voice was better left unheard. How wrong they had all been, and how many had now slipped from existence because of their ignorance. Everyone's voice held importance; it had taken the total destruction of their world, the complete annihilation of their species, and uncountable years for Ahrl and the rest of the Thirteen to realise this. Ahrl remembered the fighting, the despair and the chaos. He remembered how his planet had been ripped apart by forces that were out of their control. Desperation had formed wedges between their people, the fight for survival overriding compassion and logic. The last few souls from their home world had been doomed before they had even had a chance.

Ahrl opened his eyes as he rotated the tiny golden flower between his thumb and forefinger. Thin tear tracks like liquid diamonds made pathways down his long face. Humanity was heading for the same fate at an impossibly fast rate. Mankind had learned so much in such a short space of time. Their technology had advanced faster than the technology from Ahrl's world, though they were not quite as advanced, at least not yet. But they were young, they had barely existed for a few seconds on the universe's clock and already they were heading for destruction. There had been both Positive and Negative souls on Earth throughout the centuries, people who had changed the course of human history with a single decision, simply because they had been in a particular place at a particular time. They hadn't done it alone either. Their friends, family, strangers, even children had unknowingly guided these individuals with their own decisions.

The majority of people would never make history-changing decisions, but just because they weren't a catalyst for change, didn't mean that their decisions didn't mean anything. Even the slightest decision could have great or disastrous effects on the future. It may be that someone would do something as innocent as smile, which would brighten someone's day, which in turn could lead that person to give good advice, which would then work its way up through a chain of people until it reached someone who held a position of power, who would then execute that advice and, as a result, something Positive would happen in the world. It was as simple as that, but the balance was fine; similarly, it could happen in reverse and it often did. An ill-timed hateful gesture or an angry word could cause a Negative result. A combination of different scenarios could lead to peace or war, and often the biggest decisions were not made at the best of times.

Ahrl felt a crushing sadness against his soul and he had to fight to control his emotions. They didn't know why Alice had vanished and they feared the worst fate had befallen her. The timelines had jumped forwards and the fountain now focussed on new souls, people who hadn't even been born yet. However, even if the deceased souls could help these new souls to make positive decisions, their decisions would not prevent the devastation to mankind in the way Kyle's and Alice's would have. They would merely delay the inevitable. It would be a repeat of what had happened to their world, only this time they would be watching it unfold before them as opposed to being wrapped in the middle of it. There would be mass panic and the afterlife would lose all connections to Earth, causing them to drift aimlessly through space in search of another planet with conscious life. They had been lucky once, the fountain had guided them, but he wasn't sure they would be so lucky again.

He became aware of a flutter in his soul, accompanied by the warm gentle heat of Positive energy. Ahrl's ancient consciousness prickled and all of his seven senses stretched out beyond his soul, and beyond the confines of his imagined body. Something small had disturbed the timelines again, sending a ripple through the dimensions of time and causing the balance to waver along the dividing line. This was unexpected, yet desperately needed. Instantly, he placed himself next to the fountain, and then gazed down into the pool. He let out a low, long breath as he slowed down his thoughts to the gentle pace of a trickling stream. Colours formed and blended together across the fountain's surface, *Alice, Kyle.* The tremors of clarity wracked through his soul. He reached for her immediately, sending out the energy from his core through the pathways in his mind, and then outwards from the shell of his body and into the universe beyond. He guided his energy with a mere suggestion and found her quickly; she was amongst the stars. He could see her in his mind and he focussed all of his will and intent on her, wrapping the lines of energy around her and forming a net, then he pulled her back from the edge. Alice still existed.

She appeared before him suddenly and fell to his ground with a *thud*; her body stuttered wildly as she faded in and out of existence. She groaned and rolled on to her back and stared up at the sky through cracked eyelids. Her hair pooled out around her head like a halo, glinting bronze in the light. He saw Negative darkness in her slowly dissipating and lifting from her body like smoke trails.

'Alice?' Ahrl said as he stood above her. She opened her eyes and sat up quickly.

'Where am I?' she asked as she whipped her head from side to side and then groaned and clutched her forehead.

'You're in the garden,' Ahrl replied smoothly. He had never heard of a soul being claimed by Negative and then making it back to Positive before. He realised she must have been teetering on the fine line between the two, bouncing back and forth too quickly to be claimed by either side.

'I thought I was dead,' she said slowly. 'Like real dead, not just afterlife dead.'

'You vanished. But it seems you must have been on the very edges of both forces.' Alice pulled a puzzled expression as she looked up at him; she was remarkably calm for someone who had almost lost her entire existence. *Had she done this to herself?* 'We couldn't sense your soul,' he added.

'How long have I been…' she paused as she searched for the right term, 'absent?'

'Weeks, maybe months, I'm not totally sure. What happened to you, Alice? What did you do?' Ahrl said. Alice looked at her hands and frowned.

'I didn't actually do anything, but I wanted to.' Alice got to her feet. 'Is Kyle OK?'

'Yes.'

'I guess I should start at the beginning and then we can see if we can make any sense of it,' she said.

'That would be a good idea,' Ahrl said, inclining his head once.

Alice took a few moments to order her thoughts. She explained the disturbance she had felt right at the beginning of Kyle's last year. She talked about the grey emotions surrounding Kyle's soul, making it difficult for her to use any form of Positive suggestion, and inevitably making it easier for Negative to screw things up. She talked about her suspicions concerning Sophia Leto and she talked about her notebook which Kyle had received in the post. She spoke about Kyle's nightmares and studies, how he had been plagued by Negative in his dreams. She explained about the near miss at Halloween and how even then, Sophia Leto had been acting strangely and eventually she came to the incident with the van. She described the Negative energy and its line of intent, she admitted to her feelings of panic and fear and she reluctantly told Ahrl how she had managed to push Kyle out of the way. Alice then described her state after the event and how her awareness had returned slowly, and then she spoke about the futures for Kyle which had presented themselves one after the other. When she had finally finished describing the very last possible future scenario for Kyle she gazed down at the floor and began to twirl her thumbs around one another.

'Interesting,' Ahrl replied finally.

'I'm sorry. I know I'm not supposed to interfere, but I just couldn't let him be hurt or…' her words trailed off. Ahrl rubbed his jaw.

'You were incredibly lucky, Alice. Manipulating things in the physical world requires Negative energy and as you know, that takes a terrible toll on the soul. You could have been lost to us forever.'

'I know.'

'You saw Kyle's genuine future pathways. I don't know how you managed that without the fountain, but you did.' She did a double take on her surroundings and panic flashed across her face, their reality distorting slightly as though it were experiencing an extreme heatwave.

'Have I crossed over completely now? Can I go back?' she asked desperately. Ahrl frowned.

'I don't know,' he said. There had never been a scenario like this in the afterlife before. 'Your energy levels are still too low to return. We will need to speak to the others, they probably want to know what has happened, if they don't already know, of course.'

'Do they know I'm back?' Alice asked.

'Well, I sensed the disturbance you caused so I'm sure they did too,' Ahrl replied.

'I caused a disturbance?'

'All the time.' Ahrl grinned.

'Do you know who Sophia is?'

'I do, she is another troublesome soul, but I'm afraid I can't tell you much there right now. The fountain has been quite indecisive lately.'

'Why?'

'Something changed and a couple of well-timed and well-placed suggestions have come to light. There's been a remote possibility thrown into the mix for Kyle's future, an anomaly of sorts. It was something which we didn't think was possible before, but now, it is.'

'What? What is it?' Alice said.

'I think you know what it is.' Alice frowned but slowly, realisation dawned upon her.

'My notebook?

'Yes.'

'But why?'

'Because it could make him stop, and think.'

TWENTY

The festive period for Sophia was different. The Letos celebrated both Christmas and New Year as a family and with a few select friends. However, just because a large portion of the world was on their holidays, there was no respite from their gifts. In fact, Sophia had spent most of her time deep within visions and disagreeing with everyone.

A small Christmas tree stood in the corner of the lounge, its white lights flashing slowly. Sophia's uncle and aunt had come back from Dharamsala in India for a brief visit; they were helping the monks there. Elias, Sophia's brother, had just recently returned from America; there was a girl out there who passed regularly through their thoughts.

'So how is she?' Flo asked Elias.

'Fine,' Elias replied. 'I stopped a couple of Negative souls from reaching her, but she was completely oblivious to it all. She's a semi-famous blogger now and has been picked up by an American fashion magazine.'

'A fashion blogger?' Sophia asked incredulously. It didn't sound like the occupation of someone who could help the world.

'Yes, little sister, not everyone out there can be a scientist like you.' He grinned. 'Though I have to admit, our work is a little underwhelming at times, it would be way cooler if we had some sort of weapon, or fought actual demons.' Flo shook her head and tutted.

'Your imagination is too big for your head sometimes; you

wouldn't want any of those things to be true. Besides, the real demons are within the mind.'

'Yes, but most people have psychologists to deal with those,' Elias replied. He pushed his long, dark, unruly locks out of his eyes. Sophia laughed.

'We're hardly superheroes; we can't even show most people what we see, but we have a moral duty to help, even if it is only one small step at a time,' their father said.

'Cassie, Paul, how is his Holiness?' Flo asked, ignoring Elias and turning to their aunt and uncle.

'Travelling a lot,' Cassie replied.

'Still going strong for his age,' Paul said. 'The monks are doing all sorts of scientific research up there, some of it Sophia would be interested in.'

'What about Kyle, Sophia?' Flo asked.

'He's OK, despite the near miss with the van,' Sophia said. 'His soul is still incredibly grey and I still think he saw Alice.'

'We must bring him in,' Elias said. 'If Kyle truly did see Alice then he shares our gifts.'

'That might be our only option,' their father agreed.

'Let's not be too hasty,' Flo said. 'He had a nasty shock; he could have seen anything and he would have believed it.'

'Gran, he was adamant that Alice was there,' Sophia said for the umpteenth time. 'You should have seen him - he was frantically looking and calling for her.'

'Maybe, but Alice is gone now, Sophia. We've had no memories, no visions, no dreams, nothing. I'm sorry.'

'We thought she was gone for good once before and she surprised us by coming back. I was right about Red Oak.'

'Yes, you were right,' Flo said. 'But crossing over Positive and being a Deykashee soul claimed by Negative are two completely different things. She's not coming back this time.'

'But…'

'No buts, Sophia. Not this time. We have to be realistic.' An uneasy silence fell across the room.

'We should watch him regardless,' Elias said finally. 'If he saw Alice, he may see others, and if that's the case we'll need to keep an eye on him.'

'Elias is right, Mother,' Cassie said.

'Yes, yes.' Flo nodded unhappily. 'Sophia can't transfer now anyway; she will complete her master's at Red Oak and keep an eye on Kyle.' Flo looked directly at Sophia as she spoke. 'I would suggest that you watch him from a distance and be less involved, we don't want a repeat of last time.' Sophia winced at her grandma's words, she knew she had screwed up once before. She had to live with the guilt every time she saw Avery and his crippled legs.

'That's going to be difficult,' Sophia replied. 'I gave Kyle my journal.'

'Your journal?' Flo said.

'Yes, I gave it to him after the incident with the van.'

'Is this your journal with all of your physics theories?' Elias asked, sitting up straighter.

'Yes.'

'But…' Elias' face paled. 'Doesn't your journal contain some of the theories for the afterlife?'

'Sort of,' Sophia said.

'Sophia, this is dangerous; you know how people react to our knowledge and gifts. We've tried to talk to people before about what we know,' Flo said.

'Don't worry, I've been careful. This journal doesn't mention any of our gifts, or the afterlife, or souls. It only talks about time and how humans exist and observe the universe. Kyle seemed interested in it and it felt like the right thing to do. I thought that maybe if he read my notes he might reconsider picking up physics again.'

'We definitely need to keep an eye on him now,' Elias said.

'You're right, maybe we should send Elias back with Sophia,'

Flo said. Sophia was about to protest; she wasn't a child anymore. She didn't need Elias to look after her. A spark of hot energy shot down her spine and she gripped the side of the sofa. An image jumped into her mind and knocked out all of her other thoughts. A man was lying on the floor of a small cramped room, lined with shelves and files. She then saw Kyle in an exam scribbling away as the minutes ticked by, then a sea of people dressed in black, a gravestone, and Kyle dressed in a suit amongst the mourners. His face was devoid of all emotion; he wasn't crying but he wasn't truly there either, whatever small shred of Kyle that had been left was now completely gone. The images faded just as quickly as they had arrived and she found herself staring at her grandmother.

'What was that?' Sophia asked, blinking repeatedly.

TWENTY-ONE

Talia did reply to Hailey's email, but she couldn't tell them anything that they didn't already know. Talia had found the notebook amongst Alice's belongings in a box in the attic and since it had Kyle's name written on the front of it, she had sent it across right away. She knew nothing about the torn pages.

The days drew on and the nightmares were just as frequent as always. Kyle stared blankly at the champagne flute in his hand. The New Year was about to begin in… he checked his watch, thirty-five minutes. They had been invited to his aunt's house this year and the whole family had descended on the smallholding. His Aunt Claire lived just twenty miles to the southeast of Elbridge, and owned a country-style house which had a couple of acres, several stables, and horses.

Kyle's younger cousins were sitting on a large rug on the floor, playing a game on a large flat screen television. Kyle stood behind the brown leather sofa with half an eye on the television; his grandparents had gained first dibs on the sofa and armchairs due to their age. Out of the corner of his eye he could see his uncles chatting merrily away, discussing the latest sports results. Kyle grimaced. Alice notebook's and missing pages filled his mind with strange questions and confused feelings. He had spent the last few days trying to revise for his upcoming exams but at his thoughts had derailed themselves and wound up on Alice. His eyelids tightened as she flashed through his mind; her face and smile were like dazzling sunlight tearing through his grey clouds. He gazed down at his fizzy alcohol and was wondering if he should upend his glass when a heavy hand fell on his left shoulder.

'So…' his father's low voice rumbled. 'How are you, Kyle?' Kyle turned to face him.

'I'm good,' Kyle said.

'How's the studying coming along?'

'Fine.' Kyle shrugged.

'Good. One year left now, keep up the hard work.' His father squeezed his shoulder and then went off to join Kyle's uncles' conversation. Kyle felt his insides twist. *Yes, one year left* but the thought brought him no warmth or excitement. He watched his father go and was relieved that he had finally switched off from work long enough to relax for a few hours. The room was hot and Kyle needed some air. He left his glass on a small side table and picked up his coat as he headed out the front door.

Kyle eased open the door, trying to be as quiet as possible, and he stepped out onto the porch. Hailey was sitting on the step below his feet. She glanced up at him as he shut the door behind him and then went back to staring across the snowy driveway.

'Oh, hey,' he said as he sat down next to her.

'Hi.' They sat in silence for a few moments and then Hailey turned to him. 'You know I'm sorry about what happened over dinner a couple of weeks ago, before Christmas.'

'What are you talking about?' Kyle said.

'When Dad was lecturing me about writing and I brought up you and physics.' Hailey looked down at her hands.

'Oh, that.'

'Yes, that. It's been bothering me ever since and I just wanted to tell you that I'm sorry.'

'Don't worry about it. I know you were angry.' Hailey sighed.

'How can I get Dad to listen to me? He won't even entertain the idea of writing.'

'He's just worried about you, Hails. We all are,' Kyle said. 'He's just trying to help.'

'I know that, but every time I try to speak to him he just shuts me down or gives me that look, you know, the one where you know he's not happy and you feel stupid.'

'I know what you mean.' Kyle chuckled.

'It's annoying.'

'Why do you want to write?'

'Well, I enjoy it. I like being able to build worlds and characters. I feel like I have something to say but as I've become older I've realised that I'm not a natural speaker. I can't convey my ideas and thoughts through the spoken word so I write them down. Stories are much more powerful, they're personal, and you can weave all your secrets and concerns into a story. When I read other books it makes my imagination fire up and I just want to write something better, I want to be able to write something that others will enjoy and say, *wow*. Sorry, I'm probably not making much sense, am I?'

'No, it does make sense. It's just not something I've ever thought about before.'

'You don't read much, do you?'

'Only text books.'

'Can I ask you something? You don't have to answer if you don't want to, I know it might be difficult.'

'You can ask me.'

'Why did you want to do physics?' Kyle let out a deep breath. 'Sorry, I shouldn't have asked. I'm sorry.'

'No. It's OK,' Kyle said. He stared out across the fields and rubbed his hands together as he thought about how to reply. 'I didn't choose physics just because of Alice. I used to feel excited when I studied physics. I used to enjoy thinking about all the strange questions in the universe and imagining that I could find an answer. It was a passion, I guess. The more I learnt the more I wanted to know. The idea of discovering something new or coming up with a new idea that others accepted, used to motivate me.'

'And now?'

'Now it just makes me sad.' Kyle knew this was true, he couldn't think about anything physics-related for very long without his thoughts somehow trailing back to Alice, but if he was completely honest with himself, Alice was never far from all of his thoughts.

'How I feel about writing, is how you used to feel about physics.'

'You know Dad isn't trying to be cruel. He just wants to know that you're thinking about your future seriously. Even if you do write, you'd have to find a publisher.'

'I know,' Hailey said.

'You should really consider doing a degree that opens doors for you.'

'I'm not even sure I want to go to university; what's so good about being in all that debt anyways?'

'Hailey...'

'And even school, school doesn't teach you anything about the real world; it teaches you to recall facts. It's a shame English doesn't teach you how to write books or articles or about journalism. It doesn't teach you how to proof read or edit, the things you'd need even for university or office work. It should teach publishing and opportunities.'

'I know, but school is important,' Kyle said.

'Yes, it is, but we've been doing it all wrong. It just seems out-dated.' She hugged her knees to her chest and frowned at the snow. They fell silent again for a few long moments; they could hear their cousins laughing and the adults chatting. Kyle could smell the warm pastry from the mini sausage rolls cooking in the oven. 'It's Alice's birthday soon, isn't it?'

'Yes,' Kyle said. He had been trying not to think of it but it had been the only thing on his mind since Christmas.

'Are you going up to visit her grave this year?' Hailey said. Kyle stiffened. *Grave.* It was so cold, so final, so definite.

'I don't know. I haven't decided yet,' Kyle replied, his warm breath fogging up in front of his face.

'I'm going to light a candle, but if you want, if you decide to go, I'll come with you.'

'Maybe, but we've both got exams.'

'I can take a day out for that. It's important,' Hailey said. 'Mum said you might want to go up on your own.' Kyle saw a faint flash of gold cross over Hailey's irises and he blinked twice.

'I'll think about it.'

'OK.' Hailey nudged him with her shoulder. 'I'm proud of you, brother.'

'What for?'

'For talking about Alice again, it's… different.' She smiled a thin sad smile, but it was still a smile. 'I miss her too.' Kyle nodded, not trusting himself to speak, and Hailey sighed as she rested her head on his shoulder.

'Come on, we better go inside and see the new year in.' Kyle hugged Hailey's shoulder and they stood up and shared a brief smile before going inside.

Kyle chinked glasses with his relatives and was embraced in many hugs and sometimes kissed on the cheek. He didn't know why people insisted on celebrating the end and start of the year. Most people carried the same failed resolutions and promises forward from the previous years anyway. He didn't usually see the point in making them, but as his grandma kissed him on the cheek, he realised he did have a resolution of sorts. The idea had been planted into his head, so he silently promised himself that he would visit Alice's grave.

TWENTY-TWO

Kyle returned to university and the day after his last exam he boarded a train to Scotland. Alice's body had been cremated a week after she had died. Her parent's marriage had been difficult from the start; even Alice herself had said she couldn't believe they had stuck it out so long. After Alice died, the stress and pain of the situation didn't help to bring them together, it just pushed them further apart. It was inevitable really, and they had filed for a divorce. Alice's father eventually took half of Alice's ashes back to his Scottish roots and interred them next to his father's grave. Elaine and Talia, moved to the other side of the world for a new start in Australia shortly after.

Kyle set down a bouquet of white roses on the empty seat next to him. He pulled off his scarf and gloves and tucked them into his rucksack, and then he pulled out Alice's notebook, sat down and flipped through the pages. He recognised a lot of the drawings and doodles; she had drawn similar things in other notebooks, on scraps of paper, and on her hands. There were a couple of realistic sketches of himself too and one of Alice; she had a way of capturing the life in people's eyes with her drawings.

He paused on a page where Alice had drawn a vortex spiralling up through the middle of a page. She had written all the lyrics to The Dead Soul's song, Vortex, next to this sketch. He scanned the first few lines but he knew the song off by heart, he had heard it a thousand times. They had even gone to see the band at a small gig in London. *Look for possibilities, you're the vortex surrounding me. Burning pathways in my mind, we must have travelled a thousand times.* The song was playing in his head now, he could recall the deep soft tones of the lead singer's voice, the twang of the electric guitar, the deep tones of the bass and the beat of the drums. He could hear it all perfectly inside his mind, as though he were sat listening to them playing live right in front of him.

'Possibilities,' he murmured under his breath. He had recalled reading that word in Sophia's journal. He pulled the journal from his rucksack and opened it to the page with the diagram of the circle and the strange star. He put the two books side by side and let his gaze flick back and forth between the two pictures. *Vortex, star, circle, vortex, star, circle, vortex, circle.* An idea struck him. He flipped to the next blank page in Sophia's journal. *What if it's not a circle, what if it's a vortex?* He drew the rough shape of a vortex. *A slice through this vortex would be a circle, but that's not how humans recognise the passing of time. Humans recognise the passing of time on a linear scale, a straight line from the past, to the present and into the future.* He drew a line right down the centre of his vortex and realised he had not one, but two interacting timelines.

His nerves felt jittery and his fingers trembled, not from the cold but from excitement, something he hadn't properly felt in years. He felt tender illumination shine through the dullness inside; for the first time in years he felt excited by an idea. *Sophia's stars, no, all the possibilities, are inside this vortex. Each loop of this vortex would relate to a single moment in time and each loop would contain every possibility in that one moment.* That was what multiple universes were; there was a theory that stated every possible version of you existed in other parallel universes, but what if it was simpler than that? What if every possible version of you was just another possibility on one single loop in this second timeline Kyle had drawn? He started to draw more ideas and cross sections through his spiralling vortex, thinking of the big bang and what time was like before. His thoughts wandered down numerous pathways as he considered the mathematics involved.

He didn't notice the train speeding away past fields and alongside the motorway, he didn't notice anything until the train pulled into Glasgow Station. He hurriedly packed away his things, picked up the bouquet and caught another smaller train to Larrick. His excitement had sobered to a much calmer, and sombre state; he was here for one reason, and it wasn't a happy one. Once he arrived in Larrick, he hailed a taxi to the cemetery. It was all coming back to him now as the taxi passed down roads and streets to the outskirts of town, where the land became more open and the houses were sparse. He remembered the day Alice's father James had interred her ashes; it had been a warm summer's day at the end of August. The Hunters had stayed at a hotel the night before and then they had attended the afternoon ceremony the following day.

The taxi pulled in by a brick wall just before a pair of huge iron gates. Kyle paid the driver and climbed out, shouldering his rucksack as his shoes squelched against the slushy snow. He walked slowly to the entrance; the cemetery was more of a large hilly field with a brick building and a small carpark at its centre. Trees were stippled throughout and little paths zigzagged through the rows of graves. He headed to the centre and then took a path to the right which curved up and round a small rise. Not many people had been to the cemetery lately; the snow was virtually untouched in most places. He passed white, grey and black marble gravestones, and the faces of stone angels and saints watched him with empty eyes. He rounded a corner and passed a bare willow tree and then her grave appeared before him.

His footsteps slowed as he approached Alice's grave, with its white marble headstone carved along the edges with intricate roses. Next to it was a much larger, grey headstone belonging to James' father, grandmother and grandfather. Kyle stopped in front of her grave, his eyes refusing to read the carved letters even though he knew from memory what had been engraved there. His eyes were traitors: *Alice Lynam, 21st January 1991 - 18th June 2009, Beloved Daughter, Sister and Friend.* He said nothing for a while as he stared at the grave; he knew in reality that only half of what had been Alice was buried beneath him. He knelt down and put the bouquet of white roses on Alice's grave, they had always been her favourite. He stood slowly and prepared himself for the wave of emotion which he was sure would swamp him, but minutes passed, and nothing happened. There was calm, he realised. He gazed around at the silent graves and let his shoulders relax. He didn't know what he had been expecting, if the dead had voices, the living would never hear them. He stuffed his gloved hands into the pockets of his coat. He felt that he ought to say something, he really wanted to say something. 'Happy Birthday, Alice,' He said. He gulped, his throat felt like it was collapsing in on itself. 'I miss you.' The calm feeling was bubbling now, he could his emotions as though they were trying to climb up and out from the pit of his stomach. 'I'm sorry. I'm really, really sorry.'

He bowed his head. In the silence he could hear his heartbeat thudding between his ears. He felt the remaining warmth in his limbs disappearing as he shivered there in front of her grave. Tears made tracks down his cheeks and splattered on the ground and his shoes. *He missed her,* he admitted to himself. He missed her so much that every living day hurt and every second without her dragged on for eternity. Every breath was painful, every waking hour felt like a chore and when he went to sleep at night, he just wished he would never wake up again.

Kyle rubbed his eyes and wiped his face before turning away. He started to head back out of the cemetery when he heard a familiar voice call his name.

'Kyle? Is that…?' He turned around and was surprised to see Paula, wrapped up warm in a fur coat and hat, approaching Alice's grave from the opposite direction. She had wellies on her feet and a large handbag tucked under one arm.

'Paula?' Kyle hadn't seen Alice's grandmother since the interment of the ashes.

'Oh, it is you, Kyle!' She smiled brightly at him as she approached, then gripped him in a tight bear hug. 'Come, join me,' she said as she continued the brief walk to Alice's grave. 'They're lovely by the way, Alice would have loved them.' Paula smiled at the roses. She clasped her hands in front of her and murmured a quick prayer under her breath. Kyle stood awkwardly beside her, his legs shaking slightly as he tried to keep warm.

'Feels like it were only yesterday, don't it?' Paula said finally.

'Yeah,' Kyle nodded. They fell silent again for a few moments; no traffic noise or even birds chirping sounded here.

'How are you managing?' she asked.

'I'm OK,' Kyle said, shrugging off the question and changing the topic. 'How's James?'

'James still struggles,' Paula said on a low sigh. 'Though he's met someone new now and he seems a little bit happier.'

'That's good.'

'What about you? Have you met anyone new?'

'No,' Kyle said.

'Ah, well, you're still young,' Paula replied, her lips pinching into a tight smile. 'How did you get up here?'

'I came by train this morning,'

'That's a long way; when are you heading back?'

'This afternoon,' Kyle said.

'You only came up for the day?'

'Yeah.' He shrugged. He glanced at Paula and wondered if she would know anything about Alice's notebook; it was a long shot but… He opened his rucksack and drew out Alice's notebook.

'Do you recognise this?' he asked. Paula's eyes went wide as she took the book from him.

'Yes, yes, I do,' she said. Kyle felt a rush of warmth inside; the thought of finally having some answers thrilled him. 'I gave her this notebook in the hospital as a birthday present.'

'Oh,' he said. Paula flipped through the pages and smiled. 'She was a good artist, our Alice, she had a wild imagination. Physics was an adventure for her; she liked studying the smallest things. She liked imagining what they would look like.' She paused when she hit the last page and her smile faded slightly.

'Yes, she did.' Kyle remembered Alice's drawings. She would often create an artistic impression of the forces and particles that Mr Blakely taught them about in their lessons as a way of visualising them; she said it helped her to remember them better. If she didn't have a notebook, she would draw them on her hands.

'My granddaughter really loved you, Kyle, truly loved you. It wasn't just that little crush that most teenagers go through, but true love.' He felt his cheeks flush. 'True love goes beyond physical attraction and having a few things in common.' She fixed him with a hard stare. 'It's when you put your partner's needs above your own, and they do the same for you. You become each other's priority, physically and emotionally, you care about that person's dreams and future and they care about yours.' She smiled and her blue eyes dropped to Alice's grave. 'When you and Alice were together it was obvious that you loved each other that way.' Kyle didn't reply; he wanted to smile but was scared his eyes would betray him. 'I'm sorry; I shouldn't be talking to you about all of this.'

'It's OK,' Kyle said.

'No, sorry, it's not. I'm just a foolish old lady who remembers too much. Keep your head up, Kyle; my granddaughter didn't fall in love with just anybody. She saw the good in you; compassion, strength, honesty, and that passion for life.' Paula handed him Alice's notebook. 'If you're looking for answers, you won't find them at her grave; they'll be in her drawings and words.' Kyle raised an eyebrow, was she reading his mind? 'It's experience, we old people know things; most of us are still looking for our own answers,' Paula said. Kyle returned Alice's notebook to his rucksack. They stood there silently for a few minutes, and then Paula sighed, as though she were exhaling her emotions. She turned to Kyle. 'Would you like a lift to the station?'

'Yes, please,' Kyle said. He took one last, long, look at Alice's grave and then he followed Paula to her car.

TWENTY-THREE

The Thirteen were not human. Neither were they gods or goddesses, nor did they possess what humans would call magic, and even though they were technically deceased aliens, they had never been able to abduct a human, use mind control or had wanted to do those things. The movie images were grossly inaccurate. The Thirteen's planet still existed, though it was now uninhabitable and unfortunately unreachable by humans.

Alice stood before them; she had told them everything that had happened in the last few months and now she was waiting for their reply. It was strange watching them; sometimes the light would fade from their eyes and Alice would know that they were holding a private conversation with someone, silently within their thoughts. Others were talking, openly projecting their conversations around their reality whilst a few murmured under their breaths. A couple of them were creating small objects and images seemingly from nothing, which hovered above their hands as they spoke to each other, explaining their thoughts and opinions by simply creating and showing them. It was how the afterlife worked; when your whole existence was worked through thoughts, memories and emotions – technically the soul – these were the tools you could use to communicate. The Positive force simply held the energy that these souls used to fuel their conversations and to create their realities, similar to the way the living had to breathe in order to survive.

They were in a large circular room with pale walls. The Thirteen sat behind a large curved table which looked like it had been cut from one white block of solid stone. This was quite likely, since the only limit to what you could create in the afterlife was the imagination. The majority of the Thirteen were taller than a human, pale and slender with only two belonging to a different race, and hence half the size with darker skin tones than the rest. Alice knew the faces of all of them and she had been told the history of their world, but she hadn't been shown everything like other deceased souls. It was one of the things that happened when you crossed over properly; all of the knowledge in the afterlife was given to you, carefully infused into your mind so that you could understand the inner workings of your new existence. The Thirteen and their planet's demise was just a small part of the new knowledge you gained. It usually took newly deceased souls about a year in human time to properly process and understand their new knowledge. Alice hadn't had this luxury; becoming a Deykashee soul meant that certain information had been withheld, just in case it affected her suggestions and, therefore, the choices of the living. However, she didn't think that really mattered now; she had seen all of Kyle's future pathways.

Alice tried to imagine what it would be like to lose your planet, to die and cross over to find an afterlife that was finely connected to life on your former planet. Then to realise that the total destruction of life on your former planet would bring about the end of your afterlife too and could completely erase your soul from existence. It was mind boggling; Alice had barely managed to come to terms with her continued existence, let alone the idea that her existence could be wiped away again, along with billions of others. The Thirteen were the only souls who had survived the destruction of their world; the rest had given into despair and had been claimed by Negative. The Thirteen had endured hundreds of millions of years in isolation with no real way of knowing if they would ever reach another planet with conscious life, whilst maintaining their

Positive energy through Positive emotions. When the Thirteen had stumbled across Earth, mankind was barely walking, yet the fountain had been correct, humans did have the capacity for a soul and the afterlife was reborn.

'We agree with Ahrl,' an elderly male said at last. His name was Ioel, another from the tall and pale race. He had short grey hair and silvery eyes. 'You must have been caught between the forces.' The others nodded in agreement, their eyes brightening as they returned their full attention to their current reality. 'The question is, what would you like to do now?'

'I would like to return to Kyle, as a Deykashee soul,' Alice said.

'We thought you might say that,' Ioel said. 'If that is what you wish then we won't stop you. You have the strongest connection to Kyle, after all. Hopefully it will be enough to steer him towards the right path.' Alice held back a sigh of relief.

'Be careful Alice, sometimes it's better to watch and let the timelines run their course,' Ahrl said.

'I know,' Alice said.

'Your energy is weak, you will need to wait for your soul to recover before you can return,' Ioel said.

'How long?' Alice said.

'We don't know. This has never happened before. It could be days, it could be weeks, it could be longer,' Ioel said. Alice gulped, the thought of being away from Kyle for any length of time was unsettling, but weeks would be torture. 'Do you have any questions?' Ioel asked. Alice blinked, she had many questions, but there was one question which she still wanted an answer for.

'Will you tell me who this Sophia Leto is now?'

'Sophia was involved in one of Kyle's previous futures, before you passed away. There is another future now where she may be involved again,' Ioel said.

'Previous futures?' Alice said. Ioel glanced at the rest of the Thirteen.

'Tell her, she already knows too much,' Myaie said. Ahrl nodded.

'Very well. Sophia and Cameron were supposed to join you and Kyle in research. You were to become a team, and together you were going to discover a force-carrying particle and with it, a new level of particle physics. At first these particles would appear to absorb energy, and they would appear to exist and decay instantly, yet these particles would also interact with each other. In reality, these particles behave this way because they are interacting with a secondary timeline; you and the others were going to start a hypothesis for this, and slowly, it would have been accepted by the scientific community.' Alice couldn't believe it, a new level of particle physics and a new timeline? She didn't need Ioel or the others to tell her how huge that would be, she knew something like that would change the world. 'As you have probably figured out, this discovery would have been important. It would have changed many aspects of science and technology, but it is also very dangerous, it has the potential to bring about technology which may destroy the entire world.'

'What sort of technology?' Alice said. Ioel glanced again at the rest of the Thirteen.

'Alice, what are we?' Ioel said.

'We're souls.'

'Yes, and what if I told you that we souls exist between two timelines. The human timeline of the past, present and future, and a secondary timeline that you and the others were supposed to discover.'

'I don't understand, how could there be a secondary timeline?' Alice said.

'Because this secondary timeline is a timeline which holds all of time, it contains everything and every possibility in the universe. Souls exist in a sort of field between these two timelines, and as you know, we can create our own fantastical realities here with just a single thought.' Alice remained quiet as her thoughts raced ahead of her, trying to make sense of everything she had just been told. 'What do you think would happen, or rather, what do you think might be possible if humans are able to access this secondary timeline and manipulate new levels of quantum physics within this field?' Alice frowned, she didn't know at first but then it dawned upon her and her expression changed from that of confusion to horror.

'They will be able to create a soul?' Alice whispered, almost too afraid to speak those words.

'Yes,' Ioel said. 'But it probably won't be their intention, they will probably do it by accident.'

'But how? What do they use? How could humanity do such a thing?' Alice said.

'It will be their technology,' Ioel said. 'They will create machines that are far superior to humans and these machines will have quantum computers. They will be so powerful that they will potentially be able to house a soul and generate free thought; they will essentially have a consciousness, but that isn't the problem. The problem comes down to how humans program these machines. If these machines are programmed to understand and recognise only a couple of emotions, then...'

'Then their whole thinking and logical reasoning will be off,' Alice said. 'They may decide that the Earth is better off without humans.'

'They may also have the power to jump freely between the afterlife and life; if they do that, then the knowledge they would gain would be incalculable. They may even learn how to harness the Positive and Negative forces and energies, and if they, themselves become Negative...'

'They will destroy everything.'

'That is our fear,' Ioel said.

'Then why don't we stop it? Why don't we stop humans from ever making this discovery?' Alice said.

'Because humans will make this discovery regardless, this will happen. It's just a matter of who, when and how. This is why you, Kyle, Sophia and Cameron were so important; your team was the best team to make this sort of discovery because you handled it the right way. You, and the people who followed you, put in all the safeguards that would protect humanity and the Earth. It wouldn't stop these machines from being created, or the birth of these new souls, but it would stop them being misused and poorly programmed. Unfortunately, you became seriously ill and nature, along with a few Negative delays, meant that you passed away, and Kyle, well Kyle gave up on life after that. It knocked all of you from that future pathway.'

'Negative delays?' Alice said.

'Yes. It is not possible to protect every living soul from the Negative force. It is an ancient force and energy which feeds on humanities destructive emotions like anger, hatred and envy, but it is much more complicated than that. It is Positive's opposite and it exists to destroy. It surges in areas where war ravages the land or natural disasters strike, but it also surges when people with Negative souls gain power. It exists all around us and within us, but it is up to the individual how they respond to it and whether or not they let it take over their thoughts and actions. Though humans are not perfect even with their full range of emotions and freewill. Imagine what it would be like for a superior machine, with a consciousness and a soul, but with limited emotions and no freewill.'

'It's a recipe for disaster.' Alice shuddered.

'Negative caused you some costly delays, using fear and apathy. If you had been diagnosed earlier, if certain surgeries had taken place earlier, you may have been saved,' Ioel said. 'Now, however, it seems the pathway has opened up again. There's a possibility that Kyle may work with Sophia and Cameron again and somehow you are involved.'

'Sophia can see me,' Alice said. 'That will be how!' She had seen all of Kyle's future pathways but she didn't know all of the details. The fountain wasn't set in stone and new details emerged all the time.

'Yes, we are aware of Sophia's gifts. As someone who has seen far too much of the future, we must warn you to be careful with the information you choose to share. Strong souls have gone Negative before by sharing too much.'

'I understand.'

'What about the father?' Myaie said.

'Whose father?' Alice asked. The Thirteen glanced at each other once more. They looked nervous and Alice felt a small pit of dread opening up in her stomach.

'There's another problem looming on the horizon,' Ioel said.

TWENTY-FOUR

The snow was beginning to clear, melting away and giving into the promise of spring. Kyle still glanced warily at the vehicles parked on the sides as he passed. He entered the university's chapel through a glass-panelled door; the warm air was layered faintly with incense and it rushed past him in a bid to escape outside. He had been told by a student in the physics department that this is where he would find Sophia. He let the door close slowly behind him and his eyes roamed around the chapel's interior. He walked down a narrow corridor. Lining the wall on his right were shelves crammed with books on all sorts of religions. Sophia hadn't struck him as a particularly religious person but he wondered if perhaps she practised Catholicism like Alice's grandmother. He came to the end of this corridor and found a little alcove with chairs and a coffee table, but there was nobody there.

'Can I help you?' Kyle jumped at the sound of the voice and whirled round to see a young man dressed in a long black robe.

'I'm looking for Sophia Leto,' Kyle said.

'Ah, Sophia. She's upstairs sitting in the balcony,' the young man said. He pointed towards an open door where Kyle could see a set of spiral stairs leading upwards.

'Thanks.' Kyle headed straight for the stairs, he hadn't even been aware that the chapel had a second floor. He reached the next floor and paused before a set of heavy, wooden doors. Through a narrow glass panel he could see Sophia sitting alone on a chair beyond the door, looking over a low ledge. He could hear muted voices floating up and echoing around the lofty ceiling, there appeared to be some sort of service in progress in the main belly of the chapel below. He saw the corner of Sophia's mouth twitch into a smile before she turned to face him. She stood carefully and joined him in the little stairwell, easing the door shut behind her.

'Hello, Kyle,' Sophia said.

'Sorry, to disturb you. I just came to return your journal.'

'Great. Let's go downstairs.' Sophia led the way down the stairs and stopped in the little alcove Kyle had discovered moments before. She pulled out a bag from under one of the chairs and sat down. Kyle took the seat opposite her. He handed over the journal.

'Sorry for making a mess of your journal. I made some notes on some things. They're just ideas really,' Kyle said.

'I'm intrigued.' She took her journal eagerly and began scanning her gaze over the pages. She was silent for a few minutes and then all of sudden she gasped; her eyes widened and her mouth hung open but curved upwards as though she had been caught in the midst of laughter.

'This is brilliant,' she said excitedly, almost bouncing in her chair. Her dark eyes gleamed with something that was both incredible and frightening.

'It is?' Kyle said, slightly taken aback.

'Yes!' she said and then she frowned at him. 'Sit down,' she said. He did as he was told and took the chair opposite her.

'This is exactly what I've been looking for,' she said, leaning forwards in her chair. 'One timeline that pushes everything along, another that contains every possibility.' She looked at his notes again and nodded. 'Yes, yes, this is perfect!'

'It was just a passing idea…' Kyle said. 'I really don't know how the mathematics would work.'

'Ah, we'll come to that later,' she said, waving a hand in the air. 'Each loop gets bigger as regular time moves forward because the information in the universe is growing, hence entropy is growing, hence the universe is expanding.' Her words seemed to be jumping from her mouth.

'I'm not sure how you would explain the beginning of time with these timelines...' Kyle said.

'Beginning?' Sophia said. 'There is no beginning, as you go back into the past the loops get smaller, the infinities get smaller and smaller, it's like trying to reach zero by continuously halving down from the number one. It doesn't work.'

'Well...'

'That maths won't work. But that's OK.' Her grin stretched wider. 'I like your ideas but I don't think these timelines have to be limited to the physical world alone.'

'I wondered about that,' Kyle said. 'I read what you put about imaginary possibilities, but what you're suggesting would be like trying to explain thoughts with physics.'

'Yes, so?'

'I'm just not sure... I don't know how the scientific community would respond to it.'

'Well, let's put it this way...' she began. 'We don't know if multiple universes really exist, correct?'

'Correct.' Kyle nodded.

'So even if they're not physical universes, we can still imagine what other parallel universes would be like if they did exist.'

'Yes, I guess so.'

'So they become imaginary,' she said. 'And I mean really imaginary, imaginary to us, like made up, in our minds, imaginary.'

'Yes, but...'

'Take one of these loops on this vortex you've drawn,' she said, pointing to his rough diagram. 'The centre is regular, human time, and each loop corresponds to a specific moment in time. If you take a cross section through any point, you would have a large circle with a dot in the centre for regular, human time.'

'OK.' Kyle nodded.

'The space in between the dot and the edge of the circle would represent every possibility that could occur in that specific moment in time. So, for instance, you right now could stay here in the chapel, or go to the Students' Union, or get on a bus to town, or go back to your flat, or go to the physics building, you could call your mum, dad, sister and so on and so on,' she explained. 'Even those are only a small number of the possibilities open to you right now and technically you could do any one of them.'

'OK...'

'However, they're only the physical possibilities, the possibilities that are physically possible for your biological body to achieve within this moment. What if you wanted to say, be in Paris, right now?' She pointed to the ground.

'It's impossible.'

'It's impossible at this moment in time because no one has built a human teleportation device yet; however it may be a possibility in the future and this is where entropy comes in. The vortex grows as the present continues onwards, each loop gets bigger because as time passes more information is learnt and processed. Information is entropy so there is more entropy in the system. Therefore, maybe on some distant loop in the future it might be physically possible to move from here to Paris in one moment.'

'These moments in time are short then?' Kyle said.

'Yes, but it depends on the moment,' she said. 'Now if we go back to the present day and back to my scenario before, you can't physically move from here to Paris, but you can picture yourself in Paris right now, can't you?'

'Yes, I guess, but that's just our imagination,' Kyle replied.

'Exactly, so technically there are imaginary possibilities too,' Sophia said. 'You could picture yourself here, or at home, or in Paris, or New York, or Israel, or in the Amazon, or by the Gaza Pyramids, etc., etc. It's not a physical possibility for you, but it is an imaginary one, because your mind can picture it instantly.'

'Right… but I don't see how this relates to anything,' Kyle said.

'It does,' Sophia replied. 'It's possible for someone to win in the lottery in one of these brief moments.' Her fingers brushed upwards against the pencilled vortex. 'Winning millions on the lottery is a massive change in anyone's life, and it's both a physical and imaginary possibility for someone who has bought a ticket.'

'The odds are very steep though,' Kyle replied.

'Which makes it all the more important. There are some possibilities no matter how remote, which can affect the course of someone's life drastically, it's technically the chaos theory,' she explained. 'I take it you saw this diagram?' Sophia turned to the page in her journal where she had drawn the shaded star in a circle with a dot at the centre.

'Yes.'

'So you know then, that some possibilities are more likely than others? And that there are both physical and imaginary possibilities in any given moment?'

'Yes.' Kyle nodded. 'But how would the maths work? There are no experiments, there's no… data we could use.' He sighed. 'I can see what you're saying and it makes sense, but it's pointless in the scientific world unless you can prove it with something, and I'm not entirely sure what that something would be.'

'It doesn't need to be proved; it's only a thought theory at the moment, nothing more,' Sophia replied. 'It's like the Schrodinger's cat thought experiment; if you put the cat in a box and you can't see the cat, and then you put poison in the box with the cat, is the cat dead or alive? No one knows for sure until the act of observing it makes the outcome fact. If you want to prove that there's a second timeline then that would be a little harder, it's not like it's something you can measure, this, what should we call it?'

'Call what?'

'This second, spiral timeline.' Sophia held up the picture he had drawn of a vortex with a line running through the centre of it.

'I don't know,' Kyle said. 'It technically encompasses all of time and everything, and it moves with the time we observe and know.'

'It's technically always now,' Sophia said. 'The past possibilities leading to the present would instantly collapse so you only really have the possibilities of the present and the future. I would call it the Now Timeline.'

'I guess.' Kyle shrugged.

'You wouldn't be able to measure this Now Timeline, you would have to find a way of measuring something which interacted with it.'

'Like a new force, or a particle?'

'Exactly. Once you have evidence like that you can start to build a hypothesis.'

'Is that even possible?'

'Of course it is. There is so much we don't know about the universe, this sort of idea, if it were proven to be correct, could really help to solve some of the biggest questions in physics. It could even help with the theory of everything.' Kyle felt something strangely familiar stir within him, but it quickly faded when he realised that there was a huge gap in their conversation.

'How does this relate to possibilities and people's imagination though? How could physics ever prove something like that?'

'That is the thought-experiment side of the idea. It might not work that way, but it is definitely something worth considering, even if we can't prove that part. You could apply these timelines to everything and every individual person in the whole world. Every second of every day is filled with possibilities and choices that we have to make. No matter what choices we make or what we do or say we will affect other people, and those people in turn will affect more people and so on. It would mean that every decision would be important, no matter how trivial a decision seemed to be. It's the butterfly effect, though there would be both little and big butterflies, so to speak.'

'It would be exactly like the butterfly effect,' Kyle said. He picked up a pencil and Sophia's journal and drew the rough shape of a vortex again with a line running through the centre. 'The decisions people make during each moment in time may or may not have huge consequences, but the decisions people made before you in the past, their decisions would affect which possibilities would be more likely for you in the future.' Sophia nodded. 'So I guess you would have fine webs of *something*,' he said vaguely drawing more lines between the loops, 'connecting people together.'

'Ah… so everyone's decisions affects each other to lesser and greater extents. A gravitational consequence of events,' Sophia said. 'Your family and friends are more likely to affect your decisions and open up possibilities for you, than say, a complete stranger.'

'Yes, and it would go much further than that, if you think,' Kyle said. 'There are people in history that changed the course of the world by making a fundamental decision at a specific moment in time.' The hair on the back of his neck seemed to stand on end; he felt a murmur of static energy running through his limbs. Warm and faint tingling sensations caressed his skin.

'Interesting, yes, you're right,' Sophia said.

'Still…' he said awkwardly. 'I don't know how you would get anyone to take these ideas seriously. You're technically branching into so many different subjects, it's almost philosophy.' He felt his excitement ebbing away again as the realistic side of his brain pointed out the flaws; there were many, he realised sadly. He put Sophia's journal back down on the table.

'True, for now,' she said with a faint smile. 'That's why they're only my personal theories. Sometimes I talk to people about them; Professor Green is one of those people. I can talk about ideas and theories for hours and hours, but you're right, it would be difficult to prove anything like this with the technology we have right now, but in the future we just might. In the meantime we have maths.'

She smiled.

Kyle glanced at his wristwatch and jumped up when he saw the time, he was going to be late for his business lecture if he didn't leave now.

'I'm sorry, I'm going to have to go. Thank you, anyways, for letting me borrow your journal.'

'It's not a problem. Feel free to come and chat to me about physics ideas whenever you want.'

'OK, sure, and I'm sorry, again, for disturbing your service,' he said gesturing to the main chapel behind him. Sophia laughed.

'My service? Oh, I don't follow any particular faith or religion.'

'Oh.' Kyle frowned. 'I thought that…'

'It was a service which intrigued me, that's all,' Sophia said. 'It was different, there were followers from all the major religions and even some from the minor religions. They were all taking it in turns to share a short piece to the whole congregation, from their individual religious texts. It was fascinating to watch, and they all have the same messages in the end.'

'Oh, right.' Kyle didn't really understand it or why anyone would bother to do that, he wasn't a religious person himself. The confusion must have still be evident on his face because Sophia laughed at him again.

'You know, if you ever get bored with business you could always switch courses and do physics instead.'

'I couldn't do that,' Kyle said thinking of his father. 'I've already spent so much time studying business and my student debt would be astronomical if I switched now.'

'Yes, but it is the rest of your life you're talking about here. It would be worth it, if it's something you enjoy.' Kyle shifted uneasily under Sophia's gaze, there was an intensity about her that sometimes unnerved him.

'Well, I'll see you around.' He waved awkwardly.

'Yes, take care, Kyle.' He hurried out of the chapel and headed straight for the business building with Sophia's words still ringing in his head.

TWENTY-FIVE

Hailey clutched her practice exam booklet as she headed back home after a long day at college. She was upset with herself. She had scored a 'B' on her practice paper for Business. Even though this wasn't bad she knew it wasn't good enough. Her father wouldn't be pleased with a 'B' grade, he was expecting A's. She was frustrated with studying business - she didn't want to run a business, she wanted to write. She ground her teeth and her shoulders stiffened within the confines of her suit jacket. *Suits!* she thought. *Who the hell thought wearing suits was such a great idea?* They were itchy, uncomfortable, restricting, and in the summer, God, they were hell.

'I'll show them,' she said to herself as she marched home. She knew there would be costs involved with writing if she couldn't get a publishing deal, so if she wanted to be a memorable author then she would need to do it herself. Whatever it took, if she had to employ a proofreader and a copy-editor, go on writing courses, find the funds for marketing. *I'll get a job, I'll apply for jobs and save up, then we'll see who's right.* She went straight up to her bedroom, changed out of her suit and picked up a pile of papers from her desk. She had completed and typed out a CV, now all she needed to do was distribute them. She picked up her bag and went straight back out.

Hailey made her way up the main street in Elbridge; she stopped at every clothing store, café, and even the science museum. She gave her CV over to many friendly and sometimes scowling faces, even if they hadn't advertised positions in their windows. She had almost run out of copies when she arrived at a small courtyard with a wishing well. This was her favourite spot in the city centre and she found her feet heading straight for the bookshop on the corner. A bell sounded as she opened the door and the familiar smell of paper and ink surrounded her. Miss Wells was behind the counter; she had run the bookshop for her mother for the last couple of years.

'Hello, Hailey,' she said as she lifted her nose from a book.

'Hi.'

'It's still a bit cold out there, isn't it?' Miss Wells removed her reading glasses.

'Yes, the winter was bad.' Hailey hesitated. 'Can I give you my CV? I know you're not advertising positions but…'

'Sure.' Miss Wells smiled. Hailey handed over the last copy of her CV. 'I'll see what I can do,'

Hailey left the shop and let out a deep breath as she stood outside; she had applied everywhere in the city, she would just have to wait. She gazed at the wishing well and smiled; she found a penny amongst the loose change in her pocket. She thought of Alice and wondered how Kyle was doing. She liked having him around and missed him when he was at university. She flicked the coin into the well. 'For luck,' she said and it landed with a satisfying *plop*. 'For Alice,' she whispered.

TWENTY-SIX

Kyle stood outside the examination hall with Cameron and his other friends. They were all in grey suits and this was Kyle's last A-level exam - physics. He could see the invigilators walking along the desks inside the hall and setting down papers as the students waited. He was nervous, but his thoughts could never stay on his exam for long. Alice was still in hospital and he worried about her every day. The doctors were optimistic about her recovery, but she was so skinny and pale, and she could hardly eat a thing.

'You're worrying about Alice again, aren't you?' Cameron said.

'Yeah. It's hard not to'

'Don't, she'll be OK. She's tough and she's made it this far. Besides, she wants you to do well in this exam so you can study together at university. You're doing it as much for her as you are for yourself.'

'Yeah, you're right, I know.' Kyle let his shoulders slump. The idle conversations paused around them and the boys looked up to see their headmaster, Mr Black, marching down the corridor towards them.

'Kyle!' Mr Black said. 'Come with me, quickly.'

'What's wrong?' Kyle asked. His thoughts immediately flashed to Alice and he felt as though a hole had been punctured through his chest.

'You need to come with me.' Mr Black gripped him by the shoulders. 'It's all right all of you, carry on with your exams.' His cheerful tones rang false and hollow as he guided Kyle away.

'What's happened?' Kyle asked. 'What's wrong? Is Alice OK?' Mr Black shook his head and wouldn't say a word until they were in his office. Kyle saw that Hailey was in the office too, her expression blank.

'You two need to wait here, your parents are here,' Mr Black told them and then he left the room.

'What's going on?' Kyle asked, turning to Hailey.

'I don't know, no one is telling me anything,' Hailey said. She stood up, her voice trembling. 'It's bad, something bad has happened.' The door opened again and their parents entered the room. Their mother's eyes were red, she had been crying, and their father was impossibly pale. He looked as though he had grown old overnight.

'Is Alice OK?' Kyle asked immediately. 'Tell me, is she alright?' His father gripped his shoulders and looked him straight in the eye.

'Kyle, I'm sorry… she's….' He hesitated, lowering his eyes and pulling Kyle to him. 'She's gone, Kyle, I'm sorry, she's…'

'No,' he said softly. 'No, you're lying.'

'She passed away this morning, Kyle. She had a heart attack. It was quick.'

'No,' Kyle said. He shrugged out of his father's grasp. He felt sick. There was no way Alice could be gone, he had just seen her earlier that morning. She had been fine.

'Kyle…' his mother said, tears streaming down her cheeks.

'No!' He ran from the room. His feet pounded down a long corridor which suddenly bleached out. The smell of strong disinfectant stung his airways and removed the hairs from his nostrils as his feet clacked against the polished floors. He pumped his legs and arms harder and willed the muscles in his body to move him faster. Alice wasn't dead, she couldn't be dead.

The school turned into the hospital, and he skidded around a sharp corner, almost colliding with a nurse. He was on her corridor now, with large windows on his left looking out at the world outside and down on the pitiful city of Elbridge. He knew this floor well, he had walked these corridors so many times, he had spent long hours between these walls. He ran and he saw her room at the very end, the door was slightly ajar, beckoning to him tauntingly. He could see her through the window, a faint smile on her lips as she saw him. Tubes were wired up through her nose and into her arms, she was painfully thin and she had no hair, but her fragile smile was the most beautiful thing in the world.

A clock appeared above the window and he saw the seconds of her life counting down. He put on another burst of speed; he could make it, he just had to reach her, he just had to be there. He felt panic firing through him and then the hallway stretched impossibly like some twisted infinity. He cried out and ran harder, sweat sticking to his sides and dripping down his forehead. Eerie red light streamed in through the windows and his head turned unwillingly to gaze upon a ruined and broken world. The charcoal remnants of a blackened Earth stood against a blood red sky. He turned back to Alice and he saw her smile drop as her eyes rolled into the back of her head; her torso jolted upwards as though it were trying to wrench itself free from her limbs and then her body went still. Doctors and nurses appeared out of nowhere and crowded around her bed. One of them began chest compressions and another was shouting orders.

'No!' Kyle screamed as he ran faster. He felt his body stumble through some invisible barrier and suddenly he was gaining ground again. He saw her father appear on his side of her window, his back to Kyle as he gazed on at the chaos surrounding his daughter. Alice's body was not responding to the emergency CPR and a box-like machine displayed the flat line of her heart. 'Alice, don't leave me!' Kyle cried, his voice hoarse as he sped down the hallway. He was almost at her door; he was almost in her room. His eyes flickered to the right as he passed her father; he had the face of a destroyed man, a nightmarish image that Kyle's mind could only create. Kyle's outstretched hand crossed the threshold; he could just see into the room and he saw the blank looks on the faces of the medical staff. They shook their heads, their eyes dull. He saw Alice's lifeless form. 'Alice!' he screamed and then the floor gave out from underneath him and he fell.

Kyle sat bolt upright with his heart hammering in his chest and sweat coating his back. He gasped in the cool night air by the lungful and almost choked as it rushed down his airways. He glanced around the dim room, his eyes adjusting slowly. He was in his bed, he was at university, his head snapped from left to right and his gaze caught the red digital display of his clock. It was gone five in the morning. He dropped back down onto his bed, his skin burning and trembling from the overdose of adrenaline. It had been the same nightmare that had been plaguing him for months; just when he thought it wouldn't happen again, it did. In reality he had never made it to the hospital. He remembered the headmaster collecting him and sitting him down in the office. Shortly after his parents had arrived and he had learnt the devastating news - the rest of the day had been a blur, the rest of his life had been a blur. He hadn't taken that last exam, so the examination board had taken an aggregate result from his previous exams and he had still been accepted at university for a physics degree. A degree he had decided against, a degree he didn't feel he deserved. He felt tears slide down his cheeks and drip into his ears and hair. *Why did it have to be her? Why did it have to be that day?* Guilt twisted up his insides until his guts felt as though they were ripping under the strain.

'I didn't know,' he whispered, 'I didn't know, I didn't know, I'm so sorry, Alice, I'm sorry.' His voice cracked as he fought to contain the mournful sob that surfaced at the back of his throat. He should have been there in her last moments, he should have stayed. He gulped but nothing would alleviate the rawness in his throat or the numbness that resided deep in his bones. His heart still hammered against his chest, as though it was knocking on the door to his ribcage, demanding to be let out or to be heard, he wasn't quite sure which. He threw off his duvet and filled a glass of water from the sink and then knocked back the cool liquid. His shoulders shook violently as he put the glass down and held onto the sides of the sink. No one was prepared for death, no one.

TWENTY-SEVEN

Kyle's business books lay ignored on his desk. Every time he tried to sit down to read them he found himself standing back up and gazing at the wall above his bed. In the weeks after talking to Sophia, he had written out thoughts from her journal pages and her drawings and stuck them to his walls. He had tacked diagrams of circles with shaded stars, and vortices with lines running through their centres to the wall above his bed. He added new additions to this wall too - graphs with jagged lines like the edges of tall mountains, and another circle diagram with a dot at its centre, and a long, curving line protruding from this dot, crossing over and looping back on itself until it finally reached a random point on the outer edge of the circle. He took a step back and gazed at the diagrams, his eyes roaming and calculating the various details.

A question was bothering him. If everything in the universe was made up of the fundamental particles, essentially tiny vibrating pockets of energy, then the Now Timeline would have to hold all forms of energy. Sophia's imaginary possibilities were thoughts, but one could suggest that even thoughts themselves were made up of the fundamental particles, and if that was the case, then why not emotions too? The problem was defining what sort of energy that may or may not involve. Kyle frowned as his brain ticked over. Another problem was the fact that each loop of the Now Timeline grew with every moment. Sophia had said entropy increased because information increased. That meant that somehow energy was increasing with every passing moment and every new loop.

However, Kyle knew that Newton's second law of thermodynamics stated that energy could not be created or destroyed. This posed a problem for their Now Timeline; if the loops got bigger, did that mean there was more energy being created? What was the energy responsible for it and where was it coming from? It would have to be an energy that had always been there, and it would have to be virtually limitless, but what was it exactly? He was deep in thought as he stared at the pages tacked on his wall, hoping the answer would suddenly jump out at him. A knock at his door drew him out of his intense focus.

'Hello?' he called. Cameron appeared.

'Hey, Kyle, what are…' He halted on the spot, the door handle in his hand as he gazed into Kyle's room with wide eyes.

'Are you alright?' Kyle asked slowly as he followed the line of Cameron's sight to the wall above his bed.

'What is this?' Cameron stepped into the room, letting the door swing shut behind him.

'Oh, it's nothing. It's just something I was thinking about.'

'This is physics, isn't it?' Cameron said pointing to the circles with the many pointed stars. 'Where did you get this all from?'

'Sophia.'

'Sophia? Since when have you spoken to Sophia?'

'Ah, well…' Kyle glanced away from his friend. Cameron folded his arms and frowned.

'I know that face. What are you hiding?'

'Do you remember the van which slid down the hill and crashed just before Christmas?'

'Yeah, of course I do. People were talking about it for days and we were at the library just before it happened. You said you didn't see anything and that you left the library just after I did.'

'Well, I may have stretched the truth a bit. I didn't leave the library until later, a lot later, and I did see the van. It almost ran me over.' Cameron stared at Kyle, his nostrils were flaring like they always did when he became angry.

'Why the hell didn't you tell me?'

'It wasn't a big deal, nothing actually happened, and besides, Sophia was there. She stopped me from getting knocked down and she took me back to her room.'

'You were in her room?' Cameron's eyes looked like they were going to pop out of his head.

'No, it's not like that, get your mind out of the gutter.' Kyle scowled. 'She was just helping me, that's all, and that's not the point. She gave me this journal thing with all her science ideas and theories and well, it got me thinking about stuff.' Kyle gestured to his wall. Cameron shook his head in disbelief.

'You're so lucky! Very lucky. Sophia doesn't stop to chat with many people; she's usually in the labs and when she's working she doesn't have much patience for anyone.'

'She doesn't?' Kyle raised an eyebrow; he hadn't really thought about it like that. Of course Sophia would be busy, but she had seemed quite happy to stop and chat in the chapel when he had returned her journal. Cameron dropped his arms back down to his side and sighed.

'What do these diagrams mean?' Cameron said, pointing to the vortex shapes.

'They represent time, or, more accurately, two different timelines. You have the straight vertical line which is what we recognise as time, and the spiral, vortex shape is a secondary timeline which we've named the Now Timeline. It holds everything and every possibility in the universe, and it wraps around our own timeline. It grows because as our time passes there is more information in the universe.'

'OK, interesting idea,' Cameron said. 'It's not new by any means, but it is a slightly different way at looking at things. What about these ones?' Cameron gestured to the circles with shaded stars.

'They're diagrams to explain a moment in time and all the

decisions and possibilities open to that person at that particular moment. The Now Timeline holds all of these possibilities.'

'What, like whether you're going to walk or run?' Cameron asked.

'Yes, that would be a tiny fraction of the possibilities,' he said. 'I mean everything though, what clothes a person will wear, who they may call, what TV channel they might watch, what they might eat or drink, whether they'll get in a car, train, plane or boat… everything.'

'Wait, why have you put imaginary possibilities on your diagram?' Cameron frowned at the diagrams.

'Those are all the possible thoughts your brain can have in that moment,' Kyle replied. 'They're not necessarily physical possibilities.'

'I see, but that could be an infinite amount.'

'Yeah.' Kyle shrugged. Cameron slowly scrutinized the diagrams and notes.

'What does this Now Timeline look like before the Big Bang?' Cameron said.

'I think it would be a single loop containing everything, and then at the point of the Big Bang, the loop broke and started to spiral.'

'That would make sense.' Cameron nodded. 'But what would it look like when the universe ends?'

'I can only think of two options. The Now Timeline either disappears because it ceases to have anything to observe itself or it will collapse again into a single loop.'

'Hmm. I don't think the maths will work under the current model,' Cameron said, picking up a pen from the side.

'That's what Sophia said, she said the maths breaks down.'

'She's right. If I understand it correctly, this Now Timeline wouldn't have a single fixed value, it would have two. This Now Timeline is always now, but it's also getting bigger with each loop. If you said that all the information in the universe and all the possibilities in the universe are equal to one, then the Now Timeline would technically have a value of zero and one simultaneously. It's complicated. You've also got the problem of trying to prove that a secondary timeline, which holds everything, actually exists.'

'I know, Sophia said we would have to discover a force or a particle that somehow interacts with the Now Timeline.'

'She's clearly given it a lot of thought,' Cameron said. 'There's a time dilation presentation tonight by the way. I'm assuming you're going?'

'I don't know,' Kyle said, gazing at his neglected business books. 'I've got a lot of work to do.'

'Alice would have been thrilled to see you like this,' Cameron said. Her name stabbed Kyle in the guts. Cameron's eyes glazed over as he withdrew to some faraway place, lost in some distant happy memory, one that Kyle would only find painful to recall. Cameron was never shy about speaking of Alice, but then he didn't have to feel the pain of her absence every day. 'She would have been bouncing off the walls, with a puzzle like this.' Cameron smiled and glanced at Kyle. 'Do you remember when we used to sit at the park and ask strange questions and try to solve them? We would go to Mr Blakely the next day and he would point out all of our problems.' Kyle winced; he could remember but he didn't want to. 'We would spend lunch breaks talking to him about our dreamt up theories of the universe; most of the time they were ridiculous but we had some good ideas. Do you remember?'

'No,' Kyle said, lowering his eyes to the floor.

'Come on, man, you do remember…'

'Leave it, Cameron.' Kyle turned away from him and headed over to his desk.

'Why do you do that? Why do you always shut her out?'

'I said leave it, Cameron,' Kyle hissed through gritted teeth. He was trying his best to supress his memories; he could feel them rattling at their doors.

'It's been almost three years now and you barely talk about her, it's like she didn't even exist.' Kyle didn't respond. He could feel his fingernails biting into his palms.

'You're wasted doing business, you know.'

'Cameron, I don't want to talk about this right now.'

'You don't even like business. We were all going to do physics, remember? We all wanted to be physicists and go into research. It didn't even matter what universities we ended up at. Alice…'

'Cameron!' Kyle snapped. He felt cold, as though someone had injected ice into his veins. The door opened behind them and Dani stood in the doorframe.

'What are you guys yelling for?' Her worried gaze flickered between the pair of them. Kyle pinched the bridge of his nose and let out a deep breath.

'I'm going out,' Kyle said, lowering his arm. He picked up his jacket and keys. Dani backed up sharply as he came out into the hallway and then he locked his door.

'What's going on?' she asked.

'It's nothing,' Kyle said. He kept his head down, stuffed his hands into his pockets and walked out.

TWENTY-EIGHT

The evening was slow. There were long pauses between the clusters of students Kyle had to serve where he could let his mind wander. He enjoyed these moments of freedom and his eyes scanned lazily through the thin crowds. The continual dull ache that reigned over his mind was back but he often felt a pleasant, warm, buzz tingling up the backs of his calves. He felt sleepy as he leant against the back of the bar and folded his arms.

'How long are you going to keep this up?' Dani asked.

'Keep what up?' Kyle said.

'You know what. Ignoring Cameron, it's been almost a week now and you're still acting like a child.'

'I'm not ignoring him, he's ignoring me.' Dani rolled her eyes.

'Whatever, just sort it out will you? I hate feeling like I'm walking on eggshells all the time.' Kyle shrugged and Dani sighed as she walked away. Kyle stared off through the thin crowds. His head was throbbing in time with the bass and he scrunched his eyes shut. His head continued to throb and every throb felt like searing hot blood was being forced through the vessels in his brain. He groaned and pushed his right palm against his forehead.

He opened his eyes slowly; the spotlights were pulsing behind the bodies in different pastel hues, pink, purple and blue. The odd splurge of orange, brown and green seemed to erupt randomly here and there, and he straightened his spine suddenly and blinked repeatedly. *Orange? Brown? Green?* He gazed back at the bodies as their shadowy outlines were highlighted again with pink, purple and blue. A green dot appeared on one of the bodies, right at the centre of their torso. He squinted and watched as the green dot seemed to twist and wriggle as it swelled like a balloon. He realised that it was always hugging that person's body, a woman who seemed to have paused and was staring in the direction of a couple. A brown splurge erupted somewhere to the left and his eyes honed in on this strange light; he saw the outline of a body which seemed to be staggering unevenly and not really dancing. All of a sudden they bent over with their hands on their knees and seemed to be taking deep breaths. An orange flash sparked up to the right and he saw a person gesturing obscenely at someone else. The colours faded from his vision but he realised that different colours seemed to be erupting from the torso of every person in the room, like their own personal ghostly cloud.

'Err… are you serving or are you just staring weirdly?' a voice said and Kyle almost jumped out of his skin as his eyes settled on a small woman who held a note in her hand. She was watching him with one dark, raised, skinny eyebrow and her lips slightly pursed. He glanced back up quickly at the crowd but the colours were gone and then he flashed an uneasy smile at the young woman.

'What can I get you?' he asked as he wiped his sweaty hands on the bottom of his t-shirt.

'Just a mixed fruit cider please,' she said, her eyes darting to the fridges behind him. Kyle nodded and whisked out a green glass bottle from one of the fridges. He popped off its lid and poured it into a plastic pint glass before handing it over to her. She paid for her drink, gave him one last strange look and then headed back off to the dance floor. He watched her go and his eyes searched through the wildly moving bodies but he saw nothing more of the strange coloured clouds. Had he been hallucinating again?

He searched through the crowds and then a flash of gold erupted behind the bodies, near the stage. Kyle stared at the dance floor, the music washed straight over him. He saw a pale arm, glowing, and then it was gone again. He squinted and leant forwards on the bar, trying desperately to see through the gaps in the dancing bodies. He caught a glimpse of a pale dress and leg, and the back of a woman with long brown hair. He blinked and she seemed to disappear completely for a moment and then she reappeared again, but closer. She turned, her body flickering like a dying flame, and then her eyes met his. His throat went dry, the edge of the bar dug into his hips as he leant forwards, unable to comprehend what he was seeing. It was a trick, it had to be. His mind was playing a cruel trick. Alice stared back at him; her body seemed unable to stay solid for more than a couple of seconds. A ghost? A hallucination? Kyle wasn't sure anymore. She smiled and then she turned away and headed towards the stairs.

Kyle was stunned for a moment, he left the bar and ran onto the dance floor ignoring Dani's protests. He squeezed through the crowds accidently knocked a couple of students. He saw Alice descending the stairs and followed. The cool night air hit him as he barrelled through the door; he took the gridded stairs two at a time as his eyes darted around the quiet beer garden. A handful of students were smoking, the rest of the garden was empty and there was no sign of Alice. He stopped when he reached the bottom of the stairs then turned in loose circles as he searched for her.

His eyes welled with frustration, and then a cold numbness waved over him. He paused, his chest rising and falling heavily, he could see where the artificial lights cast shadows across the ground, but the shadows appeared to be moving, rippling and bulging out of form. He glanced around and saw more shadows, moving like liquid over the dim background and distorting the night sky. He felt a cold sting on his arm, like an insect bite, and saw what looked like black smoke, prodding at his skin and seeping into his veins. He let out a startled yelp and rubbed his arm in panic. He stepped back quickly, eyeing the shadows nervously. They felt and looked wrong.

Three students were huddled under a lamp, staring at him blankly as they smoked. Black dots erupted from their torsos and formed little spheres, and he could see the shadows dipping into these spheres, but the students seemed oblivious to all of it. Kyle stepped away from the strange shadows, and then he felt a warm hand grasping his arm. He twisted and saw Sophia staring back at him with a concerned expression. Her gaze darted to the group of smokers and then to seemingly random spots around them.

'Hey, Kyle?' Sophia said, returning her gaze to him and forcing a smile.

'Hi.' Kyle pulled his arm out of her grasp. Sophia frowned.

'Are you OK?' You look like you've seen a ghost or something.'

'I… I'm fine. I just needed some air.' Kyle stepped around her and headed back to the stairs.

'I've been talking to Cameron lately,' Sophia said. Kyle stopped in his tracks and turned to look at her again. 'He said he saw some of my notes in your bedroom and he had some very interesting ideas.'

'Oh. Yeah. Sorry about that.'

'No, don't be. I don't mind. He's been trying to help me work out the maths, but we've realised that a cosmological constant may need to be redefined and that we would need new symbols to represent the Now Timeline and whatever field exists between the two timelines.'

'Oh. Sounds difficult.'

'It is, because we would have to define them.'

'Did he say anything else to you?'

'I asked him why you weren't at last week's guest presentation. He said that you two had had an argument.' Kyle nodded and lowered his gaze to the ground. 'I pressed him for details but he wouldn't say much, but then I asked him if he knew who Alice was? And so he told me a little bit about your history.' Kyle felt a flood of rage crashing through him.

'He should learn to keep his big mouth shut.' Kyle turned away and immediately felt a hand on his shoulder.

'Don't be angry at him, Kyle. I was the one who asked him the question. You said Alice's name on the night of the van incident. I figured that she must have been someone important to you.'

'Well, now you know.' He began to ascend the stairs.

'You know that your pain will hold you back from everything you ever wanted, and everything that you want now.' Kyle paused. His hand tightened around the cool metal handrail. How the hell did she know what he wanted? How could she possibly know anything about him? He would bet his life that she hadn't lost someone close to her, someone who was taken away way before their time. All he wanted right now was to be with Alice again, to see and talk to her, but he knew that this was impossible, so all he really wanted was for something to kill him, some tragic accident that would remove him from the planet. Something like that van, if only she hadn't been there, if only he had been walking a little faster. He would be gone by now, free from his thoughts and this hell, free from everything. 'You saw something, didn't you? Something that you can't explain,' Sophia said, and just like that, he felt his anger collapse and disappear. He glanced over his shoulder; she was standing at the bottom of the stairs with that familiar burning intensity in her eyes.

'I don't know what you're talking about,' Kyle said.

'Yes you do,' Sophia said.

'I've got to get back to work.'

'OK, but the next time you need to get some…' she held her fingers up and mimicked quotation marks, 'air, you should come and talk to me.' Kyle didn't reply, he darted back up the stairs. *I'm losing it,* he thought as he took up his position behind the bar. He rubbed his eyes. Dani stared at him.

'I'm OK,' he said, before she could question him. Dani slung a cloth over one shoulder and raised her eyebrows, still staring.

'Honestly, I'm fine,' he said, faking a smile as he checked the dance floor.

Sophia didn't bother him again, and eventually the evening came to an end and Kyle and Dani completed their chores before heading back to their flat. He said goodnight to Dani in the hallway and once inside his bedroom he quickly stripped down to his boxers and donned another t-shirt before jumping into bed. He flicked off the lamp on his nightstand and gazed upwards at his ceiling. His head ached and his mind struggled to make sense of the night. Had he seen Alice? Or was his mind really playing tricks on him? A strangled chuckle escaped him. *Of course it wasn't Alice* he told himself, *ghosts aren't real*, but then Sophia's words passed through his mind again, *'You saw something, didn't you? Something that you can't explain.'* He felt his face tighten and he turned over. Science had taught him enough to be sceptical about anything that would be considered supernatural, but still, it had seemed so real, even the strange shadows had seemed real.

His thoughts trailed to Cameron, Sophia and Hailey. He thought about what they had each said but their words just added noise into his already crowded mind. He knew his life was wrong but he couldn't see a way out of it now, there was no way to fix it. He couldn't bring back the dead and he couldn't change his past. His life was broken beyond repair, and the future was filled with countless 'what ifs' and other doubts. What if he failed? What if he could never live up to his father's expectations? What if he did switch back to physics and then failed his degree? What if he did physics but then couldn't get a research position? What if his sister became a writer and failed so bad that he had to look after her? What if his father never accepted his choices? What if he couldn't make him proud and happy? What if Cameron was right? Kyle groaned and turned over. *What would Alice think?* he asked himself as his eyelids became heavy, but he already knew what she would think, and she would have never imagined him to be in this position.

TWENTY-NINE

Hailey shrieked in excitement as she pocketed her phone. Miss Wells had just called and Hailey now had a job. *Hah!* she thought. *That'll show them! I'll show all of them.* She jumped up from her bed, picked up a book and her bag and then practically skipped down to the park.

She slowed down as she walked along the pavement above the skate park. She could see Tank on the grass below; he shouted out instructions and blew on a whistle a couple of times as the kids dribbled balls around cones. Spring was warmer now and April was just around the corner. She made her way down the concrete steps and then sat down on her favourite bench and began to read. Every few minutes her eyes flicked back up to Tank and then back down to her book. *A good book,* she thought, *but could be better.* Practise finished only a few minutes later and Tank jogged over to her with a smile on his face. Her heart fluttered in her chest and she was glad that only she could feel or hear it.

'Hey.'

'Hi, Tank.' She smiled at him, 'I got a job,' she said, her smile stretching wider.

'Really? Well, congratulations then.'

'Yup. I'm now an assistant at the bookshop. Hopefully, I can start saving up now and become a proper writer.'

'You're already a writer,' Tank replied. 'You mean an author.'

'Yes.' She blushed.

'That's great news. Hopefully now you'll get to do what you've always wanted to do.'

'Yeah, if only my dad would see it that way.' She rolled her eyes.

'Ah, you can't keep living the life your parents want, or what anybody else wants for that matter. You'll always regret it.'

'I know,' she said and they fell silent for a few moments. A soft breeze rippled across the lake and swept over them. She could see the trees on the other side and behind that, acres of farmland. She felt an overwhelming peace here, and maybe a little bit of nostalgia, but she liked it.

'You know, it was Alice who told me to keep playing football after my accident.'

'She did?' Hailey was surprised and a little envious; she wished she had been the person to encourage Tank.

'Yeah. I think she got a mini obsession with encouraging people to follow their dreams in the end.' He laughed. 'Or maybe she just saw more of a person than anybody else was able to. She just seemed to know. Though I'm sure she encouraged you to write, didn't she?' He was right.

'I... I've never really thought about it,' Hailey said, thinking of Alice's penny jar, the one thing that even Kyle could cope with. She missed Alice too; it was an injustice that she had been taken so soon. Her brother had found someone special who deserved to be remembered, and she felt sad that Kyle had locked that away when so many people gained so much from her memory.

'I just think she wanted people to be happy, and one way to be happy is to do something you love doing, I guess.'

'Kyle doesn't do that, not anymore,' Hailey said.

'He used to when Alice was around. Now he spends too much of his energy trying to run away from it all.' Tank stood up and stretched.

'Your brother will be coming back soon, won't he?'

'Yes, he's got some time off to revise before his exams so he's coming back home for a bit.'

'It would be good to see him, maybe you can drag him down to the park?'

'I doubt that, he rarely comes down here anymore.' Hailey sighed as she gazed towards the skate park. She could almost imagine them all sitting there now, talking about school, music, and nothing really important, but it had been fun.

'She would be happy for you, Hailey. I mean, Alice would be happy for you.'

'I know,' Hailey said, she tried to muster a smile but she felt it fall from her lips.

'I'm sure everything will work out OK, you'll see.'

'I love how you're so optimistic all the time.'

'I'm not, but I choose my moments,' he said. He glanced down at her book. 'I'm guessing that book isn't so good, you've not stopped staring at me this time.' The air rushed out of Hailey's lungs and she felt heat rush up her neck. *He knew? How did he know!* Tank laughed again. His dark eyes sparkled with amusement. Hailey nodded slowly.

THIRTY

Kyle stared out of his bedroom window and tapped his pen against his notebook. His brain was saturated with the meaning of opportunity cost, the role of central banks, and ethical challenges that business face. The end of the semester had flown by and he hadn't spoken to Cameron at all. It had been surprisingly easy; they were both busy and their lectures were in different buildings and at different times. Cameron had more work on being in his third and final year, he hadn't taken a year out like Kyle had, and he would probably leave Red Oak and set up roots elsewhere after their exams. Cameron had spent the last few weeks going through the pain of dissertations, sleepless nights and meals being replaced by junk food. Kyle knew this because he had heard Cameron's door opening and closing in the early morning hours as he ventured to and from the bathroom and kitchen. He wondered if Cameron had come back home too or if he had chosen to stay and revise at university; it made sense to stay, the university library was there.

Kyle watched the sunshine streaming onto the path and could remember skateboarding down the path with Alice as they made their way to the skate park. He felt a pang of nostalgia as he recalled the sensation of the wind passing across his skin and hair, the rumble of the wheels beneath his feet and the way the board would move with his body. It had been a long time since he had gone out on his board and he wondered if he would ever experience such a simple pleasure ever again. It didn't seem likely. There was a knock on his door and his mother appeared with a tray in her hands.

'I thought you might be hungry so I made you some sandwiches,' Stacy said. He could also see a tall glass of orange juice and he moved his books aside so she could put down the tray.

'Thanks, Mum.'

'There's a letter for you too.' Stacy pulled out a white envelope which she had wedged under the plate of sandwiches.

'Oh right, thanks.' Kyle took the envelope from her.

'How's the studying going?'

'Good. I think.'

'Well, remember to take a break every so often.'

'I will.' Stacy smiled and then she left and shut the door behind her. Kyle took a bite out of one of his sandwiches and then he turned his attention to the letter and opened it. He pulled out the piece of paper inside and realised there were two pieces of paper, one tucked inside another. He unfolded the first piece of paper but it was the second piece of paper which stopped his brain in its tracks. It contained a picture, a sketch drawn in pencil by an all too familiar hand. One of its longest edges had been torn as though it had been ripped out of a book, and a date in the top corner read *10th June 2009*. Alice had drawn a sketch of Fairhaven Lake on this page, as though she had been standing on the other side of the park, opposite the skate park. Kyle remembered this spot, they had walked past it hundreds of times. In the sky, Alice had drawn a single shooting star. The memory hit him hard and suddenly, there was no warning…

'Come on, Alice,' Kyle whispered as he took her hand. The cool air whipped past their noses and cheeks and tangled in their hair as they made their way to the park.

'It's cold; my dad is going to kill me if he finds out.' She yawned into the back of her hand. He glanced back at her as they hurried along the pavement; she was wearing a pair of jeans with a hoody, her hair hanging loosely about her shoulders.

'I know, but this is the best chance to see the meteor shower,'

Kyle said. He gazed up at the sky as they hurried; there was no cloud cover tonight and the summer sun had been replaced by a half-moon. It was perfect.

Alice had been looking tired lately, he had noticed. She had been sleeping a lot too, often lying in until the late morning and then becoming tired again before the evening. Kyle stopped and let go of her hand. He knelt down in front of her.

'Hop on my back.'

'No, I'm fine,'

'Please,' he said. He heard her sigh reluctantly and he knew she had rolled her eyes even without looking. She got on his back and he lifted her up; she had lost weight, but he wasn't going to tell her that. He carried her to the park and then set her down. He took her hand and guided her to the side of the lake, it was darker there with less light pollution, and they had more chance of seeing a shooting star.

'You know, this is the part in the scary movie where the people die,' Alice said.

'It will be fine,' Kyle replied, but even so, he kept a sharp eye on their surroundings. He found the spot he was looking for, a clear patch of grass right next to the edge of the lake. They could see the skate park here and the houses and streetlamps in the distance. Behind them were just trees and then quiet fields. He reached out with his right hand and brushed the hair from her face; even half asleep and in the silver moonlight, she was beautiful. He pulled her close and kissed her properly, like she was supposed to be kissed, gently and passionately. He broke away slowly and her eyes opened reluctantly; it was as though she had been sedated by his lips. He cupped her cheeks, kissing her lightly between her eyes, then glanced up at the sky again. He could already see a handful of stars though he knew there were more there that he couldn't see. Thousands of other suns and only a tiny percentage of what the entire universe held, but no meteor shower yet.

He sat down on the grass and pulled Alice into his lap, and they sat there curled up together. He could feel his heartbeat and hers through their thin layers, almost beating in unison. The breeze kicked up gentle waves across the lake and they lapped quietly against the edge. An owl hooted somewhere in the trees but everything else was still and silent.

'They're so pretty,' Alice breathed as she gazed up at the sky.

'Yes, they are,' Kyle said. 'We're all the by-products of stars but they're the real wonders.'

'Wonders?' Alice replied. 'I think they're beautiful and terrifying.'

'Terrifying?'

'Yes,' she said as she snuggled deeper into his chest. The smell of her skin - soap and faint perfume - was intoxicating.

'Why are they so terrifying?' he asked as he ran his fingers lightly through her hair.

'There's so many of them,' Alice replied. 'There's so much we don't know about the world, ourselves, let alone the other stars and their planets out there.' She stretched her left arm up to the sky as though her fingertips could brush along the stars themselves. 'There could be anything out there,' she whispered, 'anything at all.'

'And that's terrifying?' Kyle asked.

'Everything unknown is terrifying to us, it's why humans hate change,' Alice replied. 'Even a stranger can be scary unless you get to know them, then they might become a friend.'

'Or a partner,' Kyle said as he kissed the top of her head. Alice looked up at him and smiled then. She straightened up and kissed his mouth for a few seconds, or perhaps minutes, Kyle wasn't sure. 'What do you think is out there?' he asked when she broke away.

'Life,' Alice replied simply. 'There has to be more life out there.'

'In theory and statistically, there should be life out there.'

'I wonder if there are aliens out there on a distant planet, living the way we do, thinking the way we do, feeling the way we do.'

'It's possible,' Kyle said quietly.

'I wonder if they're terrified too.'

'Probably,' Kyle replied as he hugged her tightly. They sat there in silence for a few moments.

'Have you always liked the stars?'

'I think so,' he said. 'As far back as I can remember and from what my parents have told me, I was always fascinated with space, particularly the planets as a kid.' Alice looked up at him through her long eyelashes and he felt his cheeks flame. 'I don't know what it was; I was just always drawn to the night sky. I had all sorts of books on the solar system but it wasn't until I started secondary school that I realised I genuinely liked physics.' He stumbled over his words. 'The more I learnt the more I realised I was drawn to the unknown. Theoretical and particle physics intrigues me more than stars these days, but I'll always have a soft spot for astronomy.' He glanced up briefly. 'I know Dad would really prefer it if I studied business.' He paused and smiled at her. 'But I think he's ok with physics too.'

'You shouldn't listen to your dad all the time. He isn't you.'

'No, I know, but I'm afraid that I'll let him down. I'm afraid that…'

'Afraid of what?'

'I guess I'm afraid that I'm not making the right decisions. Afraid that I'll mess up and fail or that I'll make mistakes and not know how to fix them.'

'It's OK to be afraid, and it's OK to make mistakes,' Alice said. 'Sometimes the bravest thing in the world is to admit when you've made a mistake, but it doesn't mean that it's the end of the world, it just means that you're going to have to go in a different direction, adapt to new changes.'

'I'd love to discover something one day, be a real scientist, help the world, maybe even win that Nobel Prize.' He could feel her eyes watching him as he stared out across the water; he felt foolish, perhaps even a little bit childish, but he had spoken the truth

'Your eyes sparkle,' Alice said softly as she reached up a hand and cupped his cheek, drawing his eyes to hers. She was smiling softly and gazing at him with so much affection. 'You don't need to be afraid, Kyle,' she said. 'Life isn't perfect and neither are we. You shouldn't be afraid of getting things wrong or changing your mind. No one knows what they're doing really; all we can do is try to be the person we can admire in the future.'

'As long as I'm with you, I'm sure I'll admire the future Kyle,' he said and she smiled.

'There!' Alice said suddenly and pointed up at the sky. He gazed up and caught the tail end of a shooting star, a silvery streak against the night sky.

The memory let go of him and he blinked as dark circles exploded across his vision like confetti. His heart hammered in his chest and he gasped as though he'd been running. His arms hung uselessly by his sides and he waited for his vision to clear. He could feel the tears falling down his cheeks and he wiped them away before he picked up the second piece of paper. There was a note written in a flowery handwriting which he didn't recognise.

Dear Kyle,

I'm sorry that I didn't tell you about this sooner but I had to check and confirm my suspicions first. When we last met, I realised that Alice's notebook had a missing page. I recalled seeing a page with a picture on it that looked like it had been ripped out of a book amongst the things James had kept. I didn't know where it was, but I managed to convince James to let me look through Alice's old things. It wasn't an easy task, he had put most of her stuff in a box in the attic and boy did he have to move a lot of boxes. I guess that's what happens when you get divorced and move house suddenly. Anyways, he found it eventually, and I went through everything and sure enough I found this page. I think it belongs in the notebook you have, so I have enclosed it with this letter. I don't know if this is what you're looking for, or if this will make anything better for you, but at least Alice's notebook is complete and you rightfully have the last thing that she ever drew. Take care Kyle, I send all my love and wishes to you and your family.

Paula.

He heard someone shouting downstairs. He put the note down, left his room and stood at the top of the landing.

'I'm not working in a bookshop so I can work in an office,' he heard Hailey shout. He saw her run for the stairs, taking them two at a time. Hailey ran past him and shut herself in her room.

'Hailey Hunter!' Matthew yelled and then he started to wheeze and cough. Their father appeared at the foot of the stairs, bracing himself on the bannister, his face flushed red and his right hand gripping at his chest. His mother was beside him.

'Stop it now, Matthew, come on, you need to rest.'

'I will not have our daughter speak to me like this. She's rude. After all the help I give her; the sacrifices I make. I work damned hard, Stacy.'

'Later, Matthew, shouting isn't going to help anything,' Stacy said. Kyle caught his father's gaze.

'At least one of our kids is being sensible about their future,' Matthew said loudly and then he looked at Kyle. His father looked haggard and old; behind the thin veil of anger Kyle could see desperation and fear etched over his father's face. Kyle thought about his future, about his degree, and he felt something he hadn't felt in a long time, uncertainty. Alice's words echoed through his head. *'You shouldn't be afraid of getting things wrong or changing your mind.'*

'Come on, Matthew, you need to rest,' Stacy said. She guided him away and Kyle was left staring at the empty spot they had left behind.

THIRTY-ONE

He stood outside the doorway but the doors kept changing. One minute it was the wooden door with glass panes, looking into the examination hall at school, and the next it was Alice's white door, the door to her hospital room. He could see her in the white room, in a single little bed. She was so weak, so pale and ill. He could see her chest struggling to rise and fall, a thin film of sweat on her forehead and her eyelids fluttering. The doorway switched again and he saw rows of desks occupied by students, bent over exam papers. He tried to move to the doorway but his feet and arms were locked by his sides. He glanced down and he could see rusted chains around his ankles and wrists, holding him firmly in place. The hospital door appeared again, only this time Alice was surrounded by frenzied medical staff.

'Alice, no!' he yelled, 'Alice!' He pulled against the chains. The doorway switched back to the examination hall, and he saw the students from his college physics class. Cameron was there, and Mr Blakely was patrolling the desks as an invigilator. The doorway switched and Alice's hospital room came back; he saw the medical staff but they weren't doing anything. They had all stopped and were all looking gravely at the bed. Alice lay there, still and unmoving. She was gone. 'Alice!' Kyle screamed and yanked on the chains; he could feel the cold metal biting into his wrists and tearing his skin. The doorway cracked and suddenly the floor gave out beneath him.

Kyle fell, the strange doorway fading into a starry sky. He felt the wind whip past him and curl around his body, pulling at his clothes and hair. His stomach lurched and he saw the park below, rising to meet him. He panicked and flapped his arms desperately, as though he were trying to fly like a bird. His body slammed painfully into the cold icy lake water, and he saw a stream of bubbles mark his descent. He kicked back up to the surface, and just managed to gasp a mouthful of air when he felt his legs being yanked back down. He screamed as he went under, and an angry stream of bubbles erupted from his nose and mouth. He looked down at the metal, rusty chains, clamped around his ankles and weighing him down like an anchor.

Kyle's lungs screamed for air as he was pulled down and he thrashed fruitlessly. He felt his body slowly giving up as he gazed out through the deep water; there were more bodies, all of them in suits and being pulled down by chains. Voices jumped into his mind, thousands of voices, and he heard them, he heard them all. *I hate my job,* one voice said. *My boss is an ass,* said another. *Why did I decide to do this?* All of them were fighting to speak first. *I'm so miserable. I'm so tired. I wish I could do something that makes me happy. Why are we here? I bet my colleagues are paid more than me. What if I'm pregnant? There's so much paperwork. It's just the same day in and day out. I never get to see my kids. Is this really what life is about? I wonder if I'll get that promotion. I really need that promotion, everything is so expensive these days. I bet the trains will be delayed. There are too many bills to pay this month. The traffic is always a nightmare. God, why does she look so miserable, she's got nothing to be miserable about. I'm so scared of screwing up the rest of my life...* A final breath escaped Kyle and then the drowning world grew dim. He heard his chains hit the bottom of the lake with a muted clink, and he saw the corpses of everyone else, sprouting up from the ground like flowers. His lungs burned and ached; everything was so heavy. His vision narrowed, and he only just about caught the wrinkled, decomposing face of his father, staring back at him.

Kyle gasped and choked as he sat bolt upright in bed. His eyes darted around the room wildly, trying to recognise the darkened details but not really registering anything at all. His heart thundered in his ribcage as though it was being struck by lightning every other second. His lungs burned, oh god, they burned. He groaned and hugged his chest as he doubled over and pushed his face into his mattress. He turned his head to the side to concentrate on his breathing and slowly his dimly-lit room revealed itself. *Why did dreams hurt so much?* His gaze travelled down and across the room to his bedside table where the red letters on his digital clock cast a devilish semicircle across the floor. It was 03:06am. He groaned again and pushed himself up. He sipped some water from a glass on his bedside table and then lay back down again.

He drew his hands over his face and pulled at his cheeks. He had never drowned in the lake before, and there were all those voices, and all those bodies, his father's body… he shuddered. There was no use in sleeping now, the exam period had come round too soon and he had his first exam in six hours. He got out of bed and opened up his business books. He read over the same paragraphs he had read a hundred times and would surely forget once the exam was over. The hours passed and then his alarm sounded. He showered, ate, picked up his things, and then left the flat and headed across the campus to the sports centre. He heard the heavy, quick thud of feet hitting the ground behind him but he didn't turn around.

'Kyle,' he heard Cameron yell. 'Kyle, wait!' Kyle kept walking and Cameron fell into step beside him, panting heavily. 'Hey, are you heading to the sports centre too?' Cameron said. Kyle nodded.

'Cool, me too. Do you feel prepared?'

'About as prepared as I can be, but I didn't get much sleep last night.'

'No, me neither. I was up all night revising. I wouldn't recommend it.' Cameron yawned into the back of his hand.

'Do you feel prepared?'

'Am I ever?' Cameron grinned. 'Did you go back home over the study break?'

'Yeah. The family wanted to see me and it was nice having someone cook my meals. Did you?'

'Na, I stayed here but it was completely dead. There was hardly anyone around. Perfect for studying really.' Kyle nodded and they said nothing for several steps. 'Look, Kyle, I wanted to apologise for being such an ass.'

'Forget it.' Kyle said. 'It doesn't matter, I've forgotten about it.'

'OK, but I'm still sorry.'

'I know.'

'So are we cool?'

'We're cool.'

'Thank god, because if they hadn't worked I was going to get down on my knees and beg and offer any forfeit to get you to talk to me,' Cameron said.

'I should have stayed quiet then.' Kyle laughed.

'I heard your sister got a job at the bookshop.'

'News travels fast.'

'Tank told me. He messages me from time to time.'

'Oh right. Yeah. She wants to be a writer and she thinks working in a bookshop will help her.'

'That's cool. I mean, it's cool that she wants to be a writer.'

'Yeah, I guess, but Dad's not too happy about it.'

'No, I can imagine what your dad would say.' Cameron laughed and shook his head.

'Hailey refuses to listen to him, she's braver than me.' Kyle said as they approached the sport's centre.

'Good for her.' They stepped through the doors of the sport's centre and entered a long corridor where other students were standing around, cramming in last minute revision sessions. A group of students waved at Cameron and Cameron waved back before turning to Kyle. 'Well, good luck with your exam.'

'Yeah, you too.' Kyle watched as Cameron walked over to the

group, and then turned to the lockers behind him. He retrieved his pencil case from his bag and dumped everything else inside a locker.

The hall had been filled with row upon row of single foldable desks and chairs. Kyle's desk was number forty-two and thankfully it was near the back of the room; he hated being near the front. Kyle sat down in his seat and switched off as the other students found their desks. His thoughts strayed to Hailey; she was brave, he realised. She was trying so hard to achieve her goals and she fought their father every step of the way. Hailey was determined; she had a bounce in her step and a wildfire in her eyes, but their father, he had wrinkles on his face, a receding hairline, constant circles under his eyes and tight lips. He hardly smiled these days; he didn't seem to have much time anymore and he looked ill with stress. Kyle felt sick as a thought passed through his mind, was that his fate too? Would he become just like his father? Was that the epitome of working life? He remembered his nightmare and all the drowned bodies in suits, held to the bottom of the lake by chains. He hadn't seen Hailey there, or Cameron, or Tank, or Sophia.

Kyle looked down at the exam paper before him; he had barely heard the invigilators announcing that their time had begun. *Focus, Kyle,* he told himself firmly. He answered the first question hastily, his pen almost ripping through the paper as he moved onto the next. Memories continued haunting him, He recalled Alice's sickly, weak body, the tears and groans, her hair falling out, her body expelling everything it was supposed to be taking in, her skin drawing thin and pale over her bones. He remembered her hours of pain as the fight slowly drained out of her and he remembered her frustration at being bed-bound. He remembered her battling with everyone and pushing herself too hard in a bid to get outside, just so she could see some sunshine. He felt his head pounding harder and his knuckles whitened. *No, not now, please not now!* He gritted his teeth as a memory surfaced from the depths, accompanied by a sharp pain that made his brain feel like it was splitting in half...

Eighteen-year-old Kyle sat in his suit by Alice's bedside, it was the morning of the 18th June 2009 and he was visiting the hospital just before his last A-level exam. Alice was propped up in bed with a blue beanie on her head, hiding her very short hair which was just starting to grow back. She owned a wig, but the wig was itchy and uncomfortable.

'Do you feel confident?' she asked. She was bony and uncomfortably thin, her clothes loose sacks on her frame.

'Yeah, I'll nail it,' Kyle replied. He was sure he would do well in his last physics exam; he had been revising for months. The backs of Alice's hands were bruised from needles and tubes puncturing her skin. He took her right hand gently between his; she was cold, she always felt cold.

'Just do your best,' she said and she smiled. Despite the chemotherapy and surgery destroying her body and poisoning her veins, her smile remained unchanged.

'I will.' He kissed her hand gently.

'When I'm better we'll make a great team. I can't wait to join you.'

'OK.' He smiled, 'but first I'm going to help look after you.' She rolled her eyes and he chuckled.

'I'm getting a bit sick of being looked after,' she said. 'I'll get stronger again, I'm going to beat this…' Her eyes started to well and her lips trembled.

'Shh, it's OK.' He reached forwards and cradled her bony cheeks. 'It will be OK, there's plenty of time, just be patient.' He kissed her between the eyes. 'I'll be right back after this exam and then I'm not leaving again for the rest of the summer.'

'OK,' she whispered. Kyle hugged her gently.

Kyle's vision wobbled and he felt bile lurch up into his throat. He blinked and gripped the desk as he tried to stop the swaying dizziness in his head. He felt sick, and cold, and heavy. He felt his body tilt to the side and he gripped the desk tighter to straighten himself. He hunched forwards, closed his eyes and put his head in his hands as he willed his mind to clear again. That morning had been the last time Kyle had seen Alice alive, the last time he had spoken to her. He focussed everything on the shadowy light behind his eyelids and let the sensation of his breathing calm down his mind.

When he felt calm enough he opened his eyes and realised he had lost fifteen minutes. He leant back in his chair and gazed blankly ahead. He could see row upon row of students, all bowed over desks, scribbling frantically into paper booklets. *Why am I here? Why are any of us here?* He heard Alice's voice echoing at the back of his mind. *'You're going to do great things, Kyle.'* Followed by his father's voice. *'At least one of our kids is being sensible about their future.'* And then Cameron's voice. *'You're wasted doing business, you know.'*

The scratching of pens, the rustle of paper, the creaking of chairs and the sighs from students rushed back to him. Pens woven between fingers, synchronised turning of pages to some inaudible beat. *Tick, scratch-scratch-scratch, tick.* A student coughed behind him. *Great things?* Kyle frowned. He hadn't done anything he had promised to do; he had been selfishly compassionate and an honest liar. He had spent so long trying to avoid his past, cutting himself off from Alice, and trying to protect himself under the guise of moving on. He hadn't realised he had actually cut himself up and buried the parts that had made himself, well, *him.*

He gripped his hands into fists; *I'm not supposed to be here. I'm not supposed to be doing this.* He thought about it and he realised he couldn't see himself working in any old office until the end of his days. He had no desire to work his way up some invisible career ladder. That was not what he wanted to do. The universe and life was much bigger than that. Alice had shared his interests and encouraged him, but physics had always been there even when he had been a kid. He may have not always realised it was physics but his interests had been there from the very beginning. He shot his hand up into the air, feeling slightly giddy. This was his life, his degree, his choices; he didn't care what his father thought or what society wanted. He was a person, a human being, a mind with thoughts and a body with emotions, he was a living creature, and he had one life to live. He would leave the exam, call his father, and then talk to Professor Green. He would switch his degree back to physics and he would put his energy back into the things he had once loved. He did *deserve* it; he deserved it for himself and for Alice. He would stay up and study long hours if he had to; he would spend every day in the library, and he would watch the postgraduates in the labs. A spark of hot energy erupted from his core and out through his veins. He felt alive for the first time in years.

He watched as one of the invigilators approached him. They were moving too slowly so he stood up and picked up his paper and belongings. *'Don't be afraid.'* Alice's voice rang loud and clear in his mind, but the initial leap was always terrifying. The invigilator frowned but Kyle was beyond the point of caring. He thrust the exam paper at her and marched out of the room as quickly as he dared.

Once he was outside, he collected his bag from a locker and called his father.

'Hey Kyle, has your exam finished already?'

'No, Dad, I need to talk to you,' Kyle said.

'What did you say? Sorry I'm in the back room with all the files; the signal is pretty poor in here.'

'Dad, I'm not doing business anymore, I'm switching back to physics.'

'What did you say? Physics?'

'I'm switching to physics Dad. I'm sorry.' There was silence for a few moments.

'Now Kyle…' his father paused. 'WHAT THE HELL!' he shouted suddenly and then he began to wheeze and cough.

'Dad?' Kyle said. He could hear his father gasping for breath and then he heard a loud clack, as though something had been dropped. 'Dad?' Kyle said, louder this time. He heard a heavy thud and then nothing. Kyle lowered his phone, the call had disconnected and he felt a chill of panic stir the hairs on the back of his neck. He tried to call his dad again, but there was no answer. Kyle cursed and ran out of the sports centre. He called the office and Zack answered the phone.

'Hello, this is…'

'Zack!' he yelled.

'Kyle?'

'Zack, there's no time to explain. Go to the back room now, the one with all the files.'

'What's wrong Kyle?'

'My dad! Go now!'

'Alright, Alright.' He heard Zack leave the phone on his desk but Kyle kept his mobile up to his ear and strained to listen for the slightest sound. A few seconds later he heard Zack's distant yelling. 'Someone call an ambulance!' It was all Kyle needed to hear. He called his mum but there was no answer so he called Hailey.

'Hey, Kyle.'

'Hailey, Dad's in trouble. I'm not sure what happened exactly but you need to get hold of Mum.'

'What?'

'The office has called an ambulance. You need to get to the hospital. Now. I'm on my way.' Kyle made it back to the flat and hastily shoved belongings into a holdall. He packed his wash bag and Alice's book, and then he ran to the bus stop.

THIRTY-TWO

The last thing Matthew remembered was talking to Kyle on the phone with one hand, and reading an alarming email on his tablet with his other hand. He wasn't even sure what the email had been about exactly now, only that he had felt angry all of sudden and his chest felt like it was being crushed. The next moment he had felt nothing but utter peace and bliss. His body was weightless or didn't exist and he was surrounded by a strange, warm, golden light. *Where am I?* was his first question, but he found he didn't much care. The peace was overwhelming; he felt like a child again, asleep and safe within his mother's arms. He closed his eyes, nothing mattered here; he was free of all pain and physical needs.

'You're stubborn, Mr Hunter,' a voice called, echoing around the empty space. He opened his eyes; he recognised that voice. 'You haven't changed a bit,' the voice said and she appeared then, and the light shifted as though she were stepping through golden clouds.

'Alice.' She wore a cream dress and her hair hung down around her shoulders, her pale skin glowed and he could see the veins in her arms shimmering beneath her skin, like lines of fireflies or twinkling stars. Her eyes were incredible; her deep blue irises shifted into lilac, red, gold, and pale blue hues, the colours never remaining still.

'Hello, Matthew.' She smiled.

'Alice? Where am I? Am I dead?' he asked. He felt panic trying to override his system but the warm peace kept it at bay.

'No, you're not quite dead,' she said as she stopped before him. 'You're in the divide.'

'The divide?'

'Yes, between life and the afterlife. You're lucky, I only just caught you. I was just on my way back.'

'Back? Back to where?'

'I don't have much time to explain. There's something you should see before you go.'

'Go? Go where?' he asked. Alice ignored him, reaching out and putting her palm on his forehead.

'You need to see time as the deceased do; all of it, past, present and future.'

'I don't…' He gasped as a bright light erupted from her chest, blinding him temporarily as it travelled up her arm and into her palm. Colours bloomed behind his eyes forming images, memories he had mostly forgotten about. He could feel, touch, see everything with such clarity it was like he was there again, only his eyes were everywhere and he saw everything he hadn't seen before.

Matthew saw himself as a young child with his younger brother; he saw their tiny one bedroom flat and his mother and father. There was nothing of note in their little home, but he saw clearly the souls of his family; he understood all of the colours, their thoughts and emotions. He and his brother were happy and content, scribbling with broken crayons on old newspapers on the floor. His mother was calm, filled with an enormous amount of love as she looked on at her children. His father was a different story; he was miserable, his soul shrouded in greys and browns. He was worried, tired, frustrated. Matthew wanted to talk to him, wanted to show him how happy and content his family were, but he couldn't change the past now.

He saw his father surrounded by a cold, black energy. It dipped into his soul, dimming his colours and squeezing out all of his positive emotions.

'What is that?'

'Negative energy.' Alice replied. 'It comes from harbouring

negative emotions; it cripples the soul and fills people's minds with self-doubt. Sometimes it feeds anger and resentment, other times it whittles people away, convincing them that there are only bad decisions that they can make, feeding life with regret.' He watched horrified as it consumed his father; time continued forwards and he saw his father's soul dim with sickness.

He also saw himself, slightly older and passing the music shop on his way to and from school. He could see the shiny, red drum kit in the window and its price tag. Both Matthew and his brother looked at the drum kit with a mixture of awe and longing, but both knew they would never be able to afford it. Matthew saw the secret time he had spent saving money in order to someday buy the drum kit; he had had paper rounds, washed pots, anything, but it had never been enough. They had always needed every penny, whether it was for rent, food or bills. Then he saw his father pass away and Matthew was no longer a teenager anymore. The colours which had once been so vibrant and bright within his soul dulled and became thin. He saw himself change from the hopeful and determined teenager into a frightened and demoralised man.

He applied for his first office job; he was rejected by many companies then finally accepted by one. He became wrapped up in his working life and obsessed with money. Then one evening, after he had stayed on late at the office, he passed a bar where he could hear live music playing. He stopped as he heard the drum beat, the bass, the guitar and the voice; the singer's voice was like nothing he had ever heard before. He walked into the bar and that was when he had met Stacy for the first time, it was like her voice had called to him. A sudden surge of youthfulness burst through his soul; he could remember the drum kit he had always wanted. He caught her eye and she smiled. The rest became a new history.

The years moved on and Matthew watched himself age. He watched his soul dull and dim, the colours moving slowly compared to his childhood days. He noticed that nearly everyone in the offices around him became this way, the colours in their souls fading, as though they were slowly dying. He saw himself and Stacy move to Elbridge; they were married and for one day he saw his soul shine brightly, but it was brief and short lived. He watched as he immersed himself in work and again his soul colours faded. At the births of his two children his soul shone again, briefly, but it never lasted long enough. Stacy was different; she continued to sing and play in bands, she toured all over Europe at small events, and she still had time to look after the family. He marvelled at Stacy's soul, the vibrant hues of lilac and aqua, and the deep crimson for love. She was brilliant like the sun and Matthew's soul was like the far side of the moon. He saw the effects of every decision he had ever made, every chance. He saw Negative and Positive in the air, shadows and golden light. He saw how emotions and decisions were so finely intertwined.

He watched his kids grow up. He saw their souls mature, obtaining new and more colours as they got older. He knew instantly what interested them, what drove them; he felt their emotions as though they were his own. Their thoughts and questions passed through his mind; he began to realise that he had never understood his kids. He saw their souls dim when he told them what to do, when he tried to push them down certain paths because he feared for their futures. He saw their features crumble and their motivation dwindle. *This was wrong.*

He saw Kyle and Alice, how their souls bounced off one another, their colours almost dancing around their cores. He knew their relationship had been genuine, he could see it in their souls, in the red that dominated their outer layers every time they were in each other's company. It was both incredible and enlightening to see such a relationship between two young people, but it had been there, he could see it now. He saw and felt their dreams and ambitions, he saw their colours brighten and grow every time they talked about their futures and plans. He saw a fire in his son that blazed in Alice's company, and suffocated in his own.

Then he saw Alice weakening, being diagnosed with gastric cancer. He saw the toll her death had taken on his son for a second time, and in a cruelly intimate way. He knew the secret feelings and thoughts Kyle had hidden from everybody. Kyle's soul became smothered by grey, and the despair that crashed through Matthew shocked him right to his core. He saw Kyle give up on everything he had once believed in, everything he had loved, and he saw the dead, blank eyes of his son staring back at him, just nodding and agreeing with Matthew's plans. The very life had been ripped out of Kyle when Alice had died; he was miserable.

He saw Hailey, her defiance and determination. Her soul blazed brightly in comparison to Kyle's but still dimmed and dulled under Matthew's words. He saw her struggling, and then at the park with her nose in a book and her soul shining in an array of different colours. He saw Tank at the park with her, both their souls a mixture of pink and red. He would have frowned but then Alice's voice jumped into his mind.

'They're good together, look,' she said. Matthew held his thoughts and followed her advice, he looked and he saw. He saw Hailey and Tank talking and laughing, like they had been at the bonfire event. He saw their souls, the colours shifting and blending into different Positive hues until they almost resembled Alice's and Kyle's souls. The same spark was there, the same one he had seen between himself and Stacy, between Alice and Kyle; it was there between Tank and Hailey too.

The images drifted away from him and then stretched thin; he saw time in a way he could have never envisioned. The images split and stretched upwards like the branches of a tree, and downwards like the roots. With each split he was aware of the decisions and choices that governed the doorways to each tiny branch. He could see his own past, the decisions which had guided him to where he was now, but he could also see the decisions he could have made, the choices he had decided against. He saw his younger self buying the drum kit and practising long hours on it with his brother, teaching themselves with second hand books. He saw himself take music at school, and the music teacher helping him with the drums. He saw himself playing at different events and gigs, his soul a bright rainbow of colours. He looked happy, healthy, and youthful; he was nothing like the haggard and tired youth who had taken on an office job. He saw himself at a big event, and he saw Stacy there too, playing with her own band. He realised then that some things were just meant to be; he would have still met Stacy even if he had pushed and followed his dreams. His vision blurred as tears sprung into his dark eyes; he could see his mother and brother in the audience too, smiling as they watched him play.

'If you want something bad enough, there is always a way to make it happen,' he heard Alice say. He could see the branches of his tree growing and overlapping, twisting around one another. The whole structure was glowing gold, and then he saw more tree-like structures, twisting and growing, into what looked like a giant bird's nest. He was pulled back further and he realised that there were more of these strange structures, like great webs depicting everyone's choices, decisions, lives, all of them interwoven with the next. A central line split down the centre of these webs and another curved around like a spiral, creating a vortex shape. He could see every choice every person had ever made; he could see the major decisions that had altered the course of humanity; he could see the minor decisions from everyday life too, both Positive and Negative. He saw a future version of Kyle, in a high tech lab, working alongside other scientists. He could see his son's research and all the good it could do for the world and the future. He saw a future version of Hailey too, writing and happy. They would be OK, he realised, his fears were all groundless, they really would be fine.

'I was wrong,' he whispered.

'You were right to care, but sometimes care lends itself to fear and fear becomes a prison. They will make mistakes, everyone does, but they are more likely to succeed following their dreams than following somebody else's vision,' Alice said.

'Yes,' he said, 'yes, you're right.' The finely interwoven lines of energy and time blurred before his eyes, his body felt heavy all of a sudden, as if he was being weighed down by an anchor. Alice appeared again before him; she removed her hand and smiled at him.

'Tell Kyle that even though he has dropped his penny, he only needs to reach out and pick it back up again.' Matthew stared at her, dumbfounded. He was about to speak when he was suddenly yanked down. Alice and the golden landscape faded, revealing the frightening beauty of the universe. He felt his body falling, passing the stars and planets as the peaceful warmth disappeared from his limbs. He closed his eyes and waited, waited for it all to end.

* * *

Matthew felt heavier than he had ever done in his entire life. His head was fuzzy and an irritating high beep sounded regularly. He forced his eyelids to open, but it felt like he was trying to lift weights at the gym. Everything was blurry and disorientated at first; his head pounded and his chest felt stiff and sore.

'Dad?' he heard Kyle say. He turned his head to the sound of his son's voice, but it only made him feel sick and dizzy. 'Dad? Can you hear me? Are you awake?' Matthew tried to speak but his mouth wasn't cooperating and his throat was dry. 'I'm so sorry, Dad, I'm so sorry; I didn't mean to stress you out. It's all my fault, I'm so sorry. I will stay on my course, I'll do business…'

Matthew tried to speak but he was incapable. He was aware of the hustle and bustle around and the nurses and doctors but Kyle remained beside him as he drifted in and out of consciousness. Eventually he could feel the sedative effects wearing off enough to speak.

'No.' he said softly. His vision was hazy but he could see his son, sitting by his bedside, leaning forwards anxiously with tears still falling down his face. 'It's not your fault.'

'Dad?' Matthew pushed himself up slowly and Kyle stood quickly to help him.

'I'm alright,' Matthew said. 'Water? Please, Kyle.' Kyle picked up a plastic cup from the side and eased it to his mouth, enough to moisten his lips enough to whisper. 'You won't do business… you'll do physics.' Kyle's eyes stretched wide.

'What?'

'You'll do physics, Kyle, you never liked business anyway.'

'Dad, you should rest; you don't sound like your usual self.'

'Hey… listen to me. You should study physics, Kyle, it's what you enjoy, and it's your passion. I see that now… I see it more than ever.' He pushed for words, it was taking every ounce of energy but he knew he must. 'I was wrong, and I'm sorry.' Kyle stared at him with a look of utter bewilderment. Matthew felt a little foolish but he remembered Alice's message and he repeated her words. 'You've dropped your penny, but you only need to reach out and pick it back up again.' Kyle's eyes bulged.

'Dad? Who told you that? Where did you hear that?'

He smiled but was overwhelmed with tiredness. 'I'm tired now, son,' Matthew said. 'Just know I will always support you. You and Hailey.' Matthew closed his eyes and found, for once, that sleep came easily to him.

THIRTY-THREE

'I swear to god, you're one of the hardest people to track down sometimes,' Cameron said. Kyle looked down from his spot on the ramp. He was balancing his board over the drop and he pulled back as Cameron climbed the smooth curve to join him.

'Hey,' Kyle said.

'So I go to your house expecting you to be there, and Hailey tells me that not only have you gone down to the park, but you also took your board with you. I couldn't believe my ears at first, I had to get her to repeat herself three times and then I ran back home and grabbed my own board.' Cameron grinned. 'It's been a long time, hasn't it?'

'Yes.' Kyle smiled.

'So I heard the good news too. Sophia told me you have transferred from business to a physics degree. How did your dad take it?'

'He suggested it.'

'Really? Wow.' Kyle nodded.

'How did your physics exams go?' Kyle asked.

'Good, I think, but you're not getting rid of me that easily. I've signed on for a master's course at Red Oak but I haven't heard back yet.'

'I'm sure they'll accept you.'

'They better,' Cameron said. He glanced down the ramp. 'What made you change your mind? Why did you decide to switch to physics again?'

'It just didn't feel right in the end, but if I'm totally honest, it was Alice who changed my mind.'

'Alice?'

'Yeah. Talia sent me a book which Alice had made for me for my nineteenth birthday, it was three years late, but she sent it to me. It had photos, drawings and notes inside and well, it got me thinking about things. That, and almost being knocked down by a van and a couple of nightmares.' Kyle chuckled.

'I should have known that something was up. You've had a rough year again, haven't you?' Cameron said.

'Yes and no. It's been nowhere near as bad as 2009.'

'No, I suppose nothing will beat that. Sophia has come up with a research proposal which involves Quantum Entanglement.'

'Oh, that doesn't surprise me.'

'We've also been working on the Now Timeline idea.'

'Oh good. I've been thinking about that a lot lately.'

'Well, we'll continue to work on it. Hopefully I'll get onto the master's course and then we'll all be at Red Oak for the next year.' Cameron glanced down the ramp again and gulped.

'Are you going to skateboard?' Kyle said.

'Yeah, in a minute. I'm a bit rusty.'

'You don't have to, you know.'

'I'm going to do it. I just need a sec that's all.' Cameron put his board down over the edge of the U-shaped ramp. He balanced there for a couple of seconds and then he descended the smooth concrete curve. Kyle watched as Cameron raced up the other side and then he wobbled and the board slipped away from him. Cameron let out a cry and he fell, rolling down and onto the ground. Kyle skidded down to his friend.

'Are you alright?' Kyle said as Cameron twisted and groaned.

'I forgot how much it hurts to fall.'

'You should be padded up and wearing a helmet.'

'I know, I know.' Cameron sat up slowly.

'Some things just never change.' Kyle heard Alice say. He froze, and he felt as though shockwaves were rippling through his entire body. He turned round and saw her. She was perched on the edge of the ramp, wearing a white dress and glowing like an angel. Her eyes widened when his gaze locked with hers. 'Wow. You can see me, can't you?' she said, leaning forwards. Kyle nodded wordlessly; was he hallucinating again?

'I wonder what Alice would say if she were here right now.' Cameron laughed, oblivious to Alice's presence.

'She would call you an idiot,' Alice said with a grin.

'She would call you an idiot,' Kyle said softly. He couldn't believe his eyes and tears started to roll down his cheeks.

'Yeah. You're probably right.' Cameron frowned and he pushed himself up to his feet. 'Are you OK? What are you staring at?'

'We'll talk later, OK?' Alice said.

'Yeah,' Kyle said, rubbing the tears from his eyes. 'I'm fine.' Alice smiled.

'You don't look fine. You look like you've seen a ghost,' Cameron said. He grasped Kyle's shoulders and stood directly in front of him, blocking Kyle's view of Alice. Kyle glanced around Cameron to the spot where Alice had been sitting, but she was nowhere to be found. Had he really seen and heard her? Had she really been there? He didn't know, but he could feel all of his emotions crashing around inside of him.

'Kyle?' Cameron said.

'I'm fine.' Kyle tore his gaze from the empty spot and focussed his attention on Cameron. 'I'm fine. Let's just skateboard, OK?' Cameron stared long and hard at Kyle and Kyle fought to keep his expression as blank as possible.

'OK.' Cameron released Kyle and turned around to pick up his board. Kyle looked once more at the spot where Alice had been sitting. He didn't know if what he had seen had been real or a figment of his imagination, but they were both possibilities. A small smile passed over his lips, riding on a fragile wave of hope. He was sure he would find out the truth in time.

* * *

Sophia opened her eyes and sat up slowly in the armchair; her neck was stiff but this wasn't unusual for her. Flo was sitting opposite her on the large sofa; she too had just opened her eyes and straightened up.

'Did you see?' Flo asked.

'Yes, yes, I did,' Sophia replied. 'He can see her.'

'So he can.' Flo's dark eyes sparkled with amusement.

'What now?' Sophia asked, as her Aunt Cassie came in, carrying two glasses of water.

'Well, I believe we'll just have to wait and see,' Flo replied. 'The pendulum has swung, Positive is in control for the time being.' Cassie nodded as she handed Flo and Sophia a glass each. 'Cassie here is going to write about Alice's and Kyle's story, though she'll change the names around to be sure.'

'Write a story?'

'Yes, a fictional story of course.' Flo replied and winked at Sophia. Sophia bit back a chuckle; her grandmother was sly. 'I'm assuming Kyle has been accepted for a physics degree now and Cameron will be accepted on the Master's course?'

'Yes, I've seen to it,' Sophia replied.

'Good. You can work with them. Now I guess we must look to the souls of the future. It always seems we have too little time.'

'All time is now,' Sophia reminded her. 'There is only the future.'

'Too true, too true,' Flo said as she pushed herself up from the sofa. Sophia watched as Flo and Cassie left, then stood up and walked over to the window. Somehow, among the chaos, Kyle and Alice were on the right path again. Elias would insist on bringing Kyle to their home and teaching him all they knew about the afterlife, but it could wait. She was looking forward to working with

Kyle in the future. Sophia could feel the buzz, the slight vibrations, of a thousand thoughts, memories and emotions clambering around her mind and begging for her attention. She only had to let her mind reach out with its invisible fingers and focus on one, and again, like a raindrop heading for an ocean, another decision, another moment, another life, would fall into her knowledge. The uncertainty in the world would become a little more certain, and a single moment in time could change everything. The Letos would be ready; they were always ready.

* * * _ * * *

ACKNOWLEDGMENTS

I am eternally grateful to Emma Pritchard, Steven Greening, James Stoddah and Bruce Nicholson at Outlet Publishing for your continued faith and investment in my work. I would also like to express a huge thank you to my assistant, Hannah Hudson and my wonderful editor, Alison Williams. Thank you too to Catherine Cousins and the team at 2QT for getting the book prepared for release.

Moreover, I'd like to thank all of my family and friends for being so encouraging and patient with my writing.

And finally, my heartfelt thanks to you, the reader, for investing your time in me. I hope to get Book 3 (Lost Frequencies) and Book 4 (The Quantum Messenger) released within the next twelve months.

CAITLIN LYNAGH
ONLINE

www.caitlinlynagh.com
Facebook: https://facebook.com/caitlinlynaghauthor
Instagram: https://instagram.com/caitlinlynaghauthor
Twitter: https://twitter.com/caitlinlynagh
Tumblr: http://thesoulprophecies.tumblr.com
Pinterest: https://pinterest.com/caitlinlynagh
ALSO find me on: Goodreads, Amazon and Booklaunch.io
Feel free to send a photo of yourself with the book and I'll include it on my *Hall of Fame* across my social media.